I0718206

INTO WINTER

The Armed Invasion

INTO WINTER

The Armed Invasion

A Novel by

Larry Landgraf

Fresh Ink Group

Guntersville

Into Winter: The Armed Invasion

Copyright © 2017
by Larry Landgraf
All rights reserved

Fresh Ink Group
An Imprint of:
The Fresh Ink Group, LLC
Box 931
Guntersville, AL 35976
Email: info@FreshInkGroup.com

Edition 1.0   2017

Book design by Ann Stewart / FIG

Cover by Stephen Geez / FIG

Except as permitted under the U.S. Copyright Act of 1976, no part of this publication may be reproduced, distributed, or transmitted in any form or by any means, or stored in a database or retrieval system, without prior written permission of the Fresh Ink Group, LLC.

All characters appearing in this work are fictitious. Any resemblance to real persons, living or dead, is purely coincidental.

BISAC Subject Headings:
FIC000000   **FICTION / General**
FIC055000   **FICTION / Dystopian**
FIC028070   **FICTION / Science Fiction / Apocalyptic &
Post-Apocalyptic**

Library of Congress Control Number: 2017952357

Hardcover ISBN-13: 978-1-936442-56-0
Paper-cover ISBN-13: 978-1-936442-57-7
Ebook ISBN-13: 978-1-936442-58-4

Table of Contents

Prologue

Welcome to my Four Seasons Series. *Into Autumn - A Story of Survival* opens the show with Eileen Branson, a San Antonio stock analyst, fleeing the city when the grid shuts down and chaos erupts around her. Out of gas, she meets Lars Lindgren, a Davy Crockett type, and his few neighbors deep in the woods of south central Texas. There, they defend against hordes of intruders who know only one way to survive—take from those who have the skills to provide for themselves.

Melissa escapes the chaos in Waco and finds her way to her parent's home, Reggie and Emily Carston. The Carstons are Lars Lindgren's neighbors upstream from his homestead. James Lindgren makes his way from Conroe to rejoin his dad and Eileen.

Ronald and Sara Weston live downstream from the Lindgren homestead. Samuel and Sally Lin live across the river from the Lindgrens and have two small children, Sean and Debra.

James and Melissa find love in the aftermath of their ever changing and challenging world. They have twin boys, Robbie and Ronnie. Lars Lindgren is killed by a rattlesnake bite to the neck when the boys are four years old. His widow, Eileen vows to teach the boys all she can and to make certain the twins know their grandpa as well as if he were there.

There is a shortage of women in the area they eventually name Peaceful Valley. When the kids grow up, Debra chooses to marry Ronnie, leaving Robbie and Sean out in the cold. They decide to go on a quest to Corpus Christi in search of wives.

Sean and Robbie set out for Corpus Christi in *Into Spring - The Next Generation,* on a quest to find women. The boys are in their late teens and there are no available women for them at home in Peaceful Valley. They have spent their entire lives in the country, in and around home, and had no idea what was in store for them nearly two decades after the grid shut down and the world descended into chaos.

What they find in Corpus Christi is a society ruled by a ruthless dictator, Sandra Hawkins. The boys thought they were prepared for anything, but are spotted by Sandra's henchmen on a roof at night. The boys are surveying the city under the cover of darkness, unaware that Sandra's men have night vision scopes.

The next morning, when the boys try to enter the city, they are captured and become slaves to Sandra, the mayor of the city. She is a big ol' southern gal, who takes a shine to Robbie, but is mean and cruel to most everyone else. Sandra has Sean castrated, as she's done to most of the men, and she forces him to work on a shrimp boat at the Bayfront, one of six compounds within the city. The remaining compounds are the Farm, Hospital, Airport, Police, and Contractors.

Robbie is more fortunate. Sandra recognizes him as good breeding stock for her population control program. She needs strong men for her ladies to produce healthy babies for Corpus Christi's future.

Robbie has to work, but his primary job on weekends is to impregnate Sandra's chosen women at her Farm, her home, and headquarters for her regime. The Farm is run almost entirely by women. Robbie grows to like some of the ladies and even Sandra gets in on his action, but the whole process feels like a form of slavery. He is used to being free, but here he is a prisoner.

Everything gets complicated as Robbie is drawn into Sandra's web. Though Robbie likes most of the young ladies at the Farm and impregnates many of them, he never loses sight of his plan for him and Sean to escape the clutches of Sandra and make their way back to Peaceful Valley. Sean eventually decides to stay in Corpus Christi, but Robbie and two of his lady friends find a means of escape and take the chance.

Into Winter opens as Robbie and two female allies are trying to escape in a Cessna Skyhawk at the Airport.

Introduction

In Corpus Christi, Texas . . .

The sun was just peeking over the horizon on another beautiful early autumn day along the Gulf Coast in south Texas. A few puffy clouds claimed the orange sunrise, folding into the blue sky overhead. But Sandra's attention was focused on the asphalt turning into concrete ahead. She gripped the steering wheel and pressed hard on the accelerator.

She yelled over and over, as she quickly gained on the yellow Cessna Skyhawk. "I'll get you, you little bastard!"

It took only seconds to overtake the plane. The Jeep sped past and ahead. Sandra pulled hard on the emergency brake locking up the wheels. She had one leg out of the Jeep before it came to a full stop in a cloud of smoke in the middle of the runway. She drew her pistol, pulled back on the hammer, and pointed toward the yellow Cessna as it leaped into the air and over her head. Before she could get off a shot, she ducked realizing her mistake, but one of the tires on the plane clipped her hand. Sandra screamed in pain as the pistol slammed into her face and fell to the pavement.

"Son-of-a-bitch!" she yelled, as she watched the plane come back down and bounce on the runway a couple of times before lifting off and climbing into the sky. She touched her cheek and looked at the blood on her hand. Her gaze returned to the end of the runway when she heard the shots. She watched the plane weave left and right, but it continued to climb. "God dammit!"

Sandra reached inside the Jeep for a rag to wipe the blood trickling down her face. She picked up her pistol and stuck it back in her holster. She watched as the plane made a wide swing over the Bayfront and circled back toward the Airport.

Sandra leaned up against the Jeep and squinted her eyes trying to recover from the blow to the side of her head. She looked back to the north and stared at the little plane as it made circle after circle near the edge of the city. Then the plane lined out and faded from sight.

That has to be the direction to Peaceful Valley. I'll get that little bastard!

Sandra turned her attention to the truck driving toward her from the end of the runway where the shots were fired. The pickup pulled up beside her and the current sheriff of Corpus Christi, Mathew Helms, got out.

"I did the best I could," he said.

Sandra stood and stared at him for a moment, her left hand on her left hip and the other on her pistol. "Yeah, I guess you did, but you know what, maybe your best just isn't good enough around here." She quickly drew her pistol and fired two rounds into his chest. Mathew's eyes popped open wide and the surprise was evident on his face.

Nope, your best just isn't good enough!

Sandra turned and climbed into her Jeep, cranked up the engine, and took one more look at Mathew lying in a growing puddle of blood before she headed toward the Farm. Halfway there, she remembered Russ and Jorge at the Airport and turned around to check on them.

Sandra walked into the hangar and yelled out, "Russ! Jorge!" There was no answer and she headed through Russ's office and into his sleeping quarters, flipping the lights on as she went. She gasped and covered her mouth with her hand when she saw Russ's face covered with blood, his eyes frozen in time, staring into space. She turned and headed to Jorge's room. She flipped his light on and immediately turned it back off and closed the door.

"Dammit!" echoed through the hangar.

Sandra shook her head in disgust as she walked back outside, climbed into the Jeep, and headed toward the Farm.

Sandra was grinding her teeth as she slid to a stop in a cloud of dust in front of the farmhouse.

"Kim! Brenda!" she yelled, as she stormed up to the house. They met Sandra at the already open front door.

"Florence is not in her cell," Kim said.

"I know," Sandra replied, "Robbie is gone too. It looks like Beka left with him as well. Her car was in the middle of the runway at the Airport."

Sandra pushed her way through the door and headed toward the kitchen. Kim and Brenda followed. "Robbie killed Russ and Jorge at the Airport too."

Brenda almost hesitated to add, "we drug the dead guards into the barn."

Sandra covered her forehead with the palm of her hand. "Two of my best guards too. Robbie was a busy beaver last night. I'll get that bastard though."

"How are you going to do that?" Kim asked, raising her eyebrows.

Sandra grabbed a soda out of the fridge, rolled some ice in a hand towel for her face, and sat down at the table. "I know the direction he headed off and I know he lives along a river. It may take a while, but he shouldn't be that hard to find. I need some scouts. And I'll take care of Sean in the meantime."

"What did he do?" Kim asked.

"Nothing. Guilt by association."

Kim and Brenda didn't say a word. They just stared at Sandra, both afraid to say anything else with the obvious mood she was in.

"I'm going to clean up my face and lie down for a while. I need to think a bit."

Sandra tossed the ice-pack into the sink and headed for the bathroom.

"Anything we can do?" Kim asked.

"Bury the guards," Sandra replied, not turning around.

She flipped the light on and looked into the mirror.

Looks like this is going to leave a scar.

When she finished in the bathroom, the throbbing in her head sent her to the bedroom to lie down.

What the hell am I going to do?

Thirty minutes later, Sandra rolled out of bed. She rested, but her mind was churning with anger. Sleep was not possible.

Sandra finished and headed for the front door. "Didn't I tell you to do something?" she yelled to Kim and Brenda who were still sitting and talking at the kitchen table. "Get off your asses!"

"Yes, ma'am," Kim replied, as the front door slammed shut.

Sandra sat in the Jeep and massaged her sore hand a second. She turned the ignition and crammed the gearshift into gear. The tires slung gravel and dirt as she left in a cloud of dust.

Fifteen minutes later, she screeched the tires on the pavement as she pulled up in front of the office at the Police compound. The second of two men exiting the building held the door for her as she stepped inside.

A large counter stretched across the center of the room, but no one manned the station. A plain-clothes man was staring at a bulletin board on the back wall. Two uniformed officers were sitting at desks to the left.

"I'm looking for Conrad Baker," she announced.

"He's in the can," one of the men behind the desks replied without looking up.

Sandra walked over to where he sat rustling papers, still mostly ignoring her.

"Something I can help you with, Sandra?" the officer at the other desk asked.

"Do you have any maps of the area?"

He leaned over pushing at his heavy black glasses to keep them in place as he pulled open the drawer. He slammed it shut and pulled open another drawer. He grabbed a handful of folded roadmaps, laid them on the desktop, and spread them out. Sandra reached down and picked one up with *Texas* across the top. She walked over to an empty chair, plopped down, and shook open the map.

As Sandra studied it, Conrad walked in from a hallway. He immediately recognized Sandra sitting in the line of chairs along the front wall of the office.

"To what do I owe the pleasure of your visit?" he asked and sat in the chair next to her.

"I need a new Chief of Police," she said without hesitation.

"Oh!" Conrad replied.

"You up for the job?"

A smile formed on his face. "Yes, ma'am."

"All right then. Your first job is to get a few men over to the Airport to bury some bodies. Mathew is on the runway and Jorge and Russ are in the hangar. There are two dead guards at the Farm, but the girls are taking care of them."

"What the hell is going on?" Conrad said, with a questioning look on his face, his mouth never fully closing, as he looked at Sandra for answers.

"It seems Robbie hijacked our Cessna Skyhawk and flew back to Peaceful Valley with Florence Ingalls and Beka Livingston this morning."

"How?" When she didn't respond, he just sat staring at Sandra with a surprised look on his face.

She wasn't in the mood to provide him with the answers. She folded the map back up, though not exactly as she found it, and stuck it in her britches pocket as she got up and headed toward the door. "Meet me out at the Farm tomorrow morning," she said over her shoulder as she walked out.

"Yes, ma'am," he replied, as she pulled the door shut behind her.

Conrad stood confounded at Sandra's lack of explanation and the quick exit. "Well, at least I got a promotion," he muttered to himself.

Chapter 1

Back at the Farm, Kim ran out to the bunkhouse after Sandra left and instructed two ladies to bury the guards, while Brenda made some snacks and tea. Kim joined her and they sat at the kitchen table discussing Sandra. They had never seen her so upset, not even when Jade tried to topple her regime a few months back. And the nasty cut and bruise on her face didn't seem to faze her a bit.

The ordeal with Jade had lasted a few hours and Sandra was once again back in control. However, Robbie would be more difficult. He was far away, and it would take a while for her to find him if that was her plan. Even longer to deal with the problem.

"I think Sandra's gone off the deep-end," Kim said, as she spooned some sugar into her glass.

"I think so too. It looks like she's going to kill Sean. I don't know what happened at the Airport, but Robbie, Florence, and Beka have put her into a tailspin."

"There are way too many people dying around here for me," Kim stated and took a sip. "If we rub Sandra the wrong way one day, we could end up on the chopping block too."

Brenda swallowed her bite and rinsed it down. "You're reading my mind, girl."

Kim and Brenda sat across from each other, both staring at the other. They nibbled their finger sandwiches and sipped their teas, but both sat quietly.

It may take weeks, if not months before Sandra can find Robbie and deal with him, Kim thought. *That's a long time for her to be on edge. She could shoot me for looking at her differently, or burning a slice of toast.*

They finished their snacks and got up to clean the dishes.

"I'd like to see Robbie again," Kim said, out of the blue.

Brenda rolled her eyes. "Damn, he *was* hot wasn't he?"

Kim smiled. "I wonder what Sean looks like. No one can be as good looking as Robbie, but I'll bet he's easy on the eyes too."

"He's a *neut,*" Brenda reminded Kim.

"So were some of the other guys I've been with. It just takes a little more to get them going, but when you do…"

Brenda smiled. "I guess all of us around here who have been with Robbie immediately fell in love with him. Can we see him again? You know what we're thinking is crazy, don't you? If Sandra gets wind of anything suspicious around here, she's going to bury us. I hate to see Sean die for no good reason, but he can't protect us, can he?"

"I don't know," Kim replied, her forehead wrinkling in thought.

Their ears perked up when they heard a car door slam. "I'm going to do some laundry," Kim said, sliding back in her chair.

"And I'll get started on dinner."

Brenda heard the front door and moments later Sandra appeared at the entryway to the kitchen.

"You working on dinner?" she asked, slamming her keys down on the table.

"Yes, ma'am," Brenda replied, without looking over while she put her apron on. She couldn't help her lips curling up into a smile.

It wouldn't hurt you to miss a meal or two.

"I'm going to take a shower and get cleaned up. Where's Kim?"

"She's in the laundry room," the smile fading quickly, but it returned when she looked over to see Sandra's fat ass disappear around the corner.

Just over an hour later, Sandra joined Kim and Brenda at the kitchen table for dinner. With everything that had been going on the past few weeks, Sandra put everyone else out in the bunkhouse. She only wanted her two most trusted ladies by her side and in her house. She always slept with her door locked and her pistol on the pillow next to her so she could sleep better.

Brenda and Kim sat eating quietly but keeping an eye on Sandra while she picked at her food and muttered to herself. Sean, Robbie, Beka, and Florence's names came up often, along with 'bastard', 'son-of-a-bitch', and 'kill'.

"Meatloaf was a little over-cooked," Sandra grumbled. She got up. "I'm going to bed," she added, on the way out.

Kim and Brenda didn't say a word except 'yes, ma'am' as Sandra left the room. They took nervous looks at each other, then got busy on the dishes and cleaning up.

Over-cooked meatloaf? Kim thought. *Sandra's not going to be satisfied with anything we do. Sooner or later, we'll pay for the slightest mistake or error. We've got to get out of here.*

Brenda took the trash out to the container on the back porch, then she and Kim headed to their rooms.

"Want to stay with me tonight?" Kim asked.

Brenda grabbed a pair of panties and a nightie out of her dresser and followed Kim to her room. They took a shower together, each giving the other a good back scrub. After primping in front of the mirror a while, they crawled into bed, but it would be hours before they finally fell asleep. They had a lot to talk about.

"Do you think Sandra will really kill Sean?" Brenda asked.

"I don't know, but we need to warn him," Kim replied. "She was certainly mad enough an hour ago and she's still steaming, but she'll cool down. I think she'll consider her options for a while. With all that's been happening here at the Farm, she'll be busy here for a bit."

"I certainly hope so," Brenda said. "We need time to plan our escape. If we go off half-cocked, we'll get caught and we're dead. So, how are we going to get out of here?"

"We can take one of the tractors with a forklift. We'll put a pallet on the forks and say we're going to the ice plant for a load of ice. That we're going to butcher a couple of the calves from the milk cows. I think that'll take care of the curious. I think it takes about an hour to get to the Bayfront by tractor. All we need to do is avoid Sandra."

"So, when are we doing this?" Brenda queried.

"Let's see what Sandra does in the morning. If she's calmed down and attending to business, we may have time to plan a successful escape. If she's still acting crazy, I think we need to take the chance and just run."

"And how are we going to get out of here once we warn Sean?" Brenda asked.

"Maybe on Sean's boat. We can go out to the Intracoastal Waterway well out of sight, sink the boat in deep water, and swim to shore. No one will know where we went."

"Do you know how to drive a boat, Kim? I know I certainly don't."

"No, but I bet Sean does. The plan will depend on Sean being on the boat, so we'll need an alternative just in case he's not."

"But Kim, it will be suspicious for us to go out on the boat during the middle of the day. And we don't even know which boat Sean might be on."

"Robbie said Sean was on Sonny's boat. I don't know his last name, but there can't be but one 'Sonny' down there on a shrimp boat. Someone will know which boat he's on and even if they're suspicious, that won't be a problem once we're on the bay. We've got to watch out for Marcia though, Sonny's wife. She's one of Sandra's spies and they have a teenage daughter, Lola, I think. Unless they're shrimping, I think Lola will keep Marcia home. They won't be hanging around the boats for no reason."

"How did you find all this out, Kim?"

"I keep my ears open," she replied, with a smile, "and I remember stuff."

"And if we run into Sean, Sonny, and Marcia at the same time?"

"I think that is always a possibility," Kim replied. "If we do, we'll have to deal with that when the time comes."

"It would be great if we had a foolproof plan. All I can see is a plan riddled with so many holes that we're both going to die a miserable death if Sandra gives us no choice but to leave immediately."

"Have a little faith, Brenda. If Sandra is calmed down in the morning, maybe we can have the time we need to do a few trial runs."

"How long do you think it'll take to iron out a good plan?" Brenda asked.

"My best estimate would be a couple weeks at least, with all the other stuff we have to do around here, but will Sandra give us that much time?"

"Are we doing the right thing?" Brenda asked, tears beginning to form in her eyes. "This is so sudden and the plan sounds crazy at best."

"I know, Brenda." Kim put her hand on her arm and gave it a squeeze. "If we stay here, we will work ourselves into an early grave. That is if Sandra doesn't kill us sooner. We had Robbie to look forward to for months and we had fun. But now that he is gone, we have nothing to look forward to. No one can replace Robbie. No one!"

"Or maybe Sean will surprise us. He may be a hunk too. If we can get to Peaceful Valley, we'll have the freedom to do what we want. Maybe we can even have Robbie again."

Kim smiled at that prospect. "We may have to work hard, but we will be free. And our babies will be free. If we have sons, they won't be castrated by Sandra. They can live full lives."

Brenda changed her position in bed so she could see Kim a little better. "How far along are you?"

"About four months," Kim replied.

"Yeah, me too. I hope we're making the right decision."

"If we can get out of here, and if we can make it to Peaceful Valley with Sean without killing our babies, it will be the right thing to do," Kim said.

Brenda sighed. "We better get some sleep."

"And fix Sandra a big breakfast without her asking."

Brenda giggled. "Right!"

Brenda and Kim were hard at work in the kitchen when Sandra walked in. "Smells good," she said.

Brenda handed Sandra a cup of coffee. "Bacon is ready and eggs are in the pan."

Sandra sat down and sipped her coffee, while Kim put several slices of bacon on her plate. Kim retrieved a bowl of fruit from the fridge, cut up just like Sandra liked it, and set it in front of her. Brenda slid four eggs onto their boss' plate and a couple on hers and Kim's plates. Kim added a few more strips of bacon to Sandra's and grabbed two more bowls of fruit for themselves.

They were all quiet as they ate. Kim kept one eye on Sandra, but she never looked up or said a word. The girls ate slower than Sandra, so they finished their smaller portions at the same time she did. When Sandra pushed her plate back and wiped her face with her napkin, Kim got up and gathered the dishes and carried them to the sink.

No mistakes; keep Sandra happy.

Sandra sat finishing her coffee watching Brenda and Kim clean up. They avoided eye contact with her.

Sandra downed the last of her coffee and pushed back in her chair. "I've got work to do." Without another word, she headed toward the front door.

Brenda and Kim stopped what they were doing and watched through the window as Sandra went out to the barn.

"Well, it looks like she's going to work, and not after Sean," Brenda said.

Kim nodded. "We'll keep an eye on her every day. As long as she's tending to her business, we'll continue to work on our plan."

Chapter 2

For the next several days, Brenda and Kim watched Sandra's every move and fixed her the best meals they could, pulling out all her favorite recipes, making certain they stayed on her good side. They spoke only when spoken to and made a big platter of fudge. Sandra loved fudge and would stay in a good mood until it was finished. She ate half the fudge by late the first evening. By noon the next day, it was nearly gone.

When they received word of a hurricane coming in, it really got busy around the Farm. Sandra had to make sure everything was tied down. She was so busy with preparations she appeared to have forgotten all about Sean and Robbie.

Four days later, Hurricane Alexandra, the first one of the season and named by Sandra, slammed into the coast just south of Corpus Christi, close enough that Corpus got the brunt of the storm. Fortunately, it appeared no more than what used to be graded as a category two, and while it was not catastrophic, it caused plenty of damage.

Band after band of heavy thunderstorms lashed at the city. Winds near a hundred miles per hour snapped trees and took roofs off some of the older buildings. The storm surge brought the sea water into all the low-lying areas including the salt and ice plants. The storm chugged along at a slow pace dumping rain, unlike any hurricane in decades.

The shrimp boats were taken to a safe location. Damage to the salt and ice plants was minimal—the plants would need to return to production quickly, particularly the ice plant. They could do without salt for a while, but the ice was necessary for food storage. Foods needed to be kept cold during harvest and transport to the processing plants.

The processing plants on the Bayfront, the Farm, and the Police compounds all needed ice as well. The one at the Bayfront processed all the seafood, the Farm processed veal from the dairy cattle's calves, and the Police compound wild game and cattle from the surrounding area.

There was also damage to a couple of the wind turbines. Electricity was out at the Bayfront, and the Police compound had minimal power. The lack of electricity at the ice plant complicated repairs.

The power was on at the Farm, but there was roof damage on some of the barns. Tree limbs were scattered everywhere and the place was a general mess.

Two days later, the sun came out and the wind died down. The storm surge receded and people began to mingle about. The gulls, terns, and brown pelicans resumed their daily routine.

Over the next three weeks, the Farm was buzzing with activity trying to get the place back in order, as was the rest of the city. The ice and salt plants, and the refinery, were top priorities. The Fall shrimping season was open and they needed ice and fuel.

The storm really stirred up the bay. When the shrimp boats were able to get back out on the water, their catches were minimal at best. They couldn't do without the seafood completely, so they accepted their meager reward for their hard work.

One morning during breakfast, after everything was back to near normal, and things had settled down, Sandra made the remark that it was time to find out where Peaceful Valley was. "I'm going to the Police compound and then down to the Bayfront," she said. She finished her coffee and headed out the front door without another word.

Kim looked over at Brenda. "She's going to kill Sean today."

Kim and Brenda had worked on their plan for a month. Sandra had given them the time they needed to come up with what they thought was a foolproof plan.

Due to the meager shrimp catches, Sandra advised the shrimp boats that they would only be allowed to work three days a week to conserve fuel until such time as the refinery got back to full production. The girls had no idea which days these would be, but they had a better than fifty percent chance to catch Sean and Sonny at the harbor working on their boat. 'Shrimp boat captains are always working on their boats' she'd heard Sandra say numerous times.

Kim and Brenda watched out the window as Sandra got in her Jeep and drove away. They immediately ran to their rooms and changed into their jeans and best sneakers. They each grabbed a parka as there was a slight chill in the air this morning.

Brenda followed Kim through the kitchen and each pocketed a utility knife, then headed outside and across the yard to a tractor with a forklift on the front. Kim checked the fuel. It was full enough and she started it up. She hopped off and helped Brenda put a pallet on the forks.

"These things seem heavier when you're pregnant," Kim remarked.

"I thought it was just me," Brenda replied.

Both girls put their hands on their hips, straightened their backs, and smiled at each other.

Kim climbed back up and sat down. She raised the forks so the pallet wouldn't fall off and Brenda hopped up on the drawbar.

"Let's get the hell out of here," Brenda whispered.

"Hold on tight."

They both looked around the yard as they headed toward the Bayfront. No one seemed to care what they were doing.

"So far, so good," Kim said, looking back at Brenda.

Kim drove toward the Bayfront by the shortest route possible without getting on the main roads. The tractor would only go twenty miles per hour and the trip seemed to take forever. Brenda kept looking over her shoulder to see if they were being followed and Kim kept a sharp lookout both front and to the sides.

There was a little fog this morning—not enough to hinder driving, but just maybe enough to help conceal their escape. Kim hoped Sean and Sonny would be working on their boat this particular morning.

Please let Sean be at the boat, Kim thought. *What if he's not there? We are so screwed if he's not. Are we doing the right thing? Yes, we are, but if Sean's not there or if Sandra catches us, we are dead and so are our babies.*

At last, they made it to the ice plant and Kim pulled the tractor alongside and killed the engine. They got off and looked around. There were not a lot of people stirring this morning.

Likely because this is not a shrimping day, Kim thought. *Please let that be it!*

The girls walked briskly to the T-head where the shrimp boats parked. Men were working on about half the vessels. They walked past the first several boats until they reached one with two men working on their nets and rigging.

"Excuse me," Kim said, "which boat is Sonny's?"

Both men looked up and stared for a moment. One of the men turned and looked down the line of boats, then extended his arm pointing, "the one with that kid standing on the back."

"Thanks," Kim said and headed in that direction.

Brenda followed, but after a dozen steps, she turned to look at the men they had talked to. They were both still staring at them. Brenda turned back around and kept walking.

Though Kim never looked back, she could feel their eyes on her.

"They're still watching us," Brenda said, nervously.

Kim didn't reply and kept walking. When she reached the back of the boat the man indicated, she asked, "Are you, Sean?"

"Yes," he replied, with a quizzical look on his face.

"Can we talk?"

Sean turned and looked over his shoulder. Sonny was still below deck. Sean walked over to the side of the boat and motioned for the girls to come over onto the ramp.

"I'm Kim and this is Brenda," she whispered. "We work at the Farm. We knew Robbie. Did he ever talk to you about us?"

"No."

"Well, Sandra went on a rampage when Robbie left with Florence and Beka. She calmed down quickly and the storm kept her really busy over the past month, but this morning she mentioned you again. We're scared. We're sure she's going to kill you."

Sean's jaw dropped open and his eyes opened wide. "What? Never mind; I heard you."

"We want you to take us to Peaceful Valley," Kim added. "Right now."

Sean looked back toward the cabin to see if Sonny had come topside.

"I mean right now!" Kim reiterated.

"But Sonny is below deck," Sean stated.

"Kill him, throw him overboard, or take him with us, it doesn't matter, but we need to go now or we're all dead," Kim said, anxiously.

Sean's eyes darted left and right, his mouth slightly ajar. "I don't know," he replied.

"Listen, Sandra went ballistic when Robbie flew the coop," Kim explained. "Robbie killed Russ and Jorge at the Airport and two guards at the Farm, but the worst is that Beka, Florence, and especially Robbie flew off. I think Sandra really went nuts because of Robbie. She trusted him and he screwed her over. She said she was going to kill you out of spite. The storm and repairs afterward kept Sandra busy and gave us time to come up with a plan. This morning, Sandra said she was coming to the Bayfront to remedy a problem. I assumed she meant that problem was you."

"So what does it matter to you?"

"We like Robbie. We like him a lot. With all the killing going on around here, we thought we might make a better life for ourselves in Peaceful Valley."

"Not just us," Brenda added, "but for our kids—Robbie's kids."

Sean looked at the girls, then down toward their stomachs. "Both of you?"

"Yes."

Brenda looked around at the other boats to see if they were attracting any attention. No one seemed to be paying them any consideration, except one of the men they talked to earlier. "That man we talked to is staring at us again."

Sean and Kim glanced over.

"We've got to go," Kim said.

"Okay, get aboard," Sean said, "and start taking the ropes off . . . quietly."

Sean walked over to the cabin, then stepped inside. He stuck his head through the opening to below deck. "You about finished up down there?"

"I'm finished," came the reply from Sonny.

Kim walked over to the cabin door. Sean grabbed a skillet off the mini-stove and waited for Sonny to appear. When Sonny stuck his head through the opening, the last thing he saw was a strange girl standing in the doorway.

Sean turned to Kim. "Now what?"

"The boat is untied. Let's get out of here."

Sean took another quick look at Sonny crumpled up on the floor, dropped the skillet, and turned toward the controls. He hit the starter button and the engine purred like a kitten. He slipped the gearshift forward, maneuvered out of the stall, and toward the opening in the jetty.

"Is he dead?" Kim asked, looking down the stairway to below.

"I hope not. Keep an eye on him and as soon as I get out of the harbor you can hold the wheel while I bring him topside. We'll tie him up if he's still alive."

Sean made the turn and pointed the boat east. "Where are we going?"

"To the Intracoastal," Kim replied.

Sean lined out the direction and told Kim to take the wheel. He then pointed to the compass and told her to keep it at 110°.

Kim steered while Brenda kept an eye on the compass. Sean pushed Sonny up through the opening and Brenda grabbed his arms and tugged. Sean followed Sonny up through the doorway and grabbed some rope to tie him up. He checked his pulse first and found a steady beat. He hog-tied him and relieved Kim at the wheel.

Sean turned his attention back to driving the boat. He glanced back regularly to see if anyone was following. No one was trailing. He looked down at Sonny, then back at the girls.

"How are we supposed to get out of this mess," Sean said, his voice stressed. "Do we have a plan?"

"I think so," Kim replied, with a little uncertainty in her voice. "We take the boat out to the waterway, sink it in deep water, and swim to shore. We then walk around Corpus Christi and on to Peaceful Valley. Can you find your way home?"

"Yes, if I can find the road we came here on."

"Well, then that's the plan."

"We can't sink the boat though," Sean said. "This is his livelihood."

"If we don't," Kim replied, "someone will find the boat and know where we got onshore. They can track us down."

"And what about Sonny?"

"I don't think we have a choice," Kim said.

Sean didn't say anything and turned his attention back to driving. He knew what she meant.

You've been a good friend for a long time, Sonny. We can't . . . there has to be another way.

Sean tried to come up with another option, but he couldn't think of one. Sonny didn't fit into the plan.

"I've never been on a shrimp boat," Brenda said, looking a little green in the gills. "Is the water always this rough out here?"

"This isn't rough," Sean replied. "Just a slight chop. We're headed crosswind so the boat rolls a little, but this isn't bad at all. I've seen it a lot worse."

"Well, it's rough to me," Brenda said, putting her hand to her mouth. She then turned and threw up on the floor next to Sonny.

Sean laughed and turned to take another look out the rear as they approached the Intracoastal Waterway. He breathed a sigh of relief no one was following them as he turned toward the northeast and up the canal. To Brenda's relief, the water was not so rough in the protected channel and the boat cut through the water smoothly now.

Sonny began to stir and Sean turned to look at him. Even if he woke up, he wasn't going anywhere, but Sean picked up the skillet and whacked him on the head again. He felt guilty enough hitting him in the first place; he didn't want to feel he needed to explain his actions to him.

"How far do we go?" Sean asked.

Kim squeezed her chin with her thumb and forefinger. "Two or three miles should do it."

"And what about Sonny?"

The girls looked at each other. Were they going to become accomplices in a murder?"

"We can't take him with us can we?" Kim asked, her expression turning sad.

Sean shrugged his shoulders, hopeful, but knowing otherwise.

The girls looked at each other and shook their heads. If they could have thought of another option, they would certainly have taken it, but time was running out and a decision had to be made.

"Three miles," Sean announced and pulled over toward the shoreline and shallower water. "It's time."

The girls jumped overboard and swam the short distance to the bank, while Sean backed the boat to the center of the waterway. The wind was light enough that the boat wouldn't drift far before it sank. Sean went below deck and grabbed a small sledgehammer from the toolbox and started busting holes in the hull. Two minutes and he had water rushing in through several holes.

Sean climbed back up the stairs and took another look at Sonny. He was still out. Sean then re-centered the boat in the deepest part of the waterway and waited for the boat to list. Confident the boat was about to go under, he killed the engine and went to the back deck closing the door behind him.

"Sorry, Sonny," he murmured. He turned, jumped in, and swam to shore.

When Sean reached dry land, he turned to see the vessel roll on its side and quickly sink. Sean looked up and down the waterway for boats. No one had seen his foul deed. He then pointed the direction to the girls and he followed, wiping the tears from his eyes.

He took a last look where the boat sank, before going over the hill. Sonny stayed down with the boat, only a few bubbles rising to the surface marked the spot.

Chapter 3

Sandra pulled her Jeep in front of the office at the Police compound and got out. A couple of men had the hood up on what appeared to be the car Beka left on the runway at the Airport. Conrad came out and met her halfway to the door. "I was just on my way out to the Farm."

"You get the mess cleaned up at the Airport?" she asked.

Conrad gave her a two-finger salute. "Yes, just as you ordered. And we brought the car over here. We need a new car. You okay with that?"

"Whatever!"

Sandra turned with a miffed look on her face and wiggled a hook finger over her shoulder. "Now, come over here."

Sandra walked back to her Jeep and spread the map she got yesterday on the hood.

"I want you to send some men out to locate Peaceful Valley," Sandra said. "You were with Richard when they first picked up Robbie and Sean."

"Yes, ma'am."

"So you know where they entered Corpus. Look at this map. They came in on this road," she said, pointing. "Follow the road about a hundred miles. There is a river here and here. Peaceful Valley has to be somewhere along one of those rivers. This one is closest to the highway. Check that one out first."

Conrad stood back scratching his head. "What do you want us to do when we find it?"

"Nothing; and don't let anyone see you. If they spot you, they'll know I'm looking for them and that'll ruin the surprise attack. Just locate them and report back here. Then I'll decide what to do."

"Yes, ma'am. Anything else?"

"Find a few of your best men and send them out as soon as you can. I want to find Peaceful Valley before the end of next week."

That's not enough time, but I can't tell Sandra that. I'll end up like Mathew.

"I have some men in mind, but it'll take some time to round them up. I'll have them on their way in a few days."

"You *do* have another one of these?" she asked, pointing to the map.

Conrad nodded and Sandra folded up the map and stuck it in her pocket. She crawled into the Jeep, drove to the Airport, and made a quick inspection. Everything was just as Conrad had told her. She smiled and headed for the Bayfront.

Sandra stopped by Marcia and Sonny's house first. Lola was playing on the swing set in the front yard. "Where's your mama?" she asked.

Lola looked up and pulled her dark curly locks out of her face. "Inside," she replied, timidly.

Sandra walked to the side door and knocked. Marcia appeared with a wooden spoon in her hand.

She pushed the screen door open. "Come on in."

Marcia handed the spoon to Sandra. "I know you like chocolate," she said. "I'll send some fudge along with you. I just finished up a fresh platter."

"Sonny and Sean around?"

"They're down on the boat. They're taking care of some maintenance and sewing on their nets. They don't want to have any problems when they're out in the bay." Marcia couldn't help noticing the fresh scar on Sandra's face. "What happened to you?"

"It's a long story. Don't plan on having Sean around for the rest of the fall shrimp season."

Marcia gave her a quizzical look.

"Robbie flew the coop last month just before the storm blew in."

Marcia turned the fire down on her pot of stew and gave Sandra her undivided attention.

"Robbie took one of the planes and left with Florence and Beka. I'm sending some men out to find Peaceful Valley."

"And your face?"

"It's nothing," Sandra said, lightly touching her cheek.

"What are you going to do with Sean?"

"Feed him to the crabs."

Marcia stared at Sandra but had nothing to say. She got a knife, cut the fudge, and wrapped up a small package for Sandra.

"I'm going to the harbor," she said getting up. "Thanks for the fudge."

Sandra pulled up to the stall where Sonny parked his boat, but the slip was empty. She got out and looked around, but the boat was nowhere to be seen. Sandra heard a whistle and turned her head down the line of boats. A man was standing on the stern of a boat staring at her. She walked over.

"You looking for Sonny?" he asked.

"Yes, as a matter of fact, I am."

"He left about an hour ago. Had a couple of pretty ladies with him too."

"What!?"

"Yeah. I don't know what he'd be doing going out this time of day, but that's what he did all right. He didn't say a word to anyone. Just left and headed out across the bay," he said, motioning with his arm. "None of my business."

"Shit! Who were the girls?"

"Never seen them before," he replied. "Right pretty though."

Sandra walked back over to her Jeep and looked across the bay. She couldn't see the boat.

What the hell is he doing?

Sandra paced back and forth trying to come up with a reason for Sonny to leave. She was clueless.

She walked over to one of the other boats where there were men working, commandeered the captain, and took him over to the man who whistled at her.

"I want you two to take your boats and see if you can find out where Sonny went. He wouldn't go out in the Gulf without Marcia, so he has to be somewhere across the bay or up and down the Intracoastal Waterway. I want you to find him and bring him back."

Sandra crossed her arms across her chest and the two captains just stood staring at each other. "Well!"

"Now?" one asked.

"Yes, right now. I want Sonny back in port. Don't give him a choice. I'll send someone down here to take Sonny, Sean and whomever into custody when you get back this evening."

The men got on their boats and started them up. Sandra watched until they exited the jetty. She got in her Jeep and headed to the Police compound.

What the hell is going on? And who were those girls? Could Sean be trying to escape? Sonny can't be a party to that. He wouldn't leave Marcia and Lola. I'll have his hide if he did.

Sandra filled Conrad in on what was happening at the Bayfront and that Sonny and the rest were to be arrested and held when the two boats brought them back that evening. "I'll be back in the morning to interrogate Sonny."

When Sandra finished her business with Conrad, she drove back to the Farm. It was getting late and she was hungry. She walked into the kitchen expecting to see Kim and Brenda hard at work on dinner. Instead, she found a sink full of dirty dishes and an empty house. "God dammit!" She checked in their rooms and they were empty as well. "Shit!"

Sandra stormed to the kitchen and stared at the empty room. Deflated, she sat down at the table. She grabbed the last piece of fudge from the platter and pounded her fist on the table. The reality of what was happening was finally sinking in. Then she remembered the fudge Marcia had given her and got up to retrieve it from the Jeep. Chocolate was the only thing which could help soothe her pain.

Chapter 4

Sean followed the girls, giving them directions from time to time, then he took point for nearly two hours. They meandered around old buildings overgrown with brush. It seemed like there was no one around and the walking was easy much of the way, but they were not concealed very well. They would be readily spotted, should they wander upon someone.

"Sean has a nice ass," Kim whispered to Brenda.

"Yeah, I can't stop staring either. Moreover, he's not bad looking. Maybe not as good looking as Robbie, but I wouldn't mind crawling into bed with him."

Kim giggled. "That's what I was thinking. It's been a while since I've been with a man and I'm getting downright horny."

"I doubt he's had a woman since he's been here," Brenda added. "You know they don't do much but work after they're castrated. Maybe he's about ready for a little one on one."

"Or two-on-one," Kim said, turning around with a sly smile on her face and giving Brenda a wink.

Sean kept glancing back at the girls. He couldn't hear what they were saying, but their constant giggling piqued his curiosity.

Sean spotted some larger trees and dense brush and led the girls in that direction. "We should make camp here and get our clothes dried out. The wet shoes are going to give us blisters and we have a long way to go. It's going to get chilly tonight and being wet will make us even colder. I don't think we can risk building a fire."

Sean led the girls into a clump of trees and brush. "I think this is good enough." He looked around. "No one could see us in here even if they walk right by us."

Sean sat on the ground, removed his shoes and socks, and hung them on a tree limb. He took his shirt off next and draped it over another branch.

The girls looked at each other, then followed Sean's lead, first with their shoes, then their tops.

Sean pretended to not look when they took their bras off, but he couldn't help himself. He tried to contain his smile when the girls removed their jeans. Sean turned away so they wouldn't see him drooling, but they did see him.

Kim smiled. "Take a good look, Sean. We don't care. The human body is probably the most beautiful thing on this planet, and there are a lot of wonderful things."

Kim stepped over to Sean and touched his arm. "Turn around." Sean turned back and gazed into Kim's smiling face. "It's okay," and she kissed him on the forehead. "We're going to get to know each other probably more than we should over the next couple weeks. We'll be peeing and pooping, bathing I hope, and there is nothing to be bashful or ashamed about."

Sean relaxed a bit, but the flush returned when he took his underwear off. He covered himself and sat down on the ground. The girls joined him forming a circle, all totally nude as the sun slowly crept toward the horizon. The girls didn't try to conceal their breasts and Sean tried not to stare, but he couldn't help but get a good look. He'd never seen such a beautiful sight.

Sean changed the subject to help him not gawk at the girls. "We can do without food for days, but we'll need water. Tomorrow is going to be difficult. We need to find a freshwater source and something to carry it in."

"I'm already hungry and thirsty," Brenda said.

Sean nodded. "It'll get worse. There was no food on the boat. We always boiled a few shrimp or grilled fish. You didn't give me a choice, but why didn't you bring food?"

Kim shrugged her shoulders. "I guess we thought you'd take care of us once we found you."

An hour later, their clothes were dry, but their shoes would take the rest of the evening and night at least. They got up and dressed. Sean watched as the girls put their clothes back on, taking another good look at their bodies before they were covered.

After the girls finished dressing, his mind, however, could still see them as they were before and he couldn't help smiling every time he looked at them. Their beauty burned into his memory and teased his manhood.

Sean eventually snapped out of his dream and pulled some weeds to make the best bed he could under the circumstances. They then huddled together, Sean in the middle, Brenda in front of him, and Kim against his back with her arms wrapped around him.

The girls squirmed for a little while and he could hear them giggling as they tried to get comfortable. They soon drifted off to sleep.

Sean felt a tug on his leg and raised up to see what was happening.

"You little bastard! You thought you could kill me and get away with it?"

"Sonny!"

"I'm not so easy to drown," he growled. "I've got you now and you're gonna pay. And you sank my goddamn boat!"

"No, Sonny. Please! I didn't mean to. I didn't think you'd come with us. We didn't have a choice. I couldn't let you tell Sandra where we went. She would torture and kill us."

Sonny laughed an evil laugh and grabbed Sean by the throat. His hand felt cold, tightening around his neck, and Sonny's eyes were balls of fire. "I can't breathe. Please . . . no . . . I'm sorry . . ."

Sean's body jerked and his eyes popped open, a cold sweat on his face. The girls squirmed. He looked around. All he could see was darkness and the silhouette of the trees above. Sonny was not there.

Sandra awoke at daybreak. She rolled out of bed and hurried to the bathroom. Since she hadn't taken a shower last night, she put on the same clothes. She put a little deodorant on and washed her face, but if she still smelled, then anyone she ran into would have to put up with the odor. She really didn't care. She hadn't slept well at all and all she was interested in at the moment was Sean and where in Hell he was. She had crabs to feed.

When Sandra reached the kitchen, there was no sign of Brenda and Kim. How could she have forgotten they took off with that renegade Sean? She grabbed a soda and a banana to eat on the road, but when she crawled into her jeep, she found herself just sitting there staring out of the window.

Did Kim and Brenda warn Sean that I was out to get him? Why would they do that? They never even met Sean. Was it Robbie who started this whole mess? Maybe the girls just wanted a way to get to Peaceful Valley and Robbie. Where could they be going on the shrimp boat? What the hell is going on?

Sandra cranked the Jeep up and headed for the Bayfront. She kept going over and over the reasoning for Sean leaving on the boat.

He's going the wrong direction. Maybe he was afraid to cross Corpus Christi. Brenda and Kim were born and raised here. They couldn't be leading him somewhere else. For some reason, he thought the boat was his best option, but he's definitely going to circle around and head toward Peaceful Valley.

I could never find him out there. There are a thousand square miles of real estate between here and Peaceful Valley. I'll just have to hope we can catch him at home when we go there for Robbie, Beka, and Florence.

Sandra pulled up to the stall where Sonny's boat was supposed to be. It wasn't there. The two boats she sent out to find him were in their stalls. She got out and walked over to the one where the captain whistled at her. He was not on the boat and neither was his deckhand.

When Sandra got to the other boat, it was vacant as well. "Where the hell is everyone?" There was absolutely no one around on any of the boats, and if there were, they were still asleep.

Sandra walked back to her Jeep and plopped down in the seat. She zipped her jacket. She was chilled by the cooler weather despite the fact she was burning up on the inside. She gripped the steering wheel, laid her forehead on her hands, and closed her eyes for a minute.

Shit! My world is crumbling around me and there seems to be nothing I can do about it.

She felt the tear trickle down her cheek.

Tap-tap-tap on her window. She wiped her tear quickly and raised her head. She was startled to see a face peering through the glass at her. It was the captain who whistled at her.

Sandra rolled the window down. "It's about time someone showed up around here."

"It's cold and there's not all that much to do on the boats. Why get here at the crack of dawn?"

"Well, where's Sonny, Sean, and their passengers?" Sandra asked.

"We didn't see anyone or anything. Buddy went ten miles south in the Intracoastal and I did the same to the north. There was no sign of the boat or its passengers."

"Nothing at all?" she asked, with a confused look on her face.

"No, ma'am."

Sandra didn't say another word. She rolled the window up and started the Jeep. She ground the gears in frustration as she headed toward the Police compound.

"Conrad!" she yelled, stepping through the door into the office.

Conrad walked in from the hallway. "Why is it dark in here?" He walked over to the door and flipped the switch with no result.

Sandra walked out the door and Conrad followed.

"I drove to the Bayfront," she said. "Sonny's boat has not been found. Sean has to be heading for home, but we'll never find him between here and there. We will catch up with him at Peaceful Valley. When we track down Robbie, we'll bring both the boys and all the girls home."

"I want you to check with all your men and make certain they report anything suspicious. I want Corpus wrapped up tighter than a drum. Check with me in a few days and I'll make sure everything and everyone are shipshape at the Farm."

"Yes, ma'am."

Sandra drove back to the Farm and rounded up a few of the ladies she thought she could trust. She invited them into the house and asked a couple of them to prepare some drinks and snacks for the meeting that would start as soon as they were ready.

When the hors d'oeuvres and drinks were brought in, Sandra started the discussion. "There has been way too much shit hitting the fan around here lately and it's going to stop . . ."

One of the girls raised her hand.

"What?" Sandra snapped.

"Where's Brenda and Kim?" she asked, obviously wishing now that she hadn't interrupted Sandra.

"Gone," was the only explanation she gave. Sandra pointed her finger at the girls one at a time, naming tasks for each. "Anyone stepping out of line ever-so-slightly will be shoveling manure for the rest of your life."

No one said anything except to respond to Sandra's assignments with a polite 'yes, ma'am'. Sandra was in no mood for even the slightest dissent. The ladies knew what she was capable of and that she would revel in slitting their throats or lining them up in front of a firing squad. They had all seen Sandra at her worst. Shoveling manure would be little more than a slap on the hand.

Sandra stood up and most of the ladies scurried out of the house. The two exceptions were Sandra's new cooks. They went to the kitchen and got started on lunch. Outside of the clatter of dishes, they were quiet for fear Sandra would overhear them. The new orders that they would only be allowed in the house to prepare, serve, and clean up during mealtime said Sandra meant business. Outside of meals, the house would be locked down and to herself.

The next morning, Sean woke abruptly. The wet tongue of a large black dog lapped at his face. He appeared to be a cross between a black Labrador and a German Shepherd. Sean rolled over and reached out to pet him. He shied away, but with Sean's urging, he returned to be petted.

Sean got the girls up and they both showered the canine with affection.

"Where do you suppose he came from?" Kim asked.

"Your guess is as good as mine," Sean replied.

"Do you think he belongs to someone around here?" Brenda inquired.

Sean shrugged his shoulders.

The dog sniffed at Sean's hand.

"I'm sorry mutt but we don't have anything for you to eat. All I can do for you now is give you a good scratch on the back. Come with us if you want, but we can't feed you."

Sean looked around and determined the direction he wanted to go and led the girls out of the brush. The dog followed. Two hours later, the dog was still tagging along.

Sean, Kim, and Brenda made good time. Sean led the way around all the obstacles he thought could give them a problem. The ladies slowed him down at first, but that was expected. They did, however, make better time after they worked their stiffness out and warmed up a bit.

Sean stopped and knelt, urgently motioning to the girls to do the same.

"What's the matter?" Kim whispered.

"See that house over there," he said, turning his head back to the structure, nodding to indicate the direction. "There are people living there. We need to avoid being seen. This could be where the dog came from."

Sean pointed his finger toward their new intended direction and the girls followed quietly. He led Kim and Brenda through a couple of vacant houses where he found one pot which would hold a gallon of water and two glass jars but no lids. If they were to find a water source, they would need to boil the water and be able to take some along with them. Sean found some string with which to make a bow drill, but they couldn't risk building a fire until they got well away from Corpus Christi.

As careful as they needed to travel, they would have no food or water today. Both Kim and Brenda complained of thirst. They were not used to going long without something to drink. Their thirst did take their mind off their hunger. Sean was surprised that by late afternoon the dog was still following. At least he was not thirsty. He found a couple of small puddles to get a drink. The puddles weren't big enough to get water for Sean and the girls, but even if they were, they would not be able to boil the water for safety.

Sean decided to travel only during the daytime and sleep at night, remembering back how he and Robbie were caught. At night, they could be seen with night-vision scopes. During the daytime, there might be more people to spot them, but at least they would have an equal chance of seeing them first.

By the end of the day, Sean thought they had made it over halfway around Corpus. Another day and they should be in heavy enough brush to be able to build a fire and boil some water. They found a vacant house, but the old carpet and bedding were covered in animal feces and stank so bad, he thought it best if they slept outside. The girls agreed.

Sean gathered leaves and grass to make a bed just as he had the night before and the girls snuggled up against him. He was the meat in their sandwich.

"Sean?"

"Yes, Brenda."

"I'm having second thoughts about leaving Corpus."

"It'll be alright. We'll find some water and food soon. Be glad it's not summertime; I'd be doing a little complaining myself."

Sean moved Kim's hair out of his face and noticed the softness. He'd never touched a girl's hair before.

"I would probably be dead now if not for you two. There would have been no escape if Sandra had caught me on the boat. Thank you for that. Now, let's get some sleep. We have a long day ahead of us tomorrow."

The next morning, Sean was up early. He was a bit sore since he wasn't used to sleeping on the ground. The girls felt worse and complained, not only about having to sleep on the ground, but about their growing hunger and thirst. The mutt was still with them, lying nearby, but not in any hurry to get up.

Sean rubbed his nose as he caught a whiff of his body odor. He sniffed his underarms and immediately put his arm down.

Why don't the girls stink? They have to. I just can't smell them over me. They haven't said anything.

Sean kept giving the dog regular back scratches hoping he would continue to follow them until they got food.

"Dogs are a little more trouble," Sean said, "but they are good assets. Robbie and Ronnie had a dog when I was little. He was fun to play with, but mostly he helped to keep us safe. I miss having a dog. I hope this one will keep following us. If we don't get some food soon though, he may leave."

"And we need to eat too," Kim said.

"And water!" Brenda added, getting upset.

Sean took a quick breath. "It was your idea to go to Peaceful Valley! Didn't you know it would likely take a couple weeks to make the trek?"

"We didn't think that far," Brenda said, with watery eyes. "We weren't sure we could even make it out of the city. If we found you and did get out, we thought you would take care of us. You're a good hunter. Robbie told us so."

"I am, but the best place to find food is along a stream. I can't snap my fingers and make water appear. You have to be patient. I *will* find water and I *will* get food, but we have to get a safe distance out of Corpus first."

Sean pressed onward and the girls followed. He looked back occasionally and the girls lagged further and further behind. Directly, he stopped and waited for Brenda and Kim to catch up.

I shouldn't have raised my voice. They are pregnant and they're not used to cross-country hikes. I have to be more considerate.

Toward the end of the day, Sean made it to the highway he thought led toward Peaceful Valley.

"We've got to follow the pavement back toward Corpus to find the building where Robbie and I entered the city. I have to make certain this is the right road."

"We're pregnant, have blisters on our feet, our ankles are swollen, and we're starving. We can't!"

"I don't have a choice. Stay here then, and hopefully, I'll be back before too long."

Kim whispered in Brenda's ear. "Would he leave us out here?"

Brenda's eyes grew wide and she shrugged. Kim nodded to Sean and they trudged along behind him.

A couple of hours later, and Sean found the building and made it back to where they originally found the roadway. It was dark by the time they returned to the spot where they found the road and decided they would venture into the woods some ways to make camp. They still had not found a water source or food.

"If it were hot, we would be severely dehydrated by now," Sean told the girls, "but the air has been cool. I know you're thirsty, but you're not going to die. We'll find water tomorrow."

Sean hugged the girls to mollify them. He didn't know why, but the mutt continued to follow them and he gave him another scratch on the back and some gentle words.

By morning, Kim and Brenda appeared to be getting quite weak from lack of food and water. Due to their weakness, however, they complained less. Sean remembered the stream he and Robbie crossed not far ahead, just before getting to Corpus, and lifted the girls' spirits with this news. It took only a couple of hours to find the water source and the girls were elated.

Sean heard a noise and turned to see a car on the road. He hurried the girls into the brush and they hid behind a large tree and waited. A minute later, a green car sped by. Sean thought the car looked familiar, but this one had men inside, a rifle sticking out of the front window. Once they passed, Sean crept to the edge of the brush to make certain they kept going. He sighed with relief when he saw the car disappearing on down the road.

Conrad's posse took Beka's car since it ran well and would seat the five men comfortably with their rifles. Steve checked the odometer at the edge of the city and steered down the highway. Conrad picked Steve to lead the team because Steve always kept his mind on business. He would not be distracted and would not quit until Peaceful Valley was found.

There were a couple of trees across the roadway, which slowed them down a little, but overall they made good time. However, they were not familiar with the area. They knew Corpus Christi like the backs of their hands, but none of them had ever been more than a couple of miles out of the city in this direction.

Steve pulled the car off the road. The trip only took two hours. Max scrutinized the road map the entire trip, asking Steve for odometer readings at regular intervals, and asking stupid questions to his annoyance. Max wasn't the smartest kid on the block, but he never got lost.

The men in back slept the whole trip, one annoying Steve with his snoring despite the other two poking him from time to time. They had come in early that morning from an all-night hunt. They were the best game trackers Conrad had on the police force and he insisted they be a part of the scouting party.

Steve got out first and looked around. Then he looked up at the sky and took a deep breath. "It smells better out here," he commented.

Max got out with the map and followed Steve to the front of the car. Steve grabbed the map and spread it out on the hood. "Okay, Max, where are we?"

Max pointed his finger at the line representing the highway. Steve leaned over and turned the map so the black line indicating the street lined up with the roadway.

"Where again?"

Max pointed and Steve leaned over and scrutinized the map closely, occasionally looking around at the trees. "This is the river, Max. It's closest to the highway here. How far away is that?"

Max bent down for a closer look. "Two more miles."

They got in the car and Steve checked the odometer. A few minutes later, he pulled off the pavement and rousted everyone out of the car. Now they would have to make the rest of the journey on foot. Steve looked around and pointed in the direction they should go.

Near the highway back toward Corpus, Sean and the girls followed the stream to put some distance between themselves and the road. Sean decided to spend the day on the stream to boil water and find some food. He selected a location but advised the girls they should not build a fire to boil the water until dark, to their dismay. Sean made a spear using the blade off one of the knives the girls had and left Kim and Brenda alone, while he made his way along the stream in search of food.

"Don't be concerned if I'm gone most of the day," he told them. "And keep the mutt here too. I don't want him to scare off any game I might find."

While Sean was hunting, Kim and Brenda constructed a makeshift lean-to and piled the leaves up to soften the hard cold ground a bit. With Sean out of the way, they also had some time to talk about him.

"Sean is so tough," Kim said, "but he is also caring. Though we've done nothing but complain, he's not had a sour word cross his lips."

"I'm liking him better every day," Brenda added. "I bet he'd make a good husband."

"For who?" Kim asked. "You, or me?"

"Either . . . or both."

Brenda and Kim cleaned up in the stream a bit, while they waited for Sean to return.

"I want a drink so bad, I'd drink from the stream now," Brenda said.

"Yeah, me too," Kim replied, "but Sean said it could kill us and our babies. The way I feel now, I wouldn't care so much for myself, but I couldn't live with myself if I killed my child."

"That's the only thing keeping me from taking a drink," Brenda said.

The girls wandered back toward the lean-to and stretched out in the shade on the leaves. They were asleep in minutes.

A couple of hours later, Brenda's eyes popped open when a bird flew into the tree above them and started chirping. When she looked over at Kim, she found her still fast asleep. She gave her a nudge to wake her. The sun had moved some distance and they were both lying in the sun now.

"I wonder what's taking him so long?" Kim asked.

Brenda didn't reply. She could visualize the intensity in Sean's eyes when they first met. He had skills she couldn't imagine and she was sure he would return with food.

You won't let us down will you, Sean?

"I wonder what it'll be like when we get to Peaceful Valley?" Kim asked, rubbing her tummy with thoughts of the child and a new home.

Brenda's eyes sparkled with hope on her face. "Well, we know there's a river and Robbie. I bet it's heaven on earth. I guess our diet will be changing a bit too."

Kim giggled, then her nose crinkled. "I hope we don't have to wear animal skins. Do you remember when Robbie first came to Corpus? Moccasins and a coonskin hat. He did clean up well though, didn't he?"

Sean was surprised when he returned several hours later with dinner. The girls had some rocks piled up in a circle for a fire, a little wood pile going, and a nice bed made.

He had already gutted the opossum and when he got back to camp, he skinned the marsupial, while the girls gathered more wood for the fire. Sean started the fire, cut sticks for a rotisserie, and skewered the animal. Kim filled their pot with water and set it by the fire. The girls watched while he roasted the meat to perfection.

Thirty minutes later, the meat was done and the water boiling.

Sean set the water aside to cool, then handed each girl a leg. "Tastes just like chicken."

Brenda frowned and took her first bite. "Not quite, but not bad."

Sean bit pieces off his portion of meat and tossed them to the dog. He missed the first chunk, smelled it, and gobbled it up. He didn't miss another morsel.

Kim didn't say a word until she finished. "More please."

Sean smiled and cut another piece for each. Sean, Brenda, and Kim took turns tossing bits of their meal to the dog until the last bite of opossum was finished.

The group took turns giving the canine a scratch as he came around each begging for more food. Sean told him to sit and he sat. Sean then grabbed a stick and tossed it. "Fetch!"

The dog returned with the stick and laid it beside Sean. "Good boy!" Sean gave him another scratch.

When their pot of water cooled, they quenched their horrible thirst.

Brenda made a face when she took her first sip of water. "Could use a tea bag, but I guess I shouldn't complain."

Sean and Kim chuckled.

They boiled an extra pot of water for the morning. They were all tired and all four cozied up now with relatively full bellies and the dog keeping their feet warm.

Chapter 5

The next morning, Sean woke up with the vision of Kim and Brenda in their panties, a wet ear from the dog, and holding onto one of Brenda's breasts. Kim's leg was wrapped around his and she had her hand on his crotch. Sean jerked his hand back from Brenda. "I'm sorry." He scrambled to untangle from the girls.

Kim giggled. "I felt a tiger in there!"

Sean managed to get free from the girls and made his way to the stream to wash his face and shake the embarrassment.

"Hey Brenda, he's got real potential."

"Yeah, I woke up several times and he kept squeezing me."

"Probably every time I squeezed him. How about we swap sides tonight?"

The girls contained their giggles and excitement when they saw Sean coming and they went to the stream to clean up a bit. When they returned, they drank all the water they could hold and started on their way.

Everyone was in a much better mood after having a meal and their thirst quenched. They made excellent progress over the next seven days. Sean killed a couple of large snakes, another opossum, and a raccoon for food, and they crossed more streams and boiled plenty of water.

Sean insisted the girls help him skin the raccoon. The skin was tough and the knives they brought weren't as sharp as what he was used to. Also, if the girls were going to be staying in Peaceful Valley, this was a task they'd need to learn.

"This is yucky," Brenda said, turning her face away when he cut the critter open.

"Just hold on tight. If you want to eat, this has to be done."

While the meat cooked, Sean looked at the blisters on the girls' feet. He knew they hurt, but there wasn't much he could do.

The mutt continued to follow and Sean was certain now that they had a new companion and partner.

"We need to give him a name," Brenda said.

"Mutt works for me," Sean replied, which drew a frown from her, but she let it go at that.

Though food and water weren't a big problem, the girls were getting worn down to the point of total exhaustion. They never slept well at night and they were not used to walking so many miles each day.

"I think I have a fever," Kim said.

Brenda felt her forehead. "You feel the same as me. I think we both have a temperature. And these damn bugs . . . they're eating me alive."

Sean ignored the complaints. "We have to keep going. Everything will be better when we get to Peaceful Valley."

The girls balked and sat down on a log.

"What's the matter?" Sean asked.

"We can't go any further," Brenda said.

Kim looked up with sweat dripping off her face. "We should have stayed in Corpus. Maybe we should go back before we die. The mosquitos, ticks, wasps . . . and my feet are killing me!"

Brenda pressed her fingers on her eyebrows. "And I have a headache. I think I'm going to die."

Sean could feel their pain. He had pushed them too hard. They were both pregnant after all. "I'm sorry. Maybe I've been too demanding of you. We're not in a race. You can't go back though. We're over halfway and besides, Sandra would kill all of us if we go back."

The thought of Sandra killing them didn't faze the girls. They were dying now, or at least they thought. "I tell you what, how about we stay here the rest of the day, rest up, then get an early start tomorrow?"

They nodded and made camp.

Sean got the girls up early the next morning and they trudged along at a much slower pace.

The following day, Sean recognized the house where he and Robbie had stopped on their way to Corpus Christi and talked with Charles. He had no intention of checking on Charles, but considering the condition of the girls, he decided to stop by and see what had happened to the old man. Sean knew where he was now and that they were only two days from Peaceful Valley, but if he killed the girls by pushing them too hard before he got home, he didn't think he could live with himself.

Sean told the girls to remain behind while he checked the house. He carefully made his way to the side and peered through a window. He saw no one. He had the same result with another window. Then he heard Mutt barking around back. Sean walked around the corner of the house and saw the body near the wood shed. A closer examination revealed that it was Charles. He had an ax in his hand and lay face-down in the dirt alongside the chopping block. His pistol was still in its holster, so Sean assumed he might have had a heart attack.

He was chewed on a bit by some wild critters, but still recognizable. Sean headed for the house and peered through the window on the back door. He turned the door knob and walked in. The house looked pretty much as it did when he and Robbie were there so many months back. It still had the odor of smoke and sweat. However, the house was empty. Sean opened a couple of windows as well as the front door. He left the back door open when he went out.

He returned to where he left the girls. "We have a place to stay for a few days until you two get rested up a bit."

Kim and Brenda were happy with this news. They wrapped him up in a group hug, whispered in his ear, and kissed his cheeks, again to his embarrassment. "Thank you."

Sean led the girls to the front porch.

"You go on inside and maybe you can clean up a little. I've got a burial in the back to take care of."

The girls looked around inside and Sean went around the side of the house. He found a suitable location to bury Charles near a large pecan tree. He thought about how friendly the old man had been when they met him months back, but also how he stank.

His heart probably gave away from whatever he'd been smoking.

It took Sean a few hours to dig Charles's grave, but finally, he finished covering him up. He stuck the shovel into the ground at the head of the grave and tied a crosspiece to the handle. He did not have any words for the old man because he did not know him. He only said 'sleep well', and went inside.

The house smelled a little better thanks to the cross-breeze and the girls had straightened up a bit, so it now felt downright comfortable. There were two bedrooms and each had a bed free of feces, unlike the ones near Corpus. One had obviously been slept in for too long, but they did find some relatively clean linens and made the beds as fresh as they could under the circumstances.

"Kim and I will sleep in here on the larger bed," Brenda told Sean. "You can sleep in the other bedroom."

Sean nodded and took a peek at the room he'd be staying in. It was straightened up and ready for him when he was inclined to go to bed.

I was just getting used to sleeping with them snuggled up against me. They made me forget the hard ground. Maybe it'll be good to sleep alone.

He turned to the ladies and smiled. "Thank you."

Sean looked around in the old man's belongings and kitchen. He found two boxes of ammunition for the gun he got off Charles's body, which was a good find. He found a thermos and canteen, which would also come in handy, but no food.

What was he eating? Maybe he wasn't . . . maybe part of the reason he died.

It was getting late in the afternoon and would be dark in a few hours. Sean decided he'd take a good look around the neighborhood to make certain there was no one nearby. He also told the girls to keep their eyes open. "You never know when someone might show up around here."

Sean strapped on Charles's gun belt, stuck some extra ammunition in his pocket, and walked out the back door. He felt good to be armed again. He had not carried a gun since he and Robbie were caught entering Corpus Christi.

Sean made a big loop around the house. He didn't see or hear anyone. He did spot a buck and a couple of doe as dusk fell, but not close enough to get a shot at one. Seeing nothing which might cause them harm, he made his way back to the house.

When Sean walked in the front door, the girls were wearing only their panties, which quickly got his attention.

"We drew some water from the well and decided we had to clean up a little," Brenda announced. "Stop staring. You've seen us wearing this outfit before."

Sean smiled.

"Our clothes will be dry soon," Kim added. "Then you won't have to stare at our ugly bodies."

"I never thought you two were ugly for a second," Sean said. "To the contrary, I think you two are gorgeous."

"Even with our bellies sticking out?"

"Especially with your big bellies. I think you two look beautiful."

Kim smiled and gave him a smirk. Brenda blushed.

Sean walked over to a desk in the corner. There was an oil lamp nearly full of oil, but nothing to light it with that he could see. Probably why it was still nearly full. "I'll see if I can get this thing started tomorrow evening and we can have some light tomorrow night."

"I would like that," Brenda said.

He picked up a wooden perpetual calendar. The month was set on September. "What month do you think it is?" he asked the girls.

"It has to be November," Kim replied. "I don't really know, but my guess is at least the middle of the month."

Sean scratched his head and laid the calendar back down.

It appeared as though Charles had been dead at least a couple months.

"Yeah, that sounds about right," he said.

"We brought in enough water for you to take a bath if you'd like, Sean," Brenda said.

"Yes," he replied. "I'd like that very much. I probably stink to high-heaven."

"Get undressed," Kim said. "We'll wash your clothes for you."

Sean stripped down to his shorts and handed the clothes to Kim. She grabbed the clothes and stood looking at him with raised eyebrows and her head cocked a bit.

"What?"

Kim looked down at his underwear. "All of them."

Sean sighed, slipped them off, and handed them to her. She giggled.

He went into the bathroom and grabbed a washcloth and began cleaning, while Kim took his clothes to the kitchen sink.

When he came back out with a towel wrapped around his waist, Kim had his clothes hung up over a length of twine she'd stretched across the room.

They couldn't find any food in the house, so it looked like they would have to go to bed hungry. At least they weren't thirsty. They had to use the hand pump, but Charles's well still worked. The girls drew not only enough water for them all to take a sponge bath, but to wash their clothes with plenty left over to drink.

"I'll go out early in the morning," Sean said. "I saw a few deer when I took a look outside. Now that I have Charles's pistol, I should be able to bring some meat back early."

"Maybe we can stay here a while and get fattened up a little," Brenda stated. "My ribs are starting to show through my skin. Even with my big belly, I must have lost ten pounds. That's probably not good for our babies. This place isn't great, but it's much better than we've had the past couple weeks."

"Are we in that big of a hurry to get to Peaceful Valley?" Kim asked.

"Not really," Sean replied. "The main thing was to get away from Corpus Christi and we've certainly done that. I guess for the health of you two and your kids, we can stay until you think you can make it the last two days to the Valley."

Brenda stretched her arms up high and yawned. "Who's ready for bed?"

It had gotten completely dark outside and they could just barely see each other now. Sean closed and locked the doors, then closed all the windows they'd opened, leaving only a small opening at the bottom of two for a little air circulation.

"Good night," Sean said.

"Sweet dreams," Kim replied.

Sean lay in bed, tired, but even with a comfortable bed under him, he had trouble drifting off to sleep. Mutt crawled up beside him and laid his head across his arm. Sean stroked Mutt while his mind wandered back to the ordeal when he and Robbie got caught entering Corpus Christi, to the doctors who butchered him when they castrated him, and to himself thinking of killing himself long before he had healed.

Over time, however, he did heal, both from his surgery and his predicament, thanks mostly to Sonny. He regretted having to kill him, but he saw no way to let him live. He would miss shrimping, but he would get over that. If there is blame to be placed, it has to be with Sandra.

Sean recalled the time he spent with Robbie at the Airport and working on the jets. A smile worked its way across his lips at the thought of the time they shot holes through the side of the hangar with the guns on the plane. His smile broadened into a grin as he remembered how angry Russ was.

His mind drifted to the Playboy magazine Robbie gave him, then to Brenda and Kim who were better looking than any of the girls in the magazine. The last memory he had was of the girls sitting across from him while they were waiting for their clothes to dry, their breasts fully exposed and them not caring, and even enjoying, that he was looking at them.

Sean was up at first light. He slipped out of the house quietly so he wouldn't wake the girls. There was a little ground fog and the air was crisp and cool, but not overly cold. He knelt down and smeared a little dirt on his face and ears to remove the shine.

Sean told the dog to stay in a stern voice. He didn't want Mutt to be running around all over the place as he had been doing ever since he got a little food in his belly. Sean walked the short distance to the highway and into the brush on the other side. He didn't want to venture too far from the house because he didn't want to carry a deer any further than he had to. Sean was surprised, but also pleased the dog stayed at his command.

Not far into the brush across the pavement, he heard the faint sound of a limb cracking. He stopped and squatted down next to a tree to listen. When he heard the noise again, he focused in the direction of the sound. He thought it might be a deer or feral hog, but then he heard 'son-of-a-bitch!'

Sean moved over behind a bigger tree and watched. Five men, all with rifles, were making their way through the brush. The men walked within fifty feet of Sean's position but were paying more attention to the briars and brambles than to their surroundings. They walked on by and didn't see Sean.

Sean followed them back to the highway. When they reached the roadway, they looked in both directions, then headed off to the right. Sean followed them nearly a mile. They rounded a curve and the men found their green car. They got in, started the engine, and turned around. Sean concealed himself a little better and a minute later the car sped by him headed back toward Corpus Christi. Sean watched until they faded out of sight over the hill to the south. He hoped that would be the last he'd see of them.

Sean was puzzled by the men. He didn't recognize them, but remembering the green car, suspected they might be some of Sandra's men.

What the hell . . . are they looking for me and the girls? Did they think they could find me, or maybe even Robbie? Did Sandra send them to find Peaceful Valley?

Sean had lost a lot of hunting time. He assumed the men were gone for now and wouldn't be a problem until they returned to invade Peaceful Valley, if that was what they were after. Hopefully, that wouldn't be until the spring.

It was a long loop around Charles's place for nothing. He apologized to the girls when he returned empty-handed. "I'm sorry, but I had to see what those guys were doing. I think Sandra sent them out here to find our valley."

"Do you think they found it?" Kim asked.

"I don't think they'd be headed back to Corpus unless they had," he replied. "Sandra wouldn't have been pleased. There wasn't enough of them to attack; only a scouting party. I think sooner or later, they will come back and they'll have an army."

A look of fear grew over Brenda's face. "When do you think they'll be back?"

"It'll take them a while to organize and plan. Maybe a few weeks, or even a month or two. I wouldn't want to attack someone this time of the year when the weather can cause a lot of additional problems. Certainly, by spring, they'll be back."

"And they'll kill all of us," Kim said, with tears welling up in her eyes.

"Don't worry, girls, Robbie's grandpa, Reggie, was an army contractor when he was younger. You'll be surprised how well Peaceful Valley can take care of itself."

Sean gave the girls a consoling embrace. "Don't worry about it too much. You'll see after we get there and you meet Reggie."

The girls smiled and relaxed a little, but they both knew and feared Sandra for the kind of woman she had shown everyone she was—a ruthless, cold-blooded killer.

"Will you start a fire, Sean?" Brenda asked. "It's a little chilly in here."

"I think we can risk that." Sean stepped outside and gathered up a big arm load of firewood, a handful of kindling, and a bird's nest he spotted in a nearby tree.

Sean picked up his bow drill and knelt down at the fireplace. "Sandra's men are long gone now and I doubt there is anyone else around." He had an ember with his bow drill in no time.

The girls gathered around. "I'm amazed you can do that so fast," Brenda commented.

Kim ran her hand under his arm and onto his chest, kissed him on the cheek, and pinched his nipple. "You know what I think!"

Sean, embarrassed again, added a couple more logs to the fire, then went outside and looked at the solar array on Charles's roof.

It looks okay. If it's working, there should be some electricity somewhere.

He then opened the water closet on the backside of the house, where the water equipment was stored. He opened the faucet on the hot water heater and it was hot, but no pressure. He checked the water pump and found a corroded connection. He cleaned and tightened the nut, flipped the switch, and the pump came to life. He watched the pressure gauge as it slowly climbed up to 50 p.s.i. He then went inside to the bathroom and turned on the faucets. Soon there was hot and cold running water. He checked the shower and it worked as well.

"No more sponge baths," Sean announced, with a big smile for his ingenuity.

It was late afternoon, prime hunting time, when he got the water going and they needed some meat. Sean grabbed the canteen. "I better go hunting. I'm hungry and I know you two are as well."

Sean filled his canteen, took a big drink, and headed back outside. He again told the dog to stay. Sean headed out back this time and ventured a little farther from the house. He found a small creek that was mostly dry but spotted one hole with water and a lot of tracks around it. He added some weeds to his camouflage and took a position alongside the most prominent trail. He waited, leaning up against a tree.

Just before dark, Sean heard a noise. He slowly turned his head down the trail to see a yearling coming up the path. He readied his spear and waited. Though he could have used the pistol, he was just as confident he could take the animal with only the spear. He had done it many times back home with Robbie and Ronnie. The young deer was heading for the water hole. Sean was inches from the trail and well-concealed.

The deer stopped just before getting to Sean and took a look around. Sean watched as the critter moved its ears around trying to detect any noise. It tested the air for strange scents while its eyes stared ahead. Then it moved forward. It walked right in front of Sean and never knew he was there.

Sean could feel his heart beating in his chest, but he'd done this before. While he was excited mainly due to the fact they needed food badly, he quietly waited for the right time. With the skill and accuracy of an experienced knight on a jousting run, Sean's muscles snapped and he drove the spear deep into the young buck's ribcage just behind the front shoulder.

The deer bolted and ran, and Sean held onto the spear tightly to pull the shaft out of the animal's side to open up the wound, so it would bleed freely. He watched as the deer disappeared into the brush.

Sean looked at the bright red blood trail on the ground. The foamy blood spurting from the deer's lungs was quite noticeable and he knew he had made a fatal stab. He walked over to the water hole and washed the blood off his weapon, while giving the deer a few minutes to bleed out and die before he followed.

It was getting dark and Sean followed the blood trail in the fading light, but luckily the deer had not gone far. The young animal only weighed about sixty pounds, so he threw it over his shoulders without taking the time to field dress it.

Sean went inside to tell the girls he was back and that he had dinner. The girls were thrilled they wouldn't be eating opossum again, though it did taste good. It's hard to enjoy a meal when all you're thinking about is how ugly the animal was before it was cleaned.

"We didn't hear a shot," Brenda said, with a curious look on her face.

Sean pointed to his spear leaning up against the door frame. "I didn't need to waste the bullet."

"You *are* good," Kim said, smiling. "I had no idea you could kill a deer with only a stick."

Sean smiled. "I know you're hungry. Get some coals out of the fireplace, start a fire in the stove, and I'll get after dressing the thing."

Sean returned a short while later with the heart, liver, and some wild onions he'd pulled and gave them to the girls so they could get started on dinner. He then went back outside to finish processing the deer. He fed the dog a generous amount of the scraps, which he gobbled up. After he'd eaten all he wanted, he crawled under the house. When Sean returned, the girls had dinner ready.

"We found some flowers out front," Kim said, with a loving glint in her eyes and pointing at the table.

Sean felt the flush returning to his face. "It looks great and smells good too."

Brenda was still chewing on a morsel she was sampling. "I couldn't help myself. We found some salt. That was the only spice we could find, but believe me, it's good . . . much better than the ugly critters." She clapped her hands together. "Let's eat!"

The meat was stir-fried with a little fat from the deer's stomach cavity and wild onions from around the house, which brought out the flavor of the meat.

The ladies enjoyed the venison much more than their previous meals. They'd eaten venison before and not having to watch Sean clean the thing also helped.

After they finished eating, Sean trimmed all the meat off the bones and put it into a large pot to simmer. "It'll keep a couple days after it's cooked and we won't get hungry between here and Peaceful Valley."

"Can we stay here tomorrow too?" Brenda asked. "Please! My feet are killing me."

Sean stood and stared at her, trying to come up with a reason for not staying here a while longer. He couldn't think of one. "I don't see why not. We're not in that big a hurry. I think we'll be safe enough here."

The girls squealed and wrapped him up in a group hug. Kim squeezed his butt. "We'll be much easier to get along with if we're not so tired. You deserve a reward."

Kim didn't indicate what that reward might be and she and Brenda got busy cleaning up the table. Sean started to help, but Brenda told him that he needed a shower.

Sean went into the bathroom. A big smile formed on his face when the hot water hit him. He stood with his eyes closed for a few moments reveling in the moment. He realized he was wasting water, quickly finished, and fell into bed.

They had a roof over their heads, a comfortable bed, plenty of water, and their bellies were full. There was nothing to worry about that he could think of and there was no reason for him to not get a good night's sleep tonight. The girls were giggling in the other room, but he couldn't make out what they were saying.

Are they talking about me?

It had been a long day and soon the girls' voices faded away.

Sean got a good night's sleep, but still was up well before the girls and slipped out onto the porch to pee. He then sat down on the rickety chair on the stoop and stared toward the highway.

Sonny was a good man. I wish there'd been another choice. What will happen to Marcia and little Lola? Sandra will come for us sooner or later. How many men will she bring? Can we handle them?

Sean walked up to the highway and stood looking up and down the road. A red-tailed hawk screeched and Sean looked upward. A woodpecker then caught his attention and he watched it going about its busy morning. Sean strolled back to the house. He took one last look around before going inside.

He walked in to find both girls completely nude. He couldn't help but stop and admire their bodies.

"We had to wash our panties," Brenda said, pointing to their make-shift clothesline. "You don't mind us going without for a while, do you?"

"No," he replied. "It's a little awkward though."

"And why is that?" Kim asked.

"I've never been around naked girls. You seem more comfortable around me naked, than I do around you fully dressed. I'd never seen a naked girl until I saw you."

Sean blushed.

Brenda cocked her head. "You look old enough to me. Are you telling us that you've never been with a woman? What about before you came to Corpus and . . . they cut you?"

"No, dammit!"

Sean wiped his eyes with his arm. "There was no one to have sex with in Peaceful Valley. That's why we came to Corpus. We were looking for wives. I've never had sex with anyone and now I don't even know if I can."

They think something's wrong with me, that I'm a freak. They'll hate me now.

Kim stepped back in shock.

Wow! No wonder he's been acting like he has. The doctors butchered him and now he's afraid he'll never be able to be with a girl again.

Brenda wrapped her arms around him. *I can't imagine what he's been going through. We didn't know. I didn't think he'd mind, and at times he didn't seem to, but we were making things worse. We've got to help him. If he's not going to get better, we need to know now.*

"Want to find out?" Brenda asked, with a devious little smile on her face.

Sean blushed. "I've never seen girls who are so uninhibited. This is new to me."

Kim raised her eyebrows. "Well?"

Sean stared back. *I was certain I could never do it again . . . that I'd never have a wife and certainly not kids . . . there's been nothing but an occasional tingle . . . that's not enough. I've put this all behind me. It took a while, but now these two beautiful girls . . .*

"I don't know. What if I can't?"

"Then we find that out here and now."

"Come here," Brenda said, as she walked into the bedroom. Sean hesitated and Kim took him gently by the hand and led him over to Brenda. Brenda sat down and pulled Sean closer. She pulled him down by the front of his shirt and kissed him, then releasing him, she reached down and slowly undid his britches a button at a time. She slid them down over his hips as she hooked her thumbs in his shorts and brought them down with his jeans. Kim was working on his shirt. She had reached around from behind and was unbuttoning it. With each button she undid, she pulled his shirt further off his shoulders and kissed him a little lower on his back. When they had him free of all his clothing, Brenda grinned and pulled him down on the bed.

She took his limpness in her hand and felt what was left of his scrotum. She squeezed and massaged to get some blood flowing. She could feel the fluids beginning to pump and the organ expanding, though slowly. Kim scooted up against his backside, put her arms around him, and pressed her breasts against his back. She titillated his nipples. Sean instinctively reached for Brenda's breasts.

He started to quiver when Brenda wrapped her lips around him and began to work her magic. Kim nibbled at his neck and ears.

Sean closed his eyes and enjoyed the sensations, which were new to him. He slowly relaxed and accepted the closeness with Kim and Brenda he had only dreamed about until now. Since the first time the girls took off their wet clothes and hung them to dry, he imagined what it would be like to have sex with them. But up to now, this was only a dream. He had thought about the girls often as they trudged through the woods, but his fantasies always led to failure on his part.

"Looks like it's working," Kim noted.

Brenda kept at it and Sean moaned and jerked against Brenda's face. Kim held on tight as Sean exploded into his first orgasm.

He relaxed and Brenda and Kim snuggled up against him.

"Well, looks like it still works," Brenda stated.

"Works pretty damn good too," Kim added and slapped Sean on the butt.

Sean looked up at Kim, then over to Brenda. They both had big smiles on their faces. His lips curled up into a big sheepish grin. "I didn't think I'd ever have sex. There has been nothing since . . ."

"Well, you can now," Brenda said. "We just proved that. I guess it just takes a little extra motivation."

"Yeah, I guess. You two are some great motivators for sure."

Brenda and Kim smiled. Brenda then stretched out on the bed and Kim grabbed Sean's hand and pulled it toward Brenda's tender spot. Kim took his finger and guided it around and into the softness. Brenda squirmed at their touch.

Before long, Sean had the hang of it and Kim turned her attention to Brenda's breasts. Brenda took his hand and pressed it into her warm moist area. His fingers pressed deep into her and it wasn't long before she tightened up, pressing his hand hard into her. She squealed and moaned as her pent up desires flowed freely.

Brenda took a few minutes to recover and she and Sean worked their magic on Kim. She was already juicy and ready for her turn, when the others started to pleasure her. Kim finished almost before Sean and Brenda got going.

They stretched out and wrapped their arms around each other, snuggled and molded into one.

After they got their breaths, they stirred and looked around. Kim got up first. "Maybe next time you can go inside of us."

This got Sean's attention.

Can I really do that? They felt so good inside—so warm . . . inviting!

Sean's eyes closed and his mind drifted off into new territory. He could be a new man—a whole man. He could be doing so much more than just surviving. He could be truly living. Brenda's sweet voice snapped him out of his dream.

"How about we all go take a shower together?" she asked, raising her eyebrows.

Kim and Brenda helped Sean up. His knees were still a little weak. They got on either side of him and led him to the bathroom. They cleaned him from head to toe and he enjoyed cleaning them too, though he spent most of his time on their breasts.

But what now? Sean thought.

He stopped what he was doing and his smile disappeared. Brenda noticed. "What's the matter, Sean?"

"Where do we go from here? Does this mean . . ."

"That you're our boyfriend?"

"Yeah, I guess that's what I meant."

"I'm good with that. How about you, Kim?"

"I'm certainly available." She rolled her eyes and toyed with the idea, teasing Sean more than anything else, but her mind was already made up. "I guess I could think of him as a boyfriend. How about you, Brenda?"

"Yes, I think a boyfriend is in order. Looks like Sean is the only real man around. I guess he'll have to do."

"But which one of you?"

Brenda and Kim looked at each other, then they giggled. "Both of us, of course," Brenda said.

They took turns lavishing Sean with kisses. By this time, the water was barely lukewarm. Kim turned the water off and they got out.

As they were drying, Kim wiggled her breasts at Sean. "You can play with these anytime you want."

Brenda slapped him on the butt. "And these too," as she took hold of her breasts and jiggled them at him.

Sean couldn't help but smile.

I have two girlfriends . . . and I can have sex! Two pregnant girlfriends . . . with Robbie's babies.

"What about Robbie?"

"What about him?" Brenda asked.

"You're carrying his babies."

Brenda thought for a second. "Florence is also pregnant with Robbie's baby and so are a lot of other girls back in Corpus. I guess we'll have to wait and see what he thinks, but as far as I'm concerned you're our man if that's okay with you."

The smile returned on his face. "I'm fine with that."

The following morning, they were well-rested. They dressed, ate, and packed their remaining meat into some containers they found.

"Thank you, ladies, for yesterday. I feel like a new man now."

"You're welcome, Sean," Brenda said, tugging on his arm and kissing him on the lips. "We did it for ourselves too. Girls like sex as much as guys do."

"Yes, we do!" Kim said, with a big smile on her face.

Sean extended an arm to each girl. "Well, shall we go to Peaceful Valley?"

They hooked their arms through his. "Lead on, kind Sir."

He led the way with a little more vigor in his step. The girls felt much better and not a complaint was heard. Once they crossed the highway, Sean got his bearings and the girls fell into step behind him.

Now that he was well-rested and his overwhelming worries were behind him, he started pointing out the dangers of the woods as they made their way through the brush, which was quite dense at times.

"There's some poison ivy. Take a good look at it. That's some nasty stuff. And always watch the ground in front of you. There are a lot of snakes around here. There will be more when we get to the river. One mistake and you're going to have a big problem.

"I know it's hard to watch where you're going and where you're walking at the same time, but work on it. This is probably the most important thing I'll ever teach you. You will learn in time and it will save your life one day. You can count on that."

"Ahhh!" Brenda yelled as she started swinging her arms wildly as if she were fighting a ghost.

Sean looked back and saw the spider web in her hair and on her face. He laughed to the annoyance of Brenda.

"Sorry," he said. "Not everything you will encounter is on the ground."

By dusk, they made it to the river and found a good place to spend the night. Alone, Sean could have made the trip in six hours, but with the girls, it took all day. He didn't care though. Brenda and Kim had given him the love he'd been longing for well before he and Robbie went to Corpus Christi.

The girls could hear the excitement in Sean's voice. At long last, he was going home. "All we have to do is follow the water downstream. We'll get to Reggie and Emily's place first. They are Robbie's grandparents on his mother's side. We'll stop there and you'll meet them. Then we'll head on to Robbie's parent's place, which will be the next and final stop."

Brenda patted Sean on the butt. "I never had a doubt you'd get us here."

Sean turned and frowned. They made eye contact and both burst out laughing.

"Thank you for getting us here without killing us," Kim said.

Sean cleaned off a spot under a large tree and piled up leaves and grass to make a bed. The girls gathered some sticks and when Sean figured he'd made the bed as soft as it was going to get, he gathered rocks from the river bank to line the fire pit.

It took him nearly five minutes to get the first flames with the bow drill. Shortly thereafter, the fire was established and he cut some sticks to put chunks of venison on to heat over the flames. He gave Mutt a cold piece of the meat as well.

The girls gathered around the fire as Sean tended the meat. Brenda scooted up next to him on one side while Kim did the same on the other.

Sean pulled two of the sticks from over the fire and handed one to each of the girls. "Dinner ladies." He grabbed his stick, took a bite, and looked over at Kim and then Brenda. *I've never felt this good in my entire life. Am I dreaming?*

Sean woke early the next morning. Being a shrimper for the past few months had really ingrained early rising into him. He rose slowly trying not to disturb the girls and went off to relieve himself. When he returned, they were still fast asleep and had cuddled around each other to fill the void he left behind. He watched the girls as they slept and smiled as his mind drifted back to his first orgasm.

The girls awoke when the birds started chirping in the trees. Brenda rolled over. Kim sat up first and looked into Sean's smiling face. "What?"

Sean grinned. "You get more beautiful every day."

"I'm dirty, I haven't had any deodorant in two weeks, and my hair is a mess. How can you say that?"

"Maybe it's love," he said without thinking first and his face turned red.

She got up to her knees and wiped her eyes, then scooted over and took Sean's arms. She pulled him close, took his face in her hands, and gave him a tender kiss on the lips. She then turned to Brenda and poked her, leaving Sean dazed and with a befuddled look on his face. Brenda got up, wiped her eyes, and looked at Sean still on his knees. "You going to just sit there all day, or are we going to go to Peaceful Valley?"

Sean snapped out of his trance, got up giving her a smile, and gathered up their stuff. The girls followed him down the river bank. He stopped here and there pointing to an alligator at one spot, a moccasin at another, and a pair of squirrels chattering in the trees.

They weren't as far as Sean had thought from their first destination and in the mood they were in, it seemed like the trip only took minutes. They reached the Carston's before noon and Sean signaled with a loud wolf howl a couple of times, but received no reply.

He led Brenda and Kim to the house. He knocked on the door several times, but again there was no answer.

"I guess you'll have to meet them later," Sean said, shrugging his shoulders. "They're not home."

The girls moaned.

"We'll head on over to Robbie's place. We'll find someone there I'm sure. We can get cleaned up and get some regular food."

Kim's enthusiasm was fading. "How much longer?"

"Only an hour."

Brenda took a deep breath. "We can make it another hour can't we, Kim?"

They came upon another house Sean had not seen before, about halfway to the Lindgren's. It was brand new and he didn't know who it belonged to, but that it wasn't there when he and Robbie left for Corpus. Sean knocked on the door and looked in the windows. It too, like the Carston's home, was empty.

Sean scratched his head with a confused look on his face. *What's going on? Did Sandra's men kill everyone? But where are the bodies?*

Brenda and Kim detected Sean's confusion. Brenda grabbed him by the arm. "Where is everyone?"

Sean didn't want to alarm the girls. "There will be someone at the Lindgren's. No problem."

Inside, Sean had a knot in the pit of his stomach.

Damn, we walked all this way and no one is here? It'll be alright. Can't scare the girls.

Sean and the girls reached the edge of the Lindgren's meadow and knelt behind a large tree. The cabin looked quiet, a trickle of smoke rising out of the chimney. He could see no one around. Mutt started barking and Sean hushed him. Seconds later, he saw a man with a rifle step out of the front door. Sean recognized James and gave the wolf howl signal. The man turned and looked directly at him. Sean stood up and gave the signal again.

James returned the howl and Sean helped the girls up and they headed in the direction of the house.

"That's close enough," James said.

"You don't recognize me?" Sean said. "Well, I certainly know you, James."

"Sean?"

"Yes."

James took his finger off the trigger and relaxed.

"Sam! Sally!" James yelled over his shoulder.

Sam came to the door with Sally on his coattails.

"I think you know him," James said.

Sam squinted as he eyed the man. "Sean?"

Sally recognized him immediately and yelled, "Sean! Oh my God! Sean!" She ran to him, tears flowing freely down her cheeks. "Oh my God!" she repeated over and over. She wrapped her arms around his neck and rained kisses over his face.

Sam followed Sally and wrapped them up in a group hug.

By this time, everyone was out on the porch. Robbie immediately recognized the ladies. He walked out and gave each a big hug. "Welcome to Peaceful Valley."

"Thank you."

He looked down at their bellies.

This is going to complicate things.

Brenda could feel his coldness.

He said the words . . . but he doesn't seem all that happy to see us.

Kira went over to the dog, knelt, and pet him behind his head. The friendly canine returned the affection, licking her in the face.

"I just love dogs," she said. "What's his name?"

"He doesn't have a name," Sean replied. "I just call him, Mutt."

Sean noticed her frown and said she could name him whatever she wanted.

Robbie turned to Sean and gave him a big man hug. "Good to see you, Sean."

"It's good to be home, buddy."

"We're just sitting down to our Thanksgiving meal," Melissa said. "Come on in."

Kim looked down at her dirty clothes. "We sure are hungry, but we're a mess and stinky."

Melissa smiled. "That doesn't matter. We're so glad Sean is home and you girls are most welcome. You can clean up after."

As they all headed into the house, James put his rifle away and grabbed more chairs. Everyone squeezed in around the table while Robbie made introductions.

"Welcome Brenda and Kim," Emily said.

"How in Hell did you get here, Sean?" Reggie asked.

"It's a long story," he replied.

"There have been a lot of long stories around here lately," Robbie stated.

"I'm sure there have," Sean replied, with a smile. "I've got a real whopper to tell you guys."

"Let's eat," James said, "before it gets any colder."

Everyone agreed. The stories could wait.

Chapter 6

After everyone finished eating, including a bowl taken out to the dog by Kira, the ladies ran the men out of the house. The kitchen was too crowded with all the women present. The men went out onto the porch and James grabbed a few more chairs from inside. Kim and Brenda were getting in the way in the small kitchen, so they joined Sean and the men.

"Looks like you've lost a little weight since I last saw you," Robbie said.

"Maybe so," Sean replied. "It was tough getting here, especially for Brenda and Kim. We did eat pretty good the last couple of days, but before that, it was slim pickins."

James rolled a couple of cigars, one for himself, and handed a second to Reggie.

Reggie lit his smoke and blew a smoke ring. "So, how did you get out of Corpus Christi?"

Sean leaned forward in his chair. "All in good time. There is something more important to discuss. After we got around Corpus and to the highway, I saw a car headed this way with some armed men inside. Then we stayed at Charles's house a couple days to rest up and find some food.

"While I was out hunting, I saw the same men I spotted earlier in the car. They were stumbling around in the woods headed back to the road. I'm pretty sure they were some of Sandra's men. I think they were looking for Peaceful Valley."

"Do you think they found us?" James asked, leaning forward in his chair.

"I don't think they would have gone back to Corpus unless they had," Robbie said. "If you knew Sandra Hawkins, you'd agree with me."

"Yeah," Sean added. "Sandra would kill them if they'd have come back without all the information she needed. I expect they found this place and scoped it out from end to end."

Robbie shook his head. "Dammit! I guess we'd better get prepared for a war. She'll send more than enough to take care of us."

"Yeah," Reggie said, "but she doesn't know us very well, does she?" He gazed over at Robbie with a concerned look on his face. "Or does she?"

"I didn't give anything away about our strengths," he said, a little defensive.

"I didn't either," Sean added.

Robbie got up and ran his fingers through his hair, unsettled and pacing the porch. "All I can recall telling anyone, including her girls, is that I live on a river to the north."

"Excuse me," Kim said, raising her hand. "You said you lived in Peaceful Valley."

Robbie turned to face Kim. "Maybe so, but Peaceful Valley isn't on a map. That wouldn't tell her where we're at."

"Just the fact that you told her we're on a river and the direction would help her find us," Reggie said, "especially if she has a map. It appears they did find us, but hopefully they don't know much more than that."

"I don't think she really knows much except what her men might have seen here," Robbie replied.

Reggie leaned forward with a troubled look on his face. "It will take her a while to mobilize enough men to take us out and they will need supplies for at least a couple of weeks. They'll need trucks, fuel, ammunition, and then they'll need to get here."

"They have all that and more," Robbie said, with a bit of panic in his tone. "They can be here in four or five days if they really hurry."

Sean's eyes opened wide. "And they have a plane and bombs if they choose to use them."

"I don't think they'll use the C-23 for a mission like that," Robbie said, not totally convinced himself. "It's too important for the livelihood of Corpus Christi. They trade with Brownsville and I think they need that trade. It wouldn't be rational to use the plane."

Brenda stood up, scared and irritated. "And you think Sandra is rational about now?"

Robbie sat down, deflated. "Good point." He propped his elbows on the table and his face in his hands.

What have my loose lips gotten us into? Sandra knows where we live and she's one crazy bitch. She proved that by swerving in front of the Cessna. She'll be here . . . and she'll want blood.

"I don't think she would try to come here this time of year," Reggie stated, "not if she's smart. I think she will probably wait until the spring, but we can't take that chance. We'll have to start preparing now and expect her to be here in a few days. We should stay on high alert. We need to be prepared for whenever she chooses to show up. What we need is an early warning system."

"Like what?" James asked.

"I have a lot of surveillance equipment," Reggie said. "I can probably put something together."

"Can they get one of the other planes going?" Sam asked.

"I don't think so," Robbie replied. "I tore up the planes good before I left. Sean couldn't get the F-15 started, so I didn't do anything to it, but the others will never fly."

"Do you think they could get the F-15 going if they robbed parts off one of the other planes?" Sam inquired.

"I guess they could," Robbie said, being defensive again, "but they don't have any mechanics."

"They have men who work on cars," Sean reminded him.

"Yeah, but working on a jet is a lot different," Robbie replied.

"Maybe so, but we don't really know what kind of expertise some of the men might have," Sean said. "We didn't know anything either and I got one going. You didn't know how to fly, yet you did. One or two guys with a little ingenuity and they could do a lot of things we might not expect them to do."

"There's only one way to be totally prepared," Reggie said, leaning back in his chair, "and that's to be prepared for anything. If they don't show up in a couple months, we have to be prepared for an air attack as well. We'll have to assume they got the jet going and will hit us from the air. They can do a lot of damage around here with one plane. Then they can take us out with their men on the ground."

Robbie hit his fists on his forehead, defeated, knowing he'd made mistakes and that their little valley was in big trouble. "In which case, we're all dead."

"Not necessarily," Reggie added. "I have a couple guns, which will take an F-15 down."

Brenda's eyes perked up with a renewed sense of hope. "Really?!"

"You'd be shocked about some of the stuff this country boy's got," Reggie said, smiling. "Maybe I can give you lovely ladies a tour one day."

Kim and Brenda didn't say anything but gave Reggie a courteous tight lipped smile. They both were a little uneasy with his 'dirty old man' tone and grin.

Brenda and Kim got up, excused themselves, and went back inside. They'd heard enough talk about guns and planes.

Reggie resumed his discussion on his favorite subject. "Someone will have to practice to hit something though. By the time they get here, we need at least a couple experts on the guns."

James rolled more cigars and handed one to Reggie and another to Lance.

Reggie lit up, leaned back, and took a big drag off his stogie. "Brenda and Kim seem like nice ladies."

James nodded and looked over at Sean who gave him a smile. Sean's gaze then turned to Robbie. "I saw a new house up stream."

"Yeah, Florence and I are staying there with Ronnie and Brooke."

"Nice big house too; you're going to need it. Looks like you're going to have some more kids, Robbie."

All eyes focused on Robbie. He blushed and gave Sean a hard 'I don't want to talk about this' stare, but Sean wouldn't let it go at that.

"Yeah, seems like Robbie planted quite a few seeds around Corpus Christi. No telling how many kids he's going to have."

"That's enough," Robbie said, growing more aggravated with Sean by the second.

"Well, it's the truth!" Sean added.

Robbie got up and went inside, but this didn't solve his dilemma. As soon as he walked in, Brenda and Kim immediately grabbed him by the arms and led him out the back door. When they saw the pier, they dragged him down to the river. Florence saw what was happening and tagged along as well.

"What's going on," Robbie asked.

Brenda and Kim got google-eyed at the sight of him and forgot all about Sean.

"We still like you, Robbie," Kim said. "We like you a lot and we're going to have your babies."

"Yeah," Brenda said. "We just thought we'd see if we could get back together. We've missed you since you left Corpus and . . ."

"And that's not going to happen," Florence broke in.

"Oh!" Kim exclaimed.

"No, Robbie and I are together now and I'm pregnant with his child," Florence added sternly and her face turning red.

"Well, if you haven't noticed, we're pregnant with his babies too," Brenda said. "We just thought . . ."

"Well, you thought wrong," Florence interrupted.

Florence grabbed Robbie by the arm and pulled him back toward the house, leaving Kim and Brenda standing on the pier.

"Guess we'll be getting to know Sean a little better then," Brenda said.

"Guess so," Kim agreed.

Florence looked over her shoulder with a frown, at Kim and Brenda still standing on the pier.

"Guess we'll be talking about this later tonight," Robbie said, Florence still dragging him along by the shirt sleeve.

Florence turned her attention back to Robbie. She gave him her 'damn right we'll be talking about this' look, but said nothing.

I know what you were used for in Corpus, but you're mine now. I'll set that straight tonight.

Robbie grabbed a drink from the house and went back onto the front porch with the men. He thought he was getting out of the skillet by going inside, but jumped right into the fire with Brenda, Kim, and Florence.

I'll take my chances outside with the guys, he thought.

The discussion had reverted to battle preparations by the time Robbie returned to the porch. He gave Sean a stern look, then turned his attention to his dad and grandpa who were discussing turrets, 50-caliber ammunition, and mortars. Robbie didn't look at Sean again and the discussion grew more intense, but about preparations rather than about the girls.

I'm glad Sean's home, but why did he bring Kim and Brenda? I'm not responsible for the babies . . . well, I am, but I'm not, dammit! They're Sean's responsibility now, not mine.

Later that night, however, after they had gone to bed, Florence and Robbie resumed their discussion about Brenda and Kim.

"I don't like those two women carrying your babies here, wanting you back," Florence said pouting.

"That was something that happened a long time ago before we got together," Robbie said, going on the defensive again.

"Four months is not a long time ago," she replied in exasperation.

"It was still before we got together."

Robbie knew he was in a predicament, but he wasn't quite sure how he was going to get out of it. He was trying to survive and keep from being castrated. Though he did like the girls, what he liked most was the sex. Well, mostly anyway. The only one of Sandra's girls he felt a real attraction to was Jade, and she was dead now.

"Do you still want me?" Florence asked, with an anxious look on her face, her eyes glistening in the candlelight.

"Of course, I do. You know I love you, baby. We're still going to get married in the spring . . . unless you don't want to."

"I do, but I guess that really depends on you," she said. "You keep your mind on me and we will, but . . ."

"I always keep my mind on you," he replied, running his fingers through his hair and pushing it out of his face. He then focused on Florence's flush and hurt expression.

Florence was quiet for a minute, but she didn't close her eyes to go to sleep. Robbie watched as her eyes told him the gears were still churning in her mind.

"Sandra's going to try to hurt us, isn't she?"

"I'm afraid so," Robbie replied.

"Should we be scared?"

Robbie scooted a little closer and gave her a squeeze on the arm. "Sandra will have a formidable force when she comes. Her men are ruthless and if she brings enough of them, they will be a power to be reckoned with."

Florence got quiet again. Robbie saw the tear run down her cheek. She rolled over and scooted back against him. He wrapped his arms around her and held her tight.

This should do it. Show her I love her and we'll be alright. If only dealing with Sandra could be this easy.

"Now let's get some sleep. We have a long day ahead of us tomorrow."

Chapter 7

In Corpus Christi . . .

Conrad dropped the man off who was on patrol with him at the office and headed toward the Farm. Sandra was in the main barn supervising the overhaul of one of the tractors when he arrived.

"Everything is secure around here," Conrad said. "I've got my men on high alert."

"And Peaceful Valley?"

"Steve hasn't returned yet. I'll give you a full report as soon as he gets back. He's my best man. I have confidence he'll find the place and give us a rundown of what we might be up against."

"They're a bunch of scavengers living off the land," Sandra said. "They can't be hard to handle, especially if we catch them with their pants down. They won't expect us."

"It's wise to never underestimate your opponent," he replied.

"Have you found someone who can work on the jets?" Sandra asked.

"Some of the mechanics are over there now. A couple of the guys said they knew a little bit about planes, but jets, I don't know. I got three of the pilots over there too. If they can be fixed, I think they'll get one going."

"I want to hit Peaceful Valley first from the air if we can. We've got all kinds of explosives in a couple of the warehouses at the Airport. If one of the planes will fly, I don't care how safe it is for the pilots, I want it in the air as soon as possible." She gives Conrad a wink. "You don't have to tell the pilots though."

"I think they want to fly one of those badass jets so bad, I don't believe they'll care if they're safe or not," Conrad said.

"Keep me apprised of their progress," Sandra added.

"I'll be back as soon as I hear from Steve and I'll fill you in on everything."

Sandra walked to the house, grabbed a soda, and strolled out to the back porch.

Those two little rednecks will wish they'd never tangled with me. And Brenda and Kim will be buried right alongside of 'em. I should have gotten rid of Florence when I had the chance. All in good time. And Beka. The double-crossing little bitch! I'll get them all. They'll pay with blood this time. All of them!

How many of them are there? Robbie only mentioned his parents and a couple neighbors. Can't be more than a half-dozen or so, plus the women. Maybe twenty at the most. I can take forty men off the Police force. That should leave enough to take care of the city while we're gone. Maybe not more than a dozen if they can get the jet flying. Should be able to take most of them out with the plane. Still better take forty, just in case. This is going to be fun. I wish I could see their faces when my men and I show up.

Sandra got up and walked back into the kitchen. "When's dinner going to be ready?"

"About an hour," her cook replied.

Sandra figured she had time for a shower. It would help calm her nerves. She stood there letting the hot water hit her in the back of her neck. She was feeling the strain of the recent events. The water felt good and relaxed her body, but her mind continued to churn.

Dammit! I'll get it all worked out and life will be much easier around here from now on. No more leniency. Everyone walks a tight rope, or they fall. They fall hard. They can count on it.

By the time Sandra finished dressing and made her way to the kitchen, dinner was ready. As usual these days, she ate in the kitchen and she ate alone. She only needed one cook, so she fired one, and the one she kept lived in the bunkhouse. Sandra stayed in the house alone at night. She kept all the doors locked and her pistol next to her on the other pillow. She trusted no one.

Sandra got up early and let the cook in. She then went to the bathroom to finish dressing. She ate a quick but hearty breakfast, checked on work in the various barns, then went back into the house to let the cook back out after she cleaned up the dishes and kitchen. This was her regular routine these days until she was certain she could trust all the ladies around her. That would take some time.

Sandra wandered out to the fields for a while to check on the progress of an early crop of potatoes some of the ladies were planting, then made a trip through the strawberry patch. She never said a word to any of the girls, but merely watched what they were doing.

She was bored after a while and headed back to the house for an early lunch, which she made herself. After a couple of ham sandwiches and a tall glass of milk, she went outside and got in her jeep to head for the Airport.

Sandra always spun gravel when she left and she always screeched her tires when she stopped somewhere. Her mood was constantly tense and she moved a little faster than she should for someone in their fifties and moderately over-weight, but she was a woman on a mission. That mission was to make certain everyone in the city obeyed the rules and followed her without hesitation for fear of their lives. She didn't care if anyone liked her or not. She only wanted their absolute acceptance of her rules. Fail to do so and she would squash them like they were bugs.

Sandra screeched to a stop at the side door into the hangar. By the time she reached the door, the workers inside were busy as bees. They all heard her tires squeal and knew they had better be working when she reached the door.

"Any progress?" she demanded, walking into the office.

"I think so," Arnold 'Shadow' Wilson replied nervously, jumping up from his chair and laying a sheet of paper over the tobacco on the desk. "The boys tore up the wiring in the Raptor badly. They also damaged some of the electrical parts for which we don't have replacements. They didn't touch the F-15, probably because as you said, it wouldn't start in the first place. I think we found why it wouldn't start. A simple relay to the JFS. I think it's the same part number as the one on the Raptor. Even if it's not, they may be interchangeable. I'll know by tomorrow."

Sandra motioned for Shadow to sit down. "And then it'll be ready to fly?"

"No, not by a long shot, but if it works, we'll get it started. Even if the relay works, there are so many systems on these jets, it's going to take at least a month to get them all checked. We've got to make sure the guns will shoot, the rockets will target and fire, and that the navigation systems work. Then on top of that, there are hundreds of other little things."

"Okay, Shadow, I believe you. You've been my best pilot around here for a long time. You get it fixed up and you'll be the one to fly it."

"That's what I wanted to hear. I'll do my very best, Sandra."

"I know you will." She looked down at the desk. "That doesn't look like the regular tobacco we get from Brownsville."

Shadow turned red and Sandra turned, walked out of the hangar, and crawled into her jeep. She didn't know why, but she had the urge to drive to the Bayfront.

Sandra pulled out to the end of the T-head and stopped. Sonny's boat was not in its stall when she drove by, but it's not like she really expected it to be there. She got out, walked to the edge of the concrete, and looked out across the bay.

Where the hell did you go, Sonny? Did you double-cross me too? I can't see you taking Sean anywhere. It just doesn't fit. If you didn't have a choice, maybe. That's the only thing that makes sense. Are you alive?

Sandra looked around and didn't see anyone on any of the boats. The only life around were the laughing gulls, terns, and a few pelicans floating in the harbor.

Sandra's weight, aggravated by the latest events, and plans for revenge kept her in a constant state of hypertension these days. The breeze across the water felt cool on her face. She ran her fingers through her hair, pushing it back off her forehead and closed her eyes. She breathed in the salty air and exhaled slowly.

She sat down on one of the short pilings next to the concrete edge and gazed across the water. The waves lapping against the bulkhead soothed her mind for a short while as she drifted off to a place it seldom found—tranquility.

It was my thirteenth birthday and I was the happiest little girl around. Daddy had just brought out my new pony. It was solid white with a shiny new saddle. Daddy gave me a boost up. I was in heaven.

I had always dreamed of a pony of my own. Now I could go riding with two of my friends who also had ponies. They always thought they were queens of the north-side. Now I could join the club.

I loved living on the edge of town on five acres. The pasture was lush and my new pony would have plenty to eat. I fed him a handful of oats every day and sometimes an apple. I loved Lightning and he loved me.

The years seemed to fly by and life was a dream. Daddy always brought a little candy home on Mondays, but Mama doled it out so it would last all week. I didn't need candy on weekends as I had Lightning to ride.

For a brief moment, she felt serene, but it didn't last. Her mind always drifted to the nightmare.

I had just turned fourteen. Daddy got fired as Harbor Master and came home drunk. He had quit drinking when I was eleven. He yelled at Mom and me all the time, but with help, he stopped. We were a happy family and dad's new job provided us with many of the niceties of life, including a new pony on my birthday.

When he came home on that dreadful night, I was now old enough that I didn't whimper like the little kid I was when he drank three years earlier. I stood my ground when he yelled at Mama and me, and he got mean. This was the first time he slapped me.

Mama screamed at him and when he came at her, she grabbed a butcher knife. He laughed when he took the knife away and tossed it in the sink, but that wasn't the last of it. Why did he hit her so hard? She screamed once and then she was quiet, but he wouldn't stop.

He hit Mama over and over until her face was bloody. I watched as he beat her to death with his bare hands.

I looked at Mom lying there, still and lifeless. When Daddy turned back to me, I scrambled for the door. Had he not been drunk, he would have surely caught me, but I was too quick for him. I ran until my lungs made me stop and I walked. I kept looking back to see if he followed, but I was alone in the dark city, only lit by a few street lamps. In the middle of the night, I fell asleep on the steps of a church.

I cried all through Mom's funeral and Dad went to prison. One of the elderly ladies at the church took me in and I got a good education, after which, I went to college and got my law degree. I made top marks and got a job with the county attorney's office.

I worked my way up the ladder and became their top prosecutor. This was fun and easy, but the best part of the job was that I was sending mean and cruel men to prison. I was the best at what I did and I sent many sorry bastards to their just reward.

Richard Ingalls, who was the Chief of Police, became an ally. He brought the trash in and I disposed of it. We were a good team for close to ten years, but he wanted more. Finally, I gave in and we were married.

The marriage was good for a few years and we were the power in Corpus Christi. Six years later, the marriage was dead and I found how much of a sorry son-of-a-bitch Richard was. I couldn't have kids, which I think made things worse, but the marriage wasn't going to survive because of his attitude. We remained civil, however, despite his views, and we ruled the city with an iron fist. When suddenly the grid shut down and the world went to Hell, we saw this as an opportunity, or at least I did.

It took us two years to rid Corpus of everyone I thought needed to go. Most killed each other over food, but Richard and I got rid of the rest. That's when I confronted him and he learned of my true plan. He didn't want me anymore than I wanted him as far as the marriage went, so I gave him a new wife and promised I wouldn't castrate him like most of the other men, as long as he took care of my dirty work.

This agreement went well and I got exactly what I wanted. I'm the boss; men will never again be allowed to rule my world. But even with everything precisely like I'd planned, one little bastard thought he could tear down everything I've worked so hard to build.

Robbie, the little shit, will get his, as soon as I get everything in place. He'll die, as well as Florence and Beka. He'll regret the day he came to Corpus Christi.

Sandra knew better than to think about her past. It had been years since the thought of her mom and dad crossed her mind, but long-ago suddenly caught up with her and she couldn't keep it out. A few moments of delight when she thought about Lightning and the fun times she had riding with her girlfriends, but then the memories of her mom and dad slapped her in the face.

Sandra got up and she slowly headed for her Jeep. She opened the door and took one more look across the water. "Dammit, I wish I knew what happened around here."

Sandra got back to the Farm early enough to let the cook in to prepare dinner while she took her shower. After she finished her veal, potatoes, and salad, she let the cook out and locked the doors.

She went to the living room and read for a while, but she couldn't keep her mind on the story. When she crawled into bed, her memories continued to taunt her with thoughts of Robbie, Florence, and Beka. As her mind drifted to the repairs on the jet and her impending invasion of Peaceful Valley, Sandra continued to toss and turn until she finally decided to get up. She took four aspirins and made her way back to bed.

As she lay in bed, she felt the trickle down the side of her face and rolled over wiping her eyes on the pillowcase. Soon the aspirins kicked in and she was able to relax enough to fall asleep.

The next morning, Sandra awoke tired, but after a large breakfast, she felt much better and got to her morning chores. During Sandra's daily instructions to her girls in the main barn, she was interrupted by the arrival of a car.

"She's in the barn," she heard one of the gals working in the flower garden tell someone.

Sandra hurried to finish up when she saw who arrived. She moved toward him, pushed her sunhat back, and glared at him.

"You have something for me?"

"Yes, Steve got back yesterday and gave me a full report."

Sandra nodded her approval. "Let's get a soda and we'll go out to the back porch where we can have some privacy."

Conrad followed Sandra through the house, then out to the patio. Sandra pointed to a chair. She sat on the porch swing and opened her bottle. Conrad pulled up the chair.

"They found Peaceful Valley," he said, pulling out the map. "They didn't have much trouble finding the place. It's about ten miles off the highway, right here."

He pointed to the map, Sandra leaned over, and took a look.

She runs her hand over the map like it's a treasure that has finally been found. "What kind of fortifications do they have?"

"Just looks like a few farm houses. Cabins and gardens. The first place they came to had a wind turbine and a big concrete building in the back. The rest are typical country cabins with a few out buildings. They have minimal electricity with solar panels. One with a big garden had no fortifications they could see. There is a new home and another under construction. The houses are scattered around about a mile or two apart. I would assume they are well-armed. The two boys had an AR-15, a carbine, and .357 magnums when they came to Corpus. They're sure to have hunting rifles too but other than that, I don't think there is anything to worry about."

"They're close enough, that if we attack one place, the others will hear the shooting," Sandra said. "We'll have to hit them all at the same time. If we can get the jet flying, we can blow the shit out of all of them and then go in and pick up the pieces."

"How are the jets coming along?" Conrad asked.

"Shadow seems to think they can get the F-15 running," Sandra replied. "He said they could rob some parts off the Raptor. It'll be a month or so at best. I'll come up with a plan of action long before then and I'll let you know. I want all your men to know exactly what they need to do when we get there. I want to take forty men."

"Forty?" he asked. "That's a lot to take out a few farmers."

"On second thought, let's take eighty. You said yourself to not underestimate them."

"Yes, I did," he replied, "but eighty is most of the Police force. Can you afford to leave the city that under-protected?"

Sandra's glare at Conrad intensified and her face turned a little red as she leaned forward in the swing. "The most important thing is to wipe out Peaceful Valley. When we get back, we'll worry about things around here. So, make a list of your best shots and have them sharpen their skills even further. I'll let you know when I have something about the jet."

Sandra walked Conrad back to his truck. The ladies in the barn had things under control when she checked in, so she headed back to the porch for another soda and some hard thinking. She needed a solid plan.

Chapter 8

In Peaceful Valley . . .

All the neighbors gather on the front porch at the Lindgren's to discuss a plan of action for Sandra's impending invasion of Peaceful Valley. Reggie, Emily, James, Sam, and Sally are sitting around the table. John and Kathy are seated nearby. Melissa comes out of the front door with a platter of cookies she'd baked that morning, followed by Brooke and Florence with glasses and pitchers of tea. Robbie and Ronnie are sitting on the steps, while the rest are scattered about sitting cross-leg on the floor or on the remaining chairs. Emily frowns at Reggie when he takes three cookies.

"I think the main thing is that we don't let them surprise us," Reggie stated. "If they get the drop on us, we're all dead, whether they get the F-15 going or not. We could probably handle a few men one way or the other, but if a big army sneaks up on us, which I'm sure she'll have, we won't have much of a chance."

"How are we going to know?" Robbie asked.

"Yeah?" James queried.

"We'll use the surveillance equipment I told you about," Reggie replied. "We'll have to set it up where we think they might try to come in."

"But what if they surround us?" Melissa asked. "They could try to hit all of us at once."

"I have enough equipment," Reggie said. "We'll have to set up receivers in all our homes. I have beepers we'll all carry in case you are not in the house where you can hear the alarm on the receiver."

"And you have enough of that stuff for all of us?" Sam asked.

"I think so," Reggie replied. "The equipment is packed away somewhere and I'm not sure exactly what I have, but I'll dig it out. I may not have enough beepers for everyone, but I think I do have enough receivers for each household. You may have to share beepers. If you're in the house, you won't need one. Only if you're going out. The receivers will beep and light up too."

"Do you know how to hook all that stuff up?" John asked.

"Not really," Reggie replied, "but I'll figure it out."

"I know a little about electronics," John said.

"Really?" Reggie replied, with a surprised look on his face.

John cleared his throat. "I've always had a knack for electronics. I took a few classes in college and played around with everything from radio equipment to computers. I'm no expert, but I tinkered around with the stuff for many years."

"I can use all the help I can get," Reggie said. "If we hear a jet though, we'll immediately know they're here and can assume an army of men will follow. Since our homesteads are scattered out and we have a good amount of tree cover, even with the jet they won't be able to come in and wipe us out easily. If they don't get a plane going, we'll still know they're here if we can get an alarm system set up."

"And what are we going to do when they get here?" Ronnie asked.

"Kick some ass!" Robbie exclaimed.

"Don't get too cocky," James said. "That'll get you killed."

"All right, Mr. Cocky, you can help me with my explosives," Reggie said. "We have a lot of bombs to make. We'll make enough to hang them along the tree line around every home."

Reggie always liked to talk about his nitroglycerin mixtures and boast about his invention known as *volleyballs*, because of their size, which saved his life years ago. He loved chemistry, especially dangerous stuff like nitroglycerin. After he got out of the army, he set up a small laboratory in his home and worked on all sorts of concoctions. His best invention was what he referred to as volleyballs. The core is a stabilized nitro compound wrapped up much like a fireworks explosive, yet unstable enough that when shot with a rifle, it will explode.

Reggie measured and tested the mixtures until he had devised a bomb, which would kill anyone within fifty feet and immobilize others within a hundred feet of the explosion. Painted green and hung in trees, he had the perfect weapon for dealing with violent intruders. After the grid shut down, a large group of intruders invaded his property and Reggie equalized the playing field with his explosives.

"I'll set up a shooting range at the house," James said. "All you gals will need to start getting good with guns."

"When?" Brooke asked.

"Starting tomorrow morning," James replied. "We've got to get all of you up to speed now. Reggie, can you supply us with guns and ammo?"

"I'm not sure," he said, with a somber look. He burst out laughing when he saw the surprised look on James's face. "I'm down to twelve hundred pounds of powder and I think I only have eighteen hundred pounds of lead left. Maybe I can spare a little." He slapped James on the shoulder. "Of course, I'll bring a rifle and pistol over for each of the women and plenty of ammunition first thing, while you're getting the shooting range ready."

"One thing we haven't discussed," James said, "is a leader for our efforts to defend Peaceful Valley from Sandra Hawkins. I would like to nominate Reggie for this task. While I think several of us could handle the job, I feel like Reggie, being an ex-army contractor, his experience with explosives, and his maturity in general, makes him the most qualified amongst us."

"I'm honored, James," Reggie responded.

"All in favor?" James asked.

Everyone knew Reggie was the perfect candidate for the task at hand. Reggie had tools and gadgets, most of which the other men and women were clueless about, but they all knew about his competence with explosives.

"I am humbled and honored for your trust in me," Reggie replied, looking over the crowd. "I will do my level best to not let you down."

Reggie delivered guns and ammo to James the next morning, then returned home with John and Robbie, aka Mr. Cocky, to get started on their early warning system and the volleyballs. Reggie cleaned off his workbench first, which was always cluttered with various projects. Then he got Robbie started on mixing ingredients while he and John went through boxes and boxes of electronics.

"Mix that stuff exactly, Robbie," Reggie said.

"Is this dangerous?" he asked.

"Not if you don't drop it," Reggie replied, with a smile. "No, it's not dangerous yet. The ingredients will need to chemically react a while, then I'll extract the nitro. That's the dangerous part. I'll do that myself."

Robbie put his hands on his hips. "What, you don't trust me?"

Reggie smirked. "It's not that."

Melissa will kill me if I hurt Robbie with this shit!

"Then what?"

Reggie sighed. "Okay, I don't trust you. It's something which has to be done very carefully. I'll get it stabilized somewhat, then you can take it from there and make the volleyballs."

"This is much better equipment than I'm used to working with," John stated, as he dug through the boxes. "And some of these items I've never seen before."

"The army always has better shit," Reggie said, "and some of this stuff is top secret, or at least it was when I lifted it."

Reggie pulled out an aerial map of the area. "It's about ten miles south to the highway," he said, pointing to the map. "We need to get a signal from there to here. Radio waves will not travel very far through all the brush, so we need to figure out a way and also block the road so they'll have to stop where we want them to stop. Then they'll need to come the rest of the way on foot, which will give us a couple hours at least to get ready."

"How are you going to get a signal from there to here?" Robbie asked.

"I can put an antenna on my turbine tower, but we need a tall tree on the other end."

"There are some tall pines at Charles's house."

Reggie grabbed a magnifying glass and scrutinized the map closely. "Is this his house?"

Robbie stopped what he was doing and looked at the map. "Looks like it. It's about the right place I think, but I don't see any tall trees."

"This is an old map," Reggie stated. "The trees may not have been all that big way back then and besides, when you have an aerial view of trees, they don't look very tall. I guess someone will have to check them out."

"You want me to bring Ronnie with me when I come back in the morning?"

"Yes," Reggie replied.

"And I'll bring one of my boys back with me," John said.

"Tell them to bring a machete," Reggie added. "If they can find a tree, they'll need to trim up the top where the limbs won't interfere with the signal."

John picked up a motion detector and stared at the little box with a plastic lens and two wires coming out of the side. "What's the range of these things, Reggie?"

"About sixty to ninety feet. A deer, hog, or even tree limbs if it's windy can set them off. We'll need to set up a video system so we can tell if Sandra's army is really here."

"How are you going to power this stuff?" John asked.

"I have a couple of car batteries charging," he said, pointing under the end of the workbench. "When those are charged, I'll get two more ready and we can swap them out once a month. This stuff is mostly solid-state and doesn't draw much electricity."

John gently tugged on the red and black leads of the detector. "This one's wired."

"Now build another one just like it. We always double-up in the army."

"I'm done," Robbie said.

"Good," Reggie replied. "Now do that a dozen more times and you're finished."

"A dozen!?"

"Yes, we're going to need over a hundred volleyballs. We don't know how they'll come in, so we need about twenty for each homestead."

"Geez!"

"We're going to war, Son," Reggie added. "If it's a war they want, we're damn sure going to give them all they can handle."

"And if they get a jet going?" John asked. "Do you have that figured out too?"

"Of course," and Reggie walked over to a box and opened it up.

John stepped over and looked inside, his amazement written all over his face. "Rockets?"

"Not just any rocket, but surface to air (SAM) missiles."

"What don't you have in here?"

"I'm a little short on walking room, but I think I've just about got everything else covered," Reggie said, with a big grin on his face.

John just shook his head and got back to work on his motion detectors.

By late afternoon, Reggie decided they had done enough for one day and John and Robbie headed back home. "Your grandpa certainly has a sizeable stash of equipment," John told Robbie.

Robbie grinned. "He can take care of just about anyone. Sandra and her men will surely be surprised if they try to tangle with us."

"Tell me more about Ms. Hawkins. Is she really that big a threat?"

"Whatever she says goes in Corpus Christi. When someone crosses her, she's ruthless and cold-blooded. She was mostly nice to me, but I never crossed her except when I left. I think she knew all along that I would never stay there, but she thought she was smart enough to catch me before I left. I would love to have seen the look on her face when she knew for certain I was on my way. I bet she nearly blew a gasket.

"I think she was a little crazy when she swerved the Jeep in front of me on the airstrip. She should have known that if I hit her, she could easily have been killed too. But I don't think that mattered. She wanted me to die even if it cost her life! She *will* be coming for me especially, and everyone else here just out of spite. She is one crazy bitch!"

"Well, if your grandpa is as good as he thinks he is, Sandra will certainly be surprised at how well a few farmers can defend themselves when she arrives."

"Yes, she will. The only problem is the women. I'm not sure they can take care of themselves. I hope we can keep them safe."

"If they get one of their jets going, even with all that Reggie has, we may not all come out of this unscathed."

With that thought, Robbie and John were quiet the rest of the trip home. They both knew that in war, people died on both sides. Neither could expect that their families would come out of this ordeal unharmed.

When John and Robbie reached the Lindgren homestead, Robbie let out his wolf howl signal, which was returned by James.

"How's it going, Dad?" Robbie asked.

"Some of the girls are going to need a lot of practice," James whispered.

John walked over and gave Kathy a hug. "How are you doing, sweetheart?"

Florence wrapped her arms around Robbie and gave him a sloppy kiss. Robbie immediately turned red in the face. Florence giggled.

Ronnie set the tin cans back up on the logs they had arranged for the girls' shooting lessons.

Brenda, Kim, Charlotte, and Kira got ready for another round at the targets with Sean, Sam, and Lance's help.

"How are they doing?" John asked James.

"Brooke does really well. She and Ronnie have been practicing since they met. Ronnie takes her out hunting with him some mornings and she's been killing a few squirrels and rabbits. Kathy does well too."

"Yeah," John replied, "she doesn't like to kill stuff, but she definitely likes shooting. When we came here from San Antonio, she would kill a squirrel from time to time, so I know she can shoot, but she never killed anything bigger."

"Of course," James continued, "Debra can shoot as well as the boys. She's been hunting with Ronnie and Robbie as long as I can remember. Lance has been helping Beka, and Robbie helped Florence when they moved in together, so they do well too. Charlotte, Kira, Brenda, and Kim need the most work. Look at Brenda and Kim. They haven't hit a can yet."

James looked over when Charlotte hit a can. "See, Charlotte and Kira at least hit one from time to time."

John nodded. "Charlotte and Kira always carried guns when we were in San Antonio and on the way here, but I don't recall ever seeing them shoot anything. Maybe I assumed too much. They always went out to hunt with Lance and Zack, but I guess the boys were doing all the work. I think I assumed the boys would teach their sisters how to shoot."

James pointed at Kira when another can went flying off the log. "At least your girls are getting the hang of it now. They'll get better. I don't think Brenda and Kim ever shot a gun before today. They had trouble loading and handling the guns at first. They're getting better, but they still need a lot of practice."

Kim grabbed James and John's attention. "I can't do this," she said, stomping her feet.

Sean took her gun and wrapped his arms around her and pulled her close. "Sweetheart, you can. I know you can."

He kissed her on the lips and Brenda looked over. James and John looked at each other and smiled.

Sean helped Kim put the rifle back to her shoulder and with one arm around her, showed her how to aim again.

Brenda cleared her throat. "I need some help too."

"Coming." Sean stepped over to her and Kim started shooting. Brenda immediately gave him a wet kiss on the lips.

James and John exchanged grins again. James pointed when Kim hit a can.

Sean noticed the can flying off the log as well. "See, I told you!"

Kim smiled. "I do better with kisses."

Brenda threw her gun up, aimed, and fired. The can shot into the air. She giggled. "Me too!"

John turned his attention back to James. "If they're going to have men shooting at them, that's going to be different than shooting at cans."

"I remember Eileen having trouble killing a man, but Lars worked with her. After a big battle over at Reggie and Emily's, she was quite upset. She did what she had to do though."

John and James looked over at Kim, Brenda, Kira, and Charlotte as they began firing.

James nodded.

At least they are starting to hit some of the cans.

Then he chuckled as he thought about what Lars had told him about Eileen. "John," he said, "I'll never forget what Lars said Eileen was telling herself when she shot her first intruder, 'They're just cans! Big goddamn cans!'"

John laughed and patted James on the shoulder.

"Later, when all the mayhem was over, she cried. But she toughened up and became stronger for it. Many of us are alive today because of her."

"Maybe we need to have a meeting to discuss the mental aspects of going into battle," John suggested.

James nodded. "I think that's probably a good idea."

"Reggie needs us for a few more days," John added. "He's going to send Robbie and Lance to scout out the highway for a tall tree to install some of the electronics on. We're going to relay the signals from that tree to a receiver on the top of his wind turbine. We'll also set up antennas on top of our houses, or on nearby trees so we can get signals from Reggie's equipment."

James scratched his head and frowned. "This seems complicated."

John sighed. "It is."

I certainly hope this works.

"Let me know when you and Reggie are through with the electronics and we'll set up the meeting."

"Will do," John said, "but Reggie's also going to get the boys to set up a couple 'jet killers' he called them. He has two turrets where he wants 50-caliber machine guns mounted. The turrets are heavy and so are the guns and boxes of ammunition. He wants one at Robbie and Ronnie's place and the other at Lance and Zack's place. Reggie wants his SAMs set up at his home. He said he'd take care of the jet most likely, but the boys and the other two guns would be his backup."

"Maybe Reggie needs another hand or two then," James said. "Debra probably can handle most anything the boys can. She may not look strong, but she grew up with tough boys and always held her own with them. I'll talk to her."

The next morning, Lance and Robbie made the ten-mile trek from Reggie's to Charles's place. Lance carried the post hole diggers and the little package of explosives Reggie gave them, while Robbie led the way. At the tree line next to the highway, Lance laid down the posthole digger and metal canister with a fuse out of the end. The boys walked over to Charles's house across the road.

They both stopped and eyed the treetops. "Looks like that's the one," Robbie said. "It's the tallest I see."

The pine tree was big enough around at the base, Lance could just barely reach around it. He slipped Robbie's machete into his belt, Robbie gave him a boost to the lower limbs, and Lance scurried up the tree like he'd been doing it all his life. Afraid the top might break if he went any higher, Lance trimmed a few limbs off to make room for the electronics which would be attached to the main shaft, then climbed back down.

"Looks like that should do it," Robbie said.

Lance nodded and the boys walked back over to the highway.

"Well, since you climbed the tree, I'll dig the hole," Robbie said.

Lance handed Robbie the posthole digger. Robbie dropped his backpack and got to work. In the center of the roadway, Robbie chipped away at the asphalt, then the gravel base, and finally into the hard dirt below. He wiped the sweat from his brow and Lance offered to help, but Robbie insisted it was his job. An hour later, he had dug down as far as the length of the digger would allow.

Lance retrieved the cylinder "This thing's not very big. You sure it will do the job?"

"Grandpa said it would."

Lance placed the cylinder in the hole, remembering Reggie's instructions not to drop it, including when he placed the charge. Robbie held the fuse while Lance carefully packed gravel and chunks of asphalt to the top of the hole.

They both just stood there looking at their finished project while Robbie caught his breath. "Let's do it," Robbie said.

Robbie lit the fuse and the boys scampered into the brush. Well away from the highway, they stopped and took cover behind a tree.

BOOM!

Though both boys knew there would be a loud explosion, they still jumped at the sound. Gravel rained down on them as they flung their arms up to protect their heads. When it stopped, they stood for a second just staring at each other in disbelief. They both grinned and then hurried back to the highway.

The hole was still smoking when they walked up. The crater was a couple feet deeper than Robbie had dug the initial hole and stretched ten feet wider than the pavement on both sides. They had no words. They looked at each other and their grins grew bigger.

"A tree on each side and this will be one fine roadblock," Robbie said.

While Lance notched a large tree on the brush line on one side of the road, Robbie readied his softball size mini-volleyball from his backpack. He placed the explosive in the notch and tied it securely. He lit the fuse and the boys were off again into the brush.

The explosion was not nearly as loud as the first, but when they returned, the tree neatly filled the gap between the brush and the large crater. They repeated the process on the other side of the road and returned to look at their handy work. They gave each other a high-five, a big grin, and headed back home.

With Debra's help, the boys got the heavy guns and turrets moved and mounted, and Reggie's SAM launcher in position in three days' time. Though she always considered herself as one of the boys, she insisted she shoot the 50-cal first because she was a girl. "Girls always go first!"

Reggie showed everyone how to load the gun and gave them some instructions first. "Simple as pie," he said and handed the hearing and eye protection goggles to Debra.

"What do I shoot at?" she asked.

Reggie pointed to a large tree across the meadow. With a big grin on her face, she turned the turret and took aim.

Rat-tat-tat-tat-tat-tat . . .

Reggie and the boys stood back and watched the tree. Splinters flew from the trunk of the large mesquite. Debra giggled then squealed after she stopped and saw what she had done. Then she took aim and fired a few more rounds at the tree.

Rat-tat-tat-tat . . .

When she stopped this time, the tree leaned slowly to the right, snapped, and fell to the ground.

"Ha!" Debra exclaimed.

"Just lucky," Lance said.

"My ass!" she replied and gave Zack a high-five and a smirk to the rest.

Reggie pointed to two smaller trees and the other boys took a turn shooting the gun.

Lance climbed on the turret first.

Rat-tat-tat-tat-tat-tat . . .

Debra teased them melodically. "Yours didn't fall down!"

"Shut up!" Lance scolded.

He hit the tree, but it wouldn't fall down.

Lance looked over at Reggie. "What's the matter?"

He stepped forward. "You're doing fine. You hit the tree, but it's a softer variety. Mesquite is hard and splinters. That's why Debra's fell."

After they all had taken their turn, Reggie handed each a rag and can of oil. They gave the gun a thorough cleaning and oiling, after which Reggie handed them a tarp to protect it from the weather. Reggie also gave them a few additional instructions and pointers to help them shoot down a jet.

Satisfied he had taught them all he could, Reggie sent the kids home and he headed back to his place. "See you in the morning."

While getting the big guns ready were probably the most important tasks which needed to be completed to deal with the potential jet, there were many more individual chores at each of the homes that were crucial for their defense against Sandra's men.

All the families converged upon the Lindgren homestead early. Reggie brought ice so everyone could have iced tea for the meeting. Brooke and Florence were there before the rest to help Melissa with breakfast for all.

When they heard the first wolf howls, Florence and Brooke began setting the table in the dining room and on the porch. James greeted the neighbors as they arrived and he and Reggie had a cigar while they waited for John and Kathy to show up. They were the last to arrive.

After everyone had eaten their fill, James made a pitcher of tea while Robbie and Ronnie began taking the chairs to the porch for the meeting. Melissa grabbed the bowl of pecans she'd shelled and took them out for everyone to nibble on.

Reggie knocked on the table to get the meeting started. "First of all, I'd like to thank John for all his help getting our early warning system ready. And Robbie did an excellent job with the volleyballs. A couple more days and we'll have enough for everyone to hang twenty around each of the homesteads."

"The girls are doing really well with their shooting," James added. "It won't be long before we'll be a force to be reckoned with."

"I'm sure of that, but shooting a man is a lot different than shooting a deer, rabbit, or squirrel," Reggie said. "That is the primary reason for this meeting."

Reggie paused a minute and looked at all the girls. Charlotte, Kira, Beka, Brenda, and Kim had the least experience with guns, but they were learning and wanted to learn more. Their attention was focused on Reggie.

"When Sandra and her men come here, they will have only one thing in mind. That is to put a bullet in you. They will not hesitate in doing so."

Reggie's voice was stern and he did the best he could to convey the gravity of the situation. He didn't want to scare the girls, but he could see the fear in their faces.

"When you were shooting at the cans during your practice sessions, they were nothing more than a target. When Sandra and her men arrive, focus on their chest. Most likely her men will be well-armed and experienced from what Robbie and Sean have told us. She has a police force at her command. Pretend you're shooting cans if you have to, but just think of them as a target. Don't hesitate."

Reggie couldn't tell whether or not he was getting through to the girls. Kira and Charlotte had tears in their eyes. He thought Kim and Brenda understood Sandra and were more accustomed to the ruthlessness of her ways. He thought they knew Sandra would kill them all if she could and they understood they were all in a grave situation, but fear would get them killed. He wanted them to be angry.

Reggie got up and stepped off the porch and asked Kira, the youngest of the group, to join him. He stopped and turned around. Kira walked up to Reggie and stopped in front of him. Reggie reached out and shoved her.

"What did you do that for?" Kira asked, innocently.

Reggie didn't reply and his face turned mean as he stared at her intently. He shoved her again a little harder and she fell backward to the ground. Kira began to whimper and tears ran down her cheeks.

"Get the hell up," Reggie demanded.

John stood up on the porch. "Wait just a damn minute," he hollered loudly.

Reggie turned his attention to John. "Shut up and sit down!" Reggie then turned back toward Kira. "Get up dammit."

Kira stood up and Reggie grabbed her throat. "I'm going to kill you, you little bitch!" he yelled and reared back with his other hand as if he were going to hit her.

John got back up and screamed at Reggie. "That's enough goddammit!"

Charlotte, Brooke, and their brothers were also on their feet at this point and moving toward Reggie. Kathy sat, her eyes wide and mouth open, in shock.

Kira screamed and swung her fists at Reggie. Reggie did not hold her throat tight enough to hurt her, but he shook her and she fought back, continuing to swing her arms. She landed a couple of good blows to Reggie's face and he let her go. He then backed up a bit and held out his hand to the approaching father and siblings.

Kira's tears continued to flow, but her face had turned to rage and she came at Reggie in a fit of anger. Her body plowed into him and her fists flew wildly at his face. Reggie struggled to protect himself and finally got her arms under control, but she began kicking. Reggie pushed her back and retreated. "Stop! Stop! I'm not going to hurt you."

John and his kids halted their approach and stared at Reggie with intense looks on their faces.

"I'm not going to hurt you, Kira," Reggie repeated. He walked over to Kira with his arms wide. "I promise I won't hurt you." He hugged Kira tightly. He could feel her trembling in his arms as she cried uncontrollably.

Kira settled down after a couple of minutes. John and the rest returned to the porch.

"I love you, Kira," Reggie said, in a much calmer and gentle tone.

Reggie led her back to the porch to her seat and gave her a smile as she sat down.

"I don't want you to be afraid," Reggie said to the group. "I want you to be mad when Sandra and her men show up. They are coming to try to kill us and if you're afraid of them, they will kill you."

Reggie looked over at Kira. She was still a little teary eyed and her face was still red, but he could see the newfound strength in her eyes.

"I was mostly concerned about you, Kira. You are the youngest here. I wasn't sure you could handle yourself in the face of the danger we all are going into. Now I know differently. You have it in you to take care of yourself. All of you do."

Reggie smiled at Kira and she managed a little smile in return. "And it looks like I'm going to have a black eye," he added, rubbing the sore side of his face. "But it was worth it."

Beka got up and nodded to Florence. She followed Beka around the side of the house and down to the pier.

"What's up, Beka?"

"Reggie brought up some bad memories about my old man. My daddy used to hit me. When Reggie grabbed Kira by the throat, it all came flooding back. That was what he used to do just before he hit me."

"I know what you mean, Beka. My dad always took out his frustrations on Mama and me. We don't have to worry about them anymore though."

Beka picked up some pebbles and tossed them one by one into the water. "I know, but the memories are still there. I thought they were long gone, but when Reggie grabbed Kira . . ."

Florence took a deep breath and ran her fingers through her hair, pushing it out of her face. "These people care for us. They may have different means of teaching us things, but they do things for our own good. We did the right thing coming here with Robbie. I wasn't sure at first. I thought Robbie loved me, but when we got here things changed. I thought he might have loved you, and then when Charlotte showed up, I really felt hurt."

"I've got to admit, I did have the hots for Robbie for a while," Beka said. "Who wouldn't? He's just so damn good looking. Lance is better for me though. We get along great and I love him. You don't have to worry about me."

"I don't, Beka. I don't worry about Charlotte or anyone else either."

Florence wrapped her hands around her stomach. "Robbie has made it very clear to me that we're together for good, and it's not just because I'm going to have his baby. He loves me for me. Life is never easy though. I guess there'll always be something to worry about. Daddy, Robbie, bugs and snakes, and now Sandra again with this damn war."

Beka stood up and tossed the rest of her handful of gravel into the river. "I guess we better get back to the meeting. They'll be wondering what happened to us."

"Yeah, I guess so," Florence agreed. "Have you told anyone else we killed our daddies?"

"Nope. Just you, Robbie, and me. I haven't even told Lance. I plan to keep it that way. No one else needs to know."

"Yeah. What would everyone else think of us if they found out that we're a couple of murderers?"

They were quiet as they walked around the side of the house and up onto the porch. Ronnie, Brooke, Kim, and Brenda were coming back from Lars and Eileen's graves out by the old sycamore tree.

Kira was playing with Mutt. Though she thought the dog needed a more glamorous name, he seemed to respond better to Mutt. She finally decided it was better if he chose his own name and she was content with that.

After everyone finished stretching their legs, they gathered on the porch again.

Reggie gave Kira a hand as she walked up the steps. "I'm sorry I had to put you through that earlier. I only did it because I *do* love you."

She squeezed his hand and smiled. "I understand. I love you too."

Reggie took his seat. "Well, shall we get this meeting going again?"

Melissa and Brooke went inside for more tea and ice. They refreshed everyone's glasses. They were all ready for a drink after the ordeal Reggie had put them through.

"I wish I'd have wrecked the F-15 before I left," Robbie said. "I never thought that whatever was wrong with it might be something simple. I'm worried about them getting the plane going now. I know you have some rockets, Grandpa, but from what Sean and I saw at the Airport in Corpus, a jet could do a lot of damage before we can shoot it down. The jet's machine guns are one thing, but the rockets can blow the hell out of this place."

"What are you suggesting?" James asked.

"We don't even know for sure if they can get the F-15 going," Robbie replied, "but if they can, they can destroy our homes, our electrical systems, our water systems, and a lot of other important things. The jet may even kill a few of us before the army even arrives. I think we need to know if they are trying and how successful they are at this point."

"What?" Reggie asked. "You thinking about going back to Corpus?"

"That's exactly what I was thinking," Robbie replied. "Ronnie and I can check them out. You know we can take care of ourselves. Maybe we can even blow up the planes to make certain they can only attack us from the ground. You've certainly got the explosives to do that."

"That I do," Reggie replied. "What do you think, James?"

"It's a ten-day trip on foot at least."

"Why can't we drive there?" Ronnie asked. "Can't we spare the fuel for something this important?"

"That might work," Robbie added. "We can drive out to the highway to the east, find a road that cuts across to the highway to the west, and we're on our way to Corpus."

"Lars old truck died many years ago," James said. "Eileen's old Volvo hasn't started in years. Those are our only choices."

The guys got up and walked out to the edge of the porch and stared at the Volvo.

"I don't know," James said. "Eileen insisted that Dad keep the Volvo running just in case she wanted to go somewhere. Her way of keeping a little control over him, I guess. Then after he died, she insisted I do the same. I don't really know why. Maybe because Lars did it. Several years ago, I quit trying when it ran out of gas. Eileen never said anything. I wish now that I'd have kept it up. At least it ran well until it ran out of fuel. If it hasn't frozen up, maybe it'll still start. Who knows?"

"Let's put some air in the tires and push it out of the weeds," Ronnie said. "This is our only chance of getting to Corpus Christi quickly."

James ran to the shop for an air compressor and extension cord. Ronnie, Robbie, and Sean pulled some of the overgrown weeds while they were waiting for James to hook the extension cord to his power supply from the solar panels.

Thirty minutes later, they had the tires aired up and the Volvo onto open ground.

"Looks better already," Sean said.

Everyone stood and stared at the old car. The frowns on their faces said they all had serious doubts whether the old Volvo would run again.

James took the air compressor back to the barn and returned with a battery charger. While he had the hood up, he checked the oil, water, belts, and hoses. He led the men back to the porch. He shook his head in doubt.

"Okay," Reggie said, "what's the next topic of discussion?"

"Lunch," Kira said.

"Good idea," Melissa agreed.

James ran to the root cellar and smokehouse to retrieve a few potatoes and a ham. After he dropped them off inside, he returned to the porch and enjoyed a cigar with Reggie and Lance. Most of their idle chat was about the Volvo.

After lunch, the meeting reconvened. "Now, what's the next topic of discussion?" Reggie asked and took a sip of his tea. Then he held the glass up to the sunlight and looked at the nearly clear liquid inside. "What's this?"

"Tea," Melissa replied. "Fourth pitcher with that batch of leaves."

Reggie frowned.

"How much steel plating do you have, Reggie?" James asked.

He turned his attention back to James. "Some. How much do you need?"

"Enough to protect us when we're shooting out of each door and window in all the homesteads."

"That's a lot."

"I know," James replied. "I have some and I think there's some over in John's barn. How about you, Sam?"

"I don't have any," he replied.

"We'll need enough for the two new houses too," James said.

"Take a tally and I'll look when I get back home," Reggie said.

"If we don't have enough, we can use firewood," James suggested. "Anything that will stop a bullet."

Satisfied they had covered all that needed discussing, Reggie adjourned the meeting. The next morning, they would find out if the old Volvo would start.

That night, Florence snuggled up against Robbie. "Are you really going back to Corpus Christi?"

"I think we need to. We've gotta know what Sandra is doing and how far along she is, if she is trying to get the jet flying."

"But why you? I don't want you to go."

Robbie gave her a tender kiss. "I know the layout of Corpus and how to get there. I'm the only one who can do it."

"But I'm afraid you'll get hurt, or probably worse, captured. They'll make you pay for coming back, then they'll kill you."

"I can take care of myself," Robbie replied.

"Yeah, like you took care of yourself when they caught you as soon as you got to Corpus the last time."

Robbie could see the tears welling up in her eyes. He gave her a big squeeze as he slipped his hand under her nightshirt.

"And you think that is going to make it all better?" she asked.

"I'm not finished yet," he replied, with a grin.

The next morning at the Lindgrens . . .

Sean, Robbie, Ronnie, and James stood staring at the blue Volvo.

"Well, let's see if it'll turn over," James said. He crawled into the driver's seat and reached for the ignition. He looked over at the hopeful eyes looking on.

Grrr-rrr-rrr.

"Eureka!" James yelled.

He hopped out and popped the hood. "Guess I'd better put some gas in it and prime the carburetor."

Ten minutes later, James crawled back behind the steering wheel. "Cross your fingers, boys."

Robbie poured a little gas into the carburetor just as James had instructed. "Go!"

James turned the key and the engine groaned and popped a couple times. "Again," James said, nodding to Robbie and he poured a little more gas into the carburetor.

James turned the key again and more pops and a cough of smoke out of the tailpipe.

"One more time, Robbie," James instructed.

"Ready."

"Third time's a charm," James said, as he turned the key. The engine sputtered a bit and James pumped the gas pedal.

Clunk, clunk, clunk.

On the fourth try, however, the engine ran a little rough, but more importantly, it continued to run. James pressed the accelerator and the old engine smoothed out. He turned the key off and hit the ignition again. The engine started back up and though it still ran rough, it did run.

James hopped out, grinning from ear to ear, and gave the guys fist bumps. "I'll clean the plugs, points, and adjust the timing and she should run much better."

"Then the new mission is a go I guess?" Robbie asked.

"Yeah," James replied. "You boys make your plans."

"I'm going too," Sean stated.

"I guess we need to make a trip to see Grandpa," Ronnie said.

"I'll work on the car the rest of the day and fill it with fuel. It'll be ready when you guys are," James said.

Robbie, Ronnie, and Sean headed toward the Carston homestead at a brisk pace. They made a short stop at their home. Brooke and Florence were busy in the kitchen.

"We're going to Corpus," Ronnie announced, as soon as they walked in the door. "Mmmm! Smells good in here."

"When?" Brooke asked.

"That depends on Reggie," Robbie replied, grabbing a spoon and sticking it into the pot. "Damn, this is good! The old Volvo started and Dad is fine-tuning it. We need some explosives from Grandpa and it'll depend on how fast he can get them ready."

Brooke wrapped her arms around Ronnie while Florence did the same with Robbie.

"I'm going too," Sean said. "Don't worry, I'll keep them safe."

Brooke gave Sean a kiss on the cheek. "I'll hold you to that."

"We've got to get going," Robbie said. "We'll stop back by here when we're through at Grandpa's."

Robbie let out a wolf howl at the edge of the Carston's meadow and proceeded in when Reggie returned the signal.

"Dad got the Volvo started," Ronnie said. "He's tuning it up now. We're going to need some explosives to take out the F-15 in Corpus."

"Come on out to the bunker," Reggie said. "I got all the volleyballs finished up this morning. You boys can start taking some of them back with you when you head home."

Reggie's mind was churning ninety miles per hour about provisions for the boys. "You'll need some fragmentation grenades for the jet. One in the cockpit or exhaust will make sure it stays on the ground. You'll need energy bars so you don't have to worry about food. You can take my sniper rifle too. That might come in handy. One of you can stay on the tree line and keep the other two covered. I'll send along some spotting binoculars as well."

"What about setting off a couple of volleyballs inside the hangar?" Ronnie asked. "Can you make two with fuses?"

"That's easy enough to do," and Reggie grabbed two and set them on his workbench. "Hand me those pliers, Robbie. I'll put a three-minute fuse on them. That should give you time to light the volleyballs, toss a grenade into the jet, and get the hell out of there."

"Perfect," Sean said.

Reggie reached into a box, grabbed a few propane lighters, and lit a couple. He checked to make certain they were full of gas and handed them to Robbie.

Reggie pulled Ronnie close and gave him a hug. "I'm really proud of you boys. You're smart kids. Now you take care in Corpus. Don't rush anything . . . except after you light the fuses." He smiled and gave the other boys a squeeze, then helped them load the gear.

The boys made it back to Robbie and Ronnie's home loaded down with supplies. They hung the volleyballs along the tree line with the exception of the two that had fuses. Afterward, they enjoyed a glass of berry drink with the girls.

"Why don't we get Brenda and Kim to stay here with you while we're gone?" Ronnie said. "I'd feel better with a larger group here and I'm sure you ladies would have plenty to talk about."

This drew a frown from Florence. She wasn't sure she wanted anything to do with the two gals who could potentially cause problems between her and Robbie. Robbie and she, after all, were not married yet and he had wandered before when they first arrived at Peaceful Valley.

Florence thought Robbie and she were an item, but then he strayed first to Charlotte and then Beka. Now that she and Robbie were together and seemingly getting along well, she feared he might stray again. Florence loved him with all her heart since she first met him in Corpus Christi. She was happier than she had ever been in her entire life. Robbie and her baby were the sources of that happiness. She couldn't let Brenda or Kim needle their way back into his life.

Maybe if I talk to them, I can find out what their intentions are—if they're a real threat. What if they want Robbie? I never fought back with Daddy . . . until that day. I always did what he said . . . and Mama too. Is that what life is about? Learning to stand up for yourself and fighting for what you want? Seems like it. At least I think I'm getting better at it. Robbie's worth the fight. Yes, I'll fight for him. If Brenda or Kim give me no choice, I'll fight back.

"We'll watch the Airport the day we get there," Robbie said. "We'll get a good night's sleep and hit them at daylight the next morning. If all goes well, we should be back here that afternoon."

"Just one night is not so bad," Brooke said. "We can handle that. We'll follow you to your mom and dad's and see if Brenda and Kim are up to a slumber party."

"The tires stayed up on the Volvo," James said. "I checked all the fluids and the old gal runs pretty well for her age and the fact that she's been sitting so long. When are you boys going to leave?"

"I'm thinking at daylight tomorrow," Robbie replied. "If we don't have any problems, we should be back the next afternoon. What day is it anyway?"

"Tuesday, I think," James said. "Why?"

"Their transport plane goes to Brownsville on Wednesdays about once a month. We have a 25% chance it will go out tomorrow. That will reduce the amount of resistance we'll run into when we get there. The only problem is we can't eliminate the C-23. They could still use that against us even if we take the jet out. I don't think they would because it is so important to them, but with Sandra you just never know."

The boys stowed all their gear in the Volvo and headed home. They needed to get as much sleep as possible. Tomorrow would be a long day.

Brenda and Kim agreed to stay with Brooke and Florence while the boys were gone. "We'll be over mid-morning," Kim said.

Chapter 9

Robbie turned onto what was left of the pavement on the highway to the east of the Lindgren homestead. He smiled as he drove around the wreckage of the remains of the Cessna in the middle of the roadway.

"I've never been out this way," Sean said. "The fire burned a lot of acreage."

"Yes, it did," Robbie replied. "At least it's growing back. Not much left of the tall trees, but there's plenty of grass and weeds."

"Look," Ronnie said, pointing.

A big buck, a younger buck, and a half-dozen does were grazing near the roadway. Farther up the way, a dozen turkey were standing in the middle of the highway. They took to flight and sailed across the meadow as soon as the car got closer.

"There's less game around our place now," Robbie said. "We've been hunting hard. A lot of mouths to feed. There seems to be plenty out this way though."

"Yeah," Ronnie agreed. "Maybe we'll have to make a few hunts out here, now that we don't have to carry them back on our shoulders. When Sandra comes, all the shooting may leave us no choice."

"Take that Farm to Market road to the right," Sean said, pointing.

They passed an abandoned car or truck grown up with weeds every so often, more deer, and a pack of javelina, but no sign of people. A few more turns and an hour later, the boys made it to what they thought was the main highway they were looking for. Thirty minutes later, a road sign confirmed this. Another hour and a half, and the boys arrived at the abandoned building where Robbie and Sean spent the night on the roof spying on the city so many months back.

Robbie pulled in behind the building, turned around, and parked the Volvo pointed in the direction they would make their escape.

"Lean some of this junk against the car," Robbie said. "If someone sees it, they'll think it's been here all along and hopefully, won't notice it." Robbie then reached down and grabbed a couple handfuls of dirt and gravel and scattered it over the hood, top, and trunk.

"The Airport is that direction," Robbie said, pointing.

"I've never seen Corpus Christi," Ronnie said. "I can't see much from here. There's too much brush."

"Climb up that ladder," Robbie said, "but keep down. We don't want anyone seeing you."

Ronnie grabbed hold of the rope which was still hanging in the rungs from the time Robbie and Sean were there. He pulled himself up, climbed onto the roof, and crawled over to the far side.

Wow. Big city! I expected to see more buildings though. Too many trees. Some tall buildings here and there, and a few roof tops. I bet they would hold a lot of people. Can't see anyone. I guess that's a good thing. There are some really tall towers in the distance. They almost touch the sky. I hope I get to see some of those up close.

Robbie climbed to the top of the ladder. "Ronnie! We've got to go."

The boys gathered all their gear and headed toward the Airport. "Everyone remember where we parked," Robbie said.

It took two hours to make their way to the perimeter fence through the heavy brush. Ronnie stood and stared at the little sign. *Government Property - Keep Out.* Then he took out his pliers and cut a large hole in the chain link. Robbie got out the binoculars and watched the buildings while Ronnie cut. Then they got comfortable for a long afternoon of watching and planning.

Meanwhile back in Peaceful Valley . . .

Kim and Brenda showed up at Brooke and Florence's place shortly before lunch. "Come on in," Brooke said.

Brenda and Kim pitched in to prepare lunch. Brenda took a peach cobbler out of her tote and set it on the table.

"You shouldn't have," Florence said. "Robbie will kill me if I get too fat with this pregnancy."

"Cobbler's not fattening," Kim said, with a smile.

Florence rolled her eyes. "My ass!"

The girls chatted like sisters while they finished getting lunch ready. Brooke had pulled a few radishes and greens from their garden earlier and pulled out a fresh jar of pickles from the pantry. Chunks of ham and some goat cheese she had from the Lins on top made a healthy salad for the girls.

"How far along are you?" Florence asked.

"About six months," Kim replied. "Brenda is about six months along too. How about you, Florence?"

"About five."

Everyone looked at Brooke. She had no tummy the others could see.

"I just missed my second period last week," Brooke said. "Two and a half, maybe three months. I know you can't see it, but I feel my tummy sticking out a bit more than usual."

"How are you two getting along at the Lindgrens?" Brooke asked Brenda and Kim.

"Good," Kim replied. "They have been as sweet as the cobbler, taking us in like they did. They had no idea who we were."

"Sean is working on getting us another place to stay," Brenda said.

"Oh?" Florence said, raising an eyebrow.

"Yes, we've been looking at a site across the river from you," Kim replied. "Sean doesn't want to live with his parents. I told him the three of us could live together if he'd build a cabin."

"Yeah," Brenda agreed. "Kim and I like Sean a lot. I know there is a shortage of men around here, so we decided we could share him."

"And you're okay with that?" Florence asked, looking at Kim.

"Sure," she replied. "Why not? Brenda and I get along as well as family. . . and Sean . . . well, being he was neutered in Corpus Christi . . . to put it nicely, it takes the both of us to get him going, if you know what I mean."

Brenda and Kim both smiled. Brooke and Florence knew exactly what Kim meant and couldn't contain their giggles. They sat quietly for a while as they finished up the last of their lunch.

Maybe they don't have eyes for Robbie, Florence thought. *It certainly looked that way the other day. They apparently want to get it on with Sean. But right across the river!*

"Well," Brooke said, "what do we talk about now?"

"I don't think we can top that story," Florence said. "When do you think you might want to get started on a house?"

"We're not in a big hurry," Kim said. "Melissa and James are easy to live with. They let us be ourselves. I enjoy cooking with her."

"We'll have to wait until after the war," Brenda reminded them. "We don't know when Sandra will show up. We may all be dead soon."

Brooke sighed.

That may be true, but we can't think about that now. We don't know what will happen. She may not come at all. Wrong! If we die, hopefully, it will be quick. No, we'll be okay!

Brooke turned and looked Brenda in the eyes. "Ronnie and Robbie will keep us safe."

Brenda cocked her head. "You seem mighty confident in that."

"The twins can shoot better than anyone I've seen," Brooke replied. "We've been hunting and he tells me to shoot the critters behind the shoulder because it's a bigger target, but when he shoots something, he hits it in the eye, even with his pistol. He never misses."

Florence got up. She didn't want to hear any more about Sandra or them dying. "How about a stew for dinner?"

"That sounds lovely," Kim replied.

Brooke got out a big pot and started the wood stove while Florence retrieved some meat and vegetables from the smokehouse and root cellar. Kim and Brenda jumped in to help prepare the ingredients.

Kim leaned back in her chair and let her eyes roam around the room. "Your home is so rustic."

"You think ours is bare," Brooke said, as she finished tending the fire, "you haven't seen Debra and Beka's yet, have you? There is always so much to do around here, the boys don't have the time to get everything done at once. We had to help Debra and Beka get their home built after ours. They don't even have running water yet and they are still using an outhouse. Now with the threat of Sandra coming . . . it seems like there is always something. There are not enough hours in the day."

"Have you thought of names for your babies?" Brooke asked.

"I thought Robbie Jr. would be nice last month," Brenda said, drawing a frown from Florence, "but I guess we can't *all* name our babies after him. In light of our new relationship with Sean, I thought Sean Jr. if it's a boy, or Shauna if it's a girl."

Kim gave her a gentle shove. "That's what I had in mind! Maybe I'll name mine after kings and queens. My first thought was after a knight, maybe Sir Lancelot, but we already have a 'Lance' in the valley. Maybe Arthur if it's a boy, or Elizabeth if it's a girl."

The girls worked on dinner and chatted like old friends. Florence grew more comfortable with Brenda and Kim, as they opened up about their attraction to Sean. By late afternoon, while she hadn't forgotten about the threat to her and Robbie's relationship, the notion faded to the back of her mind.

While the stew was simmering on the stove, they went down to the pier and fished for a while. Both Kim and Brenda were delighted when they caught their very first fish. They were 'city girls' and had never been fishing. However, when it came to cleaning them, they turned up their noses. Brooke and Florence had to do the honors, but told the newcomers they would have to clean them in the future if they intended to eat.

Florence clipped the fins off and Brooke gutted the fish. Kim looked over Brooke's shoulder. "That's yucky!"

Brenda backed away. "And it stinks too! Ick!"

Florence then removed the heads and Brooke washed them.

Brenda moved behind Florence but screeched and put her hands over her ears when Florence popped the first head off. "I can't stand to hear bones breaking."

Brooke sliced the fish along the backbone almost to the tail, hung the fish over a hanging rod, and looked back at Kim and Brenda. "You two have any trouble helping carry them to the smokehouse?"

They shook their heads.

"Fish is a major source of food around here," Brooke said. "They are slimy to clean, but they are so delicious. Sometimes we fry them, in which case, we'll take the skin off and fillet all the bones out, but for smoking, we just slit them down the middle to hang on the metal rod. After a while, you won't think twice about cleaning them.

"We save the scraps too. Sometimes we use the remains for gar bait, or when Mutt comes over with Sean, we have a little treat for him. Fish head soup isn't bad either."

By late afternoon, they had the beds made and the stew was ready. The girls congratulated each other on such a delicious meal, as it was a group effort. Brenda and Kim both shared stories about their escape from Corpus Christi but omitted the ordeal with Sonny. Brooke shared a few stories from San Antonio and the story of her sister, Charlotte, getting bitten by a snake.

After their bellies were full, they imparted more stories of the hardships of living in the wilderness, but there were many good stories to tell too. They shared stories of the advantages and beauties of living in the wilderness—mint for tea which grew wild in the swampy areas, serene and quiet days except for the sounds of nature, and fresh clean air.

"I especially like dusk," Brooke said. "The sunsets are so beautiful and sometimes the deer will come around to graze in the meadow. Does with one, or sometimes two yearlings, will hang around near the house unafraid and may be unaware they are being watched."

The girls laughed and had a lot of fun, something that was lacking in their lives for such a long time. The elders and even some of their siblings and friends had been nothing but serious for many months, but for good reason. Homes needed to be built, preparations for winter made, and so many chores had to be done every day.

The girls needed a little time to relax and enjoy themselves. Soon, they would be turning into their elders. They would be the grownups. They would have children and to ensure their well-being, they would need to get deadly serious. They would be good parents. They would make certain they survived and their kids thrived, but for now, they relished this carefree fun.

It was inevitable, however, that Sandra Hawkins' name would return to haunt them. War was coming and no one could predict the outcome. They feared the worst but hoped for the best. By the time they made it to bed, they had formed an alliance—the sisterhood of pregnant ladies all serving hope—(S.P.L.A.S.H.). Hope they could defeat Sandra; hope they could all live healthy and productive lives; hope that they could grow bountiful harvests and never need to worry about food, and hope they could all find or keep all the love they wanted and needed. They knew it was corny, but it symbolized their desires for happiness in Peaceful Valley.

Chapter 10

Back in Corpus Christi . . .

Sean, Robbie, and Ronnie sat watching the Airport as the sun slowly receded in the west. A tank truck rounded the corner of the hangar headed toward several tanks on the backside. Two men got out and hooked a hose up to one of the tanks.

"That could mean three things," Robbie said. "First, they filled up the C-23 Sherpa yesterday and it headed for Brownsville this morning. Two, they're getting it ready to fuel up the transport plane for a flight next week and the plane is in the hangar. Lastly, they got the F-15 Eagle going and are getting jet fuel to fill it. I don't know what's in the particular tank they are loading from. I never paid that much attention."

"The Sherpa doesn't matter, does it?" Sean asked.

"Not really," Robbie replied. "If they got the jet going, we need to take it out now."

"I agree," Ronnie said.

"I've got a change of plan," Robbie said. "In the past, when I was here, they always parked the fuel tanker in the hangar. I can sneak up in the morning just before it gets light, open the valve on the tanker, light the fuses on the volleyballs, roll them across the floor toward the fuel, and toss a grenade in the jet. The whole hangar goes up. What do you think?"

"What do *we* do?" Sean asked.

"You cover my ass," Robbie replied. "The fire should light up the sky and I'll be highly visible. I'll run like hell and if you guys see anyone, you take them out. If anyone is around, you should have no trouble seeing them. Just don't shoot me."

"Sounds like it could work," Ronnie said, "but what if someone is watching the place with a night scope?"

"The grass is tall enough. I'll crawl on my belly. They'll never see me even if they're looking straight at me."

"And when you get to the hangar?" Sean asked.

"I'll let it get just light enough to see anyone if they're around. Mechanics and pilots never get up early. At least they never did when I was here. We never got up before sunup. Early, but not too early."

"We better get some sleep," Robbie said, just as the sun was setting. "We've got a long day ahead of us tomorrow."

They didn't bring sleeping bags or even a tarp. They slept in their clothes on the hard ground. Sean and Ronnie were out like a light as soon as they got comfortable, but Robbie tossed and turned for hours. He had the hard part. All Sean and Ronnie had to do was cover his ass.

Four hundred yards on my belly. I can do that, Robbie thought. *I've got to be at the hangar before it gets light, take a good look around as soon as the sky begins to lighten up, sneak in and do my handy work and get out. Am I missing something?*

At Peaceful Valley . . .

Brooke got up first and fired up the stove. She had coffee made by the time Florence, Brenda, and Kim made their way to the kitchen. Brooke poured each a cup as they came out.

"It should all be over by now," Florence said.

"Corpus?" Brooke asked.

Florence nodded.

Robbie knows what he's doing. He'll be all right. Please be careful, Robbie.

They sat and stared at each other as they sipped their drinks. Brooke could see the tears welling up in Florence's eyes.

Kim walked in and Brooke got up to get started on breakfast before she started to cry too. "Good morning, Kim."

"Good morning."

Florence wiped her eyes. "What's on the agenda for today?"

"Why don't we go out and do a little target practice after we finish breakfast? That'll get our minds off the boys," Brooke suggested.

"Good idea," Florence said. "Not happenin', but good try."

Kim nodded her agreement.

At the Lindgren homestead . . .

James finished his plate and gave Melissa a kiss on the cheek.

"What are you going to do this morning?" she asked.

"Split some wood and fill the bins. It's getting downright chilly these days. That'll warm me up quickly."

It'll help get my mind off the boys too.

James walked out the front door and took a look around. He then pulled out a cigar, lit it up, and walked over to the porch railing.

Reggie made sure they had everything they needed to get the job done and get out of there. The boys are tough and careful. They'll be fine. So why am I so worried?

We thought they were prepared the last time they left, but instead, one got castrated and they were both held as prisoners. They had to escape. They had to kill people at an early age, which will change the way they look at things the rest of their lives. I've got a right to be worried!

James finished his cigar, stepped off the porch, and grabbed his ax. He split one log and heard a wolf howl from around the front of the house. He stuck his ax in the chopping block, walked around the corner, and returned the howl. John and Kathy emerged from the woods. Charlotte and Kira tagged along a short distance back.

James extended his hand. "Good to see you, John."

"Is it okay if Kathy and the girls stay here with Melissa today? I'm on my way to Reggie's to finish up on the electronics."

"You know it is. I'm sure Melissa would love the company. It'll help get her mind off Ronnie and Robbie."

"Thanks," Kathy said and led the kids inside.

"How's the early warning system coming?" James asked.

"We'll get it finished today. It's been a long time since I've worked on electronics and the stuff Reggie has is complicated. It's really good stuff though."

James pulled his cap down a little tighter. "Come on around the side. Let's get out of this wind."

John nodded. "It *is* a little brisk. The video is the most difficult, but we'll get that straightened out too. It's important. We can't be having false alarms and without the video, we wouldn't be able to tell. That would drive us crazy. When the boys get back, we'll get it installed."

"At that point, maybe we should have another meeting. We'll get a report from the boys and we'll refine our plan of action around here. Inform Reggie, will ya?"

John tightened his collar around his neck. "Sounds good to me. Well, I guess I better get on my way. Reggie's expecting me early. He gets a little testy when I show up late."

James laughed and John headed out. James got back to the woodpile and worked for a couple of hours before he went inside to check on the ladies.

Back in Corpus Christi . . .

"Be careful," Sean whispered.

Robbie gave them a thumbs up, then got down on his belly and started to crawl toward the hangar. Inch by inch, he scooted through the grass keeping his chin just off the ground. At the corner of the building, he paused a second to catch his breath and to check for guards.

Just as a bit of glow from the eastern sky lightened the surroundings, he made his way to the front corner. The hangar door was closed as he expected, but the side door was open. He peered inside. It was dark and he could see no light shining from under any of the doors to the sleeping quarters.

The C-23 Sherpa was not there.

They must have gone to Brownsville yesterday.

Robbie slid his backpack off and took out the volleyballs, a grenade, and lighter. He slipped the empty backpack back on, tiptoed to the rear of the F-15, and took another look around as his eyes adjusted to the darkness. The fuel tanker was alongside. He quietly lifted the hose off the hooks and opened the valve. He backed up to the hangar door, set the two balls on the floor with their fuses touching and with lighter in hand, and a grenade in the other hand, he pulled the pin with his teeth. He took another look toward his escape route and lit the fuses. He tossed the grenade, rolled the volleyballs toward the fuel, and ran like hell. A muffled bang from the grenade rang out just as he exited the door and he ran like the devil was after him.

A hundred yards away from the hangar, the shockwave hit him in the back and knocked him flat on his face. The searing heat from the fireball pushed him to try to scramble to his feet. Dazed, he made it to his hands and knees and crawled struggling to get back upright. Just as he made it to his feet and was off at full speed toward the perimeter fence, he heard the report of the sniper rifle and a few quick bursts from Ronnie's AR-15.

Robbie ducked slightly, instinctively, though he knew the others would never hit him, and turned on the speed. Another shot rang out from the sniper rifle as he neared the fence. "Let's get the hell out of here," Ronnie said.

"What?" Robbie yelled back, hearing only ringing in his ears.

Sean pointed the direction to the Volvo. The boys ran as fast as they could through the brush. They pushed the debris off the car and hopped in. Robbie got behind the wheel and Ronnie took shotgun. They were five miles down the road and on the way home before any of them had caught their breath and were able to talk about what happened.

"Was that an explosion or what?" Sean asked, jumping up and down in the back seat.

"What! My ears are still ringing," Robbie replied loudly and pressing on his ears trying to get them to pop so he can hear. "What were you guys shooting at when I was on my way back?"

Sean leaned over between the front seats. "Two men came out of the hangar on fire. We put them out of their misery."

Ronnie looked over at his brother. "And there was a truck coming across the tarmac from the south headed for the hangar. I emptied a couple clips into it."

"A couple clips?" Robbie asked. "I only heard you shoot a half-dozen times."

Ronnie gave him a shoulder punch. "Two full clips; sixty rounds."

"I guess my ears weren't working," Robbie said, laughing. "Did you guys feel the shockwave?"

"Not like you did I'm sure," Sean said, "but yeah, we felt it. I thought you were dead."

"Yeah, me too," Ronnie added.

They were quiet for a few minutes, then they all started laughing.

Ronnie held up his hand. "High five, men."

"Was the C-23 in the hangar?" Sean asked.

"No," Robbie replied. "They must have been on their trip to Brownsville. They had to have left yesterday morning. That's why they were refilling the tanker."

Ronnie looked over. "So, they still have a plane?"

"Yeah," Robbie said, "but that is her only option now. Sandra is certainly going to have a mess to clean up at the Airport."

The boys looked at each other and all burst out laughing again. Shortly after they turned off the main highway onto the Farm to Market road, there was a loud pop under the hood of the Volvo. A puff of smoke curled out and they heard a hissing sound. Robbie slowed down and killed the engine.

He popped the hood and the boys quickly spotted the problem. The radiator hose had blown.

"At least it's the top hose," Ronnie said.

Robbie wrapped up the hole with his handkerchief and tied it tight. They then filled the radiator with the last of their water.

"This will get us down the road for now if we don't tighten the radiator cap, but it won't last long enough to get us home."

The boys climbed back in and Robbie started the engine. As he drove, he kept an eye on the temperature gauge. The needle started inching its way to 'hot' long before they reached the road to their homestead.

The engine was spewing steam and Robbie stopped and turned it off. They would be walking the remainder of the way.

"I don't want to ruin Grandma's car," Robbie stated.

"We can't make it home today," Sean said. "And we're out of water."

Ronnie took the lead. "We can make it to the cutoff and then we can make it home by late tomorrow evening. I can't do anything about the water. You know as well as I do, there is none between here and home"

"Shouldn't we try to hide the car?" Sean asked.

Ronnie turned around and looked at Robbie. He shrugged his shoulders and Ronnie turned back and kept walking.

In Corpus Christi . . .

Sandra sped up to the Airport hangar, the tires on her Jeep smoking as she came to a stop. The flames had died down as there was little to burn except the fuel, most of which had gone up in several fireballs. Her Chief of Police, Conrad, was already there—he was over by a pickup truck a few hundred yards away on the tarmac. When he saw Sandra get out, he drove over to the hangar.

"What the hell happened here?" were the first words out of her mouth.

"Looks like someone sabotaged our planes," he replied.

"What makes you think that?"

"This was no accident. The two men in the truck are full of bullet holes."

Conrad led Sandra to some badly burned men by the side of the hangar. He squatted down beside one of the bodies and pointed. "Look here . . . bullet holes."

"Goddammit!" Sandra exclaimed.

She stepped toward the remains of the hangar and gazed over the field toward the brush line, her mind racing. When she turned around to head for her Jeep, Conrad had walked up behind her and she ran into him. "Get out of my way, dammit!" she said and pushed her way around him.

"What do you want me to do?" he yelled after her before she got into the Jeep.

Sandra ignored him and sped away.

"Well, fuck you too," he murmured.

Sandra headed back to the Farm. Her grip on the steering wheel turned her knuckles white.

Goddamn you, Robbie. It had to be you. No one else would have done this. You little bastard, I've underestimated you again. But no more you little son-of-a-bitch!

Sandra slid to a stop in front of her house in a cloud of dust. She pounded on the steering wheel a few times before she got out. Linda Gomez, her long-time mechanic, was working just inside the main barn and saw her pull up, pound the wheel, and heard her shout obscenities. She stopped what she was doing and headed toward the back of the barn to work on another task. She didn't want Sandra to see her. She didn't want to deal with her in the mood she was obviously in.

Sandra didn't see a soul when she got out of the Jeep. She slammed the door so hard, it almost flew off its hinges, then stomped into the house. The place was deserted, but the cook had left a cobbler on the cooling rack. She always felt better when she ate. Stress she told herself. Hell, this was stress times four! She grabbed a spoon, a quart of milk out of the fridge, and dug into the dessert directly from the baking dish. She felt a lot calmer after she finished it off.

Nothing like a little cobbler and milk to ease the mood.

She reached down and felt her full stomach.

I was never meant to be skinny. I've got big bones. Too much goddamn stress around here if you ask me. Goddamn you, Robbie!

Chapter 11

Back in Peaceful Valley . . .

As the sun set slowly in the west, Florence began to cry. Brooke and the other girls tried to soothe her, but Brooke broke out in tears as well.

"They should have been back hours ago," Florence said. "They're all dead!"

"No they're not," Brooke insisted, but you could hear the lack of confidence in her voice.

"There are a million things that could have happened," Kim said. "They'll be here first thing in the morning."

"Yeah," Brenda agreed. "They could have gotten lost."

They all looked at each other with teary eyes. They knew that wasn't an option.

"There's got to be a simple explanation," Kim said. "They could have had car trouble. Don't you worry, they'll be home tomorrow."

When they finished dinner, the girls took their showers one by one. Florence read for a while after her shower, until she decided she was having too difficult a time seeing through her teary eyes. She decided to turn in early. The rest of the ladies followed suit.

Florence tossed and turned in bed for nearly an hour before she cried herself to sleep.

I love you, Robbie. What would I ever do without you?

The next morning, Florence was the first up, followed by Brooke minutes later. They worked together to get coffee made and went out to the porch. Brooke noticed Florence's hands shaking and looked down at her cup. Hers were shaking too.

They'll be home soon, Brooke thought. *Please!*

Florence went back inside when the girls heard Brenda and Kim stirring. Brooke stared across the meadow.

What am I going to do if Ronnie doesn't come back? He'll never get to see his son . . . or daughter.

Brooke reached down and held her tummy.

Please come home, Ronnie. I need you. Your baby needs you. She looked down at the tears dripping on her dress, then closed her eyes.

Please, God!

Kim stepped out onto the porch. "Come on, Brooke, help us fix breakfast. It'll help you get your mind off things. Then when we finish eating, we'll make another big pot of stew. The boys will be hungry when they get home."

Brooke got up and forced herself to go inside. She wiped her tears away and Brenda gave her a hug. "You know they say if you worry too much while you're pregnant, your baby will come out wrinkled."

Brooke paused a second. "They always come out wrinkled," she replied, her lips curling up into a smile.

"They also say it'll grow up stupid," Brenda added.

"No, they don't!"

"Yes, they do and you know what John Wayne said?"

"No!" Brooke said, with a frown and her attention focusing on Brenda.

"Life is tough, but it's harder if you're stupid."

Brooke finally laughed out loud.

"That's better," Brenda said, with a big laugh. "Now let's get some stew going."

Before long, the pot was boiling and the girls began putting in the ingredients. The aroma lifted their spirits and the tears dried up, but their minds continued to focus on their loved ones.

By late afternoon, the girls wandered out onto the porch and sipped on glasses of mustang grape juice. The stew had finished cooking and was cold by now. The sun was dipping behind the trees and it would soon be dark. Their hopes that the boys would be home sank with the sun. The tears began to flow again, but this time they became more audible.

Brooke realized that Brenda and Kim were now also shedding a few tears. They were just as concerned for Sean as Florence was for Robbie and she was for Ronnie. Brenda and Kim had only known Sean for a short time, but he saved their lives. He also saved them from the misery of their life in Corpus Christi. They could have a life here in Peaceful Valley with Sean, but if he did not return, their lives would again be in turmoil.

The sun went down to the dismay of the girls and they got up to head inside for what would likely be the worst night of their lives. As Brooke pulled the door open, a wolf howl echoed through the meadow. Mutt started barking and the girls froze.

Brooke tried to return the howl, but failed on her first attempt. Hopeful tears of happiness got in the way. Her second came out much better. All the girls focused their attention on the direction from which the howl came. Through squinting eyes, they could see dark figures slowly making their way toward them. Brooke gave out another howl, which was immediately returned.

Brooke stepped off the porch. She could see the figures getting closer, but it was too dark to see who they were. "Ronnie," she yelled out.

"Yes."

Brooke stepped forward, tears streaming down her cheeks. The other ladies followed and Mutt darted off toward the men. All the ladies wrapped their men up in their arms and smeared salty kisses all over their faces.

"How did it go in Corpus Christi?" Brooke asked.

"We blew the shit out of their hangar and planes," Sean said, with a roaring laugh. "They won't be coming after us with their jet now."

"You guys hungry?" Brenda asked. "We have stew made."

"Starved," Sean replied, "but mostly thirsty."

Kim gave him another hug. "Good, you can tell us all about Corpus over dinner."

Mutt jumped up on Sean. He gave him a quick scratch on the back. "Did you miss me o' boy?"

Sean turned his attention back to Brenda and Kim. "You gals are a sight for sore eyes."

"So, you did miss us?" Kim asked.

"Of course!"

"We're dead tired too," Ronnie added. "We've had a long walk back. The car broke down and we had to walk at least twenty-five miles."

Brenda headed in first to get the stove fired up. The men followed, took off their backpacks, and placed their rifles in the gun rack.

"You guys need a shower too," Florence pointed out.

The stew was hot by the time Sean got out of the shower. Sean and Ronnie ate while Robbie got cleaned up, then Ronnie took his much-needed shower.

Sean got up and dipped himself more stew. "The explosion lit up the whole airport. I wish you could have seen it."

"They still have the C-23 transport though," Ronnie informed them. "If they choose, they can still bomb us with that one. It was apparently on a run to Brownsville."

Brooke grabbed Ronnie's hand and gave him a troubled look.

He looked into her eyes. "Even if they use the supply plane to bomb us, it's not nearly as capable of doing the damage around here they could have done with the jet. And if they do come with the big plane, it will be a lot easier to shoot down."

"Well, I for one am glad you guys are home," Kim said to all of them, but staring with loving eyes at Sean.

Sean caught Kim's look and turned a little red. He couldn't help his smile. Brenda got up and gave him a hug, which exaggerated his embarrassment, and whispered in his ear.

"I can't wait to get my hands, and lips, on you again."

His color intensified to beet red.

"We're sleeping a little tight tonight," Brooke said. "It's too late for Brenda and Kim to go back to your mom and dad's."

"We don't mind," Kim said. "We like it tight," looking at Sean.

Sean's color wasn't improving, and just maybe was deepening if that was possible.

Chapter 12

Sean stayed with the girls for a while to finish filling them in on all the details of the trip to the Airport after Robbie and Ronnie left. The discussion over breakfast was brief and the girls wanted to hear more. Sean planned to escort Kim and Brenda back to the Lindgrens' later and then on to see his mom and dad. He told the twins he would fill their mom and dad in on Corpus.

When Sean had finished telling his account of the trip to the girls and the ladies had gathered their stuff, Sean led Brenda and Kim back to the Lindgrens'. Mutt had apparently missed Sean as much as the girls did. He stayed at his side all the way there and then on to his mom and dad's.

The twins showed up at Reggie Carston's late morning after sleeping in after their long ordeal. John was already at Reggie's helping him in the bunker when they got there. Reggie gave his grandsons a big hug. "I thought something might have gone wrong. You guys were overdue."

"It went fine. You don't have to worry about the jet anymore," Robbie announced. "Their transport plane was not there, so I guess it was out on a run. Your volleyballs certainly did the trick. I was about a hundred yards away from the hangar when it went up. The shockwave hit me like a freight train and the fireball . . .!"

This got Reggie's attention and he turned to the boys, his eyes wide open and a big smile on his face. "So you like my toys, do you, men?"

"Yes, Grandpa," Ronnie said.

"I forgot to put in the earplugs you gave me and I couldn't hear unless the guys yelled at me for hours," Robbie added. "I still have a little ringing in my ears."

"That'll go away soon," Reggie said. "Just give it a little time."

The boys told Reggie and John all about their excursion while they worked on the electronics and reloaded more ammunition. Reggie then gave the boys instructions on how to mount the equipment in the tree at Charles's place.

"By the time you get there, John and I will have the equipment mounted on top of the wind turbine. When you turn it on, the light will blink. The light will stay on when it is receiving a signal from here. Turn it back and forth until you get it tuned in. The center will glow steadily. I'll have the equipment in backpacks and the two batteries ready for you first thing in the morning. Be here early. It's a long trip."

"Yes, sir," Robbie said.

Ronnie nodded his agreement.

"Wouldn't it be better if we all defended one place against Sandra's army?" Robbie asked.

"Yes, it would," Reggie replied. "The only problem is we don't know when Sandra will be here. That may be tomorrow or two weeks from now . . . maybe even longer. We can't all stay in the same house for that long."

"I've read a lot about divide and conquer," Ronnie added. "It just seems like we're giving her a big advantage."

"Maybe so," Reggie said, "but we can't gather in a central location after she gets here. We don't know how she will attack at this point. If small handfuls of us get caught out in the open, especially pregnant ladies, that will be trouble too. As bad as it may be for each little group of us to be isolated defending our own homes, the volleyballs, and steel plating around the doors and windows will turn the advantage back to us.

"I've thought long and hard about this, boys. I believe Sandra will try to hit us all at the same time. I think she'll figure six or eight men can handle small groups of us. She won't expect us to have anything more than a few rifles and pistols. You never said anything about our volleyballs, did you?"

"No, sir," Robbie said, "but she may figure out we used some kind of explosives at the Airport hangar."

"Do you know if they have grenades, RPGs, or any other explosives outside of what they have for the planes?" Reggie asked.

Robbie shook his head. "I never saw any. All I saw was the rockets and bombs for the jets, and they still have these. They were stored in another warehouse."

"Well, let's hope they don't bring the C-23 and that they don't have any mobile explosives."

"I just remembered," Robbie said, "they have the grenades they took from Sean and me when we got caught in Corpus. I don't know if they'll still have them, but they could. And if they remember, they'll know we might have some more."

After a late lunch, Reggie got the boys to carrying some steel plating inside the house to mount around the doors and windows. They leaned the excess against the side of the house and the boys constructed a travois to transport the metal to the other homesteads.

Ronnie wiped his brow. "It's a lot of work preparing for war."

"Yes, it is," Reggie agreed. "You remember the six Ps I've told you about, don't you? They apply in everything you do—life, growing a family, planting a garden, and yes, war."

"<u>P</u>roper <u>P</u>reparation <u>P</u>revents <u>P</u>iss <u>P</u>oor <u>P</u>erformance!" Ronnie said, mocking Reggie.

Reggie frowned. "You've got a long trip **mañana**. You damn better remember those words tomorrow and do the job right the first time. You'll be making the same trip the next day if you don't."

They all knew these were words to live by out in the wilderness. To live any other way meant doing the same chores again and wasting precious time. They could survive otherwise, but to thrive . . .

Early the next morning, Robbie and Ronnie gathered up the electronics from Reggie's place and headed to the highway. Only a few hundred yards into their trip, Ronnie noticed some movement and the boys stopped in their tracks as they were trained to do all their lives. A spike buck was grazing in a small opening in the brush.

"We could use a little venison," Robbie said.

"Then have at it."

Robbie slowly lowered his bag to the ground, eased up behind a tree, and closed the distance between him and the little buck, moving only when the deer moved. He slipped his .22 magnum pistol out of his holster, aimed, and waited. When the buck raised his head, Robbie put a bullet in his left eye. The deer dropped like a rock.

Ronnie walked over and looked at the deer, admiring the clean shot. "Even though it was a great shot, you know the rule: 'you kill it; you gut it', but be quick about it. We've got to get going. I'll help you hang him in a tree and we'll pick it up on the way back."

In thirty minutes, the deer was in the tree and the boys were on their way.

Three hours later, they sensed they were getting close to the highway. "You're the oldest, Robbie, I guess you'll be climbing the tree."

"Yes, I'm the oldest by nearly ten minutes, so that makes me the boss. You will climb the tree, brother."

"You *are* the oldest, and you have the most expertise, so as not to disappoint Grandpa, you should install the box in the tree," Ronnie insisted.

"We going to settle this like men?" Robbie asked.

They were quiet until they reached the highway ten minutes later. The boys stopped and faced each other to settle the argument.

"One, two, three . . ."

"Ha!" Ronnie said. "Scissors cut paper."

The boys always argued about who was going to do what, but once that was decided, they worked very well together. They were a well-oiled machine and seldom messed up.

Robbie climbed the tree while Ronnie set up the equipment on the ground. Robbie positioned the sending box and fastened it securely halfway between where the light blinked pointed to either side. When he climbed down, the light glowed steady and bright. They double-checked the set up on the ground remembering the six Ps. When they were certain everything was installed properly, they gathered twigs and placed them around the equipment to conceal their warning system from Sandra and her men.

They picked up the deer several hours later, swapping off carrying it back. The boys made a quick stop by Reggie's to make sure the equipment was working properly and headed home. The two of them made quick work of skinning and processing the deer. They even placed the hide in the tanning barrel to cure.

Chapter 13

At the Lindgren's the next morning . . .

Reggie handed James a cooler of ice as he stepped up on the porch. James had the chairs arranged for the meeting. Sam and Sally were the last to arrive.

"You two are getting old and slow just like the rest of us," Reggie said.

His remark didn't faze Sam or Sally in the least. They knew Reggie was a smartass and they'd learned to give him a deaf ear much of the time.

James showed Reggie his Dutch doors in front and back and the steel plating he'd installed on the bottom half and both sides. He also had enough steel for under the inside of the front windows. When the iced tea was ready, everyone converged on the front porch.

Reggie called the meeting to order, but Robbie was the first to speak. He outlined the trip to Corpus Christi, then went on to explain their success with the installation of the electronic equipment at the highway.

Reggie handed out a beeper to everyone. Then he placed sending/receiving devices on the table. "Each home will get one of these. They will pick up the signal from my place and send a corresponding signal to each of the beepers."

Reggie flipped the switch on one of the boxes and the light blinked. He carried the antenna with the trailing cable out from under the porch and held it up high. "See, the light stays on. That means it is receiving a signal from my antenna on the wind turbine. Attach the antenna to your roof and run the cable to the box through a window. Let me know if you have any problems."

"When do you suppose Sandra will show up?" James asked.

"Your guess is as good as mine," Reggie replied. "Robbie can probably answer that question as well as anyone."

All eyes turned toward Robbie.

"I think Sandra will know we hit the Airport. I wouldn't want to be anywhere close to her about now. If she doesn't have a heart attack, I think she'll be here as soon as she can. My best guess would be within a week. If she decides to use the C-23, all she has to do is load it up and it's ready.

"They likely won't have machine guns, but they can drop all kinds of shit out of the back. Jorge showed me one of the warehouses where they stored munitions for the jets. They've got all kinds of bombs. They can do a lot of damage around here with those. The good news is that they can only drop the bombs out of the rear cargo door. That means they can only guess where the bombs might land and won't be able to hit much, but they could get lucky. One well-placed shot and a house is gone."

"The SAMs I'd planned on using for the jet won't work on the transport plane," Reggie said. "They have infrared targeting and are designed to follow the heat signature from the engine. The prop planes don't put out the heat a jet does, so there's no trail to follow. The transport is a lot slower, so we'll have a much better chance of taking it out with one of the two 50-cal turrets we set up or with our rifles. We'll need to take the pilot out if we're forced to resort to our rifles.

"If they come with the plane, as soon as it's out of shooting range, get inside and wait for the men on the ground. I'm guessing they'll make one or two passes with the plane if we let it get that far. The men on the ground will be ready. If the plane is banking, you can assume it is going to make another run. If it climbs, it's probably finished and the men will come in. They know how many passes the plane will make. We'll only be able to tell by what the plane is doing."

"We'll be ready," Ronnie said.

"You're damn right, we will," Sean agreed.

Melissa got up, grabbed the pitcher, and refilled everyone's glasses.

"Anything else we need to discuss?" James asked.

"Medications and bandages," Emily said.

"Yes," Melissa agreed, "and operating tools. Anything you think you'd need to patch someone up—sharp knives, tweezers, tourniquet, whatever."

"Remember," Sally added, "you've got to stop the bleeding first. Then worry about everything else."

James nodded. "Yes, keep an eye on the others around you. It will be your responsibility to help those near you."

"And pain killers," Kira said. "Lots of pain medicine."

"We only have a minimal supply of herbal remedies for pain," Melissa stated, "along with a few over-the-counter meds we got from the nearby town. We need to gather more herbs."

Kathy took a sip of her drink. "I hope no one gets hurt, but I guess that's too much to wish for, isn't it?"

No one said a word. They were all aware of the gravity of the situation. They could hope for the best, but against the force Sandra would likely bring with her, they would be extremely lucky if they didn't all die.

"Is there anything else?" Reggie asked.

"A prayer," John said.

No one objected.

When he finished, Reggie stood up. "Before we break up this meeting, I'd like everyone to know how much help John has been in getting the surveillance equipment set up and working correctly. I thought I knew a lot about electronics, but John showed me my shortcomings. I know I have been pretty rough on him in the past about his religion and church, and my views have not changed, but I will go a little easier on him from now on."

A tear beaded up on John's lower eyelash. "Thank you, Reggie. That means a lot to me."

Reggie stepped over and gave him a firm handshake followed by a manly hug. "You're a good man, John."

Later that night, Robbie finished up his shower and crawled into bed beside Florence. He snuggled up to her backside and wrapped his arms around her, pulling her in tightly against him.

"I'm scared," she said.

"I'm not going to let anything happen to you," he whispered in her ear.

"But they're coming for us. They won't be just shooting at you. They'll shoot at everyone they see, including me."

"Keep behind the steel plates and stay calm. Take aim and shoot straight. You've been doing really well during target practice. You'll do fine. You'll be okay."

"Make love to me, Robbie, just in case."

Robbie scooted back a bit and rolled Florence over on her back. He slid his hand under her nightshirt and teased her nipples as he planted loving kisses, first on her cheek, then working toward her waiting lips.

He slid his hand downward, over her belly and down the hill to her tenderness. She was moist already and he teased her with his long fingers. "You sure we're not going to hurt our baby?"

"I'm sure," she replied.

"I don't want to give him brain damage."

"And you're so sure it's a *he*?"

"I guess all guys want a boy for their first child."

"I'm hoping for a girl."

"This is a little awkward doing it with you on your side," he said, as he rolled her over and slid into her.

"We can quit if you want."

"Never mind. Forget I said anything."

In the other bedroom on the opposite end of the house, Brooke and Ronnie had the same idea. The tension and adrenaline were making them all horny. When they finished, they both lay back staring at the ceiling.

"I hope that's not our last time," Brooke said.

"We're going to have a lot of kids," he replied. "I'm thinking at least ten. Five boys to help me when I get old and slow and five little ladies to help their beautiful mama.

Brooke leaned over and gave him a kiss on the cheek, then turned and blew out the candle. Ronnie was snoring within minutes. Brooke poked him and he turned over on his side. Brooke was tired, but she had trouble sleeping.

They're cans. I can shoot cans. I haven't killed anything since that rabbit last year. I cried for a week.

She touched her belly.

They want to kill my baby . . . and Ronnie. I have no other option. I have to kill them. They will give me no choice. For Ronnie . . . for my baby . . . I will kill them. Every damn one of them!

The next morning, after breakfast, Robbie led Florence to the back of the house. He opened the top half of the Dutch door. "A split door was a good idea," he said. "Sit down on the stool, Florence."

She sat down and Robbie helped her position her rifle. "See the four volleyballs? If anyone gets close to one, shoot it. Keep your gun here in the corner next to the door frame. Let me see you aim."

Florence aimed at one of the volleyballs.

"See, only about half of your head is exposed. That's not a very big target. The steel plating will protect you. Your clip has thirty rounds. Try to keep in the back of your head how many times you've shot. That way, you'll be ready when you know you're getting low. You have ten more clips right here beside you on the table. As soon as you run out, lean over out of the door opening and put another in. That way you won't get shot while you're reloading."

There's so much to think about, Florence thought. *I've done this before in practice, but can I remember everything while someone is shooting at me. I must, for my child. For Robbie.*

Robbie turned toward the front of the house, "Ronnie! . . . Brooke!"

They both turned around to see what Robbie wanted.

"I'm going to have Florence shoot a few rounds out toward the river."

Robbie turned back to Florence and pointed. "Okay, Florence, shoot that knot ten feet up from the ground on that tree over there . . . three shots at a time."

Florence pulled the gun tight against her shoulder and found the target.

Bang, bang, bang.

"Again," Robbie said.

Florence pointed at one of her hens running across in front of her. "Look, we're scaring the chickens."

Robbie grinned. "It can't be helped."

"Well, don't blame me if you don't have eggs with your bacon next week."

Florence aimed and fired again.

"Did you hit what you were shooting at?" Robbie asked.

"I think so," she replied.

"It's not hard," he said. "You've just got to keep your wits about you and pay attention to what you're doing. It's just like shooting at the cans. The only difference is that you have to keep concealed while you're doing it so you don't get shot."

"And they're not cans!" Florence added.

"You can't think like that. If you do, it'll mess up your head and you'll make a mistake. They're cans, or targets, nothing else."

Robbie knelt beside Florence. She had tears in her eyes. He could see she was struggling. "You'll do just fine," he said and gave her a kiss on the cheek.

Brooke and Ronnie came over to give Florence their support. Florence took the clip out of her gun and replaced it with a fresh one. She threw a shell in the chamber, put the safety on, then reloaded the partial clip and laid it with the others.

"See," Ronnie said, "you're doing that like an expert. You'll be okay, girl."

Florence managed a weak smile.

Daddy gave me no choice. I had to kill him—it was either him or me. I've done this before. Sandra's men will not give me a choice either. If it were Sandra I was shooting at, it would be easier. The damn bitch beat me and locked me up. Yes, just imagine I'm shooting at Sandra. That should do it.

The hours and days dragged on. No one knew when Sandra would show up. They only knew that she would. They all knew what they had to do when that time came—they were prepared for whatever Sandra would throw at them. But they also feared the wayward bullet, the lucky shot, or a bomb from the plane in the wrong place. But there was nothing they could do about that. They all hoped everyone would be okay, that they would crush Sandra Hawkins and her army.

Most of the inhabitants of Peaceful Valley, however, were realists. They knew some of them would die. But who would it be? The pregnant ladies were the easier targets and less experienced with guns. A stray bullet or a lucky shot, however, could take out the best of them, the most careful and experienced shot. Anything could happen and dead was dead no matter who you were or how good you were.

Robbie and Ronnie watched for the plane every morning and kept their ears tuned to the sound of a plane during the day. They cut firewood and hunted squirrels and rabbits around the house. Their rifles were always within arms-reach and they carried extra clips.

The girls hunted, chopped wood, exercised, and kept the house cleaned alongside the guys to keep their bodies in shape and their minds in check, but in between they practiced shooting.

The next day, heavy clouds turned into a light drizzle late in the afternoon. By dark, the drizzle turned into rain with occasional lightning.

The next morning, Robbie and Ronnie were up early, having the best night's sleep that they'd had in a while. The rain continued off and on, mostly on, throughout the day. The air temperature dropped fifteen degrees and the warmth from the stove felt welcome. Robbie started coffee while Ronnie began breakfast. The boys let Brooke and Florence sleep in. They were relatively certain Sandra wouldn't show up in this nasty weather.

"Brooke tossed and turned for a while," Ronnie said, "but after she got to sleep, she slept like a log."

"Florence was especially tired last night. She fell asleep immediately. She didn't kick me once during the night. Best sleep I've had in a while. I'm going to step outside and take a look around."

Robbie refilled his cup, stepped out to the porch, and sat down on the bench. He watched the little streams of water running across the yard heading toward the river.

The river will be coming up. That will make it a little more difficult to cross. That could work in our favor if Sandra shows up in the next week or so.

A large buck trotted by the house oblivious to Robbie on the porch. Robbie watched as it crossed the meadow and into the woods. Nothing else to see, he went back inside. He took a big whiff of the aroma coming from the stove as he headed toward the back door. "The river's up pretty high already this morning."

"We've been needing some rain," Ronnie said. "I thought we were going to have to carry water to fill the cistern."

"Not anymore," Robbie said, as he grabbed some plates and silverware to set the table. "I hope it keeps raining for a while. That'll keep Sandra away."

"You know, Robbie, I bet Sandra is getting a little antsy to get out here and whip our collective asses. She's had plenty of time to prepare. I've got a feeling that as soon as the sun comes back out, she's going to show up on our doorsteps."

"Yes, I agree. You may be right. I've had a feeling the time was drawing near myself."

"Good morning, sleepyhead," Ronnie said, as Brooke came in.

Brooke walked over and wrapped her arms around Ronnie and nibbled his ear. Her nostrils flared as she took in the welcome scents of Ronnie and breakfast.

Robbie stepped over to his bedroom and opened the door. The bed was empty and he heard the water running in the bathroom. "Breakfast is ready," he called.

"I'll be out in a sec."

When Florence came out of the bathroom, they all sat down for breakfast together.

"I thought the hard part would be dealing with Sandra and her men," Brooke said, "but the waiting is worse."

"I don't expect we can hope she won't come?" Florence asked.

"Hell or high water couldn't keep her away," Robbie said.

After breakfast, Ronnie decided he wanted to go pay a visit to his grandpa's.

"In the rain?" Brooke asked.

"Yeah, I need the exercise. Besides, I want to share my thoughts about Sandra showing up as soon as this weather blows over. I won't be long. A couple hours at most."

"Okay, suit yourself," Brooke said, "but if you come down with a cold, don't blame me."

"Oh Hon, I never get sick."

While Ronnie was gone, Robbie worked with Brooke and Florence on loading and reloading, as well as a little target practice from the front and back doors.

Satisfied they were doing well, Robbie also helped them practice some hand to hand combat. He wanted them to be the best they could be when the time came. Brooke handled herself well. She didn't have much of a tummy to get in the way either.

"I hope our *daughter* isn't deaf when she's born," Florence said.

"You worry too much, baby doll. I'm sure our *son* will be just fine."

They smiled at each other and couldn't help but get Brooke's attention. She snickered.

Robbie took the rifle from Florence and pulled the clip. He worked the mechanism to eject the shell in the chamber. He added a couple of squirts of oil, worked the bolt again, and shoved in the clip. One more pull on the mechanism and the gun was ready to shoot. He did this all in seconds and Florence frowned, then a tear beaded up and ran down her cheek.

"I can never do it that fast," she said. "I'll be the first one to die."

"You'll do just fine," he replied, but the look on his face was loaded with doubt.

"I hope Sandra doesn't show up in the rain," Ronnie said, as he walked in through the front door a few hours later. "You'd all be dead now."

Brooke, Florence, and Robbie froze and stared at Ronnie with that 'deer in the headlights' look. A heavy dose of reality hit them all like Thor's hammer coming down on their heads.

Brooke stepped over to the kitchen, poured four glasses of grape juice, and set them on the table. Everyone gathered around.

"You're right," Robbie said. "We think we're prepared, but just maybe we're not as ready as we think we are. Maybe Grandpa's early warning system will work just fine, but what if it doesn't? We'll get caught with our britches down, so to speak. We can't let that happen."

"No, we can't," Ronnie agreed. "I think we need to be prepared at daylight every day for Sandra. No exceptions! And throughout the day too. Here we are sitting at the table and no one is watching outside. That has to change."

"Yes, it does," and Robbie got up and grabbed his rifle. "Right now!"

From that moment on, they took turns looking out the windows. They were not going to let anyone sneak up on them like Ronnie did. If they were going to die, it would be with a gun in their hands.

Florence sat for an hour at a time looking out the back door. This was her position and she memorized every tree, every off-color spot in the bushes, every feature of her domain. If something were different, she would see it, and if it were an intruder, she would kill him.

Robbie spent his time at his and Florence's bedroom window when Florence was not at her position. Brooke had her assigned station as well, and Robbie and Ronnie manned the front porch while Florence was guarding the river view. They would not let Sandra get the drop on them early warning system or not.

The rain continued throughout the afternoon and into the darkness. Though they didn't expect Sandra to show up in the rain, they maintained their vigilance until well after the sun went down.

The next morning Robbie and Ronnie were up just before daylight. It was still raining, but they rousted the girls. Everyone got dressed and they continued their vigil. It looked like another boring day, but they didn't mind, considering the alternative.

"River's up bank full," Robbie pointed out.

Around noon, the rain came down really hard for a couple of hours. By mid-afternoon, it slacked off and finally quit. The wind picked up from the north and a short while later the sun came out.

"Looks like the rain is over," Ronnie said.

"Yep," Robbie replied. "It's usually dry and sunny for a few days after a fresh norther blows in. I would bet money that Sandra will be here tomorrow."

"I would too," Ronnie agreed.

Robbie and Ronnie spent the rest of the afternoon making certain everything was ready and that the girls knew exactly what they were supposed to do. Robbie laid a few nutrition bars and thermoses of water next to each shooting station in case the battle lasted all day and someone got hungry. As far as they knew, they had all the bases covered.

"We'll be up before daylight and ready at first light," Robbie said.

Again, Robbie and Ronnie were up first, but they got the girls out of bed immediately. Everyone was dressed before daylight and ready. Robbie cracked opened the front door and took a good look along the tree line. He stepped outside and got behind the barricade at the end of the front porch, breathed in the cool crisp air, and looked up at the sky. He recognized the constellation Aries on the western horizon. There were no clouds.

Aries the Ram relates to Ares, the God of War. Maybe this is a sign. If Sandra isn't here today, she will definitely be here tomorrow.

Robbie stepped inside and pulled the door closed behind him.

"No stove this morning," Ronnie said. "We don't want the smoke to give them a target to hit should they come at us with the plane."

Brooke handed out some fruit and gave everyone a glass of grape juice to get them going. They took their assigned positions, watched, and waited for it to get light. One hour turned into three, then four and five.

Brooke came up with the idea of moving all their mattresses to their assigned stations. The boys quickly completed this task, and they all decided they would sleep in their clothes from here on out.

They were all getting tired by late afternoon, but they kept up their guard. It looked like Sandra would not be here today as they had expected. Ronnie and Brooke, as did Robbie and Florence, took turns stretching their legs and fixing snacks, but by dusk, no Sandra.

"Maybe they'll come at us in the dark," Robbie said. "We know they have night vision scopes. They probably don't know we have them too and would think we'd be easier targets at night."

With that thought, Robbie and Ronnie decided to take shifts all night, just in case. Rock breaks scissors, so Ronnie took the first shift. Brooke stayed up with him for a while, but he insisted she get some sleep. The boys were the experts and could be at top form with only a few hours' sleep. The girls, on the other hand, needed all the sleep the boys could give them.

By morning, Sandra still had not made an appearance and the girls made breakfast while the boys kept a watchful eye on the perimeter. The girls took their positions while the boys ate.

Sandra was still a no-show by noon. The boys took turns getting a little shut-eye. They knew it was going to be another long night. By late afternoon, again nothing.

"I wonder why she's not here?" Ronnie asked. "The weather has been perfect. Apparently, she didn't care for the rain, but now that the weather couldn't be better, she's still not here."

"I don't know what's the matter," Robbie said, "but she will be here. We all know that. It could even be another month or more."

"Don't say that," Brooke said. "In a month, we will all be so tired, she can just walk right in and shoot us dead."

Florence started crying. It wasn't just a trickle down her cheek as was the usual, but a full-blown flood. Robbie held onto her tight. He didn't know what to say to Florence to console her, so he just held on until the tears slacked off.

Florence finally got her tears under control and Robbie wiped them away as best he could with his shirt sleeve. Robbie stared into her swollen eyes.

"I love you," he said.

A smile slowly formed on her lips and he leaned over and gave her a tender kiss.

Beep . . . beep . . . beep . . . beep . . .

Everyone looked at the box, then at each other. Robbie hit the reset button just as Reggie had told him. Reggie said he would check the video feed to see if it were a false alarm. If Sandra was here, they would hear the beeping again.

"But it's getting dark soon," Ronnie said. "Will she hit us at night?"

"If the plane is not going to be used," Robbie replied, "she might figure that is her best option."

"Or the plane could hit us in the morning," Ronnie pointed out, "then she would have her men in place and ready to attack as soon as the C-23 leaves."

Ten minutes passed and the beeping hadn't started again.

"Maybe it was just a deer setting off the equipment," Robbie said. "They move in the morning and evenings mostly. That could be it."

Beep . . . beep . . . beep . . . beep . . .

They all froze. Robbie slapped at the reset button, turned, and gave Florence another hug. He could feel her heart beating faster with every passing second.

Florence then took her position. She looked down at her hands and they were shaking. She gripped her rifle tighter.

For my baby . . . I can do this . . . I have to do this . . .

Robbie grabbed the sniper rifle and stepped out to the porch. He sat down on the stump he'd moved behind the barricade and scanned the trees for movement.

It doesn't make sense for Sandra to come with the plane this late in the evening, but she probably isn't thinking rationally. She's smart, but she's crazy too. How does someone in that condition think? They certainly won't fly at night. If the plane is not here soon, I'll have to assume it'll be here in the morning or not at all. I don't know what else to think.

Thirty minutes later, the sun was gone behind the trees and all that was left was the evening glow. Robbie went back inside to prepare for his all-night vigil with his brother. The wait was over, or nearly so, and they knew the war would start at daylight or shortly thereafter, that is, if it didn't start during the night.

"All right," Robbie said, "let's rig for night vision."

The girls quickly added the scopes to their rifles just like the boys had shown them and as they had practiced so many times before. The boys were ready in half the time, but the girls did well enough.

Chapter 14

By midnight, all was still quiet. Ronnie and Florence grabbed a couple hours sleep, then Robbie and Brooke. After that, both the boys stayed awake while the girls got several more hours sleep.

At first light, the boys got the girls up and they all ate a snack. When it was just light enough to go without the night vision, everyone swapped back to day gear.

Robbie stepped out onto the porch and got behind the barricade he'd constructed. He looked over to the turret near the corner of the stoop. Then his eyes fixed on the horizon to the south.

If they come with the plane, it has to come from the south. It will take Sandra's men a couple hours to get here from the highway. Maybe a little longer before they all find their positions, or they can be here now.

Robbie turned his attention to the tree line. He focused an intense stare and followed the trees from his far left to the far right.

If the plane is coming, it should be here soon. Target the cockpit or the engines? Don't start double guessing yourself now, Robbie. Cockpit! It can't fly without a pilot. Besides, the 50-cal will tear the hell out of the electronics.

Robbie stepped off the edge of the porch and yanked the tarp off the machine gun. He eased up on the edge of the stoop and strained his ears trying to pick up the sound of a plane while his eyes made another pass along the edge of the meadow. He cupped his hand behind an ear and waited.

An hour later and no plane.

Maybe they're not going to use the C-23. It's too important to Corpus Christi. I wouldn't use it if it were me. I'd just send all the men I could.

Robbie caught some movement thirty yards into the brush across the meadow and he hurried inside. Just as he pulled the bottom half of the door shut, shots rang out at the rear of the house followed by a deafening boom, which rattled the windows. A flurry of auto- and semi-auto rifle fire, the likes of which he'd never heard before, echoed around and through the house.

"Stay down and behind the metal," he yelled.

Ping, ping, ping . . . a hundred a minute it seemed.

Florence screamed and Robbie looked over. She was shaking her head trying to get the glass out of her hair. He saw the blood on the side of her face, but there was nothing he could do now.

"Keep shooting."

Dishes were breaking and splinters of wood and glass were flying every-where. Robbie crawled on his belly to Florence's position. As soon as the bul-lets shredding their home slacked off, Ronnie and Brooke launched a flurry of their own. Florence fired another shot at one of the volleyballs, which sent another deafening boom in their direction. A third volleyball exploded in the front meadow.

Robbie laid his sniper rifle on the door frame and quickly fired two shots. Florence emptied her clip and reached for another. Robbie looked over at her. Her face was beet red with a determination he had never seen before. He focused his attention back on the attackers. He spotted some movement in the trees across the river, but he couldn't sight in on them.

Robbie patted Florence on the leg. "I'm going to the bedroom. Keep up what you're doing." Robbie scooted up behind the steel plate and looked through his scope again.

A deathly silence fell over the house. The attack, however, was a long way from being over. There were still men out there. They would not stop. Sandra would kill them herself if they did. They would fight to the death.

Robbie's ears picked up the faint, but distinct, boom of a volleyball from upstream, then two more from downstream. He worked his rifle back and forth along the tree line trying to find a target. A face peered around a tree and Robbie squeezed the trigger. "Another one down!"

More shots from Florence and a flurry from Ronnie and Brooke. Again, there was silence. "Keep looking," Ronnie said. "They're still out there."

"How many did you get, Ronnie?" Robbie asked.

"Two I think." He looked over at Brooke. She was shaking glass and wood splinters off her arm. "Brooke got one with a volleyball."

Brooke threw Ronnie a kiss across the room.

"I got two," Robbie replied.

Florence's chin pushed her bottom lip up and over the top one. "Isn't any-one going to ask me?" she asked, her voice cracking a little.

"Yes, sweetheart, how many?"

"Two," she replied, with a squeaky voice.

Robbie couldn't help but smile. "I love you. You're doing great."

Ping, ping, ping . . .

"I know you're out there, son-of-a-bitch," Robbie growled. More move-ment and he followed the color with his scope. When it stopped, he squeezed the trigger again. "Damn, this 50-cal kicks like a mule, but I got another one."

"Let me have it," Ronnie said. "You can use my AR-15 for a while."

Robbie slithered across the floor and swapped guns with his brother. On the way back to his station, Florence called his name. "Robbie . . . I'm bleeding."

Robbie crawled up beside Florence and looked at her shoulder. "It looks like glass cut you. You'll be okay." He gave her a quick kiss. "I'm going to the bedroom." Robbie resumed his station and scrutinized the woods.

"You think we got them all?" Brooke asked.

"No way," Ronnie replied. "What do you think, Robbie?"

"I doubt it. We did kill a bunch of the bastards. You don't mess with Lindgrens and not expect to pay for it."

Robbie laughed and the bullets zipped through the house again. "Keep your heads down."

It got quiet again. "How many do you think are out there?" Ronnie asked. "I think there might be three on my side."

"Maybe two over here," Robbie replied.

Florence fired a single shot, which was followed by the shockwave and boom of another volleyball. "One less now," she said, exuberantly.

"I'm sure glad you're on our side," Robbie said.

Thirty minutes went by and not a shot was fired. Robbie could hear the faint reports of rifle fire from the neighboring homesteads, but nothing nearby. They all stayed alert, however, in case the intruders showed themselves again. An hour had passed and no one saw any movement and still no shots. Robbie scooted back around to Florence's position. As he did, he noticed all the holes in the walls and roof. A thin blanket of smoke hovered toward the ceiling. Rays of light cut through the layer. "Looks like we're going to need to do a little patching around here when this is all over," he said.

Florence was still focused on the landscape toward the river.

"You okay, baby?" Robbie asked.

"Under the circumstances, better than I thought I'd be. I'll cry tomorrow."

"Me too," Brooke said.

"Robbie!"

"What sweetheart."

"The chickens aren't going to lay the rest of the year!"

Robbie laughed.

Yep, she's alright.

"I know they're still out there," Robbie said. "I don't like waiting for them to come back at us again. I'm going to get my crossbow and go out."

"No! Stay here," Florence begged.

"Baby, it'll be much safer for all of us if I go after them. They'll never see me coming."

"You can count on that, Florence," Ronnie said. "Robbie can sneak up on anyone or anything."

"I'll head down to the river first and get mudded up. Then I'll make a circle around the place. Try not to shoot any volleyballs while I'm out. If you see someone, shoot them. You won't see me."

"Gotcha, Brother."

Robbie grabbed his bow and quiver and opened the hatch they'd made in the floor. He scooted over to Florence and gave her a quick kiss, then climbed through the opening, and pulled it closed behind him.

"Stay alert, Florence," Ronnie said. "You too, Brooke."

Florence watched for Robbie to exit the underside of the house, but she never saw him.

What is he waiting for? He should have crawled from under the house by now. "Ronnie."

"What?"

"How long is he going to stay under there?"

"He left a long time ago."

"But I didn't see him. How do you know?"

"But you wouldn't. No one would. Believe me, he's long gone by now."

"Is he that good?" Brooke asked.

"Damn right he is," he replied. "He's almost as good as me."

Brooke squinted at Ronnie but kept quiet.

I certainly hope he is.

Three hours, more or less, went by and they heard not a sound outside of an occasional report of a rifle from one of the other homes. Florence nibbled on a homemade energy bar as she continued to stare out of the corner of her doorway opening. "Ronnie, how long will he be gone?" she asked.

"Until he's finished. Sorry, but your guess is as good as mine. I suspect he'll make a couple passes around our perimeter to make certain he's gotten everyone out there."

Everyone jumped and perked up when the reports of a gun reached the house. "Those were nearby," Ronnie said.

Florence began to cry. "They caught him!" she screamed. "You said he wouldn't get caught."

"He's not dead and he's not caught," Ronnie said. "He's better than that."

"Then who's shooting? Robbie would be shooting his crossbow. Only those men would be shooting a gun."

"I don't know what happened," Ronnie explained, "but Robbie will tell us when he gets back."

"He's not coming back," Florence asserted and her tears turned up a notch.

"Don't bet money on that," Ronnie replied. "Wipe your tears and keep your eyes open. Robbie's okay, but this isn't over yet."

Another hour went by and all they could hear was the wind blowing through their newly ventilated home. Florence held her focus out the rear door. Ronnie and Brooke continually scanned the tree line, but Ronnie occasionally glanced over at Florence.

She'll be fine. She just needs to keep focused on the task at hand. Robbie shouldn't be much longer. Then she'll see.

Over at the Lins, Mutt started barking at daylight and shots rang out. Sean, Sam, and Sally rushed to their pre-assigned positions, quickly located targets, and returned fire.

Shots kicked up dirt around Mutt. He squealed and hightailed it under the house. Not another bark was heard out of him and he stayed under the house the rest of the day.

Those sons-a-bitches better not have killed my dog, Sean thought. *I was just getting used to having him around. The last couple weeks, he's become my best friend.*

"Damn you!" Sean yelled and laid out a flurry of shots toward movement he saw in the woods. Immediately, the shots were returned and splintered the door frame.

Ping, ping, ping, as some of the shots hit the metal plating protecting his body.

Good idea Reggie had. I'd already be dead without the metal.

A loud bang echoed through the house coming from the direction of where Sally was, as she hit one of Reggie's volleyballs.

"Give 'em hell, Mom!" Sean said.

Because of the denser trees, the intruders had to get much closer to the house to make their shots. As such, they were easier targets for the Lins. The volleyballs they had strung around the place were close enough together to form a continuous barrier. As a result, Sally took out two men at a time on three separate occasions. Sam, with his weapon of choice, his shotgun loaded with buckshot, was dead-on and extremely deadly.

Sean only killed two men by late afternoon, one with a volleyball and another with a head shot, but that was all who crossed his sights.

As the sun slowly receded and the sky turned to darkness, Florence began to cry again while she converted back to night vision. Despite Ronnie's continuing assurances that Robbie would be back safe and sound, her fears grew significantly as the last bit of light outside disappeared.

She finally managed to get control over her emotions and her tears dried up. The war was not over until they were absolutely certain every one of Sandra's men were dead. She needed to stay alert and make certain no one snuck up on the house and caught her by surprise.

Bam . . .

The hatch in the floor slammed open and Florence screamed. The crossbow appeared through the opening. Robbie's head poked through next. Florence's eyes were bulging with surprise. Robbie smiled, which Florence immediately returned. "It's all clear out there," he said.

"How many?" Ronnie asked.

"Four . . . two singles and a double."

"We heard shots," Florence said.

"Yeah, I couldn't reload the crossbow fast enough so I had to use my pistol on the second. Guess who else I found?"

"Sandra?" Ronnie replied.

"Yep, she's hog tied out across the river. She'll be okay for a while. There's still some faint shots coming from Grandpa's, and Mom and Dad's. We need to help them."

Florence hugged Robbie, her tears beginning to flow readily again, and gave him a kiss he wouldn't soon forget. "You're okay!"

"Did you have a doubt?" he replied, with a shit-eating grin of cockiness.

Florence frowned. "Well, yeah!"

Ronnie looked over. "Not a bit, Brother."

Ronnie exchanged his sniper rifle for his AR-15 and the boys scurried down the floor hatch, then helped the girls down.

"Now you know why we built this little bunker under here," Robbie said. "You two stay in there until we get back. We'll likely be the rest of the night. Keep quiet too."

Ronnie handed the girls a couple thermoses of water and they were off.

"North or south?" Ronnie asked.

"South. We'll get Grandpa out of trouble and our backs should be clear. Grandpa can come with us and Grandma can stay with Brooke and Florence."

"Works for me."

Being the eldest, Robbie led the way. They made a sweep on the far side of the river making certain Reggie couldn't see them and take one of their heads off. Ronnie smeared a little mud on his face, ears, and hands as soon as they made it to the river.

The sky was partly cloudy with nearly a quarter moon. The moon would set long before sunrise, so the next few hours would give them the best light. After that, they would rely only on starlight—though not optimal, with their keen eyesight, this would be plenty.

There was a gentle breeze, so the fog would not rise up until at least close to morning. The remaining leaves on the trees rustled a bit to help conceal the minimal noise the boys made.

As they neared the back side of Reggie's place, Robbie stopped and held up a finger at Ronnie. He leveled his crossbow and zipped a bolt through the intruder's chest. The man jumped to his feet and gasped as his rifle slipped through his fingers and fell to the ground. His head bent down, he grabbed at his shirt, and he crumpled to the dirt. He quivered a bit, then was still.

Robbie reloaded and eased toward the body. He kicked him in the ribs. There was no movement. The boys moved forward and there was no one until they got a few hundred yards past the far side of Reggie's bunker. There, Robbie saw a group of four men huddled around a small fire behind a fallen tree. They were well out of sight of their grandpa's home and bunker.

These guys may be armed and dangerous, Robbie thought, *but they're not so smart. Don't they know someone could sneak up on them? Maybe Grandma and Grandpa are dead. These guys certainly don't seem to be afraid of anything. Shit!*

Again, Robbie held up his fingers giving his brother the headcount. Ronnie moved up alongside Robbie. Robbie nodded his forehead toward a large tree to the right and Ronnie slipped over behind the trunk.

Ronnie nodded at his brother when he had his sights on one of the men. Robbie was ready and sailed his arrow to its intended target. Immediately, Ronnie fired and Robbie drew his pistol, but the men were all on the ground before he could get his handgun on a target.

The boys grinned at each other. Robbie pointed the direction and led the way to the river. They found a shallow spot and made their way to the other side. On a wide swing around Reggie's place, they only spotted one more man. Robbie took him out with ease.

They executed an additional sweep of the perimeter to make certain they cleared it of all intruders. Robbie gave out a wolf howl and waited. There was no return signal. The boys moved a little closer to the edge of the clearing so they could see the house better. Robbie gave out another signal a little louder this time. Still, there was no reply.

Robbie looked over at his brother and saw the tear, glistening in the moonlight, running down his cheek.

"Let's get closer," Robbie said.

The boys crawled up on the side where the woodshed was located, so their grandpa wouldn't shoot them. Robbie peeked around the corner of the shed and immediately noticed all the broken glass and more holes in the siding than he could count. Once again, he let out a wolf howl. Seconds later, the front door opened and Reggie returned the signal.

The boys got up and hurried to the porch. Ronnie slung his rifle over his shoulder and wrapped his arms around his grandpa. "We thought you were . . ."

"What?" Reggie asked.

"We signaled twice and you didn't . . ." Robbie said.

"What, you thought I was dead? I'm having a little trouble hearing. Can't get the ringing out of my head."

Emily walked to the door. "Come inside."

Ronnie stepped in and the others followed. Ronnie wrapped his arms around his grandmother.

Reggie slapped Robbie on the back. "It'll take a lot more than a dozen or so men to kill me, boy."

"That's what I thought," Robbie replied, "but . . ."

"No buts about it."

"All's clear at our place," Robbie informed his grandpa. "You missed six, but we took care of 'em for ya."

"Mighty grateful, boys," Reggie said. "What do you think you're doing running around out here in the dark? Didn't they have night scopes?"

"We didn't find one on any of them," Robbie replied. "To tell you the truth, I don't think they figured their little war would take more than a few hours at most. They didn't figure we'd be out looking for them either. One group had a fire going and weren't paying any attention to what was going on around them. They may be pretty good with a gun, but otherwise they're dumb as bricks."

Reggie laughed.

"We have a prize for you too, Grandpa," Ronnie said, with a big grin.

This grabbed Reggie's attention. "Sandra?"

The boys grin widened.

Robbie nodded. "You'll see the ol' gal soon."

"Brooke and Florence are in the bunker at our place," Ronnie said. "If Grandma can stay with them, we need to get over to Dad's. When we left home, we still heard shooting over that way."

"Then we better get going," Reggie said.

Reggie and Emily grabbed a few more clips of ammo, slung their rifles over their shoulders, and followed the boys. On the way, they stopped by and got Sandra before heading to their home.

Ronnie pointed, "over there, Grandpa."

Sandra was tied up and gagged where the boys left her. She started to struggle when she heard them coming. She was dressed in camouflage, dirty, her hair all mussed with sticks and grass, and mad as a hatter.

Robbie removed the rope from her feet so she could stand. Ronnie helped him get her to her feet. As soon as she got upright, Sandra yelled through the gag, kicked at Reggie, and swung her shoulders wildly trying to escape.

Reggie moved out of kicking range. "You're not going anywhere, except where we want you to go."

Ronnie headed toward home. Robbie pushed her in his direction, but she fought back. "Get your ass going!"

Sandra struggled against the ropes again and refused to budge.

"Don't make us carry your fat ass," Reggie said.

Robbie shoved her in the back again toward Ronnie. She reluctantly followed.

As he neared home, Robbie went ahead, crawled under the house, and got Florence and Brooke out of the bunker, while Ronnie and the others went inside through the back door. Robbie crawled through the hatch in the floor, then helped Florence and Brooke up. Florence wrapped her arms around Robbie and planted a salty kiss on his face. Brooke did the same with Ronnie.

Reggie forced Sandra into a chair. "So, this is the ruthless bitch you boys have been telling me about? Looks like a fat-ass coward to me!"

Sandra said something softly through her gag and he pulled it out to see what she had to say, but when he did, she screamed at him. "You're going to pay for this!"

Emily hit her in the head with the butt of her gun. Sandra's head jerked backward and her eyes rolled to white in their sockets.

Emily took a deep breath and turned toward the rest. "What an incredibly irritating voice!"

Everybody looked at Emily with surprise on their faces.

Emily's face then turned to sadness, when she looked at Sandra's limp body and felt bad for what she'd done. "I'm sorry, I'm a little stressed out."

Reggie gave her a hug. "We're all a little stressed out, darlin'."

Ronnie kissed Brooke and looked into her eyes. "One small candle near Sandra. Just enough so you can keep an eye on her. We don't know when we'll be back. When the war's over, I guess."

"Take it easy on me, boys," Reggie said, as they headed out the door, "I'm not as agile as you young bucks."

Chapter 15

At the edge of the Lindgren homestead . . .

Robbie, Ronnie, and Reggie squatted beside a tree at the edge of the meadow, far enough into the woods James or Melissa couldn't spot them with their night scopes. The moon had gone down and the sky was dark except for the faint light of a few stars.

A shot rang out from inside the house, which was followed by a flurry of gunfire from the woods.

"Well, now we know where they are," Reggie whispered.

Robbie led the way, followed by Reggie ten yards back. Ronnie took up the rear keeping an eye out to his six o'clock.

Robbie spotted the group of men, scattered about and all facing the house. He waved at Reggie and Ronnie to stop, eased up behind a tree, and peered around the edge. Reggie was the only one with night goggles. He was blind without them in the dark, but with the clear sky and the stars shining bright, Robbie could see well enough with the naked eye, to determine there were six men. He turned to his grandpa and held up five fingers, then one. Reggie passed along the number to Ronnie.

Reggie and Ronnie crept up, each picked a tree for protection, and eased into position. Robbie leveled his crossbow at the men and nodded to the others. He sent his arrow on its way hitting his intended target in the upper body. The man screamed and the remaining men turned their attention to their comrade with bulging eyes, not certain what had happened. Reggie and Ronnie opened up on the group. Robbie grabbed for his pistol and got in two shots before the last man fell.

After a few seconds and seeing no more movement and no more targets, Robbie pulled another bolt from his quiver and hurriedly poked all the bodies. Their work here was done.

"I estimate the sun will be up in a couple hours," Reggie pointed out, "so we need to get this place swept clear before it gets light. After that, we'll have to deal with the rest in the daylight. We'll lose some of our advantage when it gets light. I don't see any night scopes on these guys either. I'd have thought they'd all have them."

"Maybe they thought they'd wipe us out in a few hours during the daytime," Ronnie said. "Who knows? Lucky us."

Robbie again led his troops around the perimeter of the Lindgren meadow. They made two full rounds of the tree line and there were no more men. Robbie let out a wolf howl, which was immediately returned. They made their way to the porch and James ushered them inside.

The boys were happy to see their parents made it through the ordeal, and outside of a few glass cuts, were unscathed. Brenda and Kim were not so lucky. Brenda was shot in the arm, but the bullet missed the bone. Her arm was wrapped up and she was tending to Kim who was not so lucky. A bullet went in just above her belly but just below her ribs and came out her left side. Brenda had the external bleeding under control, but Kim was having some trouble breathing. She didn't know whether or not the baby was hit. She was certain that there was internal bleeding, but at this point in time, there was nothing she could do for her.

Kim was out cold from a bullet graze just above the right eye. Brenda was clueless as to whether there was brain damage, or how extensive it might be. If she lived, only time would tell with this injury.

"We've lost our advantage," Robbie said. "The sun will be up soon, but we can't do anything about that. We'll have to deal with the rest in the daylight."

"Stay here, Grandpa," Ronnie said, "we can take care of things from here on out. Maybe you can help Mom and Dad with Kim."

"You sure?"

"You know us," Robbie said and turned toward the door.

Robbie didn't see his grandpa's smile and the boys slipped out the back.

"Kim is going to need surgery," Melissa said. "She's in bad shape and she has to be bleeding inside. I'll need your help, Daddy."

Back at Robbie and Ronnie's home . . .

Emily, Brooke, and Florence sat across the room from Sandra huddled in the shadows. The candle placed on the floor behind Sandra made it easy for the girls to keep an eye on her, their rifles ready and pointed in Sandra's direction. She was still out cold from Emily's blow. They sat in relative darkness, ready should someone come in through the front or back doors.

"How does Robbie get around in the dark like he does?" Florence asked, looking over at Emily.

"Robbie and Ronnie are equals when it comes to camouflage and stalking. It doesn't matter whether it's daylight or pitch-black outside, they're the best. They have the eyes of owls and can see better than anyone I have ever known. I don't know how they do it. Maybe because they've been doing it all their lives.

"Let me tell you a little about your men. Lars taught Eileen all he could about survival. When Lars died, Eileen vowed to pass on the knowledge Lars gave her to the boys. Eileen worked day in and day out teaching the boys the ways of the woods. Reggie and I also taught them all we could, as did their mom and dad. Everyone in Peaceful Valley loved the boys as their own.

"The boys learned a lot on their own too, as did Sean and Debra. They spent as much time in the woods as time would allow. When they were at home, they were reading Lars's books and learning from Eileen's stories. Eileen made certain they were woods smart, but also as book smart as humanly possible with her resources.

"Reggie and I knew Lars well. Lars was Reggie's best friend. He was the epitome of an American woodsman. His skills would amaze most. I know he astonished me so many times. As skilled a woodsman and protector as he was, Lars was such a gentle soul—a grizzly bear on the outside, but the softest teddy bear on the inside. I think this is why Eileen loved him so much. Both Robbie and Ronnie take after their grandfather, but I believe their survival skills far exceed Lars's."

"I couldn't help but cry when Robbie left to help you," Florence said. "Ronnie kept assuring me that he'd be alright."

"You don't have to worry about the boys, they can take care of themselves. If there were more than ten men, maybe I'd be a little concerned, but I don't think you need to worry about a small handful, especially at night. One bright star above and they'll spot a tree frog a hundred feet away."

Florence knew Emily was exaggerating a bit, but the boys were truly amazing at dealing with Sandra's men. Florence already knew Robbie was amazing by the way he touched her in bed.

Sandra started to moan and move around a little. Florence quickly moved the business end of her rifle toward her.

"Don't worry about her," Emily said. "The boys know their knots. Sandra couldn't get loose if she were an eel."

At the Lindgren's . . .

Reggie helped James carry Kim to the kitchen table. Melissa retrieved the sharpest butcher knife she had and held it out to Reggie.

"You'll have to do this," he said.

"I can't, Daddy."

"You worked in a pharmacy."

"I peddled ankle wraps and cotton balls. I can't operate on her."

"If it can't be done with explosives, then I'm not the man for the job."

Melissa and Reggie looked over to James.

"Don't look at me. I have trouble getting a splinter out of my finger."

"Well, put a pot of water on to boil," Reggie said. "We'll need it later."

Melissa looked at the knife in her hand, then at Kim. When she turned to Brenda, she backed up with both hands in the air. Melissa took another look at the knife, stepped over to the table, and held it over a candle flame for sterilization.

"I'm going to need help."

Reggie and James held onto Kim, though she was still out from the head wound, while Melissa tore her dress open. She found the entrance wound as well as an exit hole. Both were oozing blood and fluid. From the angle and location of the holes, she determined the bullet had hit the placenta and possibly the baby.

Reggie suggested she cut her open as if she were doing a C-section.

She looked at Brenda. "Get another lamp."

Melissa touched the knife to Kim's stomach and made a vertical incision from just below her ribcage to her navel. Kim lay still and quiet.

What if she wakes up? Please . . . no . . .

The blood scared her and she looked over to her dad for guidance.

"I don't know how to do this either," he said. "You look like you're doing fine. It's going to bleed. That can be expected. Just keep your mind on what you're doing."

Melissa turned her attention back to Kim. She didn't think she had cut deep enough and looked over to James.

"Like you're gutting a deer. Stick two fingers in and use them to guide the blade so you don't cut anything inside."

Melissa had gutted a deer a few times and had watched James on numerous other occasions. She knew exactly what he was talking about, only this wasn't a dead animal and her hands started shaking.

Reggie saw her nervousness. "Steady, you can do this."

When she opened Kim up enough to see the baby, tears formed in her eyes. She could see the bloody water pouring out of the rupture in the skin surrounding the fetus.

"The baby can't be saved," Reggie said. "We need to concentrate on Kim's life."

James saw the tears dripping from Melissa's eyes and grabbed a hand towel to wipe her face.

"I can't, Daddy!"

James stepped in and pulled the fetus and afterbirth through the opening. "Get me a towel, Brenda." He wrapped the baby and laid it in a chair. He also noticed the water boiling, took it off the heat, and set it in the sink. "Brenda, run some water in the sink to help cool off the pot."

James turned his attention back to Kim. "Help me, Melissa. We've got to make sure there is no more internal damage."

James searched around inside the opening while Melissa tried to soak up the blood and amniotic fluid. Thanks to the baby, Kim's intestines were out of the way. Other than the two holes in her sides, the only damage was to the fetus. The bullet hit no major arteries or veins and the amount of blood loss was not significant for a wound of this type.

James grabbed the pot of sterile water, which had now cooled off to near body temperature and washed out the opening while Melissa continued to soak up the excess. "Towels, Brenda; lots of towels."

"I think that's good enough," Reggie said. "I don't see any significant blood oozing out anywhere."

Melissa retrieved a sewing needle and thread. As she sewed, James squeezed the excess air out of the wound. When she finished with the incision, she put a couple of stitches in the entry and exit holes and dabbed the areas with alcohol.

"It's not pretty," Reggie said, "but the bleeding is stopped. That's the most important thing. You did a wonderful job, Melissa, and you too James. You two have given Kim another chance at life."

"I'm just glad it's over," Melissa replied, tears returning to her eyes. "I've never done anything like that. Cleaning a deer is one thing, but . . ."

"You were wonderful," James said. "The next time I get a splinter, I'll let you dig it out."

Melissa smiled and went to the bathroom to retrieve the bandages they had boxed up for the war. Finally, Brenda jumped in to help with the bandaging now that the dirty work was finished. James and Reggie put a blanket on the sofa in case she bled a little or her body fluids got the best of her and carried Kim to her new bed.

"It's all up to her now," Reggie stated.

James nodded and headed for the back door. He ran to the barn and selected a deer hide from his stack and some leather cordage. Reggie helped him wrap up the little baby and secure it tightly with the leather strips. He then set the bundle on a chair next to the front door.

Brenda sat in a chair across from the sofa and stared at Kim. Her breathing was slow and steady. "I'm glad she stayed out during the operation. I hope she's going to live, but it's going to be hard losing her baby." She reached down and felt her stomach. "I'll help her."

"We'll all help her," Melissa said.

Robbie and Ronnie didn't see anyone on the way to the Lins's and after a full circle around the perimeter, there was no resistance. After a wolf howl, which was returned by Sean, the boys found everyone to be okay. Mutt crawled out from under the house and ran over to Robbie.

"Good dog," and he gave Mutt a pat on the back.

Smart dog too.

Robbie informed the Lins of their progress thus far and Sean insisted on going with the twins to their final two destinations—the Wimberley's and his sister's. Sean asked about Brenda and Kim.

Robbie looked at his brother, then back at Sean. "They're okay—a few nicks and cuts, but fine." He quickly turned away so as not to give away his lie.

Sean made Mutt stay with his parents. He had to put him inside for a while because the dog always insisted staying with his master, but one bark from him could give away their presence to the men they were hunting.

A half-mile from the Wimberley's', the boys spotted smoke filtering through the brush. When they drew near, they saw three men sitting around a campfire. They did not seem to be overly concerned anyone would be out in the woods at this time of the morning. They smoked their cigarettes and chatted amongst themselves, without a clue they were being watched.

Robbie double-checked his crossbow and the boys spread out and crept upon the men. At thirty yards, suddenly the men scrambled for their guns when someone yelled. Two other men were watching their perimeter, which explained why the men at the campfire were so relaxed.

Robbie got off one shot with his crossbow before the bullets zipped through the trees near his head. He hit the man in the arm and he screamed in pain, but the man fired back and Robbie scrambled for cover and reached for his pistol.

Sean and Ronnie each emptied a full clip at the men and reloaded. The men did not try to rush their position and Robbie signaled Ronnie and Sean to regroup. The three scurried back into the woods toward the Lins's from whence they came.

Robbie reloaded his crossbow. They did not know how these men would react. They didn't know if they would scatter or try to hold their position, but they did know they would be a force to be reckoned with in the daylight. They kept a sharp lookout as they discussed their options.

"I got the one you hit with the crossbow," Ronnie said.

"Then that still leaves four," Sean noted.

"Yes, four that know we're here and can see us as well as we can see them," Ronnie said.

"Unless . . ." Robbie said, cocking his head a bit.

Ronnie knew exactly what he was talking about as Robbie started gathering vines and limbs to further camouflage himself.

"You guys stay here and keep your eyes open," Robbie said. "I'll circle their camp and see if I can sneak up on them, hopefully, one at a time. If they scattered out, it'll be easy to pick them off. If they are dug in at their campsite, it will be more difficult, but I'll get them. It'll just take a little longer."

"Good luck," Sean whispered, as Robbie headed out.

Robbie made a wide circle around where they had encountered Sandra's men. As he came to within forty yards of their campsite, he spotted three men. Robbie lay and watched for a while. The men were mostly concealed behind trees and brush. After several minutes, he finally located the fourth man twenty yards on the other side of the first three. He was well-concealed too.

Robbie eased back into the brush and took another route toward the men where he was certain he could get a good shot at one of them. He carefully moved up behind a large tree thirty yards from the closest man. He had a clear line of sight and though one of the men looked in Robbie's direction, he never saw him sneaking up.

Robbie looked back at his escape route, then focused on the nearest man. He positioned his crossbow, aimed, and sailed the bolt into the man's ribcage resulting in a loud gasp as he fell to the ground. Robbie immediately scurried back into the woods using the large tree for cover. No shots were fired at him. It was apparent that he had escaped without being seen.

Robbie made a large circle around the campsite and nearly an hour later he was on the opposite side of the men. The men were still at their campsite but huddled closer together now, watching out in all directions.

Again, with the stealth of a grass snake, Robbie got into shooting range of the men. He picked his target and squeezed the trigger. Once again, his bolt found the man's chest cavity. He groaned loudly in pain and rolled on the ground.

The remaining two men jumped up and ran toward the river in the direction of Sean and Ronnie. Robbie reached for his pistol and got a couple of shots at them, but only hit brush.

Sean and Ronnie better be ready. The shots will put them on alert at least.

Within seconds, Robbie heard the gunfire. He stood and waited. Directly he heard the wolf howl and headed toward Ronnie and Sean.

"Where's Ronnie?" Robbie asked, as he walked up to Sean.

"We didn't have a good shot when they came running through the brush. We got one, but the other headed off in that direction," Sean said, pointing. "Ronnie went after him. He won't get far."

Several shots echoed through the woods followed by a wolf howl. Robbie returned the signal. He and Sean sat down on a log and waited for Ronnie to return.

Ronnie signaled again when he got closer.

"We're over here," Robbie yelled out.

Satisfied their work was done here, the boys continued on to the Wimberley's home. After making a complete circle around the meadow, Robbie signaled with a wolf howl. John returned the signal and the boys approached the house.

"Thank God you're here," John said.

He led the boys inside. Kira and Kathy knelt beside the sofa in tears. Charlotte was stretched out and Kathy had her head on Charlotte's chest.

"I heard shooting at the back of the house," John said.

"Yes, that was us," Robbie replied. "There were men sitting around a fire. Other than them, it seemed clear."

Sean stepped over to the sofa and looked at Charlotte. She had been shot. By the dim light through the windows, he could see her left eye was red and a dried blood streak ran down the side of her face. Sean looked over at John and he shook his head. "I'm sorry."

"They killed my baby!" Kathy screamed, looking up with red eyes and tears trailing down her cheeks. "Why God; why . . .?"

"Are the rest of you alright?" Ronnie asked, looking at John.

"More or less," he replied.

"We better get going," Robbie said. "We'll be back this afternoon. We need to get over to Debra and Beka's. That's the only place we haven't made and then we'll make another round of the valley. Keep your eyes out until you see us again."

They could hear Kathy still sobbing as they left the house.

After Robbie, Ronnie, and Sean made a thorough search around Debra and Beka's, they found no more intruders. Lance, Zack, and the girls were safe. Sean and the twins headed back to the Lindgren's.

Sean was shocked when Robbie told him about Kim as they approached the house. "Damn you!" He shoved Robbie and ran inside.

Robbie and Ronnie stayed only briefly to inform them of Charlotte's fate and that they thought they had taken care of all the intruders. They would apologize to Sean later.

Brenda gave Sean a big hug and salty kiss before she led him to Kim on the sofa. "They are not surgeons, but they did the best they could."

Sean knelt and took Kim's limp hand. "I feel like a part of me has died."

Brenda knelt beside him. "She'll be okay, Sean. We have to have faith."

Sean wiped at the tears. "I love both of you. I don't know what I'll do if I lose either one of you."

Brenda leaned her head on his shoulder.

Reggie followed Robbie and Ronnie back to their place. Robbie signaled the women and went inside. Emily hugged Reggie first, then her two grandsons. "You two have done a wonderful job."

Robbie looked over at Sandra, still securely tied to her chair, only now she was gagged.

"She wouldn't shut up," Brooke said.

"Will you stay here, Grandpa," Ronnie asked. "We need to get something to eat and some sleep. We can take turns."

"Of course," Reggie replied.

"I think we can risk a fire in the stove now," Robbie said, "but let's keep it dark inside. We need a sentry outside too, I think. I'll take the first watch while the rest of you get some sleep."

"I'll bring you a plate when it's ready," Florence told Robbie.

Florence had breakfast whipped up in no time and took Robbie a plate a little while later. He gobbled the food down, having not eaten much the past twenty-four hours. He had a little trouble keeping his eyes open now that his adrenaline level had dropped and his belly was full. He slapped his cheeks and splashed some water on his face from his glass, then his eyes focused on the tree line around the meadow.

Gotta keep sharp. I think we got everyone, but all it'll take is one to cause more problems.

Ronnie stepped outside after an hour and relieved his brother. "I got enough sleep for now. Go grab a couple and I'll keep watch."

Robbie got up and went inside. He noticed Sandra stretched out on the floor, securely tied and gagged. She was snoring.

After everyone got a snooze, the men headed back out to make a final check of the woods. They met up with Sean, and by dark, Sean and Reggie had made it halfway around Peaceful Valley while Robbie and Ronnie made the sweep in the opposite direction and met Sean and Reggie in the middle.

"Well, looks like we got them all," Reggie said. "I counted thirty-eight."

"We got forty even," Robbie replied. "I guess we need to bury them all. If we don't, they're going to stink up the valley."

"It's cool enough," Reggie said, "we've got a couple days. We've got to deal with Sandra too."

"Yeah, what are we going to do with her?" Ronnie asked.

"We'll have a meeting tomorrow and we'll all decide together," Reggie replied.

"Looks like you and Grandma are staying another night at our place," Robbie said.

Chapter 16

At the Lindgren homestead . . .

Everyone gathered early for Kim's baby's and Charlotte's funeral. Robbie and Ronnie went over to the Wimberley's to help Lance and Zack carry Charlotte's body to the old sycamore tree at the Lindgren's.

Ronnie and Robbie moved Sandra from their place to the Lindgren's and tied her up on the porch. They decided to leave her gagged until after the funeral. The people of Peaceful Valley would determine her fate at the meeting to follow the double burial.

Kim laid in bed. She mostly slept since her surgery. She lost her baby, which probably saved her life. If they could prevent an infection, Melissa was certain she would recover, but it would take weeks before she could get out of bed. She was certainly in no condition to attend the burial.

John's voice failed him every time he thought about Charlotte and he was unable to perform the service, so Reggie volunteered to deliver the eulogy. This wasn't his first memorial, but as always, he hoped it would be his last. He took his place behind Lars and Eileen's headstones.

"Charlotte struggled with all the critters here in the woods and they made her life miserable for some time. After her ordeal with the snake-bite last year, she learned to keep her eyes open and her life became much easier. She was learning to avoid the dangers and finally saw the beauty of Peaceful Valley.

"Charlotte was a beautiful woman, just emerging into the prime of her life. We'll never know why she was singled out to be taken away from us, but we do not know God's plan."

John looked up and threw a glance at Reggie. Reggie caught his movement and looked over to catch the small smile he managed at Reggie's words.

"Charlotte will be taken care of now by her Maker. She will live out eternity in the comfort of the Lord. Drop in and grace us with your presence from time to time, Charlotte."

Reggie made the service for Charlotte short. There was a lot he could have said about her, but felt there was no sense dragging out everyone's misery.

Reggie turned his attention to Kim's baby. "I can't see, for the life of me, why a child would be taken from us before it is born. We don't always have the answers to why things happen in this world, but if there is a reason, I cannot agree with it. Kim is a wonderful woman and to deprive her of her baby is mean and cruel.

"Maybe there is no rhyme or reason, but there is nothing we can do about it. Life is tough. Maybe it is a test. We'll never know. I do know that we will miss the little girl. If she would have grown up to be anything like her mother, we would have all loved her. Even though she was never born, she is a human being to us and we'll miss her."

Reggie wiped the tears from his eyes. He didn't shed them often, but couldn't help himself on this occasion.

Some of the family gathered wildflowers for the graves. They all said their own goodbyes as they placed the flowers.

After the ceremony, their attention immediately turned to Sandra and the meeting. Their agony over Charlotte and Kim's daughter soon turned to rage.

Reggie brought the meeting to order. "I think all of you know what I'd do. The old sycamore is good for a lot more than just marking the location of our cemetery. I'm sure we can find a suitable rope for a necklace, but I'll listen to any alternatives the rest of you might have."

"I think we should take a vote," James suggested. "If the vote comes out like I think it will, no further discussion is necessary."

"Okay," Reggie said, "let's take a vote."

Sean was the first to vote. He slapped his hands together. "Hang her!"

John and Kathy did not want to hang Sandra, but she had killed their daughter and this tipped the scales just enough that they agreed to the extreme measure. Reggie did not have to say a word to sway them. They made the decision on their own, saying only they could not think of an alternative option.

"An eye for an eye and a tooth for a tooth," he said. "May God forgive me."

Kathy burst into tears. John wrapped his arms around her. "Forgive us all," she said.

Sam and Sally were the last to vote. They said they would not have voted for Sandra to live, but since everyone else had voted for her to die, their vote would make no difference in the outcome. They said they would both sleep better if they cast their votes against the hanging.

"Well, Sandra, looks like you're going to dance in the air," Reggie said, with an evil grin.

Sandra strained against her ropes and tried to speak, but with the gag in her mouth, all she could manage was a muffled scream. No one cared what she had to say and it was decided to keep the gag on.

"We know the place," Reggie said. "Now all we need is the time."

"No time like the present," James said.

"Works for me," Reggie replied.

James got up and went to the barn to fetch some rope. Only two of the ladies wanted to watch the hanging. Brooke and Kira insisted. They wanted to see her pay for killing their sister.

Ronnie, Robbie, Sean, Zack, and Lance gathered lumber and nails to construct the gallows. It didn't need to be a permanent fixture and it only had to be strong enough to hold Sandra's weight. It didn't have to look pretty either, so it only took a couple of hours for them to finish the structure.

Some of the ladies watched from the porch, while Reggie and James supervised the construction and chatted.

"I don't believe I've ever heard you mention God all the time I've known you."

"What do you mean, James."

"At the funeral, you said Charlotte was in God's hands now. You getting soft on Him in your old age?"

Reggie sighed. "No, I don't think so, but the death of Kim's baby out of all of us, and the bullets flying everywhere made me think a little. It also brought back some bad memories."

"You mean the baby we killed across the highway?"

"Yeah. I still don't believe in God, but if, and I'm saying *if*, maybe we're being paid back for that and some of our other sins around here. We didn't know there was a baby over there when we killed the neighbors. How were we to know? We had a problem and there was only one way to solve it. We couldn't have known it was going to turn out that way."

Reggie looked down and kicked at the dirt. "You know there hasn't been a newborn in this neck of the woods since Robbie and Ronnie. I'm just saying that something like this makes you rethink your life. The death of an unborn baby of all things, when she was the least likely to die. We were all at high risk, but . . ."

James crossed his arms over his chest and took a deep breath. "Maybe we need to change our ways a bit."

Reggie was quiet for a few minutes. "Nah! Shit happens," and he turned and headed toward the boys who were about finished with their task.

When the men came for Sandra, the women went inside, with the exception of Brooke and Kira, who stood front and center of the scaffolding.

John and Kathy hated Sandra for what she did, but didn't feel they needed to see her die. This would not bring their daughter back.

While the hanging was taking place, John and Sam made a travois down by the river where suitable poles were in abundance. They wouldn't have Sandra buried in their cemetery, so they figured they'd take her down the road some distance. Eileen and Lars would roll over in their graves if Sandra were to join them.

Lance and Sean led Sandra up the stairs and Reggie placed the rope around her neck. She struggled a bit as the noose tightened around her throat.

"Shouldn't we let her have some last words?" Robbie asked.

Reggie removed the gag and Sandra licked her lips trying to get some moisture to return to her dry mouth. Her rage turned to fear as she realized there was no way she was going to get out of her predicament.

"You can't do this!" she yelled. "You're nothing but a bunch of ignorant farmers. You'll pay . . ."

"That's about enough," Reggie said and stuck the gag back in her mouth and tied it tightly.

Robbie cleared his throat. "For as long as I've known you, Sandra, you have done nothing but boss people around. You ruled everyone around you with merciless brutality. When someone didn't suit you, you had them murdered or flogged.

"You've never listened to anyone. It has always been your way or else. Well, now you are going to listen to me and there isn't a damn thing you can do about it.

"Your dictatorship has come to an end and that is a fact just as sure as you are going to die. We are going to change the world. If there are any more like you out there anywhere, we're going to put a stop to it."

For the first time since he'd known her, Robbie saw a tear run down her cheek.

"We didn't invite you here," he continued. "You did this, but we're going to finish it. We're damn good at finishing things."

Robbie turned and looked at the others. "Would anyone else like to say anything?"

Kira moved up toward the steps leading up to Sandra. "I was afraid of you for a long time, but no more. You are nothing but an animal. You killed my sister and I am going to watch you die. You are going to pay for what you did and I hope you burn in Hell."

Brooke walked up to her little sister and put her arm around her shoulder. "I don't have anything to say to you. Charlotte was my sister too and I just want to watch you swing. You are not worth any more of my time or words."

Robbie looked around and no one stepped up or indicated they had anything to say. He walked over in front of Sandra and he could just barely make out her words with the gag in her mouth.

"Then do it!" Sandra took a deep breath and slowly exhaled. Her body stiffened up and she stood straight.

Reggie stepped up and placed the cloth sack over her head while Robbie lit the twine holding the lever. They all stood back, watched, and waited. The seconds seemed to drag by as they kept one eye on Sandra and the other on the string.

"Burn in Hell," Kira screamed just as the string burned through and Sandra's weight snapped the noose tight. She continued to watch as Sandra's body jerked and quivered as her lungs fought for air.

Kira stood with her eyes glued to the body until the last muscle twitch was gone. "It's over when the fat lady swings!" She turned and headed to the house without another word.

Immediately after the hanging, Sean went to Kim's bedside, while the others disposed of Sandra's body. He wiped Kim's forehead and held her hand. There wasn't much else he could do.

After Sandra was disposed of well down the road, Sean joined the other men. In teams of two, they took shovels and buried some of the other intruders until dark. The ladies prepared backpacks with drinks and jerky to keep them hydrated and their energy levels up. Reggie complained that he was 'getting too old for this shit', but did his share nevertheless. The following day, he let the younger men finish the task at their farms, while he and Emily went home and he buried the bodies around his place using the backhoe.

There was no road between his place and the other homesteads. That is the way he liked it, and with the dense brush, it wasn't possible to get his equipment to the other places.

Reggie caught up on some much-needed sleep that night. At his age, he required more sleep than when he was younger, but mostly he wasn't used to all the work, which was forced upon him the past few weeks.

Robbie and Ronnie wandered into Reggie's meadow shortly after he finished burying the men scattered around his place.

Reggie took the boys inside and showed them the video footage of Sandra and her men when they first arrived near Charles's place. He then showed them the live feed from the video cameras.

"Looks like we have a bus, five trucks, four cars, and a Jeep if we want them," Reggie said.

Robbie's eyes lit up when he saw the vehicles. "Yeah. When we get our repairs taken care of, I'll talk to Dad. I'm sure he'll be happy with the extra gas. We can tow the Volvo back too. We may need to make a couple trips, but it'll be worth it."

"How's Kim?" Emily asked.

"She sleeps most of the time," Ronnie replied. "I hope she makes it. I know Sean has been over there every day. He loves her, I think."

Emily's eyes rolled around a bit. "I thought he loved Brenda."

"Yes, her too."

Emily smiled. She wasn't one to judge Sean and the girls. They wouldn't be the first *ménage a trois* around here, but that was a little secret no one else needed to know.

Kim started to stir a little on the third day. Her pain was agonizing and the medications available helped only slightly more than nothing. Melissa and James were no surgeons, but they had done the best they could to save Kim's life. Now that the surgery seemed to have been successful, Brenda worked constantly to care for Kim's injuries and daily needs. The abortion was the worst part for the ladies. Their only solace was that the bullet had hit the baby in the head and it did not suffer.

The fetus was fully developed and was a girl. Kim, though she was in a lot of pain, was conscious and in control of her faculties. She named her baby Abigail and Sam promised he'd make a headstone for her along with Charlotte's.

"You take care of yourself, Kim," Melissa said, "and we'll have a eulogy as soon as you're able. The main thing is for you to get well. It may take a while, but so far you seem to be healing. I'm sorry it hurts, but we're giving you all the pain killers we have."

Kim forced a smile knowing she was, while Melissa returned the same, wishing she could do more.

By late evening, the last of the new vehicles arrived at the Lindgren homestead. The side of the house was beginning to look like a parking lot.

The gears were turning in Sean's head all the way home as he drove the bus. As soon as he got out at the Lindgren homestead, he asked James and the rest about utilizing the bus for his new home until he could get a more permanent house built. He didn't want to stay with his parents and it was a little crowded for Brenda and Kim at the Lindgren's. Not everyone was comfortable with the Brenda, Kim, Sean trio, but no one let on. James said it was fine with him if no one else objected to him taking the bus.

"I'll get it ready," Sean said, "and when Kim gets better, she can join Brenda and me."

Sean had many of the seats out of the rear of the bus in no time. He stowed some of his gear as well as water and food inside, then made a bed in the back. He couldn't take the bus across the river near his parents and on this side of the river his only logical option was back up the road to the highway, far enough to be away from everyone, yet close enough to be convenient. A quarter-mile seemed the appropriate distance for now, but the bus could be easily moved at any time.

Robbie sat on the front porch watching the tree line. The early morning was cool and there was a thin layer of ground fog over the meadow. The eastern sky was bright, but the sun was still low behind the trees. The faint odor of gunpowder still lingered in the air.

Florence walked out after she finished dressing to enjoy her cup of faux coffee with Robbie. He leaned over and gave her a little kiss on the cheek, then turned his attention back to the tree line. He sat staring at a couple of rabbits scampering around near their garden, oblivious to the past few day's events. A few squirrels dangled in the treetops working on their morning meal.

"A penny for your thoughts," Florence said.

"Corpus Christi," Robbie replied.

Florence sat and stared at him a few moments trying to discern his meaning. She was clueless about why Corpus would be on his mind.

What?" she asked.

"Corpus has no leader now," he replied. "I doubt they know what happened here. We have vehicles and fuel to go there now. The city has a lot of resources. The only problem with Corpus Christi was Sandra and her henchmen. Most of them are dead now, but even without Sandra, whoever she left in charge knows where we live. That could cause more problems in the future."

Robbie fully grabbed Florence's attention with his words. She didn't say anything but turned to face him. Her eyes wide open now, as well as her mouth, she listened as Robbie spelled out his intentions.

"Ronnie and either Sean, Zack, or Lance can provide me with backup while I go there to talk to Linda."

"Linda?" Florence asked.

"Yes, Linda Gomez. She works at the Farm. She's old enough to be a leader. Though she mostly followed Sandra's orders, I worked with her while I was there. She's mature, knows the routine, and what needs to be done to reorganize the city. She could handle the job and we got along well too.

"Mostly though, she has a good heart. I think everyone else at the Farm would go along with her. If I could talk with her, I could help her set up a more democratic system of government. No more castrations, a real say in how their government is run, and freedom of movement within and even outside the city. I think most would like the change. If they don't, they could leave . . . not murdered like what happened when Sandra was in charge.

"I think this can work and we can capitalize on some of their resources. We don't have a lot to offer them outside of their freedom, but at least we could be on friendly terms with them."

Florence put her hand on his arm. "I think you're dreaming."

"It can work," he replied. "I know it can. If we let the dictatorship continue, only with a new leader, who's to say we are not going to have more problems with them down the road. Marcia Nguyen was Sandra's right-hand. What if she takes over? She could gather another army and come here to take revenge on us for Sean killing her husband. The threat of war will always be hanging over our heads. We have the opportunity to nip this in the bud and turn Corpus Christi into an ally instead of an adversary.

"Sean could go shrimping if he wanted. I know he really liked it and a little seafood would be nice too. And real coffee instead of the Karaicha beans. I've gotten used to the Karaicha, but it's not real coffee. The ordeal with Kim has opened my eyes that we need access to better medications, especially pain killers and antibiotics. There is so much we can gain and so little to lose."

"I could lose you," Florence said. "They could shoot you on sight when you get there."

"I don't think they'd do that," Robbie said. "There probably aren't many guards at the Farm, if any. I think they were all here. Linda is reasonable. I think she'll at least listen to me and think about it. Maybe she would even jump at the chance for a better life for all."

"And you're going to just walk in like you own the place?"

"I think that's best," Robbie replied. "It'll show them that I mean them no harm. Many of the gals out there will remember me and I think most will trust me. Besides, I'll have backup if things turn sour. I trust Ronnie can get me out if need be."

Florence took Robbie's cup and went inside for more coffee. Brooke and Ronnie were working on breakfast.

Ronnie noticed Florence's somber mood. "What's up?"

"Robbie wants to go back to Corpus Christi," she replied.

"Huh!?" Brooke exclaimed.

"I'll let him explain it to you over breakfast," Florence said.

Florence filled hers and Robbie's cups and sat them on the table. She stepped to the door and called Robbie in as breakfast was about ready.

"What's this I hear about Corpus?" Ronnie asked, as soon as he stepped through the door.

Robbie laid the plan out for Brooke and Ronnie, and immediately Ronnie was on board with his scheme.

"Brothers!" Florence and Brooke said in unison.

"When?" Ronnie asked.

"Tomorrow morning works for me," Robbie replied. "We have transportation and we have fuel. I think we should take the Jeep. Most will recognize it and not think twice about seeing it."

"Okay, I'll go over to Dad's and inform him and get the Jeep ready," Ronnie said. "You go tell Grandpa Reggie and we'll head out first thing in the morning."

Ronnie ran into Sean and Zack while at his dad's place. Sean had the bus back over to the Lindgren's doing a little welding. Zack was helping him. They liked Robbie's idea and insisted on going along in case they ran into trouble.

"The more the merrier," Zack said.

Robbie and Ronnie were up at the crack of dawn, loaded their gear, and took driver and shotgun positions in the Jeep, while Zack and Sean climbed in the back. They meandered their way to the highway to the east.

"Sure beats walking," Ronnie said.

Once they got out of the woods, Robbie was able to drive much faster. From start to finish, the trip to the edge of Corpus Christi took three hours. Robbie stopped the Jeep in the middle of the highway.

"The Airport is about a mile and a half to the south of here. The Farm is about five miles that way," he explained to the newbies, pointing northerly. "I'm not sure if we should drive there from here. If someone sees us, they may shoot first and ask questions later."

"They won't know we're not Sandra until we get close," Ronnie pointed out. "We'll be ready and if they so much as point a gun in our direction, we can take them out before they can get a shot off."

"Any shooting may ruin our plan of a peaceful relationship with Corpus," Robbie said.

"I say we drive to the Farm," Ronnie insisted.

Sean and Zack agreed.

"Ha! Majority rules." Ronnie was always pleased when he got the better of his older brother.

"Okay, but keep a sharp eye out," Robbie said and put the Jeep into gear.

They didn't see anyone and made it safely to within a quarter mile of the Farm. Robbie stopped the Jeep to let Sean and Ronnie out with their sniper rifles, and Zack with an AR-15. Robbie pointed out the direction he wanted them to go to provide cover should he need it.

As he watched them head into the brush, Robbie sat in the Jeep and went over his plan. He really didn't have much of a strategy. Basically, he had to find Linda quickly. He hoped she would be in the barn working on a tractor or something as she always did when he was there. He couldn't be certain what she was doing now, but he could hope.

Robbie started the Jeep and eased forward.

Here I go again, out of the frying pan and into the fire. I've got to find Linda quickly. I hope there are not many guards around. What will I do if there are?

Robbie drove up to the front of the barn where he hoped Linda would be. He was pleasantly surprised that there were not many people outside. He could see a few ladies in the fields, but there was no one around the house.

As soon as he walked into the barn, Sally Beecher, who was sitting working at the workbench, jumped up with big eyes. "Robbie!"

He smiled. "Surprised?"

"To say the least," she replied. "What are you doing here? How did you get here?"

"I need to see Linda."

She laid her screwdriver down. "Where's Sandra?"

"Sally!" he said more sternly. "I need to see Linda."

She frowned. "Linda's out in the fields."

"Will you take me to her?"

Sally gave him a suspicious eye as she walked over. She nodded and they headed toward the door. Robbie stopped at the doorway and scanned the area again for sentries.

"Sally, where are all the guards?"

"There haven't been any for some time."

Robbie followed Sally out to the strawberry patch near the rear of the house where there were two dozen women tending the plants.

Linda saw Sally and Robbie headed in her direction and walked over to greet them. Linda held out her hand. "I'm surprised to see you, Robbie."

He gave her a friendly handshake. "To tell you the truth, I'm a little surprised to be here myself. Can we talk?"

"Sure, let's go up on the porch."

Robbie followed Linda's lead and Sally tagged along. "Something to drink?" Linda asked.

Robbie nodded.

"Sally, will you get us some tea?"

Sally went inside while Robbie and Linda got comfortable.

"What's on your mind, Robbie?"

"When I was here before, I got the feeling that most of the people didn't really like the way things were run. Most everyone just tolerated the system because they were afraid to stand up against Sandra. Jade tried to change the order of things, but paid the price. When Sandra eliminated Jade, that just strengthened her position."

Sally came back out with their teas and a soda for herself.

"Have a seat, Sally," Linda said, "you may as well hear what Robbie has to say too."

She sat down beside Robbie as she had many times before at breakfast and dinner when he was there.

Robbie looked over and nodded. Her pretty face always brought a smile to his lips.

"Sandra is dead. She came to Peaceful Valley and tried to kill me, Sean, and all our families. I assume you knew about her plan."

Linda nodded, but didn't interrupt.

"Sandra brought seventy-eight of her thugs to Peaceful Valley the other morning. We captured her and killed every one of her men. One of our neighbors' daughters was killed and Kim got shot and lost her baby."

"I'm sorry, Robbie." Linda put her hand on his and the look on her face showed her genuine sorrow for their loss.

"We voted to hang Sandra. She'll never bother anyone again. Now that Sandra is gone, you have a chance to change things around here, unless you like living under a dictatorship."

The look on Linda's face was one of confusion, but she believed every word of Robbie's spiel and didn't interrupt. Sally sat dumbfounded, but also in awe of the defensive abilities of the residents of Peaceful Valley.

"I remembered you. I know you were afraid of Sandra, but I also know you have a good heart. You care for people.

"It was cruel and brutal what they did to Sean. I would like to see castration eliminated here. I think you can do this. And the ladies, they work, they make babies, and they eat and sleep. There is so much more to life than that. Under Sandra, everyone here was a slave. You can't be truly happy like that. A more democratic society would benefit everyone."

Robbie leaned back in his chair and took a sip of his tea.

"That works for me," Sally said. She looked at Robbie first, then her eyes fixed on Linda.

Robbie could see the gears turning in Linda's head, but she was quiet for some time.

"I understand what you're saying, but that's a lot easier said than done. Sandra still has a few loyal followers. Marcia went ballistic when Sonny didn't show up after Sean left. She'll be a real problem and there are a few others."

"But how do you feel?" Robbie asked.

"I never liked Sandra, but I did what I was told to do and she was good to me."

"But would you . . . could you like it better if there was less cruelty around here . . . if you had a choice in what you do . . . how you live your life?"

"I would like that," Sally butted in.

"But where do we start?" Linda asked.

"How about if we have a meeting . . . all the women here at the Farm. That's what we do back home when there's something important to talk about. How many are here now?"

"There are about two hundred at the moment," Linda replied.

"Are there any guards around?" Robbie asked.

"A couple dropped by yesterday. They asked me how things were around here. I told them everything was quiet . . . work as usual and they left. They were the first I'd seen in several days."

"Good," Robbie said. "Start rounding up the ladies and let's have a meeting right here, right now. I brought my brother Ronnie, Sean, and a neighbor, Zack, along in case things didn't go so well. They're watching us as we speak. I'll call them in if you think it's safe and we'll get started."

Sally headed to the bunkhouse while Linda walked out to the strawberry field. Robbie stepped off the porch and looked in the direction he thought Ronnie and the rest would be. He gave out a long wolf howl. This got a queer look from Linda and a few of the women nearby in the field.

Most of the women had gathered just off the porch when Sean, Ronnie, and Zack showed up. Robbie stood on the patio alongside Linda and waved his sharpshooters over to the porch. There was some giggling from the ladies as the boys walked up.

"Sandra is dead," Linda said, to start the meeting.

The crowd got noisy and the ladies talked amongst themselves. Linda began again when they quieted down.

"She took an army to Robbie's home in Peaceful Valley to try to kill him and his neighbors to satisfy her revenge for Robbie and Sean leaving Corpus. For those of you who do not know Robbie, he is here to offer us a chance at a better life."

Linda looked over at Robbie. He stepped forward to the edge of the porch.

"Robbie can make my life better any day," one of the ladies yelled out.

"I'll take any one of the other ones," another lady yelled.

The crowd got loud with giggles and laughs.

Robbie smiled and held up his hands. He then laid his proposition out to the best of his ability—life, liberty, and the pursuit of happiness for all. Work yes, but all the rights and privileges this once great country was built upon. No more dictatorship as was rigidly imposed by Sandra and her followers.

When Robbie had finished his speech, he stood and looked over the group of women. He couldn't tell what they were thinking by their faces.

"Discuss the proposition amongst yourselves for a few minutes if you'd like," Robbie said, "then we'll take a vote to see how we stand."

Robbie sat down, as did Linda, and watched the group as they mingled and chatted.

Robbie glanced over at Linda. "What do you think?"

"They'd be fools not to go along. Few of these gals know what freedom is though, so it's really hard to tell."

"I think you'd make a good leader," Robbie said. "These women know you and know that you wouldn't steer them wrong. They know you would treat them right. But do you think you can handle the job?"

"Mechanic to Mayor is a long step. All I can do is try my best," she replied. "You do make a convincing speech."

Robbie and Linda got up and walked to the edge of the porch. "Well, ladies," Robbie said, "what's it going to be? Hold your hand up if you want Linda to lead you into a more democratic society."

Half the women immediately raised their hands. Others were more hesitant, but slowly a few at a time, nearly everyone held their hands up. Robbie and Linda both took note of the few who did not.

Robbie leaned over and whispered to Linda, "Do you know those who didn't raise their hands?"

"Yeah," she replied. "They've always been troublemakers around here, even when Sandra was around."

Robbie turned back to the crowd. "You ladies that didn't raise your hands, will you please come to the front."

No one moved.

"Please, I'm not going to bite."

There were a few giggles, then one by one the ladies worked their way toward the front of the crowd.

"From now on, you will have free speech around here," Robbie stated. "You will not be punished for speaking your mind."

Robbie looked over at Linda and she gave him a nod.

"Please tell me why you didn't hold up your hand."

"Everyone here works hard," one of the ladies sneered. "We all work equally now. If everyone has the chance to 'pursue their dreams' as you put it, some of the gals are going to get lazy."

"And what if someone wants to get married and leave?" another yelled.

Linda took a deep breath. "Your work is your job now. You're not a slave. If you do poorly, you get fired. If you are fired, you don't eat. As to marriage and leaving, it's your choice, but once we get the place running right, no one will want to leave. That's the idea. It will be a place folks want to live and raise their kids. They can be happy and prosperous without living under the watchful eye of armed guards and fearing severe punishment or execution.

"There will be rules, but you will get the chance to decide what rules we need. I don't know what all those rules will be at this point, but I assure you we will iron them out together.

"There will be problems at first. Any adjustment will be difficult for some, but the change will be slow. Most of you will not notice the change at first, but over time, as we get the kinks worked out in our new system, things will get better for everyone. How do you like working fourteen-hour days?"

"And who'll make the rules?" came a voice from the crowd.

"We'll all make the rules," Linda replied. "That's the way a democratic society works. Every man, woman, and child of working age will have a voice in our new government."

Linda stood tall and stared at the group with a big smile and a determined expression on her face.

I can do this. I can make it better for everyone.

The crowd grew noisy again and Linda asked a couple of the ladies she knew who raised their hands along with Sally Beecher to go inside and fix more tea and hors d'oeuvres for herself, Robbie, and his friends. Robbie waved Ronnie, Sean, and Zack up onto the porch and they all sat and discussed the situation while they waited for their drinks.

After they finished their tea, the group settled down. Linda stood up and everyone else followed her cue and walked back over to the edge of the porch.

"Well," Linda said to the few dissenters, "have you come to a decision?"

The first lady expressed her opinion. "I think we'll give you a chance. You've been a good mechanic. Let's see how good a mayor you make. We can always vote you out, right?"

"That you can," Linda replied. "In fact, we'll have regular elections. Support me and give me a year to get us on the right track. Hopefully, we can get an election system set up by that time. You can vote me out, or you can vote me back in. The decision will be up to you. I've never lied to you before and I won't lie to you now."

"Can we see another show of hands?" Robbie asked.

The vote was unanimous, but this was just the Farm vote. Contractors, the policemen, doctors, fishermen, and many others needed to be convinced to cast their votes in favor of the change.

"All right ladies," Linda said, "I appreciate your show of support, but we still have work to do around here. Talk amongst yourselves while you're working and decide what kind of changes you want. In your spare time, write them down and we'll have more discussions. Thank you, ladies."

The women wandered off to their respective chores. Linda, Robbie, and the rest of the guys sat on the porch and began to devise a plan.

"Linda, the first thing you should do is get the Police force backing you," Robbie said. "I think we killed most of them. I don't know who's left, but you need to find a good man to help you gather a group who'll stand with you and protect you in case some of the people don't care for the new change."

"I don't know who is down there that I might know," Linda replied. "I guess the first task on the agenda is to go to the Police compound and see who's left."

"I don't think we can help you much with what you need to do here," Sean said. "We need to get back to Peaceful Valley."

"Do you have a car," Ronnie asked.

"No," Linda replied.

"We can drop you by the Police Station if you'd like," Robbie offered, "then we can head on back home. You can commandeer a vehicle for yourself to get back here."

"Let's do it," Linda said, and they headed around the side of the house.

Linda took the passenger seat at Ronnie's insistence and Robbie headed out with the others crammed into the back for the short distance.

"It's a little scary taking on a new venture," Linda stated.

"You're tough and smart, Linda," Robbie said. "You'll do just fine. Be sure to get yourself a pistol too."

"Yeah," Ronnie agreed. "That wouldn't be a bad idea for a while."

Robbie stopped a couple hundred yards from the Police compound. "I don't think we should get any closer," he said. "If someone recognizes me or Sean, or sees our guns, they may get aggressive before they know what is going on."

"Thanks, Robbie," Linda said. "And thanks to the rest of you too. It's going to be a lot different around here from now on."

"I certainly hope so," Sean said.

Robbie shook Linda's hand. "We'll come back in a couple weeks to see how things are going. I assume you'll stay at the Farm like Sandra did?"

"Yes, then I'll see you in a couple weeks."

Robbie turned around and made a beeline out of town. They all felt more at ease after they were a few miles past the city limits.

"Well," Ronnie said, "I think that went better than we could have asked for."

"I think so," Robbie agreed. "If Linda can get a friendlier society going around here, maybe you can even go shrimping again."

Sean grinned from ear to ear. "I think I'd like that. Maybe Brenda and Kim would come back here to live with me if the laws changed for the better."

What if someone gets suspicious about what happened to Sonny and put two and two together? If Marcia sees me, I think she might figure out what happened. I could confess to her, or have a good story to make it work.

Chapter 17

The boys made it back to Peaceful Valley an hour or so after dark. The headlights made the trip through the last dozen or so miles much easier, something they weren't used to. Robbie and Ronnie told their mom and dad that they needed to have a meeting tomorrow and headed home. Sean said he'd inform his parents of the meeting and Zack would get Lance and the gals here early. James said he'd run over to the Wimberley's at dawn, while Robbie said he'd go to the Carston's.

The meeting convened at the Lindgren's by mid-morning. Robbie was surprised to see Kim out and about, as was most everyone else, but she had Sean on one side and Brenda on the other. She was still hurting but said she needed to get out of bed and move around a bit. She was quite sore but recovering. The psychological healing over the loss of her baby would take much longer.

Robbie started off by filling everyone in on what was going on in Corpus Christi. He was hopeful, but also warned them there was a lot of work to be done. "Convincing a couple hundred ladies is much different than getting a few thousand on board with our plan."

"That's good to hear," Reggie said. "If we can get some relations going with the new government, we'll have access to some of the things we've been doing without for quite some time."

"Yeah," Kim said, "like maybe better medical facilities . . . and meds. No offense, Melissa and James for the work you did on me, but I certainly think we need better pain killers."

"No offense taken," Melissa replied, with a smile.

James nodded his agreement.

"Okay," Robbie said, "we need to go back and check on Linda in a couple of weeks. But what else do we need to do around here?"

"Now that we have new vehicles," James said, "we have to make sure we can keep them going for a while. We need to keep them maintained and drive them regularly."

"And roads," Reggie brought up. "We haven't had the need for roads for some time now. An easy route to the highway and roads between the places, except mine."

"And why not yours?" Robbie interrupted.

"I've never had a road into my place and I don't want one, okay?"

"My tractor is on its last leg," James stated. "If I'm going to maintain roads, I'll need a new tractor. You know, we never made it back to the city to the southeast of here. Maybe it's time we go see what the Tractor Supply has to offer, or if we can find a bona fide tractor place. I bet the county had tractors with mowers and you know how the county used to maintain them. I'll bet if we can find one, they'll be in sheds and will run. They may even be full of gas. We just need some octane booster."

"And if they're diesel?" Reggie asked.

"We'll just have to find one that runs on gas," James replied.

"Do you think there will still be good stuff out there after all these years?" Melissa asked.

"I don't see why not," James replied. "There are no people out there anymore to speak of. Things are not going to walk off on their own. Stuff inside buildings is not going to deteriorate nearly as fast as things left in the weather outside."

"If you're going to make a better road to the highway," Reggie added, "we'll need some strong gates and fencing we can lock up . . . just in case someone comes along."

"I think we'll need a bigger welder and pipe so we can make a really sturdy gate," James said. "The pre-made ones aren't very strong. Maybe we can lift one from the county. We'll either find one or we'll build one."

"Works for me," Reggie said.

"We need glass," Zack added. "Lots and lots of glass. We don't have any windows left."

"Ours are all busted out too," Sally added. "At least it's not cold and the bugs aren't bad this time of year."

"Yeah," Sam said, "but that'll change."

"Yes, it will," Reggie added. "You know what they say about Texas? If you don't like the weather, just wait a little while. It'll get colder and it'll get wet and nasty. We don't have many window panes left either."

"Maybe you can check some of the other grocery stores to see if you can find anything else we might need," Melissa said.

"Like what?" James asked.

"Well, soap, hair brushes, combs, fingernail polish, lipstick, fabric, and toilet paper to name a few," Melissa said. "Just take the bus and fill it up."

Robbie smiled. "I guess us guys lose sight of some of the smaller things in life, especially when we're talking about heavy equipment and vehicles. Thank you for reminding us. The bus will certainly make it a lot easier to haul a lot of stuff. We'll do what we can."

Kim was still quite weak and asked if she could be excused from the meeting. She was getting tired and Brenda got up to help her to her bed. Sean got up too and insisted he carry her inside. "You take care of that arm, Brenda."

Melissa and Emily decided they needed to get some lunch going and went inside as well.

James and Reggie rolled cigars. John and Kathy Wimberley walked out to the sycamore tree to visit their daughter's grave. Sam and Sally joined them.

"I found some more sandstone slabs to make headstones for Charlotte and the baby," Sam offered. "I'll need the correct spelling of her name and the dates. I've been meaning to tell you, but it's been so hectic around here. I'll make time for this though. It's important."

"That's so sweet of you, Sam," Kathy said.

"It's no trouble," he replied, "and besides, it seems to have become one of my jobs around here. If I have to make another though, it will be too soon."

"Amen," John said. "Did you get all your hogs rounded up?"

"Most of them. I'm still missing two. I hope those men didn't kill them. At least I haven't found a dead carcass."

Sean, Ronnie, and Robbie joined James at the bus. "Let's look this thing over from end to end, boys. I'll check the fluids and we'll start it up so I can check the transmission. Then we'll top off the gas tank."

So much for my new temporary home, Sean thought. *I guess other things are more important. Or maybe I just need to keep my stuff in the back to stake my claim for the times between raids on nearby cities.*

"When are we going, Dad?" Robbie asked.

"Let's go day after tomorrow," Ronnie suggested. "I haven't had a good night's sleep for a while. I need to catch up on my rest."

"Yeah," Robbie said. "Florence is feeling a little neglected too. I think a little time with her will do her and I both some good."

James nodded his agreement. "That will give me time to check the bus over first."

The next morning, Brooke got up early as usual to make coffee. When Ronnie didn't come out, she decided to go in and check on him. He was still sound asleep, so she slipped back into bed not changing into her bedclothes.

He stirred when she crawled into bed and wrapped his arms around her. She leaned over and kissed him on the cheek and he ran his hand under her blouse. Brooke rolled over onto her back and Ronnie continued his exploration of her breasts.

"You get me going and I'm not going to stop," she whispered.

"I certainly hope not," he replied.

He systematically undressed Brooke then slipped his tightie-whities off. He didn't remember when the last time he and Brooke had made love, but it had been too long.

Ronnie wrapped Brooke up in a passionate embrace and touched his lips to hers, luxuriating in the feel of her bare skin, his leg between hers, teasing her tender area. She was ready when Ronnie crawled on top of her. She was wet and touched him. He gasped and his body jumped to attention and entered the realm of ecstasy.

Ronnie pressed his lips to hers and fondled her nipples as his mind stampeded into town looking for a good time. The dance hall was open and the music loud but soothing to the weary traveler. He'd been out of town for too long and neither he nor Brooke was disappointed.

Robbie and Florence were sitting at the table sipping their coffees when the satiated couple came in. They both sat staring at their housemates with big grins on their faces.

"It's no secret what you two have been up to," Robbie said, with a big smile.

"Robbie!" Florence exclaimed. Her face turned red and she gave him a backhand across the arm.

"Sorry, guys," Brooke said, grinning like the cat that ate the canary. "We forget how thin the walls are."

"The wall thickness had nothing to do with it," Robbie said.

"That's enough," Florence said sternly, raising her hand again.

Florence and Brooke got busy on breakfast while the boys went out and chopped some wood, another chore they had gotten behind on lately.

After breakfast, Ronnie agreed to run over to the Carston's, while Robbie helped Brooke and Florence with a few more things around the house.

"I've got to get out and feed the chickens," Florence said. "We're still missing a few."

Chapter 18

At the Lindgren homestead . . .

Reggie insisted on coming along to the neighboring city. He loved exploring. He also loved browsing around in the Walmart and HEB stores on the last trip and couldn't wait to see what new things they would find.

They didn't run into any opposition on the last trip, but he suggested they go loaded for bear regardless. This included plenty of RPG's (rocket propelled grenades). He also told two of the boys to load the generator. He wasn't certain they would need it, but told them he had some ideas about how it could be useful.

Sam and John said they would stay with the ladies. Everyone else wanted to go. Most of them had never seen the city and since they had no idea about what kind of hostility they would run into, they decided more was better.

James told Robbie and Ronnie to take the Jeep as a scout vehicle. The yellow bus would stick out like a sore thumb and was not overly agile. Reggie told them, should they find trouble, to immediately head back to the bus and give them ample warning should anyone they find became aggressive.

James took the driver's seat, while everyone else got comfortable scattered in pairs on the floor up and down the bus. Sean removed all the rear seats, but this gave them more room for supplies.

Reggie sat in a front seat so he could talk to James. The big bus lumbered through the brush on the way to the highway. This slowed their progress down significantly, but when they made it to the open road, they made much better time. The Jeep followed until they got near the city.

It took nearly two hours to arrive at the edge of town. James parked the bus facing away from the city and out of sight, in case they needed to make a quick escape.

This was their first excursion deep into the city and in daylight no less. James decided they would have an equal or better chance of seeing people or vehicles, besides it would be much easier locating what they needed without stumbling around in the dark.

James got into the Jeep with Ronnie and Robbie and instructed everyone else to stay on the bus and keep their eyes open. James took the driver's seat. He trusted the boys' shooting better than he did his own.

James rolled past the HEB grocery and Walmart and into town. Several service stations, hotels, and miscellaneous businesses were burned to the ground. Their first stop was the Tractor Supply Store. The door was wide open and James took a look inside while Robbie got behind the steering wheel and Ronnie took a position at the door.

The place had been ransacked as he assumed every place in town had. All of the items that one would normally assume someone needed for survival were gone. James did find a couple of welding machines, chainsaws, and air compressors they could use. They would pick these up later though.

He joined the boys and they headed to their next destination, James again driving. They passed a couple of banks charred around the doors and windows. Insurance companies, bridal shops, and more service stations were burned to the ground. All that remained were the signs out front.

James wheeled into a strip mall, which was only partially burned. He parked the Jeep and the boys took their positions. The realty company on the end had the windows busted out and the door was wide open, but he had a hunch.

James went inside and looked at papers scattered around on the floor and tables. Something caught his attention and he reached down and picked up a folder off the floor. It was a picture map of the city. That was all he wanted and he hurried back to the Jeep to continue their search.

James studied the map. When he got his bearings, he directed Robbie to the location and got out. County Warehouse #27! He opened the first of three heavy doors. Nothing! He went to the next door and opened it.

"Yes!"

Inside sat a mid-sized tractor with a mower deck. He found another tractor exactly like the other one in the third warehouse. They were clean and looked fairly new. James shut the doors, returned to the Jeep, and cranked it up.

He took another look at the map, then headed to their next destination. As he pulled up to the front of Payne's Glass, Inc., he saw a vehicle pull out of a street a couple blocks down. James and the boys froze and stared at the blue SUV. Fortunately for them, the car turned the other direction and headed away. Apparently, they had not been seen.

James hopped out and while Ronnie again stood guard, he cautiously stepped inside the building. He found a lot of broken glass scattered all around the shop, and the racks were empty, but in a back storage room, there was more glass than they would ever need and in perfect condition. Rows and rows of glass panels of every size and thickness.

At the neighborhood Lowe's store, James found gates and all sorts of hardware, but the gates were not as heavy as he'd have liked to install across their road. If they could not find some pipe, however, these would do. There was plenty of fencing wire.

On the way back to the bus, James made a stop at an auto parts store which he'd missed on the trip in. Again, the store was a mess, but some of the items they were looking for were still on the shelves—ignition coils, ignition wires, and gauges. He'd hoped to find some batteries, but the few he found were damaged.

"One more stop," James said.

He drove to a large hotel. James made his way down to the basement where he found a locked storeroom. He drew his pistol and covered his ear with the other hand. One shot popped the lock. When he opened the door, he stood back, eyed the contents, then hurried back outside.

James crawled back in the Jeep. "Let's go."

Robbie headed back to the bus.

Ronnie leaned forward. "Did we hear a gunshot?"

James turned around with a big grin. "Yes, I had to open a lock. Boys, the ladies are going to be happy!"

Ronnie smiled. "What?"

"The basement was full of toilet paper, cleaning supplies, towels and washcloths, toiletries and lotions, but best of all, supplies for their in-store shops, including the beauty salon.

Back at the Lindgren place, Brooke and Melissa walked out to the porch with their glasses of tea.

"I wonder how the men are doing?" Brooke asked.

"I imagine they're having the time of their lives," Melissa replied.

"You're probably right, but I worry about them," Brooke said. "I guess this is the hard part—never knowing what's going on. Anything could happen out there."

"Yes, it could, but I wouldn't worry too much," Melissa said. "We made it through Sandra's army. We can handle most anything now."

"I'm sure glad Kim's going to be alright," Brooke said. "I was really worried about her with the loss of her baby and all. Has she picked a name for the gravestone?"

"Yes, I thought everyone knew," Melissa replied. "She's decided on Abigail."

"Such a pretty name," Brooke said. "I was under the impression she was going to name her baby after a king or queen, but I like Abigail better than some dead person we don't even know."

Melissa and Brooke strolled out to the garden. Melissa picked a few greens and asked Brooke to pull a few radishes and beets. "I'll make us a fresh salad."

Florence joined them when they returned to the porch. "I'm sure missing Robbie!"

"It's never easy around here," Melissa said. "Help us with the salad. That'll get your mind off him. There will be more trips here and there I'm sure, especially if this one turns out good. And the boys will be going back to Corpus Christi."

"A nail file and some fingernail polish would be nice," Florence said. "My nails are always a mess."

"Too much digging around in the garden will do that," Brooke added, taking a quick look at hers.

"... and dishes, gun cleaning, cleaning fish and rabbits, and the list goes on and on."

Melissa looked over at the girls and smiled.

A little nail polish . . . and especially lipstick.

James pulled the Jeep up in front of the bus and got out.

"Damn, you guys took your sweet time," Reggie said, with an annoyed look on his face.

"Yeah, but we found a lot of stuff," Robbie stated, grinning.

"Did you see anyone?" Sean asked.

"A blue SUV, but they didn't see us," Ronnie replied. "That's all."

"If there's one vehicle in the city," James said, "there may be more. We've got to be careful. One mistake . . ."

Reggie drove the bus while James led him back through town to all the locations they had checked out. They quickly loaded all they could carry and then squeezed in a little more. Their final stop was the County Warehouse.

"Wow!" Reggie exclaimed. "Not just one, but two tractors with shredders and they're gas. Are we going to take both of them?"

"Let's see if we can get one started first," James replied, giving him a pat on the arm.

James checked the fluids and climbed up on the first. "The battery is dead."

"And you're surprised?" Reggie asked.

Robbie pulled the Jeep up as close to the front as he could, while Sean grabbed the jumper cables and hooked them up. The tractor groaned at first, but on the third try, it started up. It took a few seconds for the smoke to die down from the exhaust, and when it did, James cranked the throttle back to an idle.

The other tractor started up as well. "We going to take both with us?" Reggie asked.

"We only need one," James replied. "The other is probably better off here in the barn. It's been fine for the past umpteen years. If we need it, it'll likely still be here."

"Who's going to drive it back home?" James asked.

Zack volunteered. Ronnie grabbed a can of gas and filled the tank. James shut the barn door behind Zack and the convoy headed back home. Zack led the way, followed by James and the bus, while Robbie and Ronnie brought up the rear.

As they pulled onto the main drag toward home, Zack spotted a blue SUV sitting crossways in the middle of their exit out of the city four-hundred yards ahead. He stopped and turned around and looked at James in the bus. James waved him over. Robbie and Ronnie pulled the Jeep up alongside.

"Looks like we've been caught with our pants down," James said to Reggie. "I guess maybe they did see us earlier."

Reggie pulled out his binoculars and looked the vehicle over. "I only see three men."

"Maybe so, but there's been too much killing lately. I don't want to get anyone hurt. To just park in the road like that, they could have snipers of their own on a building around here and we'd never see them."

"What do you think about trying to talk to them?" Reggie asked. "They're just sitting there. Maybe that's all they want. If they wanted to shoot us, I think an ambush from hiding somewhere would have been a better choice than just sitting in the middle of the road."

"It won't hurt," James replied.

"Let me have your tee shirt, Sean," Reggie said, "and I need a couple snipers on the roof just in case."

Reggie took the shirt and headed toward the SUV waving his white flag, while Robbie and Ronnie crawled up on top of the bus with their rifles.

Reggie walked a hundred yards, stopped, and waited. No one from the SUV moved and Reggie decided to walk a little closer.

Maybe they're afraid of Robbie and Ronnie. Did they see them get on top of the bus?

Reggie stopped again at a hundred and fifty yards. Then he saw one of the men head in his direction and Reggie started walking forward slowly. He walked to the halfway point and stopped again. Reggie could feel the beads of sweat forming on his forehead. He wiped his sleeve across his brow and waited for the man to make his way close enough so they could talk. The man stopped ten yards from Reggie.

James stood just outside the door with his rifle across his arm and his finger on the hammer and trigger, as Reggie made full use of his arms in his discussion with the man. Reggie and the man walked closer to each other and the pow wow continued. This went on for a half-hour before Reggie headed back toward the bus. James propped his rifle against the dashboard and hollered at the boys on the roof.

"What were the men doing at the SUV while Reggie was talking to their spokesman?"

"They didn't look overly concerned," Robbie said. "They didn't even point their guns this way. They didn't look belligerent."

James sat back down in the driver's seat and waited for Reggie. In the meantime, the men got into the SUV and drove down a side road.

"Let's get going," Reggie told Zack, as he approached. Reggie got into the bus and James started it back up. The snipers got down and got into the Jeep and the convoy continued on their way.

"What's going on?" James asked.

"Seems they were doing the same thing we were," Reggie said. "They live on a river too, about ten miles to the east of here. A dozen or so of them, all working together for their mutual needs.

"After they said there were only a dozen of them, I told them there were about twenty of us. They seemed like friendly people. I told them about our ordeal with Sandra Hawkins and the plans to make the city more hospitable to outsiders. Jake, the man I was talking to, said they sent a few men to Corpus Christi a few years back. They never heard from them again. He was happy to hear about our progress and plans there.

"He said they come here every couple of months or so, scrounging around for a few things they need. Mostly diesel for their tractor and SUV. Their needs are a little different than ours. Maybe the reason we found so many things we need. There may have been few if any people around here and that's why there is just so much that was left behind in the first place."

"Well we certainly have been fortunate," James said.

"Jake, their eldest and leader of the group, gave me directions to their place. They'd like for us to keep them informed about Corpus Christi. Jake was hungry for shrimp. He said to stick a white flag by the road and fire a couple shots into the air and back off a mile. They would come well-prepared, but if they saw the flag, they would follow the road to us with the flag waving. Just like us, their numbers are so few. They can't take chances with their safety.

"They know our vehicles now and will keep an eye out for us when they go on another scavenging party. I told him we'd do the same and maybe we can have tea or coffee together and get to know each other a little better. He asked if I knew a good coffee shop in town. We both got a good laugh at that."

The convoy drove on into the darkness. The lights didn't work on the tractor and the Jeep moved up to take the lead. One light worked on the bus, plenty for them to see the way.

It had been a long day and everyone was dead tired when they pulled into Peaceful Valley well after dinnertime. Dinner, however, was ready. It needed warming, but the ladies were thankful for the return of their men and greeted them with open arms.

Chapter 19

The next morning, the men showed off their newly acquired tractor and a bus load of welcome and badly needed supplies. Ronnie carried a single box over to Melissa and Brooke. They both squealed when he opened it up and carried it to the porch. The other ladies gathered around.

"Lipstick, powder, nail polish, combs, brushes, and lotion as requested."

Brooke gave him a bedroom kiss to his embarrassment.

"There are another dozen boxes full of stuff in the bus, plus fabric," he added, when his flush faded.

Reggie also shared the news of their potential new friends. "Maybe in time, the country can partially heal itself. Hopefully, progress, like we're making, is happening all over."

"Yeah, without all the people who caused the downfall of this country," James said.

"At least for the remainder of our lives," Reggie added. "In a few decades, maybe this country can heal itself at least before people tear it back down again."

However, the girls were no longer paying attention to the men, their story, or their tractor. They were giggling, painting their nails, and putting lipstick on. They had their girly stuff at last!

"Oooh! I like the red one."

"Pink for me!"

"This smells heavenly!"

James shook his head. "Girls!" He held up his tobacco pouch, to which Reggie nodded. He sat down on the steps and rolled a cigar for himself and Reggie.

For the first time, they saw a brighter future for the whole country. Things could change for the better. They could only hope that the new leaders would not make the same mistakes, and there were many of them, the next time around.

Over the next couple of weeks, each of the families installed new windows in all their homes and a new road was made to the highway from the Lindgren homestead. They didn't find any pipe to make a heavy gate to protect the entrance but hoped the gates they got from Lowe's would do. Maybe they could get some from Corpus Christi.

All the boys filled their woodpiles with logs and the woodsheds with split wood as well as plenty of kindling. They made certain the smokehouse was full of venison, rabbits, squirrels, and especially fish. Fish was the favorite of most of the girls.

Florence fished a little too and caught her first eel. She squealed when she brought it to the surface. She thought it was a snake, but Robbie assured her it was not. He showed her how to skin the slimy creature and hung it in the smokehouse with the fish.

Florence got curious and retrieved the eel one afternoon and decided to prepare it for dinner. When Robbie and Ronnie sat down that evening, she served the snake, as she called it, for an appetizer. Florence had never prepared eel and wasn't sure exactly how to make it, but after working on a sauce for well over an hour came up with a mixture she really liked. The boys and Brooke were pleasantly surprised at how it tasted.

"We usually use eels for bait to catch bigger catfish," Robbie told her. "I don't think Mom knows how to fix them either because I don't recall eating them before."

"Well," Florence said, with a smile, "looks like we have a new meat on the menu. And a very sweet white meat at that."

Everyone kept busy and before they knew it, it was time for Robbie to make another trip to Corpus. Sean wanted to go but decided to stay home. Kim's body had healed reasonably well, but she was struggling with the loss of her baby. Sean decided to remain by her side and try to help her overcome her depression.

Zack also decided he needed to stay with Debra, but Lance readily volunteered. Ronnie was anxious to go as well. Lance, Ronnie, and Robbie loaded the Jeep up at daylight and got off to an early start despite the short notice.

The boys laughed and enjoyed the scenery along the way, but otherwise, the trip to Corpus was uneventful. When they got to the edge of the city, there were three very noticeable plumes of smoke rising high into the air and their attitude turned sour. Robbie stopped and killed the engine. The faint yet distinct reports of semi-automatic gunfire quickly got their attention.

Robbie cranked the Jeep up and turned around. He drove the short distance to the two-story building he had spied on the city from before. From the rooftop, they glassed the area with the scopes on their sniper rifles.

"I don't know what's going on," Robbie said, "but this isn't good. I wonder what happened. I thought everything was going so well the last time we were here."

"Apparently the shit hit the fan," Ronnie added.

"That seems to be a regular occurrence these days," Robbie said. "I'm at a loss about what to do."

"Shouldn't we try to see, what's her name, at the Farm?" Lance suggested.

"Linda?" Robbie asked.

"Yeah, you said she was going to run the place."

"Maybe so," Robbie replied, "but we can't be seen by whoever started the new war."

The boys got back into the Jeep and headed to the Farm. This time, however, they stayed in the brush, zigzagging through the trees. They cut the wires to get through a couple of old fences and had to navigate a small creek, but the Jeep had no problem with the rough terrain.

Robbie parked the Jeep in the brush, they grabbed their rifles, and went the rest of the way on foot. From the edge of the brush, the Farm looked normal.

"But looks can be deceiving," Robbie noted.

Closer inspection of the buildings and barns revealed no guards. Ladies were working in the fields as usual, but Linda was not amongst them. Robbie told Lance and Ronnie to stay behind. He decided it would be best if he checked the main house alone. Lance and Ronnie could provide cover should he run into trouble.

Lance and Ronnie took positions about fifty feet apart with a good line of sight to much of the Farm and eyed the area with their scopes. Robbie worked his way around the main barn, then up to the rear of the house. When he peeked around the corner, he spotted Linda on the patio.

"Linda!"

She turned around with a surprised look on her face. "Robbie!"

"Is it okay for me to come to the porch?"

"Yes," she replied.

Robbie turned and whistled at Lance and Ronnie, then he proceeded to the patio. When they were all there, Linda offered them tea.

"Yes, thank you," Robbie replied.

Linda went to the door and asked someone inside to make the drinks and returned to the chairs.

"What's going on?" Robbie asked. "There were fires burning when we got to the city limits and we heard gunfire in the distance."

"The trip to the Police compound didn't turn out so well. I talked to the highest-ranking officer, Billy Drake, and told him about Sandra and your idea for a new democracy. He seemed okay with the new deal but told me to come back the next day. He said he'd gather up some men and that I could lay out my proposal to the group for their acceptance. Then we could get a plan of action in place.

"When I went back the next day, his tone was much different. He had about half of the Police force there and they didn't want to hear my plan. They were satisfied with the way things were and that Billy would be running things around here from now on.

"He said I couldn't have a gun, took the car back that I had commandeered the day before, and told me to get my ass back out to the Farm. When I protested, a couple of his men pointed their guns at me and said it was time to leave.

"I walked the eight miles back here. There was nothing I could do against the armed men. Only the Police force has guns. No one can stand up to them.

"Billy and some of his men came to the Farm the following day. Some of the ladies here knew Billy and his nasty attitude. When they tried to stand up to his men, they were beaten and some were raped."

Sally Beecher came out with drinks. Robbie immediately noticed the bruises on her face. Sally set the drinks down, then hurried back inside without saying a word or making eye contact.

"I haven't been away from here lately, but some news filters in from the other compounds. Several men at the Contractors compound were killed and one at the Bayfront. The men tried to stand up to Billy like we did here at the Farm, but without guns . . . I guess Billy and his men are pushing their weight around at the other compounds with their new-found power. I've heard Marcia Nguyen's name mentioned too."

"That's why everyone at Peaceful Valley is armed," Robbie said. "Your protection is your responsibility. If you have no means to protect yourself, then you are at the mercy of those who would do you harm."

"Men don't give up power so easily," Lance said. "The Police have been in control for how long? Now you want to take this all away from them."

"I guess we were a little naïve to think this would be easy," Linda said. "We can't do this on our own. We don't have any guns. Will you help us? It was your idea after all."

"Not just the three of us," he replied.

"We don't have enough ammunition to start another war," Lance added.

"How many of the Police force are left?" Robbie asked.

"I think a couple dozen . . . maybe a few more," Linda replied. "I'm not certain, but I think Sandra took about two-thirds of them."

"We have the means to take them out," Robbie said, "but this is not a decision we can make on our own. We need to go back home and see what everyone else thinks, then we'll vote on the measure and go from there."

Robbie and his crew took Linda up on the offer of another glass of iced tea. Ice was a rarity back home—only his Grandpa Reggie had an ice maker. "We'll be back in a few days and let you know how our meeting went," Robbie said, as they parted.

The boys made their way back to the Jeep and backtracked out of the city. They mostly held their breath until they were well past the city limit.

"I knew this wasn't going to be so easy," Robbie said, pounding his hand on the steering wheel as he drove.

"Another war," Lance replied. "Just what we need."

"At least their numbers are getting smaller," Robbie said. "There's only about twenty-five now. I doubt they'll expect us to be coming back after them. If we can catch them off-guard, we can finish this up quickly and go on about setting up the new government."

Robbie stopped and got out. "I've got to pee."

The others got out and relieved themselves too.

"If we can set up a trap and draw a lot of them in, we can take out most of them in minutes," Ronnie said.

"A bunch of Reggie's volleyballs will work wonders for our cause," Robbie said. "Set up a chute and run the cattle through. Burn their asses into the ground."

"Yeah!" Lance yelled. "Burn them all to Hell."

When Robbie pulled into the Lindgren homestead, it was getting close to dark. He informed his dad they needed to have another meeting first thing tomorrow. Sean and Brenda were on the front porch and he said he'd run over to get his parents early. Lance said he'd bring his mom and dad. Robbie and Ronnie headed home. Brooke and Florence were surprised to see them home early. They hadn't expected them until tomorrow.

"We're happy you're home, but we didn't prepare dinner," Brooke said. "We ate earlier and didn't have any leftovers."

"I'll take a little jerky," Ronnie said.

Both girls immediately noticed the boy's lack of concern over dinner. They were always hungry when they returned from a trip.

"Something the matter?" Florence asked.

"You might say that," Robbie replied. "Seems like the Police didn't go along with our new proposal. Linda said they have all the guns and didn't want to give up their power. They liked things like they are, with or without Sandra."

"So, what are you going to do?" Florence asked, a look of 'gloom and doom' spreading over her face.

"We're going to have a meeting tomorrow and we'll see," Robbie said. "I need to run over to Grandpa Reggie's first thing in the morning, then I'll stop back by and get you guys."

Florence could feel the tears welling up in her eyes.

We just finished a war and now we're going back to Corpus to fight in another battle with the men Sandra left behind. Robbie won't let this go. He is intent on a new government in Corpus Christi.

I know he's right and this may be necessary for the future of our babies, but why does it have to be so hard on us? There seems to be no end to the bloodshed. Every time we turn around, there's a new threat. Why can't we just leave this one alone? Why won't it all just go away?

Chapter 20

All the families descended once again on the Lindgren homestead eager to hear the latest news about Corpus Christi. Numerous important decisions needed to be made in these trying times and these meetings bonded the residents of Peaceful Valley into a close-knit group. Robbie started by informing everyone of the situation in Corpus Christi.

"I didn't think Linda was going to have a problem when we were there before," he said, "but as it turns out, it looks like Sandra's legacy is far from dead. There's a new sheriff in town . . . a guy by the name of Billy Drake."

Beka's eyes focused on Robbie. "I know that name."

Ronnie leaned forward. "What can you tell us about him?"

"He's a couple years older than I am," she said. "I went out with him a few times, but he was a nasty kid. Everything was always about: Me! Me! Me! He never cared about my wants or needs . . . only what he could get out of me."

"You mean you dated him?" Robbie asked.

Beka nodded and looked over at Lance. He had a frustrated look on his face. She knew she'd be doing a little more explaining later that evening. Bones from her past showed up once again.

"How smart is he?"

Beka shrugged her shoulders. "Average, I guess."

Reggie leaned in a little closer. "What are you thinking about doing?"

"I thought long and hard about this on the way home," Robbie said. "Corpus Christi has a chance at democracy. About twenty-five or thirty men stand in the way. If they were gone, there's plenty of guns and ammunition at the Police compound. If we can arm many of the citizens and get a well-armed police force established, then they have the chance."

Sam slapped his hand on the table getting everyone's attention. "We just finished a war. Now you want to start another goddamn war in Corpus? That's bullshit!"

Reggie ignored Sam, just as Sam ignored him much of the time these days. Reggie thought Sam was a bit of a pacifist—he never wanted to kill anyone, until they stuck a gun in his face. Sam thought Reggie was a little too quick on the trigger—killing solved everything.

"Corpus has a lot to offer," Reggie pointed out. "Coffee, tea, seafood, and salt to name a few. Besides, they know about Peaceful Valley now. If the dictatorship stays in place, the threat of an invasion will always hang over our heads."

"Sandra was ruthless," Sean said. "If Billy is no better, then Reggie may be right."

"Or Billy could be worse," Beka added. "He was always stirring up trouble when we were younger . . . his daddy was a mean son-of-a-bitch."

"Like father, like son," James said. "Twenty-five or thirty men is a formidable force though."

"Ahh!" Reggie said, "piece of cake."

"So, we going to murder more of our neighbors?" Sam grumbled.

Reggie pounded his fist on the table. "We didn't make them the sorry bastards they are. They chose to be who they are. Every member of the Police force was part of Sandra's army whether they came here or stayed behind in Corpus. They're no different. Now it's time for the rest of them to pay for their actions. It's time to finish what *they* started."

"It's still murder," Sam reiterated. "Any way you look at it, it's no different than what you did to the families across the highway."

"What's he talking about?" Robbie asked.

"Something we never told you about, Son," James said. "Some of the neighbors across the highway were always hunting around here and raiding your Grandpa Lars' garden, root cellar, and smokehouse. They shot your Grandpa Reggie. They were a problem and we came up with a solution."

"Why didn't you tell us?" Ronnie asked.

"It happened a long time ago," James said. "It wasn't something we were proud of and we decided it was something you boys didn't need to know. Maybe we'd just rather put that incident behind us. When you boys got older, we'd forgotten about it."

"Now there is a problem again," Sally said, "why do you always have to resort to murder? Doesn't that seem a little excessive to you?"

"Severe problems require drastic measures," Reggie said, pounding his fist on the table.

"But it's not a severe problem for us," Sam added.

"Ruthless dictatorships like the one Sandra started will be a problem for everyone," James said. "Maybe not now, but sooner or later, Peaceful Valley will suffer for it. Sam, Sally, you don't have grandkids yet. You will though. Debra and Lance will have kids sooner or later. When they grow up, if something doesn't happen between now and then, they will have to deal with it. We have the opportunity to nip this in the bud now. We have the chance to make certain Corpus never again bothers anyone like Sandra and her army did around here.

"They murdered Charlotte. They murdered Kim's little Abigail. Sandra's army, whether they came here to kill us or stayed behind in Corpus, are still part of her army and her ways. They are no different and they started the war and we should finish what they started. I say we deal with them now while we have the chance. Next month, next year, they may be too strong. They may be increasing their forces now as we speak. We can take them out and set up Linda as the leader."

"We don't have the right to deal with them," John said. "I know Charlotte would agree with me. God will deal with them. They came here, attacked us, and gave us no choice. God tested us and we prevailed in the war, but he took our baby to warn us. Our Maker will determine our fate. We cannot take His matters into our own hands."

Kathy reached over and gripped John's hand. "I agree. As much as I wanted all of Sandra's men to die and I was the cause of some of their deaths, we cannot go out of our way to Corpus Christi to seek revenge for what happened. The men in Corpus were not a party to Sandra's invasion. They are innocent in my eyes."

"Innocent my ass!" Robbie exclaimed. "When we got to Corpus, there were fires and gunshots. Linda said people were killed at some of the compounds and women raped and beaten at the Farm. I saw Sally Beecher's bruises. What about those innocent people?"

"I don't know them," Kathy said.

"You say you are God fearing people and would bend over backward to help others. People are suffering and maybe dying this very moment, but you say you won't help them?"

Kathy was quiet, as was John. Robbie had certainly given them some food for thought. No one expected them to go along with their proposal, Robbie included, but he did hush them up for a while.

Melissa stood up, exasperated with all the arguing. "I'm getting hungry. I think I should get some lunch going. Looks like this is going to be a long meeting."

Brooke got up as well. The meeting was getting a little too heated and giving her a headache. "I'll help."

Reggie slid his chair back. "Okay, let's take a break."

Florence and Debra also got up. Debra smiled as she went inside. She'd seen these arguments before and enjoyed them.

These people need to calm down! Florence thought.

James rolled cigars for Reggie and Lance and they stepped off the porch and strolled out to the pier.

Robbie stayed on the porch with John and Sam. He knew they were the main opposition to his proposal to kill off Sandra's remaining forces in Corpus Christi. He doubted he could sway them regardless of what he said, but he wanted one more chance.

"I think I know the city of Corpus Christi better than anyone here. I was a part of it for a while. Sean can back up much of what I say. He knows Corpus too.

"The men are castrated at birth and the young women no older than Kira are forced to work in the fields fourteen hours a day during the heat of the summer. Those who are placed with families outside of the Farm are taken back to the Farm and brainwashed from the time they turn sixteen. When they reach eighteen, they are forced to have sex and produce babies.

"Almost all the people at the Farm are women. All the Contractors do as they are told or they don't eat. The same is true for the Hospital and everyone at the Bayfront. There is not much left at the Airport, but the same was true there as well. They are all slaves. Only the Police force carries guns and everyone does as they say.

"Anyone who comes into the city like Sean and I did is castrated, killed, or forced into servitude."

Robbie paused and took a sip of his drink. The looks on Sam and Johns faces told him he was not making any headway in changing their minds about Corpus, but at least they were listening and not interrupting.

"You say you believe in God. If that is so, then God created the strong to protect the weak. The citizens of Corpus Christi cannot protect themselves. We, on the other hand, were created strong and we have the means to protect those in Corpus who cannot protect themselves. We are God's force to defend the weak."

John opened his mouth and started to speak, but Robbie held up his hand and continued. John shut up and listened.

"We must be doing something right around here. We have killed a lot of men and God hasn't struck us down yet. There were so many bullets flying around from Sandra's men, that if God wanted to put a stop to us or our ways of dealing with monsters, he could have easily sent a wayward bullet in our direction.

"I don't know why Charlotte and little Abigail were singled out, but maybe that is not for me to know. I don't think it had anything to do with what we were doing. I only know that I am still alive, healthy, and I still have a lot of fight left in me. If there is a God, then He put that fight in my heart.

"I don't know what you are going to do, but even if it is me alone, I'm going to go to Corpus Christi and kill every one of Sandra's remaining men, or die trying. People need my help and I'm going to give them all I have.

"I am doing this for us too, for my family, my kids, and everyone else here in Peaceful Valley. Yes, and even you two."

Robbie leaned back in his chair and sipped on his tea. He gave John and Sam the opportunity to speak, but they both just stared off across the meadow. He didn't know whether or not he'd made any difference in what they were going to do, but at least he felt much better getting everything off his chest. The neighbors now knew exactly where he stood and Robbie felt proud of his position on the subject, whether or not he had any impact on John or Sam.

The meeting resumed after lunch. Kim stretched out on the porch. Sitting for long periods of time aggravated her abdomen.

Reggie patted his stomach. "Great lunch."

"Yes," Florence agreed.

Sam and John were unusually quiet and somber at the start of the meeting. Robbie kept an eye on them. He didn't know whether or not he made enough of a difference for them to vote in favor of their proposal, but at least he got them thinking.

"Well," Reggie said, "I get the feeling most of us are in favor of taking matters into our own hands in Corpus Christi. Why don't we take a vote?"

When they'd finished casting their votes, the overwhelming majority voted to end the problem for all time. Sam and Sally, of course, voted against the measure, as did John and Kathy. Emily and Kira both abstained from the vote when Emily explained to Kira what abstain meant. Everyone else voted and the measure was passed.

It didn't take long for Kim to decide the porch was too hard for her. Sean helped her up and took her inside to lie down on the sofa. She gave him a wet kiss. "You're so good to me."

He gave her a wink. "I love you." He took another look at her smiling face before he went through the door.

"There will always be bad people around," Sam said, deflated. "You can't kill them all."

"Maybe not," Reggie said, "but when there is a threat to our families and our way of life, I'm damn sure going to try."

"But we killed Sandra's men," Sam said. "Her men in Corpus are not a threat to us."

"If Marcia Nguyen, Sandra's next in line, comes to power," Robbie said, "they will be back for Sean. She will want revenge for her husband's death."

"I'm not going to have any part in this," he said, and he and Sally stormed home just like they did on a couple of previous occasions.

"He's just pissed that he's always in the minority around here," Reggie said after Sam was out of earshot.

"He has different beliefs," Emily said. "You can't hold that against him. I'm not comfortable with it either, but I understand this needs to be done."

"Sam is narrow-minded," Reggie added. "He can't see past his own nose. We have to think about our futures. I won't be around here that much longer, but I do think about our kids and grandkids. I want them to have a more peaceful life than we've had. I want them to be safe and secure in their homes. I know it may be years before we have any problems with Corpus, but if we don't do something now, some of our family, friends, and neighbors may die because we were too stupid to act. I'm not stupid."

"No, you're not," James agreed, "and neither are the rest of us."

Reggie folded his arms across his chest and sat with a smug look on his face. *Same kind of people we had to help in Vietnam. You've got to stand up for yourself—fight for what you believe in. He should have learned this lesson. 'Remember the Alamo!' . . . 'Remember Pearl Harbor!' . . . You've got to remember your history. Damn good thing you have people like us who do.*

Though John and Kathy were not as rude about the prospect of the venture, they did decide it was time for them to go home. They didn't want to be a party to murder either. They politely said goodbye to everyone and excused themselves.

Melissa got a tablet and Robbie, with the help of Brenda and Kim, drew a map of the Farm, Police compound, and the neighboring structures. As they were drawing, Reggie scrutinized the area and asked many questions. He was the best person to devise the perfect plan, which would minimize the threat to all of them.

"I guess I'm going to have to do without my new home for a while longer," Sean said. "If you guys keep needing the bus for excursions like this, maybe I need to get started on building a permanent place."

"That might not be a bad idea, Sean," Ronnie said. "The bus is ideal when sizeable groups of us need to go somewhere. It's perfect for hauling large amounts of supplies from the neighboring city. If we can get Corpus settled down, we may be making regular trips there running supplies back and forth. If you pick out a spot, we can all pitch in and get it built."

"I'd like that," Sean replied.

"Back to business," Reggie said. "I think our best option is to set up at the Farm and draw Billy and his men there. We can't be running around all over the city chasing them down. That's asking for trouble."

"When?" James asked.

"I think we can get ready in the next couple days and be good to go the third morning," Reggie said. "That will give me time to think my plan over and make sure we don't forget anything."

That night, Robbie and Florence lay in bed discussing the upcoming event. She rubbed her hand across his chest. "Will there ever be peace around here?"

"Growing up, I don't remember many problems." Robbie caught her hand and raised it to his lips to gently kiss her knuckles. "We always worked hard and provided for ourselves and that was tough at times, but most of my life it's been relatively peaceful around here. This is Peaceful Valley after all.

"Maybe some of the things Dad and Grandpa did, and I'm thinking about dealing with the neighbors across the highway they mentioned, have been the reason it was peaceful around here for much of our lives. Things may have been rough lately, but things will settle down after we get back from Corpus. We're making changes, which will be better for us all in the long term. It won't happen overnight, but it will get better. You'll see. Don't worry."

"Yeah, but the last year has been a living hell." Florence snuggled up tighter against Robbie's side. "Daddy, the trial, getting locked up at the Farm, getting out of there, the plane crash, and then Sandra's men. It just doesn't seem like it's going to stop."

Robbie squeezed her tight and gave her a soft kiss on the head. "Trust me, it'll get better. I promise."

Robbie rolled over and stared up at the ceiling. From the deep recesses of his mind, a hint of doubt crept forward.

Sam, Sally, John, and Kathy . . . why are they on the opposite side of the fence when it comes to taking care of the remainder of Sandra's men and changing the government of Corpus Christi? They wouldn't budge from their position no matter what I said. Everything I've read and everything I've been taught tells me that I'm right. But why are they so dead set against getting involved in Corpus? There has to be a reason. Could they be right? They are not dumb or stupid people. Do they know something I don't?

Florence noticed Robbie staring at the ceiling. "Something you want to talk about?"

Robbie took a deep breath and turned his head to face her. "I thought of us getting out of here. Going somewhere where there wouldn't be anyone to fight. A place where we could live out our lives without worrying about getting shot . . . just you and me . . . where we could raise twenty kids and live happily ever after . . . run around naked if we wanted to."

"The fairy tale?"

Robbie chuckled.

"As much as I'd like that, you and I both know fairytales are not real."

"I know," he replied, "Life is what you make it. If you want more out of life, you have to work harder for it."

"And what do you want, Robbie Lindgren?"

"Peace." Robbie paused a couple seconds. "But first . . ." and he reached under her nightshirt and gave her a gentle squeeze.

"I'm really not in the mood," she said.

"It's been a while," he replied.

Florence scooted down and kissed him on the belly as she fondled him. The reaction was immediate. "Yes, I guess it's been a little too long," she said and kissed his little head.

Five minutes was all it took to satisfy his needs. He snuggled up against her backside and rubbed her belly. They were both asleep in minutes.

Chapter 21

The following morning, Reggie supervised the loading of the bus. He also instructed a couple of the boys to snag a few leftover volleyballs from the surrounding trees. "I've got a plan for these," he said. "They'll never expect explosives."

Melissa and Emily grilled sausage patties, creamed some corn, tossed a fresh salad, and set out a jar of pickled beets for lunch. Over all these years, Emily never tired of Lars' pickled beets. Thanks to Eileen disclosing the special ingredients to her before she died, Emily could now make the beets just like Lars and Eileen did. She would have traded the beets for Lars and Eileen's lives, but the beets always brought back special memories for her.

Reggie had to rest a while after the meal, partly due to his age, but mostly due to him eating too much as he always did during special occasions. Preparing for war was always exciting for him. No matter how much he ate, however, he never gained weight. Though he didn't labor as hard as he did when he was younger, his mind always worked overtime devising new weapons, working on old ones, or maintaining his bunker and keeping all the stock rotated whether it be his ammunition or all the guns he possessed. He shot each and every functional weapon on a regular basis and made certain he never missed a single one. He was constantly busy.

The boys installed makeshift bunks in the bus and Sean still had his bed in the rear. They packed cooking equipment and food as well. They didn't know how long they would be in Corpus, but made certain they had everything they needed. The toughest job was to install a 30-caliber machine gun on the back of the Jeep, on a 360° swivel base. The gun was fully automatic and Reggie made certain they had plenty of ammo. It used standard 30-06 shells, of which Reggie had a generous supply. They packed enough body armor and earphones for three men. The Jeep was to be used to sweep the city for stragglers in the Police force after they eliminated the bulk of the men in a single trap. They had to make certain they got every last one of them to avoid problems in the future.

Reggie had some thoughts about how to lure the cops to the Farm for the ambush. He decided a third vehicle would be necessary and the boys prepared one of the trucks they confiscated from Sandra's army to Reggie's exact specifications.

The last task of the day was to fuel up the three vehicles and check all the fluids and tires. By late afternoon, the convoy was ready, most of the plan was in place unless Reggie thought of something else, and everyone went to their respective homes to get a good night's sleep.

Melissa fixed a light dinner for James and he went to bed early.

"You take good care of everyone," Melissa said before he went to sleep.

Just after daylight, the motorcade pulled out of Peaceful Valley. Robbie and Sean led the way in the Jeep.

"The prospect of building a new home uplifted Kim's spirits significantly," Sean said. "She's getting better by the day physically, but Abigail nags at her constantly. She spends way too much time at her grave. If we can get going on the new home, that'll take her mind off the loss of the baby."

"Losing her baby like she did has to be tough," Robbie replied. "Abby was my daughter too, remember. I've thought a lot about that, but it's not quite the same for me as it is for Kim. Losing your daughter is one thing, but having your baby ripped out of your body . . . I can't imagine."

"And I'll never be able to give her another child," Sean said. "That bothers me and it may bother Kim eventually too."

"I can fix that," Robbie said. He looked over at Sean to see what his reaction might be. Sean returned the look, but he wasn't smiling. "That would have to be just between you, me, and Kim though. I don't know how Florence would feel about something like this, but I wouldn't imagine she'd be overly enthusiastic about it. It would have to be our little secret."

Still, Sean didn't say anything. He stared ahead up the highway, but Robbie could tell he was thinking about the proposition. Robbie looked into the rear-view mirror. The bus had lagged behind a half-mile and Robbie looked down at the speedometer. He was going sixty-five. The prospect of impregnating Kim again excited him a bit and his foot got a little heavy on the accelerator.

Robbie slowed down and his mind drifted back to the times Kim ravaged his body repeatedly. He couldn't help but smile.

Kim is quite a lady. Beautiful breasts . . . soft, warm, gentle at first, then . . . damn!

Robbie ran off the edge of the road and gripped the steering wheel tighter as he worked to get it back on the pavement. The Jeep swerved back and forth a couple of times before he got it completely under control.

"You forget how to drive?" Sean yelled as he gripped the door frame.

"Sorry," Robbie replied. He focused on the road for a while. Sean sat quietly watching the scenery go by. He pointed at some deer grazing from time to time, but was quiet otherwise.

"Where do you think you want to build your house?" Robbie asked.

"I thought of building it across the river from you. That would make it close enough where it would be easier for you and Ronnie to help with the project. But then again, there's a great spot across the river from Debra and Zack and that would be closer to Mom and Dad's."

Robbie looked over at Sean and frowned.

Guess the idea of me and Kim didn't sit too well. Sean can't do it. That will never be a possibility. It's not like I haven't done it before. I don't see what the problem is. Not my decision to make though. Florence can never know it was me, that's for sure. Sean can't build across the river from us. Florence would know.

The three-hour drive passed quickly for Robbie, even if for no one else. Robbie pulled behind the two-story building, which had become a regular stopping point for the boys. He got out and motioned for his dad to back the bus in behind the building.

"Sean and I will run over to the Farm to scout the area between here and there, and to check in with Linda," Robbie said. "She doesn't know we're coming yet. I'll let her know we're here and what we plan to do. Then I'll come back and get you guys."

Sean got in back on the machine gun and got it ready.

"Hold on," Robbie said.

James got out a six-foot step ladder and set it up next to the roof ladder on the back of the building. Reggie grabbed his spotting scope and headed up, while James steadied the steps for him.

Robbie drove as near as he could to the Farm without exposing either of them should police be there. He found Linda with a group of ladies in the field tending the crops.

She pushed back her sunhat. "I'm glad to see you. Billy and some of his men were here yesterday to make sure we were doing what we were supposed to. He was apparently satisfied we weren't going to cause a problem and didn't stay long."

"My dad and the rest are at the edge of town this side of the Airport. We thought we'd set up just down the road and draw Billy and his men here."

"How many are you?" Linda asked.

"Seven."

"Only seven?"

"More than enough to take care of your police," he said.

Linda looked doubtful but didn't question Robbie. Seven was all they had and would have to do one way or the other.

"So, exactly what are you going to do?" Linda asked.

"We'll set up a trap and lure in as many as we can," he replied. "When we eliminate them, we'll scour the rest of the city and take out the rest a few at a time."

"All of them?"

"They are all Sandra's men. The only sure way to end the problem is to kill every last one of them. Are you okay with that?"

"If you think that's best," Linda replied. "When?"

"Right now," Robbie replied. "I'll go get the rest and we'll set up and get at it. No advantage to waiting."

Robbie and Sean headed back to the Jeep and made their way to his dad's position. They held a short meeting before heading to the Farm.

"The Police cars are marked," Robbie said. "You can't miss them. There are only two roads into the Farm. The main road has a curve just before you get there. We can hide the bus on the Farm side of the curve and set up on the other side before they can see the bus. There is plenty of brush for us to hide in and several overhanging trees for placement of the volleyballs. We can lead them through the gauntlet and take them out quickly, I hope."

"Yeah!" Lance yelled. "Blow them all to smithereens!"

Reggie leaned over to James. "Cut back on his energy bars."

James smiled and nodded.

Reggie pulled the map out they had made back home and Robbie pointed out the details to the rest of the group. Reggie approved of the plan and their trap was set into motion.

Robbie and Sean led the septet back to the intended location and fortified their positions on one side up and down the road. Robbie instructed Sean to take the Jeep and park it just in the brush on the other road.

"If you see a cop car, Sean," Robbie said, "fill it full of holes. Don't hesitate."

Four hours later, the trap was set. Zack volunteered to be the bait. His task was to drive to the Police compound, make a ruckus, then draw as many of the cops back through the gauntlet as possible. Steel plating would protect him should they shoot at him on the way back, but it would not protect him from a side shot while at the compound.

"Don't hang around there," Reggie said. "Just get their attention and get back here. A few shots at the building should do it."

Zack climbed into the pickup and laid his pistol on the seat beside him. He cranked the truck up, turned it around, and headed toward the south. A hundred yards down the road, the truck started to sputter. He turned around and headed back.

"What's the matter?" James asked.

"The engine's missing," Zack replied.

James popped the hood and checked the fuel filter first. Zack started the truck back up and it still sputtered. James checked the wiring and distributor.

"It may be the plugs," Reggie said. "Ronnie, grab a socket set, will ya?"

James pulled and cleaned all the plugs. When Zack started the truck, the sputtering continued.

"Dammit," Reggie said. "If this thing dies on you, you're dead. You can't take the truck."

"We can use the Jeep," Robbie said.

"But then Sean can't cover our back," James said. "And there's no steel plating for protection. We can't take the steel out of the truck because we welded it in place."

The men stood looking at each other trying to come up with a solution.

"Sean and I'll take the Jeep," Robbie said. "I'll lead them through here, drop Sean off around the curve, then hump it back to help you guys."

"But you won't have the steel plating to protect you," James said.

"The steel plates on the machine gun will help some and the body armor will help too," Robbie said. "If you have a better idea, I'm open to suggestions. We'll stay far enough ahead of them where they can't hit shit from their moving vehicles."

No one came up with a better plan. Robbie jumped into the Jeep and Sean manned the turret. In a cloud of dust, Robbie turned the Jeep around and screeched the tires as he climbed back on the pavement.

"Give 'em hell," Lance yelled out.

"I'll speed through the parking lot," Robbie yelled back at Sean. "Fire a dozen or so rounds into the building. That should get their attention. If you see anyone outside, shoot them on sight."

"Got it," Sean replied.

Robbie slowed down a bit when he spotted the building they were looking for. There were no vehicles on the road thus far. He rounded the corner and went the extra hundred feet to the far parking lot exit, reserving the first exit as his escape route.

As he entered the lot, a man came out of the front door. "Get him," Robbie yelled.

Sean immediately targeted on the man and squeezed the trigger. *Rat-tat-tat-tat-tat.*

The man's arms flew into the air scattering papers in the wind. His body quivered as the bullets shredded his chest and blood splattered against the outside wall.

Robbie pressed the accelerator and sped toward the exit as Sean turned and sprayed the quickly passing building with more hot lead. Robbie swerved the Jeep trying to navigate the corner back onto the main road. As soon as he got control, he lined out toward the Farm.

"Yeeehaa!" he yelled.

Sean pointed his machine gun down the highway behind the Jeep and waited. They were nearly a half-mile down the road when the first vehicle pulled out of the parking lot. It was followed by a second . . . third . . . fourth . . . and finally a fifth car. Their lights were flashing and the sirens wailing.

"A little faster," Sean said, "they're gaining on us."

"This is all I've got," Robbie replied.

"Well, keep your head down."

Robbie scrunched down and peered just over the steering wheel. Sean ducked down behind the steel plates on either side of the machine gun.

Ping, ping, ping.

Bullets deflected off the turret shields and one hit the passenger side mirror.

Ping, ping, ping.

Robbie felt and heard the thud as a bullet hit his body armor, then he felt pain in his lower side. "Dammit!"

A groan escaped Robbie's lips, but he managed to hold the Jeep straight. Sean returned fire. *Rat-tat-tat . . . rat-tat-tat . . .* All five cars continued toward them, but he didn't want them to stop. He wanted them to make their way into the trap they had set.

Robbie was getting a little woozy by the time he drove under the first volleyball hanging in the tree. Another shot of pain in his right arm, but he continued forward. His eyes were tearing and he didn't see the second and third volleyballs.

The curve. I've got to make the turn.

Within a few seconds, after he and Sean made it around the bus to the cover of the trees, Robbie heard the first explosion behind him. Then another and another followed by rifle fire. He heard the crunch of metal against a tree, followed by the distinct muffled explosion quite different than Reggie's explosives, which were sharp and much louder.

Robbie brought the Jeep to a stop, killed the engine, and leaned against the steering wheel. Sean wheeled the turret around to point down the street in front of them and scrutinized the roadway in that direction.

"We did it!" Sean exclaimed as sporadic gunfire continued around the corner. Sean was not concerned in the least that the others could handle the men in the cars.

"I'm shot," Robbie said.

"What!"

Robbie didn't say anything else as he remained leaning against the wheel and his body began to slump.

Sean jumped out and grabbed hold of Robbie to prevent him from falling out of his seat. He kept one eye down the road while he searched for Robbie's wounds. He spotted the blood on his arm, but it was barely bleeding.

That's not enough to make him pass out.

Sean pulled the body armor off and while he was doing so, he noticed the blood on his side. He pulled Robbie back upright in his seat. "Robbie! Robbie!"

Back in Peaceful Valley at the Lindgrens . . .

Everyone except the elder Lins and Wimberleys mingled around the house trying to keep their minds off their loved ones in Corpus. Emily and Melissa prepared the beets they'd pulled earlier that morning just after the men left and got them into a pot to boil. They were making another batch of Lars' famous pickled beets.

Brenda and Kim were doing each other's nails. The rest of the girls were reading, crocheting, and sewing. Brooke was reading *War and Peace* before Sandra and her men showed up, but after their ordeal, she exchanged the heavy book for something a little lighter to read. She chose *Oliver Twist* by Charles Dickens from Lars' original collection.

Florence wandered over to the kitchen where Emily and Melissa were sitting at the table sipping on their teas and discussing the weather.

"How can you be so calm when the men are out there, maybe dying?" she asked.

"Worrying doesn't help," Emily replied. "The men will be fine, and if they're not, worrying will not change anything. All we can do is hope for the best and wait to see what the outcome is when they return home."

Florence turned her gaze toward Brooke and Debra on the sofa, then to Beka on the recliner. Brenda was tending to Kim on the day-bed. Compared to Florence, they all appeared to be comfortable and relaxed.

Why am I the only one who is upset? Why am I so nervous? Why do I cry all the time? Is there something wrong with me?

Florence turned back to Emily and Melissa.

"How can you just sit there like nothing is going on?" she asked.

"You're young, Florence," Melissa said. "In time, you will toughen up and be just like us. This isn't our first war. It all comes with age and experience. You watch for snakes now and they no longer scare you, right?"

Florence nodded.

"But not knowing is driving me up the wall," she said.

Emily reached out and grabbed hold of Florence's hand. "Listen, the men will always be going out on adventures. Trying to get a new government going in Corpus will not happen overnight. They will be going back there again and again. They will be going to some of the neighboring cities and towns too. There will always be danger in what they do, but they are strong and able.

"Believe in the boys and their abilities. I think Sandra was the worst obstacle. Getting rid of the rest of her men in Corpus will be the next in terms of danger. After that, it should be all downhill, but the danger will never go away.

"Years ago when the grid shut down, we fought many battles. Intruder after intruder showed up to take what we had because they did not have the skills to fend for themselves any other way. Ronald and Sara Weston, the first inhabitants of our valley, died as a result. This continued for years, but in time things got better.

"Now, in time, the men and women who would do us harm will be rounded up and dealt with. They may never go away completely, but they will become few and far between. Then, we will be relatively safe and you can breathe much easier. By then, you will be older and have more experience under your belt and when something does pop up, you will deal with it in a calm manner just like we are dealing with the current affair.

"It's all a learning process. The more you learn, the better you are able to deal with adversity the next time."

Emily looked over at Brooke on the couch who was changing her position.

"It's just like reading," Emily continued. "The more you read, the better you get at it. You don't learn to read overnight. You don't learn to deal with hardship overnight either. That's just life. Not quite the comfortable city life you're used to, but life nevertheless."

Florence wiped her eyes.

"Robbie is young," Melissa added, "but in the short time he's been on this earth, he has acquired knowledge and skill few gather in a lifetime. The same is true for his brother. The boys are strong and tough. You need to be strong for Robbie. Learn with him and be there for him when he returns. He will love you more for it."

Emily glanced over at the stove and got up. "Let's get some beets canned."

Chapter 22

Back in Corpus Christi . . .

The Police cars and the roadway were barely visible due to the smoke from the volleyballs and the plastic and rubber from two of the burning cars.

James put his rifle up to his shoulder and stepped toward the first car. "Cover me, Reggie."

"You know it," he replied.

James, with his finger on the trigger and slightly crouched, moved toward the upwind side of the cars. He saw Ronnie come out of the brush at the far end of the burning and smoldering vehicles. They poked and prodded the bodies of the cops who escaped the burning vehicles. Zack came out of the brush and gave them a hand. Lance held his position to provide cover.

James, Zack, and Ronnie met in the middle.

"All's clear," James announced, and Lance came out of the brush.

Reggie made his way to the roadway and stood looking at the rising smoke and flames.

James turned his attention down the road to see if there were more vehicles. There were none . . . yet.

Reggie and his men regrouped. James yelled at Robbie and Sean.

"Robbie's hurt," he immediately heard back from around the corner.

James ran toward the curve and Reggie followed. The others stayed behind to keep an eye out toward the Police Station. When James reached the Jeep, Sean had Robbie stretched out across the front seats, trying to control the bleeding.

"Reggie!" James yelled, with fear in his voice.

When Reggie came around the curve, James yelled again. "Hurry!"

Reggie examined Robbie's wound. "This requires surgery . . . and we can't do it. He needs real doctors."

By this time, Ronnie had made it around to the Jeep. "Robbie!"

"He's hurt bad, Son," James said. "Sean, where's the hospital around here?"

"But they won't help us," he replied.

"Damn right they will," James said. "If they don't, they'll die."

"I'll have to show you the way," Sean said.

"Ronnie, you, Zack, and Lance stay here," Reggie instructed. "Watch both roads. If anyone closely resembling a cop comes around, take them out."

Sean and James moved Robbie to the back seat. Reggie got in the front seat, while Sean manned the turret.

"We don't know who we're going to run into, Sean," Reggie said. "Stay alert."

James cranked up the Jeep. "Where to, Sean?"

Sean pointed forward. "At the intersection take a right."

Reggie looked back at Robbie. "Hold on, Son. We'll be at the hospital in no time."

James yelled over his shoulder at Sean. "You sure this is the shortest route?"

He nodded. James followed his directions and they soon arrived at the Hospital. There was no resistance from the police, but when they reached the emergency room, they were confronted by the hospital staff.

James carried Robbie inside and laid him on a nearby gurney.

"He's been shot," James said, to an approaching nurse and doctor.

The nurse walked over to the gurney and pulled Robbie's shirt open, while the doctor walked up to James.

"We can't treat him," the doctor said.

"Damn right you'll treat him," James replied, in a harsh voice.

The doctor crossed his arms across his chest and looked over at Robbie. "He's not an officer from one of the compounds . . . absolutely not . . . not without Sandra's permission. Get him out of here."

The doctor turned to walk away and James grabbed him by the arm and drew his pistol with his other hand. James stuck the pistol under the doctor's chin.

"You'll treat him and you'll do it right now, or this thing just might go off."

The doctor turned back with a shocked look on his face and stared into James's glaring eyes, then over to the gurney. By this time, more of the Hospital staff had gathered around and Sean and Reggie had guns drawn and ready.

The doctor looked at all the weapons. "Very well."

The doctor took one look at the hole in Robbie's side. "He'll need surgery."

"Then you'd best get started," James replied. "If he dies out here on this cart, he won't be the only one."

Two staff members wheeled Robbie down the hallway and several nurses scurried ahead. The doctor followed.

"Get back to the bus," James told Reggie. "I don't think there'll be any more problems here. I'll be okay. Come back when you can."

James hurried to catch up with the doctor. At the door into the operating room, the doctor stopped and turned to James. "You can't come in here," but by the time he got the words out, James had his pistol out and cocked. The doctor huffed a quick breath and pushed the door open.

When Reggie reached the bus, he heard gunfire around the corner. "Get ready, Sean." Up the way, there were two more police cars. Ronnie, Zack, and Lance were hiding behind the burned-out cars returning their fire. Sean opened up with the 30-cal. as soon as they came around the corner and had a clear shot. Thirty seconds later, the Police vehicles were Swiss cheese and the challenge squashed.

"Thanks," Ronnie yelled out.

"Just doing my job," Sean replied, with a big grin on his face as they pulled up close. Those guys can't compete with this machine gun and up to 700 rounds per minute."

Reggie leaned out the window. "We got Robbie to the Hospital and the doctors will fix him up. They were a little hesitant, but your dad didn't give them a choice."

Lance leaned on the fender of the Jeep. "What do we do now?"

"How many men have we eliminated?" Reggie asked.

Lance paused for a moment counting in his head. "Sixteen, more or less."

"That's only about half of them then," Reggie said. "Now, we wait and we watch."

An hour went by and there were no additional targets. Two hours and it was still quiet.

"Hello!"

Ronnie jumped and immediately leveled his rifle in the direction of the voice. Sean leaped up on the Jeep and swung the machine gun around.

"Don't shoot!"

"Come out so we can see you," Sean yelled.

When they emerged from the brush, Sean and Ronnie recognized the women. They introduced Reggie to Linda Gomez and Sally Beecher.

"Nice to meet you, ladies."

"I didn't hear any shots or explosions for a long time, so I thought we'd come take a look," Linda said.

"I think we got about half of them," Reggie informed her.

"There's only five of you . . ."

"Robbie got shot," Reggie said. "His dad is with him at the Hospital."

"And they're taking care of him?" Linda asked, surprised.

"Not willingly," Ronnie said, "but my dad is a good persuader."

"What are you going to do now?" Sally asked.

"We wait," Ronnie replied. "If no one else shows up, we'll go roust them out wherever they may be."

"They may be scattered far and wide," Linda added. "They not only take care of police work, but are our primary hunters. They hunt beef cattle, deer, and small game for the processing plant."

"And where's this processing plant?" Reggie asked.

Reggie showed her his makeshift map. She pointed to a location, which was not on the drawing. She then described the building and its surroundings.

"There could be a few cruising the city too," Linda said.

"Will you take a look at the bodies?" Reggie asked. "I want to know if Billy is amongst this bunch."

"Oh my," Linda said when she looked at the dead men in the first car and she covered her nose. The bodies were charred, but she was certain Billy was not one of the three men.

The second car didn't burn and Linda immediately recognized Billy in the driver's seat. She turned her head away as soon as she saw him. The body was soaked in blood and a portion of his face was missing altogether.

"We've got another car coming," Lance announced from his position behind a tree.

All eyes turned down the highway. A single car was approaching fast.

Reggie turned and waved the women back. "You better get to the Farm, Linda. Stay there until we come get you. We don't want you two to get accidentally caught by a stray bullet."

Linda and Sally hurried off, while Sean manned the turret and the rest hid behind trees.

"On my mark," Reggie yelled.

Though they never wanted war or to kill anyone, Reggie was very well trained in the art of warfare through his army experiences. The boys, through discussions with Reggie, learned warfare tactics, but it was only through Sandra's invasion that they truly became experts at war. They didn't like killing, especially people, but when necessary, they were probably more skilled than Grandpa Lars through camouflage, stealth, and the element of surprise. Thanks to Reggie, they were skilled at planning their warfare as well.

Five minutes later, four men lay dead down the highway, their bodies riddled with holes just like their vehicle. Reggie took the driver out on the first shot with his sniper rifle. The car swerved and rolled twice, stunning the remaining three. As they scrambled out and tried to hide behind the car, Sean, Ronnie, Zack, and Lance picked them off.

"That should be about twenty," Reggie said. "Ronnie, you better get the Jeep back around the corner. We don't want anyone sneaking up on us from that direction."

Ronnie got behind the wheel and he and Sean went around the bend. Ronnie took a position behind the Jeep while Sean stayed on the machine gun.

Three hours dragged by and the sun was setting quickly in the western sky. No more vehicles ventured their way. Reggie passed out a few energy bars and gave Lance a few extra to take to Ronnie and Sean.

"Grab a couple sets of night vision goggles out of the bus," Reggie instructed. "It'll be getting dark soon and we don't want to get caught with our britches down. On your way back, grab some for us too."

Reggie knew the boys could see well enough without night vision under most circumstances, but in city warfare, they needed the five-hundred-yard vision the scopes provided.

After an uneventful night, each swapping off taking short snoozes, Reggie made some breakfast for each consisting of ham sandwiches and pickled beets. This was quick and high in protein and carbs to keep the crew going.

By mid-day, everything remained quiet. Reggie decided they should take the bus to the Farm and hide it inside one of the many barns. Reggie and Ronnie fiddled with the truck for a couple hours while the others kept out a watchful eye on the roads. Reggie finally discovered a short in one of the plug wires, which was causing it to sputter. A little electrical tape and the truck was back in operation. The Jeep would have been a little crowded to go out on an excursion with the five of them, two of whom were packing RPGs.

A couple of hours after noon, Reggie decided it was time to go. They needed to round up more of the police. He also needed to check in on, James and Robbie.

He drove the bus to the Farm and Linda showed him which barn to put it in. The boys gathered up more ammunition and trail mix to snack on, from the bus. Reggie decided Sean should stay on the turret while Ronnie drove the Jeep.

They were to lead. Reggie drove the truck with Zack in shotgun and Lance in back with his RPGs.

The first stop was the Hospital. Reggie went in while the boys stood guard.

"Where's Robbie?" Reggie said, probably a little too loudly. One of the nurses quickly led him down a hallway. Other staff members parted to let them through when they saw the elderly man and his sniper rifle. The agitated nurse, not used to men with guns, led him to the end of the hall and pushed the door open. James jumped when the door slammed against the wall.

James motioned with his hand. "Robbie is still asleep."

Reggie pushed the door shut and walked over to the bed.

"He was torn up badly inside," James added, looking down lovingly at his son. "He lost a kidney and a couple ribs were broken. Some of his intestines were torn and he lost a lot of blood. They only had a pint of plasma to give him. The doctors said they did the best they could."

"He's a tough boy," Reggie assured James. He circled the foot of the bed and came to stand by James's side. He squeezed his son-in-law's shoulder reassuringly. "He'll recover. That's all we can ask for."

James nodded and wiped his sleeve across his cheek.

Reggie stepped over to the window and pulled the curtain back "We're going to see if we can track down the rest of the police force. We got twenty. There's got to be a few more, but they may be off on a hunt or scattered anywhere over the city."

Reggie turned back and looked at James. "What happened to your face?"

He reached up and touched the cut on his forehead. "I think there's a snitch around here. Someone on the hospital staff must have got the word out that we're here. A couple men came in late last night and tried to take me and Robbie out.

"I made my bed on the floor in front of the door and they woke me up when they tried to push their way in. I shot one immediately, but the other almost got the best of me. We scuffled on the floor for a bit and he hit me with his pistol, but I eventually took care of him."

"Do you want one of the boys to stay here with you?" Reggie asked.

"Nah, you guys do what you need to do. Make a sweep around the Hospital regularly and we should be okay from here on out. I gave the staff another stern warning last night while they were cleaning up the mess."

"By the way, we got the truck fixed and can split up to cover more area. We'll get all of Sandra's remaining police force rounded up in no time."

Reggie gave James a manly hug, then took a last look at Robbie. He joined the boys outside and they headed to the Police compound.

"Your dad got a couple more."

When they arrived at the Police Station, Lance put an RPG through one of the windows. *Boom!*

They sat and waited, watching the smoldering building, waiting for more adversaries to make their presence known.

Rat-tat-tat-tat-tat . . .

Sean took out the front windshield of a single police car and its lone occupant when it came around the corner. Zack added a few more rounds with his AR-15 for good measure.

"That should do it, boys," Reggie said.

The third stop was the meat packing plant. Sean took out another vehicle on the way there. Linda's directions were right on, but there was no one around.

The next few hours, Reggie and the boys drove up and down the main roads in a systematic pattern looking for more adversaries. An hour before dark, they had only eliminated one more. Reggie decided it was time to head back to the Farm. They got there at dusk without further encounters.

Linda offered the men dinner, which they readily accepted, but they opted to stay on the bus together when she offered beds to sleep in.

"I have some motion sensors to place around the barn," Reggie said, "so if anyone comes around, we'll know about it before they get the drop on us. Thanks anyway, Linda."

The men freshened up a bit and joined Linda in the house. The cooks served veal parmesan, creamed potatoes, and broccoli. For drinks, Linda offered a long list. The boys settled on milk. They had never had real cow's milk, only goat milk from the Lins and powdered milk from Reggie's survival food stash. They didn't care for the goat's milk but liked the powdered milk, much better. They thought they'd give fresh milk a try. Reggie took fruit juice followed by coffee. The meal was quiet except for the noise of silverware against the plates.

When they finished eating, Linda took a sip of her tea. "Why are you doing all this for us?"

Reggie washed his last bite down with a sip of his juice, wiped his face on the napkin, and leaned his chin on his knuckles. "I've got to tell you, Linda, our motive is a little selfish. Now that your city knows about us, if we'd let a dictatorship stand here in Corpus, we would always be at risk for some ruthless son-of-a-bitch . . . excuse my language . . . to attack us. If we can help you set up a friendly democracy, then we would all be much safer."

"After we get finished here," Ronnie butted in, "we want to try to establish a peaceful relationship over all of south Texas."

Linda set her glass down and turned her full attention to Ronnie. "I never thought you had such vision."

"We've only briefly discussed this possibility," Reggie said, giving Ronnie a look.

"Yeah, but I've thought about it a lot. We'll do just that when we get through here."

Reggie set his drink down and looked back at Linda. "Well, there you have it."

Linda got up and walked over to the china hutch. "I found this," she said, handing Reggie a map of the city. "It may help you. I've marked a few areas some of the police may frequent."

"Yes, this will help a lot." Reggie rose from the table. "If you'll excuse us, we better get some sleep. It's going to be another long day tomorrow. Thank you for a *very* nice meal."

"Yes, ma'am," Ronnie said, as he pushed back his chair.

The others nodded as they rose.

Reggie gave Linda a gentle handshake. "Thanks and good night," he said, as he pulled the door closed behind him.

"The cow's milk was good!" Ronnie exclaimed, on the way to the barn.

"Didn't care for the broccoli," Sean commented, with a sour face.

Reggie gave him a head ruffle. "I know you hate broccoli, but I'm pleased you choked it down politely for the ladies."

Lance came up behind Sean and mussed his hair again. "Sean eats broccoli for the ladies!"

Sean gave him a shove.

"That's enough, boys."

Reggie grumbled all the way to the bus holding his stomach. *Ate too much, again! . . . and babysitting!*

Ronnie climbed into the bus and immediately crawled into bed. Reggie noticed him staring at the ceiling. "Something the matter, boy?"

Ronnie looked over at his grandpa. "Robbie said he had doubts about what we are doing before he got shot. Now that he's lying in a hospital bed, I'm just wondering if we're really doing the right thing here. Is this fight really worth it?"

"It was his idea. You told Linda that you wanted to form a new state in south Texas. I assume you and Robbie have been discussing this."

"We have, Grandpa, and one minute it sounds good, but then the next, I think of Robbie and I have my doubts."

"We are in the middle of this mess and you can't have doubts. That will get you killed. Believe you are doing the right thing and stay focused. Put your uncertainty aside for now. You can think about the right or wrong of the matter after we're finished."

"Did Robbie get shot because of his doubts?"

"No," Reggie replied sternly, "doubt causes hesitation, which can get you shot, but Robbie did not hesitate. He got shot purely by coincidence . . . an errant shot. That's all it was. Now stop thinking and get some shuteye. We have a long day ahead of us."

Chapter 23

Reggie got his crew up at the crack-of-dawn. They slept well with full bellies thanks to Linda. Reggie looked over at Ronnie. "You okay, Son?"

"Yeah," Ronnie replied, glumly.

"Remember what I told you last night?" Reggie asked. "Doubt will get you killed."

"Yes, sir," Ronnie replied, giving his grandpa a smile.

They checked the fluids, filled the tanks with gas, and warmed up the engines. Linda came out and offered breakfast, but Reggie declined for them. However, he was happy to take a thermos of coffee each for himself and his men.

A pass by the Police compound was quick and uneventful. The next stop was the meat plant. Again, no one was there. What followed was six hours of cruising the streets. No more challenges.

"Let's make a trip to the Hospital," Reggie suggested.

Suddenly, Sean cut loose with the machine gun . . . *rat-tat-tat-tat* . . . *rat-tat-tat-tat*.

The police car came out of nowhere in a brushy neighborhood and Ronnie almost hit him with the Jeep. Sean was quick to respond with deadly accuracy. Ronnie watched the wide-eyed man splatter all over the inside of his vehicle as the tires on the Jeep squealed and smoked when Ronnie locked up the brakes.

"Way to go, Bro," Ronnie said, looking back at Sean.

Ronnie steered the Jeep around the car and made it to the Hospital without further conflict.

"I want to go in this time," Ronnie asserted. "He's my brother and I need to see him."

Reggie didn't argue the point. "He's on the first floor . . . room 111."

When Ronnie walked into the room, the first thing he noticed was that Robbie was awake. James got up from the chair beside the bed. Ronnie gave his dad a big hug, then stepped over to the bed. "You don't look so bad to me."

Robbie managed a weak smiled and mumbled. "Just don't make me laugh. It hurts like hell."

"So, I guess you're going to be okay now?"

Robbie closed his eyes and didn't reply. Ronnie looked over at his dad.

"He goes in and out. Yeah, I think he'll be alright. They say he may be able to get out of here in three or four weeks."

"That long?"

"They said if Robbie were going to a comfortable bed in a nice home somewhere, maybe in two weeks, but back into a war zone, no."

"Florence isn't going to like that," Ronnie said, looking back at Robbie. His eyes were still closed.

"Maybe you can bring her here when you get things stabilized," James said. "By the way, how's everything going?"

"We got twenty-six of the bastards. There may be a few more, but we won't know for sure for another day or two. Linda can't tell us exactly how many there are, so we just have to keep looking."

"Reggie told me not to stay too long. We still have work to do this afternoon." Ronnie put his hand on his brother's arm and his eyes opened slightly. "Good to see you getting better. I'll see you the next day or so."

Robbie moaned.

Ronnie gave his dad another hug on the way out and rejoined his grandpa and companions. "He's awake and doing okay. Looks like he'll survive."

"That's good to hear," Reggie said. "Now back to work. Let's make our way to the Bayfront, then we'll head back by the Contractors compound and on toward the Farm."

Just before dark, they arrived back at the Farm without further incident. Linda again offered them dinner.

"Thank you so much, Linda," Reggie said. "Dinner helps us sleep better at night."

"And it's damn good." Lance looked almost dreamy at the thought of another meal like the night before.

Sean, Ronnie, and Zack nodded.

Linda and the men enjoyed a bowl of pea soup while they waited for the main course. A lady came in to gather the bowls when they finished, while another set a large platter of fried shrimp and a second of French fries in the center of the table. The boys went for the cow's milk again.

There was no talk for a while, but the boys continually looked up with their mouths full of shrimp and potatoes nodding their enjoyment of the delicious meal.

Shortly, Linda called the cook in. "We're going to need a few more shrimp."

She looked over to the boys and they all nodded. The ladies then headed back to the kitchen.

The ladies served fruit and coffee for dessert to finish off the meal.

The guys all thanked Linda for another fine dinner and adjourned to the bus, Reggie moaning all the way and holding his belly.

After everyone washed off under their portable shower unit and crawled into bed, Reggie brought up the subject of a new police force.

"First thing in the morning, we'll head over to the Police compound. We've got to find guns for the ladies here at the Farm and get them trained. They're bound to have plenty of guns and ammo somewhere in the Police compound. We'll bring what we find back here and I'll stay and get started on that task. You boys can then do exactly what we did today.

"Lance, I know you like the RPGs, but I think you'll be better off with an assault rifle or a sniper rifle. Sean can probably handle pretty much anything you might come across with the machine gun. Unless you almost run over someone like Ronnie did today, most adversaries will be at a distance and the RPGs are not good for long shots. Any questions?"

"No, Grandpa," Ronnie replied.

"No, Sir," the others said.

"Okay, get a good night's sleep. I'll see you in the morning."

Reggie was right, a warehouse in back of the main office at the Police compound was loaded with guns and ammunition. Sean manned the machine gun while the others loaded up the truck with an assortment of pistols, mostly 9mm, all the holsters they could find, two dozen AR-15s, and enough ammo to train the women without fear of running out.

Reggie and the boys delivered the weapons and ammo to the back porch of the main house at the Farm. Reggie instructed the boys to follow a similar grid pattern as they did the day before and he sent the crew on their way, while he stayed behind with the women.

"Linda, we need to gather up the ladies," Reggie said. "You need an army to protect yourselves. I'll help you get started."

Linda sent Sally Beecher to the bunkhouse and fields to call everyone in.

Reggie joined Linda on the patio for tea while they waited for the women to gather around. He finished up his second glass by the time most of the gals were assembled.

Reggie and Linda got up and he stepped to the edge of the porch and looked out over the crowd. They were dressed in overalls and jeans mostly. Many had ponytails and their shirts were damp from perspiration.

"Ladies, we have pretty much eliminated the police force. But an unarmed citizenry will always be in danger. My job today is to help you create an army yourselves. Have any of you ever shot a gun? Hold up your hand if you have."

No one raised their hand.

"Well, then some of you are going to have to learn." He looked out over the assembled crowd. "To be a part of the new police force, you need to be bold, fearless, and strong of mind. I know some women are just not cut out to shoot guns. You can't be timid. I need some tough ladies to volunteer. Who will give it a try?"

A woman in the back of the crowd raised her hand. "I'll give it a go."

Everyone turned and looked to see who raised her hand. Directly, another hand raised, then another. After five minutes, nineteen had held up their hands.

"Any more?" Reggie asked.

"If I'm going to lead this group," Linda said, "I'm gonna have to learn to shoot too."

Reggie gave the ladies some preliminary instructions while some of the others dragged square hay bales across the backyard and gathered cans. He lined the women up and gave them a few additional instructions.

"Never, ever point a gun at me," was his final directive. "Alright, ladies, fire at will."

He stepped back a few yards to get away from the noise. Most of the women fired a single shot and stopped, though all the rifles were semi-automatics. Reggie stood and watched as some of them began firing two or three shots at a time. He turned and walked down the line, noting that few of the cans were hit.

While this was going on, Sally Beecher retrieved a bench from the porch and set it behind the shooters at Linda's request. She then carried numerous boxes of extra ammunition over and stacked them on the bench.

Reggie started on one end of the line helping them make a few adjustments on how they held and sighted the guns.

As the women emptied their rifles and turned around to face him, he pointed to the ammo on the seat. They reloaded and went back to the firing line. A couple of them propped their guns against the bench. They walked over to Reggie and told him they didn't want to do this anymore.

"That's okay," Reggie said. "Thank you for trying."

Linda walked over to him after she quickly unloaded her rifle on the target for the third time.

"What do you think?" Reggie asked.

"Quite fun actually," she replied, with a pleased look on her face.

"Good. Working alongside your crew is a sign of a great leader," he said. "Tomorrow we'll go get you some cars to drive. There are plenty at the Police compound. We'll bring them back to the Farm and the new all-female police force can work out of here for a while until things settle down. Then the new gals can take over the Police compound and work from there."

Reggie and Linda walked over to the shooting line. "Ladies!" he called. "That's enough on the rifles. Let's get each of you a pistol and holster and we'll give them a try."

The group turned to face Reggie and Linda.

He pointed at the porch. The women ran over and swapped their rifles for a pistol. They all found a holster to fit their sidearm and strapped it on. Slowly, they strolled back over to where Reggie and Linda were waiting, making additional adjustments to their holsters.

Reggie took one of the pistols from the closest gal, demonstrated the loading process, and handed it back.

"Remember, never point it at me or anyone else you don't want to shoot. Just like the rifle, if you're not shooting, point it either up or down at the ground."

The ladies loaded their guns and slowly made their way back to the firing line. He showed them how to hold and aim the pistols, then stepped back.

"You may proceed when ready," he said.

Again, Reggie walked up and down behind the line giving them additional instruction. He then stood back and watched. Linda walked up beside him.

"Looks like they're doing fairly well," she said.

"Yeah, they're even hitting a few cans."

Linda and Reggie watched as the ladies emptied their guns, reloaded, and returned to the firing line. After nearly twenty minutes, he told them to empty their guns and put them in their holsters.

"Gather on the porch when you're finished."

Linda and he went back to the patio and she sent Sally in for another pitcher of tea. Reggie had almost finished his glass by the time all the shooters had grouped around the stoop.

He stood up and walked to the edge.

"Okay, how many of you want to become police ladies?"

All but one held up their hands.

"I don't like this," she said.

"That's alright," Reggie replied. "If you don't think you can handle it, then you're probably not suited for the job, but thank you for your effort. The rest of you want to be cops, right?"

A couple of the ladies mumbled a 'yes'.

"I can't hear you," Reggie said, in a loud and firm voice.

A few 'yes, sirs' rang out.

"I can't hear you!" he said, much louder with his hand cupped behind his ear.

"Yes, Sir!" the group yelled loud and clear, with determined looks on their faces.

Reggie smiled. "Much better, ladies. Now that you've gotten your first taste of shooting, in the coming days I'll teach you some of the basics of being a police officer—driving, the partner system, hand-to-hand combat, things to watch out for, and the like."

Reggie gave the ladies some classroom instruction and simple demonstrations on the porch for the remainder of the afternoon. "Tomorrow, we'll start with the hands-on experience for all of you," he said, as he adjourned for the day.

When the boys returned to the Farm just before dark, Reggie filled them in on the progress with the new police force. Ronnie pulled the map out and showed his grandfather the area where they made their sweeps over the south side of the city.

"We didn't see anyone all day," he said.

"That's a good sign, Ronnie, but there has to be more. I want you to do the same thing tomorrow while I work with the ladies again. I need to give them some instruction on dealing with adversaries. We're going to bring some of the cars from the Police compound over here and I'll see how they do driving tomorrow.

"I want you to check around the meat packing plant again, the Police compound, and north and west of where you were today. The rest have to be out that direction."

"Yes, sir."

"Now you guys get a shower and we'll grab a bite to eat. It'll be another long day tomorrow."

Reggie found out the following morning that none of the ladies had ever driven a car. While the boys were scouring the city for remaining members of the police force, he spent the day teaching the girls how to drive. Some had driven tractors or combines and had no trouble driving the car. The few who had no experience on the farm equipment were a little slower to learn, but by late afternoon, most were reasonably competent. All the cars had automatic transmissions, so it wasn't as difficult as it might have been.

Teaching them to drive and shoot at the same time should be fun, Reggie thought.

At the end of another long day, Reggie and the boys joined Linda once again for dinner.

"We've got plenty of white and red paint in the barn," Linda said. "I have decided we're going to paint all the new police force vehicles pink and the name of the force will be the Pink Ladies."

Ronnie and Zack laughed, which drew a frown from Reggie.

"Be polite, boys," he said.

"Yes, sir."

"We stopped by the Hospital again today," Ronnie said. "Robbie is doing much better. He still hurts a lot, but he's eating and the nurses got him up to walk around the room."

"And he had a poop too," Zack added. "The nurses said that was a good sign."

"Not over dinner," Reggie said. "Excuse the boys, Linda, sometimes they're a little crude."

"No apology necessary," she replied.

"With that," Reggie rose, "we bid you good night. Thanks for the wonderful dinner. We'll see you in the morning."

For the next two days, Reggie worked with the women while the boys continued their rounds. On the second day, they encountered two cars and three men at the meat plant. Reggie told the boys that the plant was likely the first place some of Sandra's men would show up if they were not around town. After all, their secondary job was to provide beef and venison for the city.

When Ronnie drove up to the meat plant, the men were not in their vehicles. They wore contractor uniforms, didn't appear to be armed, and were at the side of the building working on the condensing coils.

"They're not who we're looking for, Sean. Hold your fire."

As Ronnie pulled up to the building, the men heard the Jeep and turned around. As soon as they saw Sean on the machine gun turret, they threw their arms into the air. "Don't shoot," one of the men yelled.

"Anyone else around?" Ronnie asked.

"No, just us."

Ronnie climbed out of the Jeep and grabbed his AR-15. He kept his rifle pointed at the men, but as they didn't appear to be a threat, he pointed the rifle more toward their feet, but ready should they make any sudden moves.

"We're just adding coolant to the system," one of the men said. "This is where we keep all our red meats. We check the system every day to make sure it's working okay."

Zack and Lance got out of the truck and checked the inside of the building, then around the grounds. Sean stood his position on the turret while Ronnie continued to talk with the repairmen.

"Things are going to change around here," Ronnie said. "For the better for you, I hope. If you don't already know, Sandra is dead. All of the men she took to Peaceful Valley to try to kill us are dead too. We're going to eliminate the rest of Sandra's men here in Corpus and you'll have a new leader and a new police force."

The men stood and listened to Ronnie, maybe partially because they were interested in what he was saying, but maybe a little more because Sean had a 30-caliber machine gun pointed just over their heads.

"There will no longer be a dictatorship here in Corpus," Ronnie added. "You and everyone else will have the freedom to choose your own destiny. You will also have the right to vote. Linda Gomez will be your new leader temporarily, but in time, you will be able to choose who you want to run the city. And, no more castrations."

This drew a smile from the men. "Is this for real?" one of the men asked.

"It is if we can get rid of all of Sandra's old police force," Ronnie said. "What do you guys think about a new system of government?"

The men looked at each other and whispered back and forth for a minute or more. "A change might be good," one said. The others nodded.

"Spread the word," Ronnie said, "change is coming. Democracy is coming!"

Zack and Lance got back into their truck and Ronnie into the Jeep. They left the men to their work and continued their search. By late afternoon, they had not found any more of Sandra's men. They made a quick stop by the Hospital before returning to the Farm.

Now that Robbie was going to be okay, but had to stay in the Hospital, James went back to the Farm with the boys. Before he left, he thanked the doctors for taking such good care of his son, but also gave them a stern warning. "If I come back and anything has happened to my boy, we'll bury every damn one of you."

Ronnie filled his dad in on the progress thus far. James was delighted with the news. When they drove up to the Farm, the first thing they noticed were five pink cars with 'Police' written across the side in bright red. The cars brought an immediate smile to the boys' faces. When Reggie introduced them to some of the new police force, their smiles turned to laughter.

The girls wore jeans. Each carried a rifle and had a pistol strapped to their hips. What made them noticeable, however, was their short freshly cut hair and their pink shirts. Most of the girls already had white shirts for working in the fields in the hot sun. They washed them with a couple of red towels to give them their new tint.

That night at dinner, which was a surprise and a delight to James to be eating food not constrained to hospital dietary requirements, Reggie informed Linda that tomorrow would be their last day here. One more day of training. One more sweep of the city by the boys and the new police force, then the women would have to hold the fort on their own. After all, they had work at home. They would be back to Corpus in a few days and on a regular basis until Robbie was able to return to Peaceful Valley.

"After that," Reggie said, "we'll work on setting up some friendly trade."

"I guess I'll have to make trips to the various compounds," Linda said. "I need to start explaining the new system of government to the heads of each department . . . see how much resistance I'm going to have bucking the old system."

"Do you know these people?" Reggie asked.

"Some fairly well, but others, not so much," she replied. "Marcia will probably be the most trouble."

"Marcia Nguyen?" Sean asked.

"Yes."

"Well, don't tell her I'm around, or even alive for that matter," Sean said. "She'll put two and two together and know I killed her husband, Sonny."

"I didn't know that," Linda said. "Marcia was one of Sandra's staunch supporters and her favorite spy. Thanks for telling me. She'll be tough to deal with if she finds out you're helping with the new government."

"Any more spies that you know of who might cause problems?" James asked.

"The only ones I knew of were Beka and Sally. Sally Beecher is here and I think I have her under control, but I'm keeping a close eye on her. She's not in a position of power, so it probably doesn't matter. Beka is gone now. I don't know what happened to her."

"Beka Livingston?" Lance asked, raising an eyebrow.

"Why, yes," Linda said, quite surprised he knew her. "Do you know Beka?"

Lance got up from the table. "You're damn right I know her," and he stormed out of the house, slamming the door behind him.

"Sorry about that," Reggie said. "Seems like we have another problem." He explained Beka had escaped the city with Robbie and Florence, and that now Lance and Beka were a couple.

Linda shook her head. "I'm sorry too."

Chapter 24

At Peaceful Valley . . .

Melissa prepared breakfast for herself, Kim, and Brenda. This was the routine the past several mornings. Brenda usually helped with setting the table, but other than that she helped Kim, especially with her shoes so she wouldn't have to bend over.

Kim was annoyed that she still needed help from Brenda for basic necessities. Melissa seemed annoyed at both of them for always getting in the way, but they were not really annoyed at each other. They were aggravated by the fact that their men had been gone so long. They could be dead for all they knew. They were not kids playing with toys. They were playing with fire trying to overthrow the remaining government of Corpus Christi.

The girls had confidence in the abilities of their men. All the women in Peaceful Valley did. Even Florence's confidence was growing by the day. Together, they just finished saving their community from an invading force four times their numbers. They kept their concerns to themselves most of the time when they were together, but separately they worried. This turned into depression, which tried their patience.

"What time did Beka and Debra say they were coming over?" Melissa asked.

"They didn't say exactly," Brenda replied. "Sometime before noon."

"Guess it really doesn't matter," Melissa said.

Beka and Debra finally showed up just after noon. They were concerned as well about the men being gone.

"Shouldn't they be back by now?" Debra asked.

"It's a long way to Corpus Christi," Melissa said. "You can't overthrow a city in a day. They'll be back when the job is done. Don't worry."

While Melissa sounded confident in her tone and tried to be cheerful, in the back of her mind, she was as deeply concerned about the well-being of the men as anyone.

"Have you thought about names for your baby?" Debra asked Brenda.

"I've always liked Cassandra if it's a girl," she replied. "If it's a boy, I first thought about Robbie, Jr., but that wouldn't be fair to Sean. He will be the daddy though it's Robbie's baby. Then again, Sean, Jr., wouldn't be fair to Robbie.

"I never knew who my dad was, so I can't name it after him if it's a boy. Probably wouldn't want to name it after him anyway. He was likely one of Sandra's guys. I guess it wouldn't be appropriate to name him after one of her stud muffins. Maybe I'll pick a name out of thin air. Are you pregnant yet?"

"Not yet, I don't think," Debra said. "We haven't been specifically trying, but we have been fooling around enough that it could happen."

"What about you, Beka?" Brenda asked.

"Lance and I aren't having sex yet. I'm still not certain Lance is right for me. We get along fairly well, but he has a temper."

"He's not still bossing you around is he?" Melissa asked.

"No, I don't let him, but the tendency is still there. Maybe when I'm certain he's got that under control permanently, we'll consider having kids."

Back in Corpus Christi . . .

Reggie rousted the boys early and got them on their way, while he made his way to the house. Linda had coffee ready by the time he got there.

"You wouldn't happen to have a state map would you, Linda?"

"I think there were several in Sandra's desk. Give me a second and I'll go check."

Linda came back a few minutes later and laid a map in front of him.

"Planning on doing a little traveling?" she asked.

"In order to get the area back to a more normal state after we're finished with Corpus Christi, Robbie's got it into his head to expand the democracy to the southern half of Texas. A two hundred-mile radius anyway. I don't have any state maps. If we know where we're going, we won't have near the trouble getting there."

"I think that's mighty courageous, Reggie."

"If we can stabilize a larger area, maybe we can get a substantial enough police force established that small groups of marauders can be eliminated. Re-arm the peaceful folks around us and show everyone that we won't take crap from anyone, then it will be much safer around here for all of us. I want my great-grandkids to have a future too."

Ronnie and Sean led the group back into the city. Zack and Lance followed in the truck. No sooner than they had gotten on their way, Zack asked Lance about the previous night.

"What was the deal with Beka," Zack asked.

"Beka never said a word about being a spy for Sandra," Lance replied.

"You shouldn't jump to conclusions. Maybe she was 'playing' at spying, or maybe she was forced. Sounds like Sandra made a lot of people do things they normally wouldn't have done."

"She should have told me dammit," Lance said.

Lance and Zack were quiet for the next hour, but Zack looked over at Lance from time to time. He continued to look at the scenery, but Zack could see he had other things on his mind, namely Beka.

I don't see what the big deal is, Zack thought. *Robbie never said anything about her being a spy. Maybe he didn't know. If Beka had been spying for Sandra, she would have known he was leaving and caught him. Maybe she wasn't spying on Robbie? She could have been spying for Robbie. What does Sean know?*

When they pulled into the parking lot at the Police compound, Ronnie's eyes locked on two unfamiliar cars parked out front.

He pressed hard on the accelerator and sped through the parking lot and out the other exit, the truck following close behind.

Before they made the cover of trees, bullets ricocheted off the roll-bar on the Jeep. Sean tried to get a few shots in, but Lance and Zack were in his line of fire.

Ronnie sped down the road and Lance followed closely. A few blocks down, Sean told Ronnie the men weren't following and he slowed to a stop. Lance and Zack pulled up alongside.

"You guys miss all the bullets?" Sean asked.

"I'm fine," Zack said.

Lance was holding the side of his head and when he pulled his hand away and showed it to Sean, it was covered in blood. Ronnie saw the blood too.

"Stay your post," he told Sean. "How bad is it?"

Zack pulled Lance over so he could see the side of his head. He wiped some of the blood away with his shirt sleeve so he could get a better look at the wound.

"Dammit, that hurts," Lance yelled.

Zack pushed him away and turned back to Ronnie. "He'll be fine. May have a little trouble hearing, but otherwise, he's okay."

Zack reached into his pocket and turned his attention back to Lance. "Be still." He opened his pocket knife behind Lance's back so he couldn't see what he was doing and sliced off the dangling piece of his ear lobe.

"Son-of-a-bitch!" Lance yelled.

Zack wrapped his handkerchief around Lance's head and tied it tight. Then he turned back to Ronnie and Sean, holding up the piece of an ear for them to see. "How about we go to the Bayfront when we get finished here. I've got bait."

The boys laughed. Satisfied Lance would be okay, Ronnie put the Jeep in gear and turned around. Sean swung the machine gun forward. Ronnie eased ahead and stopped concealed behind the side of a building, but just far enough that he could see the two cars still parked in front of the station.

He turned to Zack and Lance. "Get in the brush and take either side of the building. Watch for them to be in the woods too."

Ronnie gave them a minute to get into position and eased forward so Sean could get a shot at the far window, the door, then the other window. Sean showered the front side of the station with lead. Ronnie backed up to conceal the Jeep while Sean reloaded and then pulled forward again.

After Sean unloaded on the building again, the front cinder block wall crumbled and the roof collapsed inward, Ronnie heard both Lance and Zack shooting and Sean reloaded a second time. Ronnie pulled up again and Sean emptied half his canister.

The doorway and the two front windows were collapsed and the opening sealed. Ronnie sped forward to the far side of the building and around the backside. He spotted a man running down the side of the highway, a quarter mile away by now. Sean sprayed the man with the 30-cal, his arms flailed, and he went down to the pavement.

Ronnie turned the Jeep around and they returned their attention to the back of the Police Station. There was just enough room to get the Jeep between the station and the warehouse. They met Zack on the far side.

"I checked the inside," he said. "Lance and I got the man who ran out of the side door. One guy was crushed under the roof and another was in a pool of blood. Guess you got those, Sean."

"Let's make a thorough search," Ronnie said. "We don't want anyone getting away."

He and Sean headed for the roadway and made a few circles around the block while the other two searched the brush on foot. When Ronnie came around for the third time, Zack and Lance met them on the road.

"Looks like that's about it," Zack said.

"Chalk four more up for the good guys," Sean added.

Satisfied their work here was finished, the boys worked their way farther west and north. They made a big swing through the area zig-zagging the entire way. By late afternoon, they made their way to the Airport running into no more opposition.

The C-23 Sherpa was sitting on the tarmac and Ronnie decided they should check it out.

"Unless one or two of Sandra's men are out here, they shouldn't have guns," Sean said. "I don't think Russ had a gun, or at least I never saw one, and I know Jorge didn't."

Ronnie stopped four hundred yards from the plane and Zack pulled the truck up beside them.

"Move over there a ways," Ronnie said, pointing. "I'll fire a shot in the air and see what happens. Keep your heads down. Hopefully, there is only a mechanic or pilot around here."

Ronnie got out and moved behind the Jeep with his AR-15 ready. Zack and Lance did the same. Sean stayed on the machine gun. Ronnie pulled out his pistol and fired one shot into the air.

Seconds later, the hatch to the cockpit lowered and Ronnie could see a head peeking through the opening. That was the only person they could see.

"Come on out," Ronnie yelled. "We won't hurt you if you're unarmed."

A man dressed in flight clothes exited the plane with his arms in the air.

"Anyone else around here?" Ronnie yelled.

"No!" the man yelled back.

Rather than risk everyone, Ronnie decided to walk over to the plane and have a talk with the man. The rest could keep him covered.

Ronnie laid his rifle across his arm with his finger on the trigger and headed toward the plane, keeping a sharp eye out. He walked to within ten yards of the man and stopped.

"I guess you're a pilot?" Ronnie asked.

The man looked down at his flight uniform and nodded. Ronnie gave him a smirk.

"Are there any more pilots?"

"Yeah, there's one who lives over by the Hospital."

Ronnie moved closer to the man. "Do you know what's going on around here?"

"No."

"Well, Sandra is dead as are most of her men. We're hunting out any stragglers. Linda Gomez is running the Farm and the city now. There will be a democracy in the future."

The man just stood and stared, his mouth slightly ajar.

"Are you still making flights down to Brownsville?"

"The next flight is supposed to be next week. Are the vendors going to be here?"

"I don't know. I'll check with Linda when we get back to the Farm."

"And we'll need fuel too. I have enough for one more flight, but if I'm to go again, I'll need my tank filled."

"I'll let Linda know that too. Are the mechanics still coming out to work on the Sherpa?"

"Not lately, but they're not due here until just before the next flight. You look familiar."

"I don't think I've seen you before," Ronnie replied, extending his hand. "Excuse my manners. I'm Ronnie."

"I'm Arnold, but I prefer 'Shadow'."

Ronnie smiled. "Nice to meet you. I'll tell Linda about your concerns. I know how important these flights are to the city."

The man nodded with a curious look on his face and Ronnie headed back toward the Jeep.

It was nearly dark when the convoy pulled into the Farm. Linda had a big pork roast ready with all the trimmings. Over the meal, Ronnie and the boys informed Reggie, Linda, and Sally of the day's events. Sally cleaned Lance's ear. Ronnie also told Linda about the pilot and his concern over vendors and fuel.

"You'll take care of that won't you, Sally?"

Sally nodded.

Linda again offered the men a shower in the house.

"Hot water would be nice," Ronnie stated, looking hopefully at Reggie.

"Yeah, why not."

Sally showed the boys to three separate bathrooms and took their clothes after they undressed.

"How many bathrooms does this house have anyhow?" Sean asked.

"One in every bedroom and two more less private ones."

"And how many bedrooms?"

"I've never counted, but more than a dozen."

"Wow!" Sean exclaimed. "I've never seen more than one bathroom in a house. I've never seen more than two bedrooms in a house either."

"Put a robe on when you're finished," Sally told them.

When they were through, they came out in their robes and Reggie wrapped up his conversation with Linda. Sally showed him to a bathroom and took his clothes, then came back to work on Lance's ear some more, this time with ointment and proper dressings.

By the time Reggie was through, Sally had brought the boys clothes in and they changed. When Reggie returned in his robe, Linda brought out the cobbler and ice cream.

"My!" Reggie said, "this is quite a pleasant surprise."

The boys' eyes got as big as golf balls.

"Ice cream?" Ronnie asked. "Nothing like the ice cream I've ever had. This is really good."

Reggie, as well as the boys, each had a double helping of the pie, each with two scoops, and by the time they were done, Reggie's clothes were ready.

"I want to thank you very much for your hospitality, Linda. We'll be leaving at first light."

All the boys thanked Linda and they headed to the bus. Lance winked at Sally on the way out.

Chapter 25

At the crack-of-dawn, Ronnie cranked up the Jeep and Sean took his position on the machine gun. They both thought that would be a good idea at least until they got out of town. James started the bus and followed Ronnie. Zack and Lance brought up the rear. A few miles past the city limits, Sean crawled up front with Ronnie so they could talk.

"We did good, I think," Sean said.

"Yes, we did. I doubt we got all of Sandra's hoodlums, but hopefully, the Pink Ladies can take care of one or two. The next time we come back, we'll pick up Robbie and everything will be fine again. We can get some trade going and enough fuel to expand this fledgling democracy out to the surrounding areas and beyond."

"Democracy! Sounds good, doesn't it?"

Ronnie smiled.

A couple of miles from the cutoff to the homestead, Ronnie spotted a big buck in a small meadow. He took his foot off the accelerator and eased to a stop. Sean had his AR-15 ready. He made the two-hundred yard shot with ease hitting the buck in the eye. Its legs buckled and was dead before it hit the ground.

"Doing a little hunting, are we?" James asked.

"We've been tied up a bit lately," Ronnie replied. "I figured we need a little more meat at home. It was there, so why not?"

Sean laid his rifle down on the back seat of the Jeep and he and Ronnie went after the buck. The boys field dressed the deer in record time and they were back on the road within thirty minutes.

Ronnie pulled the Jeep in front of the Lindgren homestead at late-morning and honked the horn. Melissa was first out of the house. The other ladies bolted out after her with huge smiles on their faces.

Melissa wrapped her arms around James and gave him a big hug and kiss. She then hugged Ronnie. Her tears began to flow as she looked for Robbie.

"Where's Robbie?" she asked in a frantic voice.

"He's alright," James assured her, as he tried to take her in his arms again.

"Then where the hell is he?" she demanded, pushing him away.

James wrapped Melissa up in his arms again. As he explained what happened, she settled down a bit and he guided her up on the porch.

"We took him to the Hospital and he had very good doctors. He is awake, talking, and eating just fine."

"And pooping," Lance added.

"Yes, and pooping," James said, with a smile.

"And if he's fine, why isn't he here?"

"The doctors said it was best if he didn't travel. They wanted to keep an eye on him to make certain he healed properly. If he were here, he would likely have died, but the doctors in Corpus Christi saved his life. They operated on him and thanks to them we still have our son."

Ronnie and the other boys got the deer out of the Jeep and headed back to the rear of the house to process the meat.

"We'll need to have a meeting when you're finished," Reggie yelled after them.

By the time the boys butchered the deer, Melissa had settled down significantly and Reggie began the meeting.

"I think we were successful," he explained. "We eliminated most of Sandra's remaining police force the first day."

"Linda Gomez will be the new leader," James added. "I have confidence after talking to her, and Reggie working with her women, that they will be able to hold the city together. I wouldn't have left if I didn't."

"I trained a new all woman police force to deal with any threats," Reggie continued, "while the boys finished searching out Sandra's remaining thugs."

Melissa grinned. "All women? Did you have fun old man?"

Reggie frowned. "That's enough! I was just doing what I had to do."

Her grin widened. "I know you, Dad. You had your hands all over their hot, young bodies."

He got up. "You think you're too old to spank, little girl?"

Melissa smiled, put her thumb and index finger together, and zipped her mouth. Reggie had finished what he wanted to say and nodded to Ronnie. They headed upstream to Ronnie's place.

Now that the meeting was over, Lance grabbed Beka by the arm and dragged her around back to the pier. When they reached the pier, he yanked her around a little too hard for her comfort.

"What the hell are you doing?" she yelled, jerking away from his grasp.

The look in his eyes scared her.

"I might ask the same thing," he said. "Linda said you were one of Sandra's spies. The bitch tried to murder us all and you were working for her."

"It wasn't quite like that," Beka said.

"Well, exactly what was it like?"

Beka sat down on one of the chairs. "She was blackmailing me."

"How?"

"I was seeing a guy and she said she'd make sure I never saw him again if I didn't do what she said. She wanted me to keep tabs on Robbie. I did, but I never told her anything that would hurt him, Florence, or his chances of getting out of there.

"I saw Robbie as my chance of escaping Corpus. I decided that if Robbie left and I didn't tell Sandra, she'd think I helped him whether I did or not, and she would have killed me. I don't think I could have talked my way out of that, so I decided to leave with Robbie and Florence. Sandra made me a spy against my will, but I only told her a few lies, so I never really spied for her."

"Well, you should have told me," he said.

"Like you've told me about your whole life? I bet there's a skeleton or two in your closet. You want me to start yanking on your bones? And if you ever grab me like that again, I'm going to make you wish you never did."

Lance took a step back, his jaw dropping, and eyes open wide. "I'm sorry!"

Beka stormed back toward the house. After a few steps, she turned back around. "Maybe you should sit out here and think about the conclusions you jumped to, what you accused me of, and how you reacted. You expect us to build a relationship like this? If so . . . that damn well better not happen again!"

When Ronnie and Reggie made it to their house, Brooke, Emily, and Florence were sitting on the porch having tea. They returned Ronnie's wolf howl signal and the men approached.

When Ronnie saw Florence get up, he ran ahead hollering "it's okay!" As Ronnie drew close, she stepped off the porch, the other ladies following. Florence's stomach drew up in a knot and tears formed in her eyes.

"Where's Robbie?" she said, her voice trembling.

"He was hurt, but he is going to be fine. When we left, he was under a doctor's care, talking, and eating."

"And pooping," Reggie added, elbowing Ronnie in the side as he walked by. He gave Emily a hug and kiss, then turned back to Ronnie and Florence. "The doctors didn't think he should travel just yet. It was a serious injury. He lost a kidney, but he's strong. We'll pick him up on the next run."

Ronnie gave Florence a hug, took her by the shoulders, and put on his serious face. "We wouldn't have left him behind if we didn't know he would be safe. Dad made it really clear to the doctors that their lives depended on Robbie's recovery. We didn't have time to take a vote at the hospital, but the hospital staff seemed like rational people and the new democracy setup was explained to them."

When Florence settled down, everyone stepped up to the porch, and Reggie explained their progress in Corpus.

"We killed the police force and Corpus Christi has a new leader, Linda Gomez. Sandra's brutal dictatorship is no more and the city has settled down, so he should be fine there until he heals."

"I've got to see him," Florence demanded.

"Not until we make certain the new government has taken root," Reggie said.

"I'll go back in a few days and check on how Linda is getting along," Ronnie said. "I'll bring back a report and if everything is fine, maybe you can go the next time, or if Robbie is doing well enough, maybe I can bring him home. I don't think we should jeopardize his life moving him when the doctors warned against it."

Florence was hardly satisfied, but accepted the situation as it was. The main thing was that he was alive.

"Emily," Reggie said, "you about ready to get home? I need to catch up on my sleep. I'm getting too old."

"Yes, dear," she replied.

Chapter 26

A couple of days later . . .

Ronnie got up early and was sipping on his coffee at the dining room table when Florence came in dressed and ready for the new day.

"My, you're up early," he said.

"Yeah, I couldn't sleep. With Robbie in Corpus and you guys so busy these days, I thought I'd go down to the river to see if I could catch a fish or two. I'm fish hungry."

"Catch a big one for me. I'll be back in a day or so and I'll expect to see it hanging in the smokehouse when I get back here. I'm meeting Sean at Dad's."

Ronnie swigged down the last of his coffee and grabbed Brooke around the waist with one arm as he slipped his cup into the soapy dishwater in the sink with the other. He gave her a squeeze and a nibble on the neck.

"You be careful," she said and turned to give him a proper goodbye kiss.

Ronnie grabbed his backpack off the table, made a pass back by Brooke, patting her on the butt, and headed out the door.

Florence grabbed a quick half-cup of coffee and headed out the back door, picking up her fishing rod on the way. She scooped up a handful of earthworms out of the bait barrel beside the house and moseyed down to the river.

She got comfortable in the chair, baited her hook, and tossed her line in the stream still swollen from the recent rains.

As she sat and waited for a nibble, her mind drifted.

I do get a little more upset than Brooke and the rest of them when things don't go exactly like I want or expect. I don't like crying, but I can't help it . . . damn hormones! Robbie will always be in danger of some sort and if this country is going to improve, someone will have to make the effort. Nothing gets done without working at it. I know that.

Robbie and Ronnie have it in their minds they are the ones who need to put forth the effort and they are right. We are the new generation. It is up to us and other young people like us in the surrounding areas to work hard and make this country grow.

We have to be strong. Change is never easy and there will be people who will want things to stay as they are. Some will fight back and some will die, but over time all our lives will get better . . . we will be safer in the long term. But for now, life will be hard. I have to be strong. Robbie is already tough as boot leather. I have to be resilient for him . . . for me . . . for my baby . . . our baby . . . our future. I can't be crying all the time.

Florence heard a noise in a nearby tree and turned to look. A squirrel rustled the leaves as it searched for a morning meal. Florence smacked her gums to simulate a squirrel chatter like Robbie taught her. The critter stopped what it was doing and looked at her, then went on about its business.

Such a carefree life. All you have to worry about is your next meal. No squirrel wars. All you have to be concerned about is Robbie or Ronnie if they get squirrel hungry. No, I won't bother you, today anyway. But if you get shot, how will your mate feel? Maybe life is not so easy on you either. Maybe that's just the way life is.

Florence turned her attention back to her rod. She watched a log drifting downstream and her gaze followed it along until it floated around the bend.

Her attention snapped back to her rod tip as it jerked downward. She waited like Robbie had shown her for a strong tug. *Catfish nibble at first. You have to wait until they get the worm and hook into their mouth.*

Florence waited and directly the fish grabbed the bait and ran. She jerked hard on her rod and felt the fish pull back as the hook grabbed hold of its lip. Her rod tip bent sharply toward the water and Florence held on. She reeled the line in, but the fish pulled back hard. Line spooled off against the drag.

Patience. This is a big one.

She looked around for the dip net. It was laying on the cleaning table. Florence stood up and wrestled with the fish as she slowly reeled it in. The fish wanted to stay on the bottom, but she insisted it come to the top so she could dip it up.

Florence struggled with the monster.

I've never felt a fish pull this hard. Please don't get off.

Finally, the fish broke the top of the water. Her mouth gaped open and she sucked in a big breath of the fresh morning air. She'd never seen a fish this big.

"Brooke!" she screamed.

Brooke opened the back door.

"You okay?" she yelled.

"Help!"

Brooke ran down the steps toward the river.

"Hurry," Florence yelled again. "Get the dip net."

Florence reeled the fish up close to the pier. Brooke leaned over and scooped it up to pull it onto the deck.

Florence panted in quick breaths. She could feel her heart beating a battle tune in her chest. She stared at the flathead catfish inside the net flapping its gill plates, then at Brooke who had a big smile on her face.

"Wow!" Brooke exclaimed.

Both girls burst out laughing. Florence could feel the tension of the battle with the big fish fading. Her anxiety had turned to relief when she got the monster safely out of the water, to happiness of landing such a big fish, and now to dread as she knew she had to gut the critter.

"You know what they say," Brooke said, "you catch it; you clean it."

Sean met Ronnie at the Lindgren homestead. They got the Jeep ready for another trip to Corpus Christi. Lance and Zack asked to go along, but Ronnie wanted to keep the back seat open in case they were able to bring Robbie home. He was certain Robbie would be weak and would need the whole seat to stretch out if it were possible for him to make the trip.

Ronnie and Sean reached the edge of Corpus Christi shortly after noon. Sean manned the machine gun as they drove into town just in case. They worked their way to the Hospital. Ronnie took a quick look around, hopped out, and ran inside.

"What the hell do you mean he's not here?" Ronnie demanded.

Ronnie pushed the doctor up against the wall and put his AR-15 under his chin.

"This is not necessary," the doctor whimpered. "Linda took your brother. Other than that, I know nothing."

Ronnie pushed off the doctor and rushed out of the hospital to where Sean was waiting at the turret on the back of the Jeep.

"What's going on?" Sean asked.

"I'm not sure," he replied. "Robbie's not here. The doctor said Linda came and got him."

Ronnie cranked up the Jeep.

"Let's see what Linda's got to say."

Ronnie headed toward the Farm. On the way, he was met by a pink car. He stopped and waited to see what it and its occupants would do. The car stopped a hundred feet away. Two people got out, one on either side and lowered their guns at Ronnie and Sean.

"Hold your fire," Ronnie told Sean. Ronnie got out and raised his arms into the air.

"Walk forward."

Ronnie walked to within ten feet of the pink car. "You don't recognize me, ladies?"

"Just making sure," one said. "Linda told us to not trust anyone."

"And does that include me?"

"No. We owe you our newfound freedom. We just wanted to make certain it was really you. Linda is at the Farm. She said to take you to her as soon as you arrived. You may follow us, good sir."

Ronnie followed the pink car the rest of the way to the Farm. One of the two guards at the front of the house showed Ronnie to Linda inside.

"What's going on?" Ronnie asked.

"Just being careful," Linda replied. "I'm not sure who I can and cannot trust at this point. Word had gotten around that Robbie was at the Hospital. It's easier to keep him safe here. Come on, I'll take you to him. He's been asking about you. Robbie's doing much better. I have one of the nurses from the Hospital here. She's making certain he stays stable and recovers completely."

Down a long hallway, then another corridor, Linda led Ronnie to a room tucked away in the back of the farmhouse. She reached over, turned the doorknob, and let it swing open. Ronnie walked in and Linda turned the dimmer switch to brighten the room a bit. She then pulled the door shut and left Ronnie and Robbie to talk in private.

"I was worried when we didn't find you at the Hospital. At least you have a little color back, Robbie."

"It's good to see you, Brother. It gets mighty boring around here with only a ceiling to look at. The nurse tells me it'll be a couple more weeks before I'll be able to get out of here. How's Florence? Did you tell her I loved her?"

"She's okay but worried about you. If the city is safe enough, I thought I'd bring her here to see you."

"I would really like that, but you make sure it's safe for her and my baby."

"So, how are you getting along?"

"I've been able to make it to the bathroom a few times on my own. Maybe next week, I'll be able to venture outside. Then I'll be ready to go home."

"Anything I can bring you other than Florence?" Ronnie asked, with a smile.

"The heads of any remaining members of the opposition," Robbie replied. "Anyone who would do harm to me, the city, Linda, or my Florence and baby. That's all."

"I'll do what I can, but it looks like things are pretty much in control around here. There may not be any heads to chop anymore. The Pink Ladies are certainly on high alert. Looks like they're taking care of things."

Ronnie rejoined Sean and Linda in the kitchen. He was eating.

"Can I get you something to eat?" Linda asked.

"Whatever Sean is having," he replied, looking over at his plate.

Linda nodded at her cook.

"Well, how are things going in the city?" Ronnie asked.

"We've secured the Police compound," Linda replied. "You sure made a mess of the building."

"I'm sorry, but we had to get the men inside."

"I know. We moved stuff we needed from inside the office to the warehouse. No one has tried to get at the guns there, so maybe all the old police force is gone. The Pink Ladies haven't reported anyone coming around. The bad news is all the shipments of beef and venison to the packing plant have stopped. They were, after all, the ones doing all the hunting. We've got to get the operation back online before the stock at the plant runs out. Several of the ladies are working on that.

"I've secured the Airport, Hospital, and Contractor compounds. The Contractors are on board with our new plan. They are working as we speak to make sure the refinery is secure and production is stable. The shipments to and from Brownsville have stayed on schedule. All that is left to take care of is the Bayfront.

"I'm a little afraid of what Marcia Nguyen might do, but I guess there's no point in putting off the inevitable."

Ronnie finished his breakfast. "Well, let's go see if the Bayfront is going to be a problem. We'll give you backup."

Sean and Ronnie got up and Linda followed them outside. Linda got in the passenger side while Sean manned the machine gun.

"When I made it over to the Contractor compound," Linda said, "word had already reached them that Sandra was gone and that I was going to form a new government. I don't think Sandra was very well liked around there. They agreed with what I said and assured me they would back me for the first year."

When they got to the Bayfront, they checked on the seafood, ice, and the desalinization plants. Marcia was at neither, but the plants seemed to be moving ahead, business as usual.

"Now Marcia's," Linda said, nervously.

Linda pointed out the direction to Marcia's home, but instructed Ronnie to park a block away so she wouldn't see Sean. Linda and Ronnie walked to the house.

Marcia's truck was in the driveway and Linda knocked on the door. Little Lola's bright face greeted them.

"My, aren't you getting to be a big girl," Linda said.

Marcia came to the door as well. The look on her face said Linda was not welcome there, but she listened as the new mayor laid out how things were going to be from now on. The fact that Lola wouldn't be whisked away to the Farm when she turned sixteen to become one of Sandra's slaves eased the mood, but Linda's woman's intuition told her that Marcia wasn't convinced.

Linda told Marcia she would retain complete autonomy over the Bayfront and seafood packing plants.

"You run things as you see fit and report to me as you did to Sandra weekly," Linda said. "You keep things running smoothly and you can do pretty much whatever you like around here."

Marcia kept eying Ronnie. She knew he wasn't Robbie, but never asked. Either she guessed they were brothers, or she didn't care.

Ronnie and Linda left, just as uneasy about Marcia as they were before they got here, but satisfied they did all they could. They decided to stop by the Airport on the way back to the Farm.

"You boys sure made a tangled heap around here," Linda said.

"It couldn't be helped," Ronnie replied. "We couldn't let Sandra come to Peaceful Valley with a jet. She could have destroyed our homes and probably would have killed us all."

"I know. At least we still have the transport plane," Linda replied. "Looks like everything is going alright around here. They'll make another trip to Brownsville in a few days. I guess we'll be keeping the C-23 outside from now on. It won't fit in the other buildings."

Ronnie waved at Shadow. The pilot looked over and smiled.

Linda nodded to Ronnie and he cranked the Jeep up. They headed back to the Farm. When they got there, Ronnie and Sean stepped in to see his brother again before they left.

"Take it easy, Bro," Ronnie said, and rejoined Linda in the kitchen.

"We'll be back in a few days," Ronnie said. "It looks like it's safe enough to bring Florence to see Robbie."

"I'm sure they'll both like that," Linda said. "I'll set up a meeting with all the heads of the compounds and see if we can formally get our new government established. It would be great to have you boys here for that."

Sean manned the machine gun while Ronnie drove them out of town. After they were well out of the city, Ronnie stopped so Sean could ride in front with him. They were quiet for a long time.

"Something the matter?" Sean asked.

"Everything just seems to be a little too easy," Ronnie replied.

"What do you mean?"

"We just overthrew a government. All the ex-cops seem to be gone now and everyone is going along with the new government."

"What's wrong with that?" Sean asked.

"When has anything ever gone this smoothly?" Ronnie replied. "It hasn't even been that peaceful in Peaceful Valley and there's only around twenty of us. There are a few thousand in Corpus Christi and for everything to go as well as it has, that just doesn't seem natural.

"Is everyone there just a bunch of sheep? Does no one have their own opinions about how things should change? Even Marcia who seemed to be 100% on Sandra's shirt sleeve is now 90% on Linda's side."

"Maybe if they were moving in the opposite direction, there would be some stiff opposition," Sean said, "but they are moving in a direction for the betterment of all. It's a lot easier to move from a dictatorship to a democracy than it would be the other way around. I think everyone should feel a sense of relief. Things will get much better for everyone and if they're not satisfied, then they can leave upright, not to an early grave as it would have been with Sandra."

"You may be right," Ronnie said, "but things have never been effortless for us no matter what was going on. Life just isn't easy, ever. And now to change a whole city, thousands of people nearly overnight. It just doesn't seem right. That's all I'm saying."

The topics of discussion then drifted off to deer and turkey along the way, and about Florence, Kim, and Brenda. Both would be fathers before long, more or less. Though Brenda would be having Robbie's baby, Sean thought of himself as the father.

Brooke grabbed Ronnie up in a passionate embrace and showered him with kisses when he arrived home.

"Have I told you how much I love you lately?" she asked.

Florence laid her book down and got up. When Brooke was finished lavishing him with affection, she pulled him around by the arm. "What about Robbie? When is he coming home?"

"Not until we know it's safe for him to travel."

Florence plopped down at the dining room table, put her chin on her hand, and stared across the room with a forlorn look. Ronnie and Brooke sat down with her. Brooke patted her on the arm. "I know you want to see him. Think on the bright side. He's healing and you two *will* get back together soon. Now come on, you wouldn't want Robbie to see you pouting like this."

Florence wiped her tears and got up. "No, I guess not."

Here I am crying again. They're right, Robbie is alive and that's all that matters. Pull yourself together . . . and show him the fish.

She took hold of Ronnie's hand and pulled him up and toward the back door.

"Where are we going?"

"Wait and see." She giggled.

Florence pulled the door open to the smokehouse and pointed with a big grin on her face.

"You?"

"Brooke helped me land it, but I caught him all by myself."

"And is this dinner?"

"Just like you ordered."

"If that's how things are going on around here, when I get back next time, I'd like a big pork roast with potatoes and brown gravy. And with lots of onions cooked in."

Florence gave him a smirk.

"Oh, but you can't do that next time. I forgot you have something better to do," Ronnie teased.

Florence's eyebrows slid together as she squinted at him.

"What?"

"You'll need to escort me to Corpus Christi."

Florence's face lit up like a Christmas tree. "Really?"

"Yes, really. I think Corpus is safe enough to take you there now. Besides, Robbie misses you and he needs you. He'll heal faster if you're there. And just maybe he can come back with us."

Florence squealed and wrapped her arms around his neck.

"Thank you!" She gave him a peck on the cheek, then pushed him back. "Wait a minute," and she hit him. "Dammit, you made me cry!"

"I'm sorry," he said, with a snicker.

Florence hit him again, as did Brooke.

Chapter 27

Three days later in Corpus Christi . . .

Linda had the main barn at the Farm arranged with chairs, tables, and a podium up front. A table was set up with coffee, donuts, and cheesecake. Present were six representatives from the Contractors. This was the largest group representing more than fifteen hundred contractors. Four were present from the Bayfront including Marcia Nguyen, two from the Hospital, a pilot from the Airport, and half of the Pink Ladies, which had grown to thirty strong, for security.

Reggie came along with Ronnie, Sean, and Florence. Reggie was to be the representative for Peaceful Valley.

Robbie was able to attend the meeting. His wounds continued to heal, to the delight of Florence.

She wrapped her arms around him and rained kisses all over his face. "I've missed you so much. I was so worried when you didn't come home. It's been terrible without you, especially at night. I woke up every morning snuggled with your pillow."

"I missed you too," he replied. "Everything will be better now. If you have room for me in the Jeep, I'll go back home this time."

"We'll make room," Ronnie said, overhearing their conversation.

When Marcia walked in, she immediately spotted Sean with the Peaceful Valley group. She walked toward them with a sinister look on her face and shoved Sean. "I know what you did to Sonny!"

Reggie grabbed her and pulled her away from Sean. Linda, noticing the commotion, nodded at a couple of nearby Pink Ladies, who came over to assist.

"I left Sonny tied up, but alive on the boat," Sean rebutted. "I don't know what happened to him after that."

Marcia huffed and gave him a glare of disbelief. "You'll pay for what you did!"

The Pink Ladies took her by the arms and pulled her away.

"You'll pay!" she repeated over her shoulder, with a fierce look on her face as the Pink Ladies led her across the room. Linda pointed to a chair at the end of the front row where she could keep an eye on her.

When Marcia was seated, Linda tapped her gavel on the lectern. "Let's come to order." She glanced back at Marcia while everyone took their seats.

Linda took a deep breath and looked over the crowd. "The first order of business is to make certain every one of you know what is to happen here in Corpus Christi. There will be one chief at each compound who will report directly to me. Each compound will hold its own election as soon as practical. Every adult will vote if they choose to do so and the ballots will be anonymous. I will oversee the elections and the Pink Ladies will count the votes.

"I will be Mayor for one year. After a year, there will be elections to vote for my successor should the masses decide I am no longer fit to govern the city. There will be elections every four years for mayor and chief, but after two years for the chiefs in the first election only. We can't be changing the whole government every four years.

"The chiefs are free to choose their subordinates. The main thing I'm concerned about is that the work, which is necessary for our survival and to make the city run smoothly, gets done efficiently.

"In addition to being the mayor, I will stay at and manage the Farm. However, I will choose someone I can trust to get the job done there as well. Currently, I am thinking I will assign that task to Sally Beecher. My primary job will be to make sure all the compounds run at peak performance and everyone is getting along. We need to make certain everyone eats well and works hard.

"If someone is not happy with the way things work, they can leave. Their respective chief is to be notified of their request, the chief and the ones wanting to leave shall come to me, and they will be escorted out of the city. It's as simple as that. There will be no more killings like there was under Sandra's rule."

"And when the Peaceful Valley people came!?" a man remarked.

Linda took a drink of water. "They did what they had to do to get us to the point we are now at."

That was all she said and the man kept quiet. Linda stood for a moment and looked over the crowd to try to gauge their reaction thus far.

"There will be no more castrations," she continued. "It may take a while, but eventually there will be enough males so we can have a fertile population. The populace will be able to choose who they make a family with, but for the current time, due to the lack of viable males, ladies will be fertilized as I see fit. Brownsville could prove to be a feasible source of sperm, but for our current needs, Peaceful Valley can supply us with what we need. It can be done through a process of artificial insemination if they choose."

Reggie looked over at Robbie, Ronnie, and Florence. They were looking at each other too.

"I don't think I feel comfortable with you spreading your sperm all over Corpus Christi again," Florence whispered to Robbie.

"Don't look at me," Sean whispered to Ronnie. "I'm not going to be part of the process."

Robbie squirmed in his seat a little at her words. He wasn't certain he wanted to be part of the process either, after what he went through with Sandra, though he did enjoy the girls. They would need to have a private discussion about this subject a little later.

When Sean spoke up, he caught Marcia looking straight at him. The look on her face made him uneasy and he looked away immediately.

"Are there any questions?" Linda asked.

"What if we don't like our job?" one man asked.

"There's no guarantee that you'll like what you do," Linda replied. "You can discuss that with your chief, and if you can find someone to replace you, or if your job's not necessary, then maybe you can move to another job or even another compound. Chiefs will post job openings around at the other compounds, and just maybe you can make a move.

"There will be an adjustment period where your situation may not seem to change much, but over time I hope everyone can be a little happier with their work than they were under Sandra.

"I know we will need a much larger police force now that all of Sandra's men are gone. This is one area where we need to be strong, not so much for enforcement within, as for protection from intruders who might upset our new government. I will post jobs around the various compounds and anyone who is interested can apply."

A woman raised her hand and Linda nodded. "Now that we don't have much of a police force to protect us from outside threats, how do our compounds protect ourselves?"

"We have a force of thirty now, and over time that number will grow. But for the meantime, each chief and maybe a few of his subordinates will be issued guns," Linda replied. "Until we get our police force built up, it will mostly be up to the compounds to protect themselves. The Pink Ladies will patrol the perimeter and on a limited basis in the interior of the city, but the bulk of your protection will come from you. I know it will be an adjustment, but we'll manage."

"I haven't had any beef or venison for a couple weeks," another man said. "What's going on in that department?"

"The meat is at the packing plant," Linda said. "It was primarily up to the old police force to harvest and process it. The hunting and butchering have stopped, but there's plenty in storage. We'll just have to work on delivery.

"And that brings up another problem. With our small police force, the hunting of red meat has stopped. The Pink Ladies can't handle that job at this point. We need to get that going soon. You sir," Linda said, pointing at the man who asked about job changes, "maybe you'd like to change jobs now, depending upon how badly you're needed at your current position."

"I can do that," he replied.

"If there are a few more men available," Linda said, looking primarily at the representatives from the Contractors, "we could use at least a dozen men to do the hunting. Oyster production is good now, but with our meager shrimp production due to the hurricane, we need to boost our red meat supplies. So, those with hunting experience, come see me and we will form some teams."

Linda paused a few seconds and looked around at all the confused faces staring back at her. "Is there anything else?" No one spoke up though she could feel there were more unanswered questions. She glanced over to Reggie and gave him a nod.

Reggie stood up and introduced himself to the group. "Peaceful Valley has made it possible for a new future for Corpus Christi without the likes of Sandra Hawkins. We have gone to war for the city, not entirely at our own choosing, but we risked life and limb for Corpus. Now that Sandra is gone, we want a token of appreciation for all we've done. We don't want a lot, but we want something.

"Now that there is the possibility of trade between Peaceful Valley and Corpus Christi, I would like to address some of our needs. We don't have many requests, but when Robbie got hurt badly, that reminded me that we don't have access to competent medical and dental care.

"You have access to salt, sugar, tea, coffee, and a few spices we could use. We *do* have the best recipe for Pickled Beets known to man!"

A few chuckled, but most of the attendees stared with blank expressions on their faces.

Tough audience!

Reggie moved on. "I'm not sure I know what we can provide in return, but we'll do what we can."

"You have already given us a great gift in our freedom," Linda said. "You risked your lives for us and have suffered as a result. I think we can accommodate you with a few tokens of our appreciation.

"I think our greatest need from you is sperm. Richard Ingalls, Mathew Helms, Conrad Baker, Billy Drake, and three of our pilots were the only fertile men in the city. All but one of the pilots are dead now. One pilot cannot take care of our needs."

"That's all?" Reggie was shocked.

"Sandra didn't keep many 'true' men around," Linda replied. "You know about Billy Drake. A couple of pilots were in the hangar when it went up in flames, Louise Ingalls killed her husband, Richard, and Sandra took care of Mathew Helms. So to answer your question, yes, that's all."

Reggie looked over at Ronnie and Robbie. Florence had a frustrated look on her face. "We'll do what we can," he said.

Reggie wasn't sure what they could do, but he knew they had needs as did Linda and the city. They had to come up with a solution.

Shortly after the meeting, Ronnie drove them back to Peaceful Valley. Robbie went back with them, but the doctors wanted to see him again in a couple of weeks.

Sean mentioned Marcia's staring at him to Robbie and Ronnie.

Robbie scratched his head in thought. "We have to defuse this, or Marcia is going to be a problem."

"When Linda and I went to see her last week, she went along with our new plan," Ronnie said. "She seemed happy that the city would be changing. Besides, she would still be taking care of things at the Bayfront."

"But she didn't see me then," Sean added. "She now knows I'm a part of the new plan, and she didn't look happy today."

"We need to make her doubt her suspicions," Robbie said. "I don't think she'd listen now, but let's let her simmer down and we'll have another talk with her."

Chapter 28

Back in Peaceful Valley . . .

Robbie did what he could over the next couple of weeks, but that wasn't much at first. He helped Florence with meals and setting the table, but mostly what he did was read and think. Ronnie did most of the heavier chores.

Florence didn't care what he could and couldn't do. She was happy he was home and healing. Her belly was growing larger every day and her walk turned into more of a waddle. She was a contented pregnant lady with Robbie safely by her side.

Florence was like a mother hen when they first met in Corpus Christi. She nursed Robbie back to health. She loved taking care of him and fussed over every ache and pain when he tried to get up to go to the bathroom or assured her he could fix his own plate when he was hungry. She insisted on helping him, but Robbie had always been independent. It was difficult for him to ask for help, or even accept it when it was given freely if he thought he could manage by himself.

By the end of the first week at home, he had gained a significant amount of his strength back and most of his pain had subsided. His muscles steadily gained vigor due to his wife's cooking. He never complained about the Hospital food, but it wasn't home cooking.

At the end of the second week, he knew he wasn't totally healed, but he felt he could handle most anything by then. He didn't have the endurance when he chopped wood, but he could manage for a short while. He knew the only way he would get back to 100% was to work at it and that is exactly what he did to Florence's dismay. Shortly after the first week home, she gave up trying to slow him down.

After two weeks, Robbie, Ronnie, and Sean prepared the Jeep for another trip to Corpus Christi, so the doctors could give Robbie a final check, but also to check in on the fledgling democracy.

Lance decided he wanted to go along as well, so Reggie said he'd stay home. Ronnie and Sean had been handling the Corpus affairs well up to this point, so Reggie didn't see a need to accompany them.

As the boys pulled up on the outskirts of the city, things didn't seem quite right. There was the distinct odor of smoke, which they hadn't smelled before and the air was hazy. Sean manned the machine gun turret and Ronnie proceeded in the direction of the Hospital where Robbie could get checked out first.

Just before arriving at the Hospital, Ronnie spotted a pink car just off the roadway. Both doors were open on either side of the car.

As he pulled up alongside, he could see someone slumped against the steering wheel. Ronnie got out and Sean went to high alert. Ronnie spotted a second body on the ground outside the passenger door as he pulled the first body back against the seat. It was Sally Beecher. Then he went around to check on the other body. It was Linda Gomez.

"What the hell is going on?" Robbie asked.

"I don't know," Ronnie said, "but it's not good. You guys check your guns and stay alert."

"Maybe Marcia stirred up a ruckus," Sean said, with a frown.

No one said anything, but Sean did give them food for thought. Ronnie got back into the Jeep and headed toward the Hospital. Lance and Ronnie ran in to find the compound empty. There were no bodies, but though they did not check the entire building, they knew things were not normal.

Ronnie and Lance made their way back to the Jeep and headed toward the Farm. "Looks like you're not going to get your checkup," Ronnie said.

"I'm feeling fine," Robbie said. "A little scared about what is going on around here, but otherwise just fine."

Halfway to the Farm, Ronnie saw a vehicle coming up the road. He stopped and Sean aimed the machine gun at it, as did Lance and Robbie their rifles. The car slowed but continued toward the Jeep. It stopped thirty yards in front of the boys. The driver got out and walked toward them.

"I'm sure glad to see you," she said.

Ronnie recognized the girl from the Farm though he didn't know her name.

"What's going on?" he asked.

"Some men came to the Farm and demanded fuel for their vehicles. When the Pink Ladies confronted them, the men started shooting."

"Where are they now?" Ronnie asked.

"They left," she replied. "I don't know where they went. I've got to get to the Hospital. I have a nurse in the car and we need to get there for more supplies."

"We just came from there," Ronnie said. "There's no one around."

"No, they're all at the Farm."

"Is it safe there?"

"I think so. The doctors are working on the injured."

Ronnie hopped back in the Jeep.

"Okay, we're going on to the Farm."

The lady got back in her car and pulled around the Jeep. Ronnie crammed the gearshift into forward and headed toward the Farm. When they got there, the main house was burned to the ground and still smoldering. There were people scattered everywhere picking up the pieces from the mayhem which had occurred.

"Who's in charge?" Ronnie asked one of the ladies scurrying around the area.

She pointed to the main barn, then hurried away. Lance and Robbie followed Ronnie to the barn, while Sean remained on the machine gun turret, eyeing the chaos and the surroundings for potential danger.

Inside the barn were over a dozen nurses and five doctors working on numerous patients stretched out on two dozen tables. Some were quiet while others were screaming in agony. Ronnie approached one of the tables where the doctor was working while Lance and Robbie circulated about.

"Can you tell me what happened, Doc?" Ronnie asked.

"Can't you see I'm busy here? Check with the girls," he grumbled.

Ronnie turned and walked over to Lance and Robbie who were mingling around watching all that was going on, when a big gal dressed in pink walked in from the rear of the barn. Ronnie recognized her immediately from the previous visit to the Farm when Reggie was choosing the new police force. She was at the back of the crowd of ladies and was the first one to hold up her hand. She walked right up to them.

"What's going on?" Ronnie asked.

"I'm trying to get this hell-hole back in order," she replied.

"Who gave the responsibility to you?" Ronnie asked.

"I did. One of my ladies found Linda and Sally on the side of the road over toward the Hospital."

"Your ladies?"

"Yes, since I'm the new Chief of Police, the responsibility fell with me."

"Do you know who did this?"

"No one around here had ever seen them before. Just a bunch of men in trucks. Yesterday at dusk, they drove in and demanded fuel. When the few Pink Ladies here at the Farm told them 'No', they started shooting.

"There are no major farming operations going on now, so our fuel tank is nearly empty. They took what they could, but it wasn't much. They hit the Contractors too, so I assume they eventually got what they needed."

"Anything else?" Robbie asked.

"They didn't take anything from what I can see. A few of the girls were raped and beaten. As far as I can tell, they burned the house down just because they could."

"Which way did they leave?" Lance asked.

"They were headed south the last time I saw them," she replied.

"Where are the Pink Ladies?" Ronnie asked.

"Half of them are dead. They were no match for the men. The ones who tried were killed. The rest got scared and hid. Now, they're questioning people at the Contractors compound to try to figure out the extent of the damage."

Ronnie looked around the barn at the patients and a long line of bodies lined up against a back wall he hadn't noticed before.

"Have you seen Marcia?" Robbie asked.

"No."

"So," Ronnie said, "since you are taking over around here, shouldn't we know your name?"

"Sorry," she replied. "I'm Christine."

"Just Christine?" Lance asked.

"I don't have a last name. Never knew who my daddy was. No need for more than one name around here anyway."

"I don't know you very well, Christine. Are you good to continue with Linda's plan?"

"I worked with Sandra a long time," she replied, "but I never really liked her and the way she ran things. A lot of the other gals didn't either. Take Jade. I know you remember her," she added, looking over at Robbie.

Robbie blushed. "Yes, ma'am."

"I'm inclined to continue with Linda's plan, but first let's see what's needed to get order established here again," Christine said.

Ronnie breathed a sigh of relief as did Robbie.

"That's good to hear," Ronnie said. "Then I guess we'll be helping you from now on. We'll do what we can and I look forward to getting things back in order soon."

"Is there anything we can do now?" Robbie asked.

"Not really," she replied. "We can get things cleaned up around here. Some of the contractors will be here tomorrow to get a few of the bigger messes taken care of. The farmhouse will need to be rebuilt. I guess the main thing I need is to make sure those men are gone and don't come back."

"We'll take a look around today, then we'll head back to Peaceful Valley first thing in the morning," Ronnie said, seeing Christine had things well under control. "We'll be back next week though."

With that, Ronnie, Robbie, and Lance headed back out to the Jeep. When they climbed in, Robbie filled Sean in.

"I told you things seemed a little too easy," Ronnie stated.

Sean gave him a sneer.

"Do you think Marcia could be behind this?" Lance asked.

"That's certainly a possibility," Robbie replied. "But if they're locals, where did they get the guns?"

"They could have gotten them out of the Police station without us knowing about it," Ronnie said, "or someone could have had a stash of weapons and ammo all along. It could even be the rest of Sandra's men. They might have waited to mobilize until they saw us leaving. They could have been watching us all the time from afar and we'd never have seen them. We were just roaming the highways."

The boys checked their guns and Sean got back on the turret while Ronnie drove first through the Contractors compound, made a loop around the Hospital, then around the Police Station.

Ronnie saw cars at the Police Station and decided to pull in. A couple of well-armed Pink Ladies came out, but the ladies recognized the Jeep.

"There are only five of us here," one of the girls said. "We thought it better to guard the station than to go out on rounds."

"You're probably right," Ronnie said. "We're making a trip through the compounds to see if we can find the guys who shot up the city. We'll be back next week to check on how you are doing. Try not to shoot us."

The ladies smiled.

"No promises," one said, with a wink.

The boys continued around the meat packing plant and then down toward the Bayfront. They didn't see anything unusual and zig-zagged back to the Hospital as the sun settled on the horizon. That was the only place they could think of where there were plenty of beds.

The building was still empty and quiet. At dark, some of the staff filtered in. The boys informed them they would be staying the night. One of the nurses told them the third floor was empty and they made their way up the stairs. At the end of a hallway, they found two rooms to their liking. They booby-trapped the stairway, elevator, and the far end of their hall.

They had running water and decided to take showers since they had the opportunity. After the last finished showering, they played rock/paper/scissors to see who stood guard first.

The next morning, the boys washed their faces, grabbed their gear, and carefully made their way to where they stashed the Jeep. The first thing Robbie brought up was Marcia.

"If she was behind the rampage the other day, why did she burn the farmhouse? That doesn't make sense."

No one said anything and they were quiet as they drove back toward Peaceful Valley. After they got well out of the city, "you know," Robbie said, "I've been thinking about this for a while. Laid up in bed gives you the time.

"It seems we are always at war these days. Every time we turn around, there is someone who wants to stir up trouble. We need a formidable police force going in a wider area as soon as possible. It looks like Christine will take up the slack in Corpus, but we need to start visiting neighboring cities to see if someone can help out there."

"We do have dependable transportation now," Ronnie said. "If we can contact some of the communities around us, maybe they're having the same problems we are and would be willing to help."

"What about fuel?" Lance asked. "We have some, but not enough to go traipsing all over the country."

"There are a lot of abandoned gas stations still around," Ronnie said. "We've been able to get some out of them with Reggie's portable pump. There must be more around that haven't been tapped."

"We didn't grow up in the peaceful country our parents remember," Robbie said. "If it's going to be a place without war in our lifetime, I think we're going to need to be the ones to make that happen. Us and other like-minded folks like us."

"It's certainly something to think about," Ronnie said. "We should talk to Mom and Dad. Maybe it's time for a new and different kind of adventure."

"And Grandpa," Robbie said. "We talked about this a little a while back. It's time we had a more serious discussion."

In Peaceful Valley . . .

The following morning, Ronnie ran over to Grandpa Reggie's and asked him and Emily to make a trip over to James and Melissa's. Robbie went ahead to his mom and dad's with Florence and Brooke and brought them up to date on the situation in Corpus Christi.

When Reggie and Emily showed up with Ronnie, Ronnie had already informed his grandparents about what was going on in Corpus. Sean was over at James and Melissa's to see Brenda and Kim.

"I had a lot of time to think while I was recovering," Robbie said, looking at his elders. "You had your own obstacles to overcome after the grid went down."

He looked toward his parents where they sat by Reggie and Emily and nodded. "But lately it seems we just go from one battle to another. There have to be other people out there who are experiencing the same thing. There have to be pockets of survivors who would be willing to die for a chance to live in peace again. I think we need to search out those folks and band together to form a new and stronger government than we could do in the little groups we are currently in."

"You mentioned that a while back," Reggie said. "You still working on that?"

"Yes, Grandpa."

"How big an area are you talking about?" Reggie asked, with an inquisitive look.

"The whole state," Ronnie replied.

James leaned back in his chair with a big smile. "That's a mighty big area, Son."

Robbie raised his eyebrows and cocked his head. "Well, maybe not the *whole* state, but maybe a two or three hundred-mile radius around Corpus Christi."

"That's still a lot of real estate," Reggie pointed out.

"We can't have a government way out here in the middle of nowhere," Melissa said.

"That's where Corpus Christi comes in," Robbie said. "If we can get Corpus under control, that can be where the central government will be."

"And who's going to lead this government?" Brooke asked. "If you're thinking about you or Ronnie, Florence and I don't want to move to Corpus. We like it here."

"No," Robbie said, "I thought Sean would be the new governor."

"What!?" Sean exclaimed.

Robbie had not told Sean of his plan for him to become governor of the state. Robbie knew he didn't want to lead the new state and since Ronnie was a lot like him, he figured Ronnie wouldn't want the job either. But, since Sean liked shrimping and Brenda and Kim were from Corpus, Sean could take the job and maybe even get in a little shrimping when he wanted.

"How about what's her name . . . Christine?" Sean asked.

"I don't think she's strong enough to handle the job," Ronnie replied. "She's new to the Police force, and though she is the Chief of Police now, she still has a lot of farmer in her."

"But Linda had a lot of mechanic in her," Sean brought up.

"Besides Sean, you have a lot in common with all the men in Corpus with the exception of one pilot," Ronnie added. "I think they will bond with you on account of that alone. And you are a leader. You are strong of heart and mind. The job may not be perfect for you, but you *could* do it."

"The shrimping part sounds good," Sean said, "but I don't know about being a governor. Folks might think I'm too young. I think you're asking a little too much."

Ronnie reached over and gave him a shove. "You may be young, but you're intelligent. You can surround yourself with good people."

"Before something like this could work," Reggie said, "there has to be a method of communication between all the new communities and Corpus Christi. And there has to be fuel."

"This area is rich with fuel," Ronnie said. "You have told us that many times. It only needs to be pumped out of the ground and refined. Corpus has a refinery and storage tanks. Pipelines and pump motors may need to be repaired or replaced, and well-heads reworked, but I'm sure there are a lot of contractors in Corpus who could do that."

"What's going to happen to Marcia?" Melissa asked. "You said you were worried about her seeing Sean. She would never stand for him becoming governor and likely cause all kinds of problems right from the start."

"She's already seen me," Sean replied, "and she didn't seem too happy about it."

"And Marcia may be the cause of the recent problems," Ronnie added. "We can't prove it yet, but it *is* a possibility."

"Marcia will have to go," Robbie said. "Even if she's not the cause of the recent mayhem, she has to go."

"Go where?" Melissa asked, with a concerned look on her face.

"Just go," Robbie replied.

He didn't have to say anymore. She knew.

"So we're going to start murdering people again?" Emily asked.

Reggie gave out a big laugh. "I'm glad Sam's not here."

"Yeah," Sean agreed, "Dad's not too keen on killing someone unless that's the only way, and only if they attack first. With Marcia, I'm inclined to feel the same way. She has a tough shell, but inside, she has a soft spot. I saw that when I was with her on the shrimp boat."

Robbie raised an eyebrow. "You sure about that?"

Sean shrugged his shoulders. "We'll have a talk with her."

"We're going back to Corpus next week," Ronnie said, changing the subject. "We'll set Sean up as mayor for the time being, and as soon as we can get things a little more stable around there, we'll concentrate on fuel production."

"And John is good with electronics," Reggie added. "He may not be able to do all the work and there are not nearly enough resources around here, but he could supervise a communications project."

"Who's going to scout out people in the area and beyond?" James asked.

"I thought me, Ronnie, and maybe either Lance or Zack if one of them wants to come along," Robbie said. "I'll drive the Jeep, Ronnie can take shotgun, while one of the others man the machine gun."

"And how long are you going to be gone?" Brooke asked.

"Off and on, probably a week or two at a time," Robbie replied.

This drew a sour face from Florence and Brooke. Kim and Brenda weren't too happy with Sean going to Corpus either. Though they weren't married or anything, they considered themselves a threesome.

"Don't you guys think you're getting the cart a little ahead of the horse?" Reggie said. "You have a lot of work to do in Corpus and I'm talking a month or two at least."

"By then it'll be planting time," James brought up.

"We'll be having a few babies popping out along the way too," Melissa said.

"There's wood that needs to be cut at home," Brooke said, "not to mention there are still a few drafts and some roof leaks from all the bullet holes, a shortage of meat, and the toilet is not working properly . . . to name a few."

Brooke smiled. All the young men frowned, but they knew everyone was right. There was a lot of work yet to be done in Corpus and they couldn't neglect their work at home entirely. In particular, they could not neglect their women folk.

Chapter 29

The next morning, Ronnie got up before daylight and went hunting. A fresh norther had blown in during the night and the temperature had dropped into the upper thirties. He found a good deer trail and waited. An hour after sunup a doe and her yearling meandered by closely followed by a young buck. He had no trouble bagging the six-pointer.

When he got back to the house with his kill, Robbie was on the pier fishing. He'd already caught three by the time Ronnie arrived. His brother laid his pole down and helped him skin the deer, then got back to fishing. He caught two more by the time Ronnie finished processing the buck.

Ronnie grabbed his pole and fished with his brother for a while afterward, but by this time the fish had stopped biting, so they gave up and went inside.

Brooke reminded Robbie about the broken toilet. He worked on that for a while and Ronnie went to the woodshed and chopped wood, while the girls prepared a late breakfast.

After their eggs with fresh heart and liver, the boys went back outside and cut more wood.

When they came in, Brooke insisted they start a fire in the fireplace. A short while later, Reggie and Emily came over for a visit. Reggie brought the state map Linda gave him and a pail of asphalt Ronnie requested for the roof. He set the pail next to the fireplace to warm so application would be easier. Florence made more coffee and they all huddled around the table and stared at the map.

"I think you should stick to a smaller area," Reggie said. "Texas is a mighty big place and if you spread yourself too thin, you're not going to be able to adequately cover the real estate."

"What about putting the cart ahead of the horse?" Florence asked.

"It'll be a while before the boys put the plan into action," Reggie said, "but there's no reason the organization can't start now. Like I was saying, begin small. For starters, Aransas Pass, Rockport, and maybe as far as Tivoli to the north."

"Tivoli is only a small town," Ronnie said.

"Maybe so," Reggie replied, smoothing out the map so he could see better, "but it's near a river. There may be people there. We live on a river and it has been important to our survival. Also, keep your eyes out for cell phone towers. We will need communications between all the groups of people if they choose to join us.

"Farther inland, Refugio, Victoria, and Cuero would be good places for folks to have settled. West, Kingsville, and Alice are worth checking.

"We've already been to Beeville southeast of here and maybe up to Floresville toward San Antonio. I don't think you should go quite as far as San Antonio yet, but maybe eventually.

"There are also a lot of small towns, mainly along the San Antonio, Nueces, and Guadalupe rivers to check. I think this area will keep you busy for some time.

"If you're successful in this region, then you can expand out even farther. If you find some people who will help you, maybe things will go a lot faster. Hopefully, they will have a vehicle or two and some fuel. If not, maybe Corpus can supply them."

Reggie folded up the map and handed it to Robbie. "Put this in a safe place where you won't lose it."

Brooke got up and walked to the kitchen. "You guys want more coffee, or would you rather have tea now? We have grape juice too, or water."

Emily took water while everyone else opted for grape juice. Florence and Brooke watched Ronnie put a couple more logs on the fire.

"It's not warming up in here like it should," he remarked. "Guess we better get some of the drafts fixed—tomorrow."

"And the roof leaks," Florence said, as she stepped around the pots they had scattered over the floor to collect the drips.

Reggie changed the subject. "I won't be going back to Corpus Christi with you guys anymore unless you absolutely can't get by without me, and I certainly won't be going on your next adventure."

"Why not, Grandpa?" Ronnie asked.

"I'm getting too old to be running all over the country. I'm not as young as I used to be and the war with Sandra has taken a lot out of me. I've got to take better care of myself or I'll be joining Lars and Eileen soon."

"You're not that old," Robbie said.

Reggie smiled. "Okay, let me put it another way; I need my beauty sleep."

The discussion then reverted to Corpus Christi. They discussed the need for more fuel production, the installation of telecommunications, which Reggie said he'd talk to John about, and training. Robbie and Ronnie could handle just about any situation, but others like the Pink Ladies needed adequate training or they would fail.

Finally, Reggie brought Marcia back up. "I don't know whether or not she had anything to do with the last battle in Corpus, but the old gal is going to be trouble down the road. Sean made certain of that."

"We agree with you, Grandpa," Robbie said, "but Sean will have to deal with her . . . and there is also little Lola. We'll have to wait and see what kind of solution he comes up with."

Emily got up.

"I don't want to hear any more about this discussion. I'm going out on the porch. When you get ready to go home old man, that's where I'll be."

Brooke and Florence didn't want to hear any more about the subject either. They followed her outside and pulled the door shut behind them.

"I know we've done a lot of really bad things around here," Emily said, "and I've been a part of it, but I don't have to listen to it."

Brooke smiled at Emily.

Be strong, Florence thought. *If Marcia needs to die . . . Robbie will only do what's necessary. Sean will come up with another solution. I don't think he'll kill her because of Lola.*

Florence felt the tears welling up in her eyes and there wasn't anything she could do about it. The drop hit her on the arm and she looked down. Emily reached over and patted her on the hand and she peered over at Emily.

Florence wiped the tears away. *"Dammit!"*

Florence opened her eyes and all she saw was darkness. She turned her head slightly to look out the window and there wasn't a hint of light outside. She relaxed as she felt her stomach and closed her eyes, but her mind would not let her go back to sleep.

I couldn't keep from crying yesterday, but I didn't break down entirely like I usually do. I was stronger than the day before. I am not the same woman I was. I'm getting stronger. I was such a baby before that day Daddy forced me to change.

Her mind focused on the day she sat on the side of the bed holding the revolver in her hand. The steel felt cold when she touched the gun to her cheek. She knew what was going to happen. Her mother was not strong enough to stand up to her father, but she had the gun. She had the means and her dad gave her the opportunity just like she knew he would.

She would never forget the look on Richard's face when she pulled the trigger. She no longer cried about killing her dad, but the vision was forever burned into her memory.

Her thoughts then turned to her mother. Louise begged her to let her take the blame for Richard's death. Louise's love for her was unconditional, like all good moms. She would never have let her daughter pay the price for killing the abusive bastard. Her mother took the blame.

I cried every night in the tiny cell Sandra locked me up in for being an accomplice to murder. I don't think Sandra knew I really killed my daddy. Even if she did, she was satisfied to let Mom pay the ultimate price for that dreadful day.

Sandra took her whip to me. I lost count of the lashes, but I still wear the scars. I cried until I had no more tears, but then my shining knight showed up and everything changed. The tears went away mostly, except when he had to leave and the cell door closed behind him. He came to see me often and the tearful sessions grew farther and farther apart.

Florence remembered the excitement of flying in a plane for the first time with Robbie and Beka. She'd never seen such a beautiful sight as the earth from high in the air. She also relived the fear of dying when Robbie nearly crashed the plane and it exploded.

The memories were painful, but now, she no longer shed the tears for these events. New memories kept popping up though—the fire; Robbie turning first to Beka, then Charlotte, leaving her out in the cold; Sandra trying to kill them . . .

The rooster signaled the dawn of a new morning and Florence looked over at the window. The room was much brighter now and she felt her baby moving inside her. Robbie stirred and she reached and grabbed his hand.

"You awake?" he asked.

She squeezed his hand. "Good morning, Sir Lancelot."

Maybe the tears will never go away completely, but just maybe they're not supposed to. Crying is a sign that I still have feelings and that I'm still alive. I wish life would get back to normal though . . . but maybe . . . this is normal.

Florence fired up the stove and put a pot of coffee on when she got to the kitchen. Robbie brought in a basket full of eggs and a slab of bacon. Brooke and Ronnie joined them and the two girls started fixing breakfast.

"What are we doing today, Brother?" Ronnie asked.

Brooke turned around and crossed her arms across her chest. "Patching the roof and the holes in the walls."

"Never mind," Ronnie said, as he got up and walked over to the fireplace. He poked some kindling into the coals and when they caught, he added a few logs on top. He then looked over at Brooke who gave him a smile of approval.

After breakfast, the boys got to work on house repairs and when they finished, they thought they would do a little fishing before the sun got up too high, but the girls had different ideas. When they came in, the women had made a long list of other neglected chores and by the time the items were checked off, another day had ended.

"Tomorrow's the day Sam said he was butchering, wasn't it?" Robbie asked.

"I think so," Ronnie replied. "Our ham is about gone and I can't wait for some fresh sausage and cracklin' cornbread."

The boys kept busy over the next several days with trips to the Lin's and Lindgren's. The girls cheerfully kissed their men goodbye each morning and got after their chores. Robbie bagged another deer on the way home one afternoon. Their smokehouse was suddenly full. Winter carrots, beets, and tomatoes were doing well. Though the weather had cooled off significantly, they had not yet had their first frost or freeze though it was late in the season.

Before they knew it, it was time for another trip to Corpus Christi. Ronnie and Robbie packed everything up in the living room and turned in early to get a good night's sleep.

Brooke noticed Florence's cheery mood all day. She was surprised that the boys leaving had not thrown Florence into another crying stint.

"No tears?" Brooke asked.

"There's nothing to cry about," Florence said, a little indignantly. "Robbie and Ronnie are creating a new and safer world for us and our babies. They know what they're doing. I trust them to do what is right, and if maybe I don't quite agree with their means, they have to do what they think is best."

Brooke wrapped her arms around Florence and gave her a big hug.

"The boys *are* wonderful, aren't they?" Brooke said.

Chapter 30

Robbie and Ronnie met Sean, with Mutt tagging close behind, at the Lindgren's. Sean knelt and gave him a good scratching. "I'm sorry, Fella, but I can't take you with me. I'll come see you when I can." He looked up at the twins. "You guys take good care of him, will ya?"

"You sure?"

"Yeah. He'll be better off here. Besides, you need a dog to help you keep an eye out. Some other families in Corpus have dogs. Maybe I can bring a puppy or two back the next time I come. I bet Kira would like one."

Robbie nodded and they headed off.

"I thought you'd be wanting to take the truck," Ronnie said to Sean. "You'll need something to drive."

"If I'm going to be governor, I thought a Cadillac would be more fitting," he replied, with a smile.

Three hours later, Robbie pulled the Jeep up to the edge of the city and stopped to look around. He took a deep breath. The air was crisp and clean—much different than the last time he was here. Then he noticed a small plume of smoke.

Probably just someone burning trash.

He slipped the gearshift into forward.

At the Farm, Robbie was quite surprised to see all the debris cleared and a huge framework in place for a new ranch house. Busy beavers were scurrying around inside and on the frame, hard at work on the project. Christine walked over and greeted the boys.

"You have time for a meeting?" Robbie asked.

"Of course," she replied, and led the boys to a picnic table under a large tree next to the construction site.

The boys sat down with Christine and a young lady stepped over to the table and asked if they'd like drinks. Christine nodded and the girl scurried off.

"I took it upon myself to add some men to our police force," she said. "While the ladies do a fair job, I think it will take men on the force to deal with ruthless adversaries like the ones who were here last week. I hope you don't mind."

"I think that is an excellent idea," Ronnie said. "We're not here to tell you what to do. We only want to help you create your new government. We're quite pleased you've taken the bull by the horns. That's what it will take to get things going."

Christine smiled.

"So, you're feeling more comfortable as Chief now?" Sean asked.

"I guess I've always been on the tough side. It feels good to tell people what to do rather than being told and seeing tasks being carried out without question."

"Let me tell you what we've been thinking," Robbie said. "As you know, Sean was captured and castrated by Sandra. He may be an outsider, but he is no different than any of the other men here who were butchered by the bitch. I think the others, once they learn this, will accept him as the new mayor of the city. We'd like to set him up as your new leader."

Christine looked over at Sean. "I don't have a problem with that, but how will that affect me?"

"You seem to have matters well in hand," Sean replied. "You make sure everyone is safe and secure in their homes. Get as many people armed and ready to deal with any threat swiftly and professionally. You do what you need to do to that end and I'll never boss you around. If you have a problem, however, you come to me and we'll figure out a way to get it worked out to our mutual satisfaction.

"If the Contractors will accept me as their leader, I'll work with them on the fuel production. I will organize the labor force and suggest alternative procedures, so we can get fuel production going quickly and efficiently. You just take care of the security issues."

"So, what do we need to do first?" Christine asked.

"I'll set up a meeting at the Contractors to see if I can get them organized," Sean replied. "Seems like you've already headed us in that direction with the new house. I'll see if I can expand on that."

The boys jumped and their eyes grew wide as they reached for their pistols when they heard shots coming from the backside of the new construction. Christine laid her hand on Sean's. "It's alright. Let's go around back and I'll show you what's going on."

Christine got up and the boys followed her lead. The shooting continued as they walked around the carpenters.

Out near the fields, a line of men and women, all dressed in pink shirts, were lined up shooting at hay bales.

"We have another twenty new recruits," Christine said. "They'll be up to speed in no time. In addition to rebuilding the house, the Contractors are working on a couple dozen cars and trucks to get them ready for the new officers."

The boys followed Christine back around to the picnic table and resumed their conversation.

"Have you seen or heard anything from Marcia?" Ronnie asked.

"Nothing," Christine said. "Did you expect me to?"

"We were hopeful she would keep to herself and not be a problem," Robbie said. "After we left last time, I got to thinking. I think she maybe could have been the problem with the shootings and burning around here and elsewhere. She knows Sean is here with us. Sean was forced to kill her husband when he escaped. We think she may be seeking revenge. Since she was one of Sandra's spies, there is also the chance she wants to move into Sandra's controlling position. We really don't know, but Marcia could be a thorn in our side if we don't keep an eye on her and keep her under wraps."

"Don't worry about her for now," Ronnie said. "Maybe we'll go find her tomorrow and see what she's up to."

"We should run over to the Contractors," Sean said. "I need to see if we can set up a meeting for tomorrow. We should see what is on their schedule and adjust it if need be."

"Are we about through here?" Ronnie asked. "We can go over there now."

"We need a place to stay while we're here," Robbie said, looking over at Christine. "We stayed at the Hospital last time, but I'd feel better staying out here if you have room."

"I'll have a place ready for you when you get back this evening. Three rooms?"

"We'd prefer one," Ronnie replied.

"I'll have dinner ready too, around dark."

The boys dropped Sean off at the Contractors compound. They figured he'd be alright there since Linda had said they were all for a new government and the recent mayhem didn't appear to be caused by them.

Robbie and Robbie headed down to the Bayfront. They wanted to see Marcia. Robbie was convinced she was behind the men who terrorized Corpus Christi and killed Linda and Sally. He had questions he wanted answers to.

She will answer them!

When Robbie pulled up to Marcia's house, her truck was not there, but Ronnie got out and knocked on the door anyway. When no one answered, he shrugged and got back in the Jeep. They proceeded to the harbor. Robbie drove by the ice plant then on down to the boats. There was no sign of Marcia.

Robbie and Ronnie stood and watched for a while as a group of men unloaded sack after sack. Three men waited on another boat nearby for their turn to unload their sacks. It looked like there were close to a hundred of whatever they were unloading. Robbie decided he'd seen enough and they headed toward the desalinization plant. Marcia wasn't there either.

"There's only one more place she can be," Ronnie said, and they headed on to the seafood packing plant.

Robbie pulled in at the end of a line of cars and trucks and got out. He still didn't see Marcia's truck. He walked around to the entrance, Ronnie on his heels, and went inside. Several men were busy by a conveyor.

"Have any of you guys seen Marcia?" Robbie asked.

Only one of the men turned and acknowledged their presence. The other men were working on the drive motor. A curly headed kid, the youngest of them, looked about scratching his thinking cap, then back at Robbie.

"I don't know when I've seen her last," he said. "She hasn't been around here lately as far as I know."

"Thanks."

Robbie walked to the far end of the building, looking into several offices on the way.

Where the hell is she?

Robbie turned to his brother. "Any ideas?"

"Let's run over to the Police Station and see if anyone there has seen her," he replied.

When Robbie pulled up, the first thing he noticed was a line of sandbags on the roof over the doorway with a rifle and a head peering over the top. He didn't recognize the man wearing a pink hat.

"Who goes there?" he asked.

"Robbie Lindgren."

Apparently, his reputation had preceded him, as the man told them they could go in. Five Pink Ladies, including Christine, were scattered around, two seated at desks.

"You've got things under control and in order," Robbie said, looking at Christine behind one of the desks. "I like the sentry idea."

"Thanks," she replied. "Have a seat."

"We can't stay long. We just stopped by to see if any of you have seen Marcia. We drove around trying to find her. Seems she's vanished."

Christine looked at the other girls and they shrugged their shoulders.

"Well, I don't know what to tell you," Christine replied.

"Keep an eye out, will you? If you see her, take her into custody and detain her until I can talk to her."

Sean was still inside when Robbie pulled up to the Contractor compound. They sat in the Jeep for a while, but when he didn't come out, the boys went in. The place was quiet except for voices coming from a room at the back of the building.

Robbie peered inside and Sean was standing behind a podium at the back of the meeting room answering questions. When the man who was standing sat down after Sean answered his question, Sean noticed Robbie and his brother standing in the doorway. He motioned for them to come in. Robbie led the way to Sean's position and he introduced the boys to the crowd of thirty men, more or less. They gave the boys a round of applause.

"What's going on?" Robbie asked.

"Just wrapping up with a Q & A," Sean replied. "I'll fill you two in on the details tonight over dinner."

"Any more questions?" Sean asked, turning back to the crowd.

"Want some more oysters?" a man at the back of the room asked.

"Of course," Sean replied.

"Want some?" he asked, looking at Robbie and Ronnie.

"I guess," Robbie replied.

"There are plenty this time of year," Sean said.

Robbie and Ronnie had never eaten oysters before, but Sean assured them they were delicious.

The new Mayor led the boys to the doorway and the three of them followed the oyster man to a table where a sack like the ones the boys had seen at the Bayfront was open with the rocks spilling out onto the table.

"This is Hank, by the way," Sean said. "Best oyster man around."

Robbie smiled. "Nice to meet you, sir."

The others nodded.

Hank was a fifty-something genial old man. He appeared older than he was. He'd lived a hard life since the grid shut down. He was short and stout with big hands. He slipped his gloves on, picked up the oyster knife, and opened one up and handed it to Sean. Sean held it out for the twins to see, then pushed it off the shell into his mouth. Sean chewed a couple of times and a big smile developed on his face as it slid down his throat. A queer look came over the boys' faces.

The man opened another oyster and extended his hand toward Robbie. He looked at the odd creature on the half-shell, then over to his brother. Robbie's gaze then turned to Sean.

"Go ahead, they're good."

Robbie pushed the slimy looking thing off the shell into his mouth just as Sean had done. He chewed and swallowed, then his eyes lit up.

"Damn, this is good!"

The man handed one to Ronnie. He slurped it down.

"This *is* good! Salty . . . and slick as snot, but delicious."

The boys looked back at the man who already had another opened and handed it to Robbie. He then opened more for the others. The man ate one occasionally, but mostly told some old stories and continued to open oysters until all their bellies were full.

Ronnie watched carefully as Hank opened the oysters. "You make that look so easy."

"It's easy when you get the hang of it. I've been doing this for nigh on forty years. Shit comes and goes around here, but oysters . . . they grow in shallow water. You can go out and pick them up with your hands if you're not afraid to get your feet wet. When you ain't got no balls, they'll put a little lead back in your pencil, if you know what I mean."

Robbie smiled and looked over at Sean.

Grandpa needs to meet this guy. I think they'd like each other. Maybe the next time he comes to Corpus.

"I sure hope you boys get Corpus Christi settled down. I'm originally from Seadrift, up the coast from here. I'd sure like to get back there before I die.

"I came here for shrimp years back, before the grid shut down. There wasn't a lot of shrimp in San Antonio Bay that year and I heard there were a lot down here. Been stuck here ever since. Seadrift has more oysters too, or at least they did when I was growing up."

Sean looked over. "The place is probably dead by now. Why would you want to go back?"

"Fellers in that neck of the woods are tough. I bet some of my old buddies are still around. You get this town cleaned up and just maybe I'll head back up there."

Ronnie's eyes lit up. "Maybe we need to add Seadrift to our list of stops, Brother."

Robbie nodded. "I think I've had enough oysters. I'm gonna get sick if I eat too many."

Most of the rest of the men had gone back to work by this time, but a few still mingled about. Sean thanked them for their support and bid them farewell.

Sean joined the boys in the Jeep and they headed back to the Farm. Robbie drove while Ronnie filled Sean in on the missing Marcia.

"Stop!" Sean yelled.

Robbie screeched the tires on the pavement.

"Back up," Sean said.

Robbie put the Jeep in reverse until Sean said to stop again. Sean pointed to a truck down a side road and climbed in back to get on the turret. Robbie turned and headed toward the vehicle.

"It looks like hers," Sean said, as they pulled up alongside. "See, a shrimp net, rope, crab boxes . . . it has to be hers."

Robbie drove farther up the street scanning all the houses on both sides. They were dilapidated and overgrown with weeds.

"There's no one around," Robbie said, as he drove back to the truck. "See if it has keys inside."

Ronnie jumped out and looked inside. The keys were in the ignition. He opened the door, crawled in, and turned the key. The truck started right up and he shut it off.

"This is mighty strange," Robbie said.

"Want to take it with us?" Ronnie asked.

"No. Let's leave it here. We'll check it tomorrow and the next few days to see if it's been moved."

Robbie circled a few blocks on either side of where Marcia's truck was parked to see if they could spot anyone or any place where someone might be. All they found were more run-down houses and no sign of Marcia.

When they got back to the Farm, Christine was back and she showed the boys to their quarters.

"Dinner will be ready in an hour or so," she said. "Meet me in the barn when you get cleaned up."

Sean took his shower first. "I worked the hardest today, so I go first."

Ronnie gave him a slap on the arm. "Work! You call talking and eating oysters work?"

"Absolutely! That was hard getting up in front of all those guys. I didn't know whether they would accept me or not. I talked my head off today. All you did was drive around in the Jeep. That's not work."

Robbie laughed. "And the oysters?"

"I tried to open one! I worked on it for five minutes before I got the damn thing open. By the time I got the slimy little bugger out, I'd cut it in three pieces. Yes, that was work!"

Robbie conceded. "Alright, get your shower. Your odor is playing hell with my sinuses."

Christine had given them a whole section of one of the bunkhouses, which normally slept ten women. The room was huge with three queen size beds and its own bathroom. The bunks were taken out and the larger beds moved in for the boys.

Robbie and Ronnie picked their beds and relaxed while they waited for Sean, then took their showers when he'd finished. They pulled fresh clothes out of their backpacks so they could be presentable for dinner. When they headed to the main barn, the boys found that Christine had set up a new kitchen there until the house was finished.

When they strolled in, the several dozen ladies who were seated eating and chatting away grew quiet. This made the boys a bit uncomfortable.

Christine was sitting at one of the nearer tables and waved them in, then pointed to the serving line. They filled their plates and a couple of the ladies got bold and yelled 'over here', but they joined Christine at her table as the conversation around the room picked back up. Groans of disappointment emitted from across the room.

Robbie opened the conversation. "We spotted Marcia's truck in a dead part of the city between here and the Contractors compound. The keys were in it and it wasn't abandoned because it stopped running. It started up just fine. For the life of me, I cannot figure out where she might be or what she's up to."

All eyes then turned to Sean. Everyone was anxious to hear about what happened with the Contractors.

"First, seven men were killed the other day during all the mayhem around here. Their two top men were among them. They had only one gun, but before they died, they shot one of the intruders and wounded another. The dead contractors were the only ones who got a close look at the marauders, but the rest said they didn't think they were locals."

Sean took another bite of his chicken and a sip of tea. "They chose a new man to lead them and he picked a helper. They asked for more guns and ammunition. I told them they would get them tomorrow. We have to do this so I don't lose their trust."

Robbie and Robbie both nodded, then looked over at Christine. She saluted them with her glass of tea.

"They said they would have the refinery going at full capacity soon and not to worry about that, but expressed the need for a new source of crude. Quite a few men are out doing maintenance on the wind turbines and the seafood plant. They are receiving a lot of oysters now and that takes personnel to process and flash freeze them on the half-shell. You should be getting some around here soon."

"We got some in this morning," Christine said. "Twenty gallons. We'll be having fried oysters for dinner tomorrow night."

"They're damn good raw," Robbie said. "I can't wait to try them cooked."

Then Christine dropped a bombshell.

"I've got about thirty ladies lined up for artificial insemination," Christine said.

The boys froze and their eyes focused on her.

"Oysters are good for your pencil. We need to move forward in this area," she continued. "Some of the ladies remembered you, Robbie, and were a little disappointed about the new procedure."

Robbie blushed. Neither of the brothers had thought of the subject since it was first mentioned a while back. Neither was even certain they wanted to move forward with the project. Florence certainly didn't like the prospect.

"I set up an appointment at the Hospital," Christine added. "They'll be expecting you tomorrow."

Robbie and Ronnie looked at each other, then they looked back at Christine, who was waiting for their confirmation.

"Well?" she asked.

"We're not sure," Robbie said.

"If not you two, then who? If we had options, it would be different, but we don't. Maybe next month we'll get some men up here from Brownsville, but we have women ready right now. It's not like it's the first time. There are a few pregnant ladies around here right now carrying your sons and daughters."

Robbie hadn't seen these pregnant gals around and had forgotten all about them, but Christine was right.

"Where are they?"

"They stay in the far bunkhouse and do lighter chores in the barn next door until the kids are born. There is also a nursery on one end of the bunkhouse.

Pregnant women get a different diet than the rest of us, so unless you go out back, you'll never see them."

"Can I go back there?" Robbie asked.

"Of course, but what about the Hospital tomorrow?"

"Can we think on it overnight?"

"Yes, but this isn't a want or desire. Your seeds are a need."

Robbie slept in the most comfortable bed he'd been in for a long time, but he didn't sleep well. He woke up before the others and lay in bed thinking.

Florence won't like it. Corpus needs to grow, but without me and Ronnie, it can't.

Robbie looked over at Ronnie.

He doesn't seem to be having a problem sleeping.

He looked at the window when he heard the rooster crowing. Sunlight brightened the room and Ronnie started to stir. Robbie got up and went into the bathroom. Ronnie came in just as he was finishing with the razor.

"Good morning," he said, with a big smile. "Let's go scatter our seeds to the wind."

"So, you're okay with that?"

"Of course, it's not like we have a choice. They need us. That's what we're doing here—helping these people."

Robbie got dressed and laid down on his bed while the other two finished their morning routine.

"If it bothers you," Ronnie said, when he came out of the restroom, "we can ask if they can mix them together. That way, no one will know who the baby belongs to. They'll probably be mostly mine anyway. My little boys can run circles around yours."

"Our boys are as alike as we are!"

"Just trying to help you, Bro."

They both laughed, but Robbie was still churning inside.

One of the cooks offered the boys bacon and eggs. After all the roast they'd had last night, plus the oysters at the Contractors, they only grabbed a few slices of bacon. They thanked the lady for her hospitality and headed over to the new house where Christine was talking to the men.

Sean asked about a car for himself since he would be staying in Corpus. She assured him he'd have one in a couple of days.

"Pink okay?"

Sean frowned but agreed to the color and the boys headed out.

Robbie turned down the street where they saw Marcia's truck the afternoon before. They were surprised it was not there.

"Are you sure this is the right street?" Robbie asked.

Ronnie and Sean looked around.

"Yup," Ronnie said.

Sean nodded.

"Okay, then Marcia is in town. Sooner or later we're going to find her . . . or one of the Pink Ladies will."

"Next stop, the Hospital," Sean said.

Robbie leaned over and butted his head against the steering wheel. He then looked over at Ronnie and Sean who were staring back. Robbie sighed, gave them a smirk, and crammed the gearshift into forward.

Robbie was moving a little slow when they arrived at the Hospital. He was the last to get out of the Jeep.

"Come on," Ronnie said. "If your boys move as slow as you are, mine are going to eat all yours."

Sean led the way while Robbie brought up the rear. They told the receptionist they were here to make a deposit. She pointed to a nurse down one of the hallways. The nurse heard them talking and headed their way.

"I've been expecting you," she said. "Follow me."

She handed a cup to Ronnie and opened a door for him. "Bring it to me immediately when you're through. She opened a door for Sean, but when he told her he had nothing for her, she said she was sorry and placed Robbie in the room instead.

Sean sat down in a chair across the hallway, while the nurse kept busy with her cart of supplies and her chart.

Ronnie was out quickly. He gave the sample to the nurse and sat down beside Sean. Ten minutes later, Robbie was still in the room.

"We ain't got all day," Ronnie yelled.

The nurse gave him a sour look and his face turned red when his voice echoed down the hall.

"Sorry," he said.

A few minutes later, Robbie came out and handed his cup to the nurse.

"Can you mix them?" Ronnie asked. "My brother doesn't feel comfortable scattering his sperm around. If you mix them, no one will ever know who the babies belong to."

"I'll ask the doctor," she replied, shook her head and walked toward the nurse's station.

The boys followed her to the oval desk.

"That's all," she said.

She looked up at their curious faces.

"The doctor is on another floor. I'll ask him when he comes down. The decision will be up to him."

Chapter 31

Robbie, Ronnie, and Sean scoured the city for two days looking for Marcia. Midday on the third day, they spotted the truck a few blocks up, headed to their right. Robbie pressed the accelerator hard, but when he made the turn, Marcia was not to be seen. He scoured the area, but their efforts to find her were in vain. Close to dark, they headed back to the Farm.

Robbie cleaned up first and went out to the bunkhouse where the pregnant ladies stayed, while the other two got their showers.

"We heard you were here," one of the girls said. "We weren't sure you'd come out here to see us."

"I wasn't sure I wanted to. You know I like all of you . . . it wasn't you . . . it was Sandra and the fact that I was forced . . ."

"Would you like to feel it kicking?"

"I don't remember your name."

"Nancy."

She walked over and took Robbie's hand and placed it on her stomach. The other ladies gathered around and Robbie felt of each. Some kicked hard while others didn't kick much at all . . . more like a butterfly.

"He's been kicking all day," she said, smiling. "Must be a boy."

"You know I can't be a father to your baby?"

Nancy held his hand. "We all know that, but we'd be honored if you'd come around from time to time. We all love you for the gifts you've placed inside all of us. You can't be a *real* father, but just that you acknowledge they are yours . . . that you're not ashamed of us or our children is all we ask."

Robbie sat down on the sofa and the girls gathered around. *These are all beautiful women. They are all beautiful inside too. What would Florence think? Maybe if she got to know some of the ladies. Florence is no different than they are in how the babies were conceived. Can she accept all my children . . . and these women?*

Robbie looked them in the eyes and he could feel the tears welling up in his. "I'm not ashamed of any of you. We were doing a job, but I have a special place for each and every one of you in my heart. Each of you is exceptional. I knew that when we . . . you know . . . were wonderful women. You're still extraordinary ladies and I will not forget it. You will have strong children and I'll love them all."

The girls who could reach him showered him with kisses.

"Thank you," Nancy said.

"They're expecting me for dinner," he said. "I best not keep them waiting."

Nancy kissed Robbie on the cheek. "Thank you for coming."

Robbie turned back and gave them a last look before he closed the door behind him. He wiped a tear away and walked back toward the barn.

Over dinner, Robbie informed Christine they would be going home first thing in the morning.

"We haven't seen any sign of Sandra's men, so I guess we got all of them. I don't know what happened to the raiders. It's impossible to track them in the city. Hopefully, they are long gone. Sean will stay and get everyone organized, help you keep everyone safe, and assist you with whatever you need."

Sean nodded.

Robbie looked at Christine. "Can I have some more oysters? We'll be gone for a couple weeks."

"Yeah, me too," Ronnie said, with a grin. "They're even better cooked!"

Back in Peaceful Valley . . .

Robbie called the meeting to order. "I'm pleased to say the trip to Corpus Christi went very well. They're getting the Police built up with both men and women. Sean met with the Contractors and the meeting went well too. They're working hard to get fuel production back to capacity, but they'll soon need more crude oil. Sean will help them organize teams to search out and get some old wells back into service.

"The oyster boats are producing a good harvest and I've got to say, Corpus Christi was worth saving for that alone."

"Yuck!" Beka said.

"More for me," Ronnie said, slapping his hands together. "I can't wait. How can you not like them?"

Robbie continued. "All the plants are up and running and we haven't seen hide nor hair of the marauders who came through and tossed a monkey wrench into the works.

"I feel in my gut that Marcia Nguyen was behind that attack, but I can't prove it. When we catch up with her, we'll learn the truth."

"You haven't found Marcia?" Reggie asked, a little surprised.

"No," he replied. "She's apparently abandoned her home. We found her pickup once, but it disappeared the next morning. Then we came across her one day and she eluded us. Sooner or later, we'll catch up to her. The Pink Ladies are looking for her too. Hopefully, they'll have her in a cell when we get back over there."

"When's that going to be?" Florence asked.

"I'm thinking a couple weeks."

Florence smiled.

"I've been talking to John about getting some communications going," Reggie said, "and he agreed to do whatever he could. It would be nice if we could get an open line between here and Corpus."

"Can we do that?" Ronnie asked.

"The best way would be to get a line of cell phone towers working between here and there," John said.

"What do they look like?" Robbie asked.

"Tall towers with what looks like vertical bars on the top," John replied.

"I saw one between here and Corpus," Robbie said, "but I didn't know what it was."

"One's not enough," John said. "There has to be one about every ten or twelve miles at least."

"I only saw one," Robbie said.

"And we need cell phones," Reggie added. "Mine died a long time ago. I don't know if it's the phone or just the battery. Eileen had one too. Have you seen it lately, James?"

"No, I haven't, but I don't remember throwing it out," he said, looking over at Melissa.

She shook her head.

"How are we going to find the towers?" Ronnie asked.

"There used to be a tight grid of towers over most of the country," Reggie said. "It would be much easier if we could get hold of a tower map though. When you go back to Corpus, see if you can find an old cell phone store. There have to be a few around if they weren't all destroyed . . . and see if you can find cell phones and someone who can work on them.

"Keep your eyes open on the way there too. Now that you know what you're looking for, maybe you can spot a few towers. If you find some, note how far they are apart using your odometer on the Jeep."

"Can Kim and I go to Corpus on the next trip," Brenda asked. "If Sean's going to stay there now, we'd like to be with him. I'm sure he'll be happy about that."

"Are you up to it, Kim?" Robbie asked.

"Yeah, I'm doing much better now. I think being close to Sean would help. I miss him."

"Ronnie and I will make sure it's safe on this trip, then I promise you two can go on the next one."

"How long are you going to stay next time?" Florence asked.

"Just a few days most likely," Robbie said. "If we can take care of Marcia, then future trips will likely be short."

"I'd like to go too."

"The Jeep only seats four comfortably."

"You and Ronnie both don't have to go do you?"

Robbie looked over at Ronnie. He shrugged his shoulders.

"Settled then," she said.

Later that evening when Ronnie and Brook, and Robbie and Florence were alone at home, the boys sat the girls down around the kitchen table to discuss the Corpus re-population program. They knew the girls wouldn't be happy about it, but it would be much better to get it out in the open now than to have it come out later. They were certain to find out eventually. Now that Florence was going to Corpus, someone would certainly mention it.

The girls did understand the city's need and that if the boys didn't feed this necessity, trade with the city could go sour. The whole city could even crumble, the last thing anyone wanted.

"Why not your dad or John?" Florence asked.

Robbie shrugged his shoulders. "They didn't ask. We were the ones there at the time. I'm not sure John would have gone along with the program because of his religious beliefs, but Dad probably would have if he'd have been there."

"This isn't a permanent arrangement," Ronnie added. "They're going to try to get some men from Brownsville. One more round when we go back in a couple of weeks and that should be it."

Neither of the girls were overly enthusiastic, even if it was only one more time, but they both accepted the plan and without tears. They went to bed a short while later and the guys showed the girls how much they loved them.

All the while they were making love, Robbie's mind was on the girls back at the Farm.

I've got to tell her. Is this a good time? There may not be a perfect time, but when?

When they'd finished and were lying side by side, hand in hand, he figured there'd never be a better moment.

She knows I love her.

"I went to see the other girls carrying my babies," he blurted out.

Florence let go of his hand and turned on her side to give him her undivided attention. Her eyes were wide open and her stare intense, but she didn't speak. She only gave him her questioning look.

"You know Brenda isn't the only one carrying my baby. Christine told me about the others. I had to go see them. I didn't remember their names. They told me they didn't expect me to be a father to their children."

Robbie paused and returned her stare. She didn't look mad or upset, but the stare was piercing.

"They just wanted me to not be ashamed to be the father of their babies. They asked if I would stop in occasionally. I told them I would. We were just doing what we had to do . . . what Sandra demanded we do . . . just like you and me."

Robbie didn't understand why he was getting no reaction from Florence other than her penetrating stare, so he figured he'd said enough. He snuggled up tight against Florence and gave her a gentle kiss.

Why didn't she say anything? She didn't cry. What's that supposed to mean? Maybe she understands . . . maybe she now accepts things as they are. Is that possible?

The next morning, Robbie and Florence went for a long walk. They needed time together. He started the process last night, but today he needed to work on the mental and spiritual aspect of their relationship.

Robbie took Florence's hand as soon as they stepped off the porch. She looked up to him and gave him a loving smile. Robbie squeezed her hand and gave her a little tug to pull her closer.

As they wandered through the woods to the Lindgren homestead, they stopped from time to time to look at the birds chirping and fluttering from limb to limb and the occasional squirrel scampering through the trees.

The sky was clear and the air cool. A gentle breeze filtered through the woods from the northeast. A thin layer of fog lined the ground.

Robbie stopped and pulled Florence close and pressed his lips to hers. His mind was void except for her. He had been so busy since well before Sandra invaded their valley, there was little time for Florence, except to train her in what she needed to learn to deal with their ordeal. Now things seemed to be headed in the right direction, but the task was far from over.

He didn't mention the girls in Corpus Christi and Florence didn't ask. She appeared to accept the situation and he didn't dare bring up the subject again. He decided to wait and see how it all worked out. He felt relieved this problem at least appeared to be behind him. There would be more problems and he didn't need the distraction.

Soon, he and Ronnie would be off on a new adventure, but for now, his job was to take care of Florence's needs and ease all her pains. Robbie was the ultimate expert at so many things, but when it came to Florence, he was still a novice.

He signaled with a wolf howl, and moments later, his dad walked around from the back of the house and returned his signal.

Robbie led Florence halfway to the house and waved.

"We'll be in, in a little while," he yelled and turned toward the sycamore tree. His dad then disappeared around the woodshed.

Robbie led Florence to the bench at the foot of the graves. They sat down and he put his arm around her. He gave her a gentle squeeze and she leaned her head on his shoulder.

"I wish I could have known them," Florence said, as she stared at Lars and Eileen's gravestones.

"I miss them so much," Robbie said. "I wish they could meet you and see their great grandkids."

Florence reached over and gently wiped the tear from his cheek.

Robbie got up and took a deep breath, then picked a few flowers from the base of the sycamore tree and placed one each on Lars and Eileen's graves, on Abigail's, Charlotte's, and the last on Buster's.

"Outside of Ronnie and Sean," he said, "Buster was my best friend for many years. He loved to play fetch and always wanted his belly scratched, but when we went hunting, he found the dead squirrel or bird first every time with his keen nose. He would bark and look at me as if to say 'why didn't you find it?' Then when I bent over to pick it up, he would lick me on the cheek."

Robbie sat back down beside Florence and turned to face her. He put his hand on her belly. He smiled when he felt the baby kicking. He glanced over at Abigail's headstone. The smile soon faded and a tear ran down his cheek. Florence reached up to whisk it away.

"Abby was my daughter," he said. "I'll never know her now. I'll never know how beautiful she would have been; how smart she . . ."

Florence wrapped her arm around him and held him tight. She gave him a gentle kiss on the cheek and wiped another tear. He looked into her eyes. He could see her understanding.

She knows that regardless of the circumstances, or who the mother is, I'll love all my children unconditionally and she's okay with that.

They sat quietly for a few moments and Robbie took a deep breath of the cool forest air.

"This time next year, we'll have a new society around here. Corpus will be an ally and maybe we can take regular trips there to see Sean and to pick up supplies. We won't have to worry about someone shooting at us all the time. Maybe we won't even have to carry a gun for protection. We can make new friends and talk to them on the phone. We can even fly down to Brownsville and see what it's like there."

"You have some big dreams," Florence said smiling, her mood improving with Robbie's.

"And some of these dreams will come true. Ronnie and I will make certain of that. With Sean as mayor of Corpus Christi and then maybe even governor of the state, things will definitely change. We can meet new people and see new places. Maybe we won't even have to struggle so hard all the time for food. We can just go to the store and trade for what we need."

Florence patted him on the hand. "Let's go see your mom and dad."

Robbie and Florence joined James and Melissa in the house, where Brenda and Melissa were getting things ready for lunch. Kim was reading a book on the sofa. Robbie and his dad excused themselves and took two poles down to the pier to fish and do some talking. Florence stayed in the house to help the ladies.

"So, you're going to join Sean in Corpus?" Florence asked Brenda.

"Yes. I think Kim is ready to go. She really needs to be with Sean now."

Kim looked over from the sofa and nodded.

"I don't really want to leave Peaceful Valley," Brenda continued, "but we need to be with Sean. It's safe for us now, or safer anyway. I'll have better medical facilities there when my baby comes."

"It'll be sad to see you go," Florence said, "but I'll try to visit from time to time. I've got to see your new baby!"

"I'd like that."

"Me too," Kim said, looking over with a smile.

"Robbie and Ronnie will be heading off to see if they can gather some support for a new Texas as soon as all their business in Corpus Christi is finished. I don't know when they'll be here at Peaceful Valley, or when they will go to Corpus, but I'll catch a ride somehow."

"One of you gals set the table," Melissa said.

"I'll help," Florence replied, as Brenda headed for the cupboard.

Kim put her book down and got up to help too.

"You can go call the guys in," Melissa said.

Robbie and James were still engrossed in conversation when they strolled in fifteen minutes later. Their eyes were locked together and their mouths going at highway speed as they made their way to the table.

"That's enough, guys!" Melissa demanded.

They took one look at her, knew she meant business, and shut the word faucet off immediately. Robbie turned, almost ran into Florence, and wrapped her up in his arms and embarrassed himself in front of everyone else with a mushy kiss that lasted a little too long. No one else really noticed, but he thought he could feel their eyes on him long afterward.

He sat down at the table beside Florence and didn't make eye contact with anyone until later during the meal when his mother asked about Brooke and Ronnie.

"Things have been so hectic lately," Robbie said, "I thought Florence and I needed a little time to ourselves to talk and think about things. We didn't plan on staying out this long, but I figured Ronnie and Brooke needed a little time together too.

"I didn't plan on coming over here for lunch. Thank you, Mom, for inviting us. I needed to see Grandpa and Grandma too."

"Are you going to be okay, Robbie?" Melissa asked. "You know I worry about you."

"Yes, Mom," he replied, and looked over at Florence, a smile making its way to his lips. He squeezed her hand under the table. "We'll all be just fine."

"Yes, we will, Melissa," Florence said. "I'll take good care of your son."

After lunch, Robbie and Florence headed back home. Melissa gave her son a big hug as they left and he promised he'd make sure both Ronnie and Brooke made it over to their house soon.

Chapter 32

In Corpus Christi . . .

Homer and Dawn, two new recruits for the Pink Ladies, climbed into their pink squad car at 7:00 a.m. and headed toward the Bayfront. They had both gone through basic training at the Farm, but the only real experience they'd had thus far was driving the streets looking for trouble and the only problem they'd dealt with was a fallen tree across the road.

Halfway to the Bayfront, Dawn recognized a pickup truck. She and Homer had been told to keep an eye out for Marcia's truck and this morning they were certain they had found her. They kept their distance and followed Marcia to the seafood plant.

"I'll stay here," Dawn said. "You go back to the station and get reinforcements."

Dawn waited for Marcia to go inside, then she got out, hid around the corner of the building, and watched the truck.

Nearly a half-hour later, three pink cars pulled up behind Marcia's truck. Dawn came out and joined them. Her chief, Christine, led the squad.

"That's her truck alright," Christine said. "Homer, Dawn, you come with me. The rest of you guard the exits."

Christine led the way inside, their guns drawn. She found Marcia inside a conference room at the back of the plant. Marcia stopped talking when she saw Christine coming toward her. She stared at the pistol pointed at her face. She glanced over at Homer and Dawn covering the only escape route.

"What's the meaning of this!?" Marcia yelled.

"You'll come with us," Christine replied.

"I haven't done anything . . . you don't have the right . . ."

"You'll do what I say," Christine ordered.

By this time, Homer and Dawn had made their way across the room. Homer took his handcuffs out.

"You don't have to do that," Marcia said.

"Procedure," Christine said.

Homer led Marcia outside and placed her in Christine's car. Marcia led her to where Lola was staying, the other squad cars following close behind. Christine headed on toward the Farm while the others got Lola.

Christine led Homer and Marcia to a cell at the rear of the main barn.

"Where's Lola?" Marcia asked.

"She'll stay here at the Farm, but she won't know you're locked up. You'll see her when we're finished with you."

"Why are you doing this?" Marcia asked.

"You'll find out, all in good time."

It seemed like only yesterday when Robbie and Ronnie returned from Corpus, but it had in fact been two weeks, nearly to the day. Robbie cranked up the Jeep, Florence leaned over and kissed him on the cheek, while Brooke did the same to Ronnie, and the boys were once again on their way.

"Don't forget, I'm going next time," Florence said.

Robbie gave her another peck on the cheek.

As they drove, they watched for cell phone towers and discussed Marcia. The time passed quickly and Robbie stopped the Jeep in their usual spot on the edge of the city. They never really knew what to expect and had learned that stopping for a thorough review of the city was advisable before proceeding.

Within minutes, the boys noticed a pink car. It stopped for a second, having spotted the Jeep, then headed in their direction. The car pulled up alongside them and the lady driving said 'howdy'.

"Welcome back," she added.

"Everything alright around here?" Robbie asked.

"Yes. We've been holding Marcia at the Farm. We were told you wanted to talk to her."

Robbie nodded and followed the Pink Lady in. Christine met the boys in front of the new farmhouse. The guys looked the structure over and were amazed at how quickly the construction had progressed.

"It's dried in, but the men still have a lot of work inside to finish up. It'll be ready to move in, in a couple more weeks."

"I assume you will want to get your meeting with Marcia over before you do anything else?"

The boys nodded and Christine led the boys out to the barn.

"What have you told her?" Robbie asked.

"Nothing," she replied. "I locked her up a few days ago and she's been fed well, but neither I nor anyone else has talked to her. Sean said he wasn't going to talk to her without you guys."

"What about Lola?"

"I put her in the nursery. I couldn't lock her up at her age. She seems to like being with the pregnant women and they'll keep an eye on her until this is settled. I didn't tell her that her mother was being held. As far as she knows, Marcia left."

They followed her to the cells in the back. Robbie had visited Florence in the last cell many times. It wasn't a place he liked, but this time he was anxious to interrogate Marcia.

Christine led Robbie and Ronnie to the cell. She grabbed the key. The door squeaked when she pushed it open. Marcia sat up on the bed and rubbed her eyes.

"Let's take her to the front of the barn where we can sit comfortably," Robbie said.

Christine took Marcia by the arm and led her out of the cell to some tables and chairs out front. Robbie and Ronnie followed, their hands resting instinctively on their pistols.

Christine asked Marcia sternly to sit at one of the tables.

"Why am I being held prisoner?" Marcia asked, tears forming in her eyes.

"I asked Christine to hold you," Robbie said.

"But why? I haven't done anything."

"Sean is going to be running the city from now on. He's the new Mayor. We know there might be bad blood between you two because of Sonny's disappearance."

"He killed Sonny, didn't he?"

"I don't know exactly what happened. We're assuming he's dead just as you are, but that's all we can tell you. Regardless, I don't think we can trust you because of that. In addition, you have to know we are aware you were one of Sandra's spies."

"That doesn't mean I liked what she was doing around here."

"Did you?"

Marcia didn't answer. She put her hands over her face, then wiped her tears and stared.

Robbie frowned. "That's what I thought."

Robbie paused and looked over at his brother, then at Christine. He turned his attention back to Marcia.

"What do you know about the men who shot up the place a while back and burned down the farmhouse?" Robbie continued.

"Nothing. I never saw them. I didn't know the house was burned until Christine brought me here."

"Then why were you hiding? You've been avoiding us."

"I wasn't avoiding you," she replied, with a surprised look on her face. "When Sonny didn't come home and no one could find his boat, I knew something happened to him. I asked some of the men at the dock and they said he left with Sean and two women. I don't know what the deal was with the women, but I knew Sean was escaping.

"I figured he'd done something with Sonny. I couldn't stay at home. I went to my sister's house and stayed with her. She and her husband were happy to have me and Lola there with them. They have a large house and there was more than enough room for us."

"And what about your truck parked in that rundown residential area?"

"When the world went to hell a couple decades ago, my mother and father were killed. They are buried in the backyard of one of the houses. I go there to talk to them and put flowers on their graves. What's wrong with that?"

"That's enough for now," Robbie said, looking over at Christine. "I'll have some more questions for her tomorrow."

Robbie and Ronnie followed Christine as she took Marcia back to her cell.

"Some lunch?" Christine asked, on the way back to the front of the barn. Some of the other women had come in and started preparing a buffet for the workers.

Robbie and Ronnie nodded. Christine sat back down at one of the tables and the boys joined her while they waited for the women to finish preparing the meal.

"We need to get Sean over here," Ronnie said. "We need his take on what Marcia is saying. He knows her best."

"He usually comes here in the late afternoon," Christine said. "He's staying in the same room as you stayed in the last time you were here. I'll set up a private dinner for us this evening. It'll be quieter and we don't need to discuss this with everyone."

Sean showed up on cue just as Christine said he would.

"Good to see you, buddy," Robbie said, as Sean got out of his vehicle.

Sean gave the boys a big hug. "I've missed you."

Christine was in the house supervising some of the interior work and the boys had some alone time. They walked over to the picnic table and sat down.

One of the ladies who saw Sean drive up brought out a tray of tea and sat it down on the table.

"We interrogated Marcia," Robbie said. "She's convinced you killed Sonny, but she doesn't seem to be overly upset about that. She seems more upset that she's imprisoned and not allowed to see Lola."

"What are you going to do about her?" Sean asked.

"That's what we wanted to talk to you about. Now that we are trying to get a new government going, I don't think it would look good if we killed everyone who didn't suit us. Up to now, we've only killed Sandra's policemen. If we start killing citizens, we wouldn't appear to be so different from Sandra. But I don't know what we should do. We can't keep her locked up forever."

"Let her go," Sean said. "See if she'll do her job down at the Bayfront. Damn sure don't give her a gun though. We'll ask Christine to have someone keep an eye on her, and if she tends to business, let her live."

Robbie raised his eyebrows. "You sure that's what you want to do?"

"Yeah. We don't have a good alternative. You guys okay with that?"

The twins nodded.

"So, Sean, what have you been up to?" Ronnie asked.

"Eating a lot of oysters. Outside of that, I have some men working on a workover rig to see if we can get some oil production going. A crew is already out searching for wells that might produce. Also figuring out what it'll take to get them going and walking pipelines. There are still a few tanks around the refinery full of crude, but eventually, we'll need more.

"We found several phone stores and there are plenty of phones for what we need. Some men are looking at the cell phone towers around the area. They don't have a lot of expertise in communications, but I told them we have a man back home who might be able to help in this department. When you go back home, ask John and your grandpa if they'd mind making a trip here. We need to make sure everyone is on the same path.

"Oh, and I almost forgot, there's a warehouse near the Airport with several planes inside. No jets, just a few light planes. I have some men working on the Cessna like the one you flew. There are two more Piper Cubs and another I don't know what it is, but I don't think that one will fly again. It looks much older than the rest."

"Cool!" Robbie exclaimed. "I never thought I'd fly again after the last one burned up. Maybe we can use it to scout out the cell phone towers and if everything works out, with taking a look over the area where we want to expand our new government."

"We'll need an airstrip back in Peaceful Valley too."

Robbie's eyes lit up and his voice was excited just talking about flying again. Though he only flew the plane once, it thrilled him after they escaped Sandra's grasp. The thought of flying again, however, didn't stay with him long after the Cessna exploded and burned. But now, the prospect of a second chance gave him goosebumps.

"We'll need to get a fuel tank home and some fuel too," he added, a new sparkle in his eye glistening brightly.

I can take Mom and Dad flying. Maybe Grandpa and Grandma would like to go. We can get to Corpus and back in about an hour instead of three or so.

"Can you bring Brenda and Kim with you when you come back?" Sean asked. "I really miss them."

"Yeah, Brenda and Kim are missing you too," Robbie said. "They already asked if they could come next time. Florence wants to come along too. Kim is doing much better now, but I'm sure just being around you would be very comforting to her."

Christine walked out with a big bowl of strawberries. Sean scooted over and she joined them.

"I'll talk to Marcia again in the morning," Robbie said. "What we're thinking is that we'll send her back down to the Bayfront to do her job as outlined before. We don't know what she'll do, so we need you to assign someone to keep her under surveillance."

"And damn sure don't let her get hold of a gun," Sean added.

"I'll do what I can," Christine said.

"Oysters, and now strawberries!" Ronnie exclaimed. "I'm going to like Corpus Christi."

"Wait 'til you get a taste of the white shrimp in the Fall," Sean said. "Greentails on the barbie. You'll love 'em."

The next morning, Sean bid his friends goodbye after a quick breakfast. Robbie and Ronnie pushed their plates back and waited with Christine at the table until the rest of the ladies and cooks left. When the barn was empty, Christine brought Marcia out and sat her down in front of the guys.

"We talked to Sean last night," Robbie said, looking directly at Marcia. "The only problem we have with you is the way you feel toward him. You let that go and take care of what needs to be done at the Bayfront, and we won't bother you again.

"We may never trust you completely. You will be watched and you will never be allowed to own a gun. You will stay away from Sean and someone will check in with you regularly. If we feel you are a threat to Sean, the city, or any of its people, you will be dealt with swiftly and harshly."

"You'll kill me?"

"I didn't say that. We're not like Sandra, but we have methods . . . I'll let it go at that. Just don't do anything you shouldn't be doing."

"But you *are* like Sandra. You killed all her men . . ."

"You're wrong, Marcia. Yes, we did kill her men, but we did it because there would be no democracy otherwise. They were not going to change. They proved that with Linda and Sally. Sandra killed anyone—men, women, even her own police if they rubbed her the wrong way. You don't have to believe me, but we are different."

Marcia wasn't very happy, but she nodded her compliance.

Christine waved to one of the Pink Ladies stationed at the doorway to the outside. A few minutes later, she returned with Lola.

"You can go," Christine said. "A couple of my officers will follow you so they'll know where you are staying. They will check with you tomorrow and set up a schedule to keep tabs on you. Don't mess up. You're on probation until further notice."

Marcia walked over to Lola and gave her a big hug and the officers followed them out. Robbie walked over to the door and watched as mother and daughter left with two cars tailing.

"Would you like me to show you the house?" Christine asked.

The next morning, Robbie and Ronnie left just after Sean headed off to his duties. The boys bid Christine goodbye as well. Things were looking up and there was no reason for them to hang around in Corpus Christi.

On the trip home, Ronnie pulled out the roadmap and they took numerous side roads trying to spot more cell towers. They located three on the way to Corpus, but this wasn't near enough to make cell phone connection between Peaceful Valley and the city.

By late afternoon, they had spotted three more. Each time another was located, Ronnie marked it on the map.

Their ladies were surprised and overwhelmingly happy when the Jeep pulled up at the house shortly before dark. The trip to Corpus was successful and it appeared they would not be needed there for a while. They would go again to take Brenda and Kim, but the last key to their forward progress would be to locate and refurbish the cell towers.

The boys followed the girls inside and took their showers while Brooke and Florence prepared dinner. Ronnie filled the girls in on what took place in Corpus while Robbie was in the shower. Robbie didn't take long and joined the ladies at the table while Ronnie took his turn in the bathroom.

Robbie unfolded the map and scrutinized the many farm-to-market roads where a cell tower might be found. They had located six, but would need quite a few more to make the connection from the valley to the city.

After Ronnie came out and joined the rest at the table, Robbie shared their new find in Corpus. Florence's mouth gaped open a bit and her eyes bulged with the mention of the Cessna.

"I want to fly," Brooke said, her eyes lighting up.

"It's not all it's cracked up to be," Florence said, with a smirk.

"I bet it's a lot better when the plane doesn't crash," Ronnie blurted out, laughing.

"That's enough guys," Robbie said. "Maybe no one will be shooting at us next time. Flying's not all that hard; landing is what gets a little tricky. You add a little fire to the mix—it gets downright impossible. I thought I did well. We lived, didn't we?"

Robbie met with his Grandpa Reggie the next morning and showed him the map with the cell tower locations. His grandfather confirmed the need for more, so they put their heads together and guesstimated locations where there might be additional towers. They needed to get the signal the hundred or so miles from here to Corpus Christi and Reggie told Ronnie he needed at least four more.

Satisfied he had all the information he needed from his grandpa, Robbie headed to the Wimberleys. John would be their best bet in getting the towers workable should they find enough. The chore would become mammoth should they need to relocate a tower or two.

Robbie stopped by his house to inform Brooke of his intention of going to the Wimberleys. When he made it to his parent's house, they insisted he stay for lunch. James and Melissa took every opportunity to slow him down a bit and get some food in his belly. Robbie assured his mother he was eating enough, but his mother always worried.

After Robbie ate and clued his parents in on their progress in Corpus, he headed on toward the Wimberleys. John was working in the garden to get it ready for an early planting of some spring greens, cabbage, and carrots. John was happy to see Robbie, especially after he offered to give him a hand.

"Kathy got some plants started inside. I know it's still a little cold, but I'll mulch the plants if it looks like frost."

John handed him a hoe, Robbie jumped in, and they talked while they worked.

"The main thing which might be a problem, Robbie, is fire ants. Those nasty little buggers can get into almost anything. Usually, electrical equipment like what we are talking about is sealed up pretty good, but if they can get in, they will. They seem to be attracted to electrical equipment. Without power to the towers for so many years though, you may get lucky and find no damage.

"Cell tower equipment was made with good materials back then, but twenty years is a long time out in the elements. Of course, lightning could have hit a tower or two and may have caused some damage, though they are protected in this respect. Nothing is foolproof as you well know, so all we can do is take a look at them and see what we find.

"Without the power grid, you'll need to find a generator and tank for all the towers. It will also be necessary to keep them fueled up on a regular basis. Do you think Corpus Christi can provide the generators?"

"I don't know," he replied. "They have wind turbines for electricity. All I can do is ask. You know, this seemed so simple at first. It sure got complicated quickly."

Robbie informed John they still needed to find more towers to make the connection between here and Corpus. John assured him they were out there; he just needed to find them.

By the time they finished the conversation, the garden was cleaned up and John offered Robbie a snack and drink. Robbie took him up on the drink, but explained he had eaten plenty at his mom and dad's.

On his way back home, Robbie stopped in to check with Zack and Lance. Beka and Debra were the only ones home and were glad to see him.

"We don't see you enough," Debra said. "You guys are gone so much."

Beka offered something to eat.

"Do I look like I'm starving?" Robbie asked, patting his stomach. "Everyone is trying to feed me all the time. I think I've actually gained a little weight the past couple months."

Beka snickered. "You look fine, Robbie."

Zack was fishing, while Lance was setting some snares along the riverbank. When he'd finished talking to the girls, Robbie strolled down to the pier.

"Catch anything?"

Zack looked back, then reached down and raised his stringer with two fish tied to the end.

Lance showed up a little while later.

"The cell tower project has gotten complicated," Robbie said. "It's turning out to be much more difficult than I first thought. Can you two help your dad with the project?"

"But we don't know anything about cell towers," Lance said.

"You don't need to. All I'm saying is that your dad can't do it all by himself. Just help when he needs it."

"We'll do what we can," Zack replied.

"Ronnie and I will be heading off soon to see if we can find enough people to get a local economy going again. I want to get an area police force with communications so we can protect ourselves no matter what. I'm tired of fighting. I want things to be safe around here for our kids, and one day, our grandkids."

Lance and Zack agreed with Robbie totally and said they, along with their dad, would have the cell towers up and working by the time they got back if that were possible. Robbie gave them a high-five and headed back home.

Chapter 33

Over the next two weeks, Robbie and Ronnie prepared the Jeep for their new adventure. They added steel plating behind the front seats, Robbie remembering the bullet he took to the side. They also welded additional steel around the machine gun turret to give Ronnie better protection when operating the 30-cal.

The plan was for Robbie and Florence to take Brenda and Kim to Corpus Christi, check in with Sean, and if everything was like they expected it to be, they would return home and he and Ronnie would pack their gear in the Jeep and head out.

The boys worked on their list of supplies and gathered them into a spot in the corner of the living room ready to go.

Robbie memorized the map and the boys worked up a route. They would take Highway 181 down to Kenedy, cut across on 59 to Goliad, and 183 to Refugio. They'd get on 77 to Sinton, 181 to Gregory to catch Highway 35. There, they'd pick up Aransas Pass and Rockport, then on to Tivoli.

Robbie pointed at the map. "Remember what Hank said about Seadrift?"

Ronnie nodded. "It's not far out of the way. We can catch 185 off of 35. When we're finished there, we can go back up 185 to Victoria and catch 87 to Cuero. Finally, we hit 72 back across to Kenedy again and we'll be within a couple hours of home."

Robbie slapped his hand on the table. "Sounds like a plan to me!"

They gave each other knuckle bumps and grinned like Cheshire cats.

This was a lot of real estate and the trip meant they had to find gas along the way. The Jeep didn't get great mileage, but it was the best vehicle they had. They weren't certain they'd need the four-wheel drive, but it was good to have the option available.

With all the planning Robbie and Ronnie were doing, they made certain Florence and Brooke were a part of the process. The women needed to see the boys were taking everything they could possibly need on the trip, so they didn't worry about them too much.

Zack and Lance promised to come over regularly to cut firewood and kindling for the girls. James said he'd check in with them every few days to see if they needed anything. Of course, Mutt would keep them safe.

'You keep track of the days, Robbie,' Florence told him on numerous occasions. "I don't want you missing the birth of your first son." She giggled. "Or daughter."

James and Melissa asked the boys and gals over for an early dinner one evening. They would have had them over every evening if possible, but the twins had things to do and Brooke and Florence needed to be with them.

Ronnie with Brooke on his arm and Robbie with Florence seven months pregnant waddling along beside him, strolled into the Lindgren meadow. The late afternoon air had turned quite cold and sleet pellets were falling by the time they arrived. The winter thus far had been mild and they looked forward to an early spring, but this afternoon mother nature showed them winter was far from over.

Ronnie and Brooke led the way up the steps and Robbie helped Florence up onto the porch. James was waiting in the doorway to welcome them in. Brenda and Florence compared bellies while Brooke jumped in to help Kim and Melissa finish off the table setting.

James pulled the boys aside for a minute. "You sure you want to do this? It's going to be quite an undertaking."

"Mom, you and Grandma Eileen have told Ronnie and me many stories about how it used to be," Robbie said. "Though it was crowded and there were a lot of problems, people weren't trying to kill each other over their next meal. I don't think we have a choice. We have to try. The root cause of all the problems before has been eliminated—overpopulation. Now there aren't enough people for the country to function as a whole.

"John told us how polluted the San Antonio River was and I'm sure this was true elsewhere, but the rivers should have mostly healed by now. With a reasonable population growth, we can create a new world . . . a better world where everyone can live out their lives happy and free. It will start with small steps like we will be doing—trying to band communities together to make a larger and safer society."

James gave the boys manly hugs. "I'm so proud of you boys. Lars and Eileen would be equally as proud of you for the monumental task you are undertaking. I never knew you had it in you to get our little part of the country to something we could call normal."

"Frankly, Dad," Robbie said, "we didn't know we had it in us either."

Ronnie nodded.

"Sandra gave us a big opportunity," Robbie continued, "even though it seemed like an adversity at the time. With her out of the way, we have something to build on in Corpus.

"There have to be a lot of people like us with the same desire for peace. We don't have to be a bunch of savages. If we can regroup and get this country back to something near what it was before the grid shut down, where people helped other people, helped protect others' rights and property, then we would all be better for it."

James had tears in his eyes by this time. He had no idea Robbie would grow up to be such a leader and Ronnie was not much different. They were, after all, twins. They were strong willed and had a vision, but more importantly, maybe, they had the balls to carry it out.

All the while James was talking to the boys, the ladies were still busy in the kitchen, but very quiet. They were eavesdropping on the conversation in the living room. Melissa called the men to the table, but as soon as they headed her way, Melissa led the applause they all gave to Robbie and Ronnie for their bravery, courage, and persistence.

The boys blushed. They never liked being the center of attention and certainly never thought they deserved accolades. They were just doing what needed to be done. That was their job, no different than cutting firewood or carrying out the trash.

Melissa met the boys near the table, wrapped Robbie up in a tight squeeze, and kissed him on the cheek. She then turned to Ronnie, pulled him close, and showed him her love.

"I am so proud of you boys," she said, "more than I could ever tell you."

Melissa waved them into their seats at the table. The group was quiet for some time. Everyone was hungry and concentrated on the venison, potatoes, and fresh greens. There was little talk other than a few compliments on the excellent food, but Robbie could feel the other's eyes on him. He blushed on occasion when he made contact with his mother's loving stares.

Why does everyone have to make such a big deal about this? Robbie thought. *Anyone else would have done it too. We're just doing what needs to be done. I hope there are others out there with the same thoughts as Ronnie and me.*

Robbie crawled in behind the steering wheel and put his rifle in the new gun rack he'd installed between the front seats. He wouldn't have a gunner on the turret this trip, so he needed to keep his AR-15 handy. Florence got in on the passenger side with a big smile on her face.

"I'll be ready when you guys return," Ronnie said. "Take care and get back here safely."

"Give Sean our best," Brooke added.

A short while later, they were at the Lindgren's, grabbed Brenda and Kim's gear, and Robbie helped the ladies into the vehicle. James and Melissa waved from the porch as they headed toward Corpus.

Brenda, Florence, and Kim chatted the entire way and Robbie never got in more than a word or two. Florence was ecstatic she was going on the trip and Kim and Brenda couldn't wait to be reunited with Sean.

When they got to the edge of the city, there was a barricade across the road. Robbie readied his rifle.

"There's no need for that," came a voice from a nearby building.

Robbie's eyes focused on the opening in the wall. Before he could respond, a Pink Lady opened the door and walked out toward the Jeep.

"What's going on?" Robbie asked, as he climbed out and stepped to the front of the Jeep.

"We have outposts on all the roads entering the city now," she replied.

"Everything alright?" he asked.

"Everything's fine," she said. "Christine figured we needed more perimeter guards, so she posted two of us around where we might expect intruders to enter. Barricades like this are at all the highways coming into the city."

"Is it okay for us to pass?"

"Of course. We all know who you are," she said, with affectionate eyes and a loving smile.

Robbie noticed the frown on Florence's face, but he didn't say anything as he got back in behind the wheel. He waved as he pulled around the roadblock.

Robbie stopped in front of the farmhouse. All the previous activity was virtually non-existent. He got out first and stretched his legs. As he was looking around the yard, his eyes met Christine's coming out of the front door.

She gave them a wave. "Come on inside."

Robbie grabbed the girls' gear and they all followed Christine into the house.

"I'll find you a room," she added.

"We'll stay in Sean's room," Brenda said.

Christine turned with a surprised look on her face. She looked at the girls, then over to Robbie. He nodded.

After the gear was placed in Sean's room, Christine took them on a tour of the new house.

"This is really nice," Robbie said. "I especially like the new wood laminate floors."

Christine smiled.

All the bedrooms were fully furnished and each had a nice large bathroom, but one of the first things Robbie noticed was there were no longer mirrors on any of the ceilings. He didn't say anything, but his mind drifted back to the times he laid for hours staring at the nude bodies of many of the women he had slept with. Jade was the most prominent memory, which stuck out in his mind. Her jet-black hair and wonderful breasts . . . that first kiss she gave him and making sure he never forgot her name.

Robbie shook his head to force the memory out of his mind when his thoughts turned to the day Sandra whipped Jade and finally took her in front of the firing squad.

"Something the matter?" Florence asked, noticing him growing a little distracted.

"No," Robbie replied, "just seem to be a few ghosts still hanging around."

Christine offered drinks and snacks, which they accepted. She told them Sean was doing a wonderful job. This was pleasing news to Brenda and Kim. Marcia hadn't been a problem and everything was getting organized. The crews were working well getting the city back to running like a well-oiled machine.

They took their drinks out to the back porch overlooking the fields. Ladies were scattered here and there working on various tasks. Most of the crops were in and there didn't appear to be much that needed doing, but on a farm, there was always work to do.

Sean showed up and one of the yard ladies directed him to the back porch. His eyes lit up when he saw Brenda and Kim. Both girls jumped up and wrapped him in a group hug, showering him with kisses to the point of embarrassment. Christine smiled and looked over at Robbie. He shrugged and returned the smile.

Robbie and Florence got up when the girls were finished with Sean and gave their red-faced friend handshakes. They didn't want to embarrass him further.

As they sat back down, Robbie pulled their map out and laid it on the patio table. Sean scrutinized it as he ran his finger along the route they had outlined.

"How long do you think that is going to take?" Sean asked.

"It's hard to tell," Robbie replied. "I guess it all depends on how many people we find and what kind of issues we run into dealing with them. It could take a couple weeks, or even a month or more, if we encounter resistance."

Sean looked at the map again. "If you run into trouble early, you can always come to Corpus through Portland. Anywhere up to Tivoli you can make your way back here. After that, your best bet will be to keep on going."

Robbie nodded while Florence eyed the map. They had learned a lot about urban warfare lately if they ran into problems. They were confident, yet they weren't cocky. They would make certain they were not captured as easily as he and Sean were when they first came to Corpus Christi so long ago it seemed now, but the memory was still fresh in the backs of their heads.

When they finished their discussions, Robbie was satisfied they had done the right thing bringing Brenda and Kim to Corpus Christi. The city was on the rebound and headed in the right direction. Robbie and Ronnie would lead them into a new and wonderful community spanning hundreds of square miles. They gathered at the dining room table for an exquisite dinner and to be thankful for what they had accomplished.

All their new favorite entrees were served—shrimp, oysters, crab, and squid. Trimmings included sweet corn, asparagus, dinner rolls, and creamed potatoes. The dessert was to die for—blackberry cobbler with homemade ice cream. They all ate their fill long before the dessert was served. Nevertheless, all ate a hefty serving of the sweet finale.

Needing to let their dinner settle a bit before retiring, Christine instructed the kitchen help to make a pot of coffee. They all sat around in the living room listening to a little music. They got their minds off their worries with some more personal catching up on each other's lives. It had been another long day as usual and it was late before the party fizzled out.

Satisfied everything was completely under control, Robbie and Florence got a good night's sleep and headed back home bright and early the next morning.

Back in Peaceful Valley . . .

Ronnie and Brooke were pleased with the uneventful trip Robbie and Florence made to Corpus Christi. The boys spent one more wonderful night with Florence and Brooke. They packed their gear in the Jeep that evening. All they needed to load in the morning were a few personal items, consisting mostly of drinks and food, and they would be on their way.

Each of the boys took their lady's hand and led them off to the bedroom and a night of intimate good byes.

"You come back to me and your son safely, you hear?" Florence said.

"My son?"

Florence smiled. "You mean more to me than anything. We will have many kids. The first may as well be a son, but if it's not, you will have sons, many of them. I love you."

"I love you too."

Robbie laid his head on her shoulder and snuggled up close to her, his hand on one of her breasts. His hand then moved down to her tummy. He could feel the baby turning.

At the crack of dawn, Florence and Brooke fixed the boys a large breakfast consisting of eggs, plenty of bacon so they'd have leftovers to take along to snack on, biscuits and gravy; lots of gravy. The boys loved gravy. It usually took four or five biscuits to sop it all up. The boys ate their fill.

They strolled out onto the porch and gave the girls a final kiss. Robbie wiped a little trickle from one of Florence's eyes.

"That's the first tear I've seen in a while," he said.

Florence met his eyes with a steady gaze. "I'm so proud of you. I'm growing up now. I can't have you worrying about me all the time when you should have your mind on the job you have to do. I will be fine and your son will know of your bravery when he grows up. He will know his dad is the reason he is safe and secure. Now you two get going. The sooner you leave, the sooner you return to me." She gave him a kiss he would be thinking about halfway down the road. "Make us a better world."

Robbie and Ronnie crawled into the Jeep and looked over at each other with big smiles on their faces. They knuckle bumped and grinned. Robbie cranked up the Jeep and eased away from the house. He waved as he looked at Brooke and Florence in the rearview mirror standing on the porch.

"We have a couple of wonderful women," Robbie said.

"You know it, Brother. Now let's go make them proud."

The End?

Getting there, but there is a lot of story left. The final chapter of my Four Seasons Series, *Into Summer*, will be out before you know it.

Epilogue

Thanks to Robbie and Ronnie's hard work with the help of friends and family, Corpus Christi is secure and working toward a stable economy and government headed up by Sean, with Kim and Brenda at his side. Christine has security under control and much of the citizenry has been armed for their mutual protection. Their outlook seems bright.

Robbie and Ronnie are leaving Peaceful Valley with the hope of bringing their successful beginning in Corpus to the outlying area to create a new state, first near home, then throughout the region, and hopefully eventually across the entire country. This is an optimistic dream and it will not be easy.

The brothers will find many who like their plan and are easily convinced to join them in their quest for peace and friendship, but for some, change is not welcome or wanted.

One brother will live and the other will die. Will the survivor continue the quest? Will he go it alone, or will someone join him on this monumental journey? Will the Sandras of the world rule the day, will the dream of a unified new world die, or will the country find the road to democracy?

Into Summer - Dawn of a New Age will complete the Four Seasons Series. The finale will sizzle through the summer and lives will change forever. You won't want to miss this epic conclusion to the saga of Peaceful Valley.

Into Winter by Larry Landgraf (7-28-2017)

Some years it happens so quick,
The clouds roll in, cold and thick;
The days grow ever so brief,
The nights more suited to a thief.

Life is a test, you will soon see,
That is the way it's supposed to be;
No one is exempt from what lies ahead,
The only way to escape is if you're dead.

Work hard and maybe you'll survive,
Sit on your ass and later you will cry;
Be tough and roll with the flow,
Keep your eyes open and learn as you go.

Life goes on, even in the ice and cold,
Be prepared, or like a house of cards, fold;
Make certain you have everything you'll need,
Learn necessary skills even if you must read.

A sturdy shelter and warmth will get you by,
Out in the cold you will surely die;
When the polar cold dips down deep,
Looking to kill you while you sleep.

A few months out of every year,
You know winter will always be here;
Even areas where it is dry and warm,
Mental winter will hit you like a swarm.

The cold can also freeze your brain,
In a form even lacking ice and rain;
Toughness of the mind you must learn,
Or just like in the frost, you'll take a bad turn.

So prepare for all that you must endure,
Forces from within as well as from out there,
They are all as real as they can be,
Fail either and you will surely see.

Do it now before it's too late,
Fail and you'll seal your fate;
You get only one chance at life,
Give it your best shot; lose the strife.

About the Author

Larry Landgraf was born and raised in and around the swamp country of the Guadalupe River Delta on the Texas Gulf Coast. After four years of college, not wanting to spend the rest of his life in an office or classroom, he became a commercial fisherman. That played out in the late '80s, and he became a general contractor for another twenty-plus years. Due to a death-defying injury on the job, he turned to writing.

Trying to save his commercial fishing career, Larry wrote his first book in 1986. The career and book were a failure. He didn't write again until he published his second book, *How to be a Smart SOB Like Me*, in 2012. Then he got serious about writing and in 2015 published *Into Autumn* to launch his *Four Seasons* series. The release dates for *Into Spring* and *Into Winter* are 2017, and 2018 for *Into Summer*.

Larry divorced in 2006 when his wife of 38 years decided to walk out. This marriage produced three kids, all grown now. Larry met Ellen in January 2009 after a long search which spanned the globe. They now live together in the swamp where Larry has lived all his life. Much like Eileen Branson in *Into Autumn*, Ellen is a city gal, but loves Larry's swamp. Larry, much like Lars Lindgren in the story, wouldn't have it any other way. He teaches her the ways of the swamp, and she has plenty to teach Larry, as well.

Fresh Ink Group

Publishing
Free Memberships
Share & Read Free Stories, Essays, Articles
Free-Story Newsletter
Writing Contests

Books
E-books
Amazon Bookstore

Authors
Editors
Artists
Professionals
Publishing Services
Publisher Resources

Members' Websites
Members' Blogs
Social Media

Email: info@FreshInkGroup.com
Twitter: @FreshInkGroup
Google+: Fresh Ink Group
Facebook.com/FreshInkGroup
LinkedIn: Fresh Ink Group
About.me/FreshInkGroup

Fresh Ink Group
Guntersville

Into Autumn
A Story of Survival

By Larry Landgraf

Lars is living alone in the Texas countryside when the economy collapses and his world becomes a dystopian nightmare. Joined by outsider Eileen, he and his neighbors band together for survival in their "Peaceful Valley." They must learn to scratch out sustenance while fending off predatory invasions in an increasingly violent and lethal world. *Into Autumn* is a sweeping adventure, a thought-provoking saga that could happen to us all.

Paper-cover ISBN-13: 978-1-936442-54-6
Hardcover ISBN-13: 978-1-936442-53-9
Ebook ISBN-13: 978-1-936442-55-3

INTO SPRING
The Next Generation

By Larry Landgraf

Twenty years after *Into Autumn*, Sean and Robbie leave Peaceful Valley for Corpus Christi, hoping to find women who will join their fiercely protective group back home. What they find is a fight to survive the violent dictatorship of ruthless Sandra Hawkins. Meanwhile, a new family joins the group in the Valley, except that what seems like a safe addition might bring the worst kinds of change. *Into Spring* continues the Four Seasons saga about building a new life in Texas after the collapse of civilization.

Paper-cover ISBN-13: 978-1-936442-44-7
Hardcover ISBN-13: 978-1-936442-43-0
Ebook ISBN-13: 978-1-936442-45-4

How To Be A Smart Sob
Like Me

By Larry Landgraf

Work, money, food, relationships, life in general—these are the everyday struggles for billions crowded into our challenging world. Larry Landgraf tells us his story and the many lessons he's learned for finding extraordinary happiness. *How to Be a Smart SOB Like Me* is a stark but heartfelt examination of a life well-lived. You might like him, and you might not, but you can't help but learn ways you, too, can achieve your best.

Paper-cover ISBN-13: 978-1-936442-51-5
Hardcover ISBN-13: 978-1-936442-50-8
Ebook ISBN-13: 978-1-936442-52-2

www.ingramcontent.com/pod-product-compliance
Lightning Source LLC
Chambersburg PA
CBHW071734190726
48292CB00003B/745